Quadrille in Kenya

Quadrille in Kenya

Enid Dawson

Pearl Press

First published in Great Britain by Pearl Press

ISBN 978-09566518-7-7

Printed and bound by Good News, Ongar, England

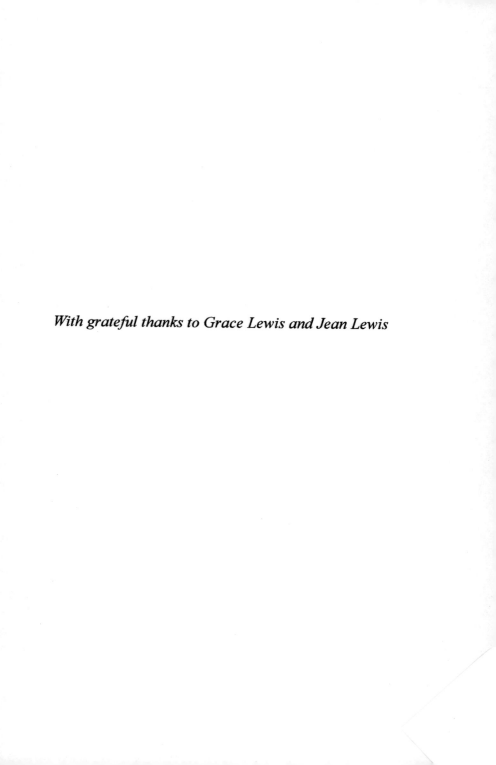

With grateful thanks to Grace Lewis and Jean Lewis

Contents

Prologue 1

Chapter 1 9

Chapter 2 21

Chapter 3 37

Chapter 4 51

Chapter 5 63

Chapter 6 75

Chapter 7 89

Chapter 8 101

Chapter 9 115

Chapter 10 125

Chapter 11 139

Chapter 12 151

Chapter 13 163

Chapter 14 173

Chapter 15 187

Chapter 16 201

Chapter 17 213

Chapter 18 227

Chapter 19 241

Chapter 20 255

Chapter 21 269

Chapter 22 283

Chapter 23 297

Chapter 24 311

Chapter 25 323
Chapter 26 335
Chapter 27 351
Chapter 28 365
Epilogue 375
Glossary 379

PROLOGUE

KENYA

1941

Three pairs of eyes were looking down.

Two pairs belonged to Libby, aged thirteen, and little Lew, just eight, who were sitting on a ledge of the great, long kopje that was the highest place they were allowed to go.   Reared on adjacent ranches they were bush children to the core but always enjoyed the annual Neighbourhood Picnic that was going on below them.   They were watching noisy people spilling out of the three big tents, some with beer mugs, others chattering as if they'd not seen each other for months, which was probably true.

It was Lew who was conscious of a shadow passing over them. He looked up. A huge eagle, gliding nonchalantly, was caught in an up-draught of air.

'It's a *crowned* eagle!' he said.

'How do you know?' Libby could just see a big bird.

'It's from the forest up the escarpment at our place. There's been a pair there for years, feeding off the monkeys. Libs, you know them! Don't be thick! They fly up and down the valley all the time.' Lew missed nothing.

The third pair of eyes belonged to the eagle who could see a lot more than the two on the kopje. The whole length of the Backlands valley was open to him, a wide stretch of big ranches, running west to east. The thousand feet rise of forested escarpment lined the south of the valley whilst the north was enclosed by the long line of the Littet Hills. Beyond those hills, stretching forever, was simply wild Africa. Above the southern escarpment lay the neat fields of the mixed farming community of Chemchem, whose river, of the same name, cascaded down the scarp and fed the whole of the ranching valley.

Living in the Backlands Valley was a quartet of ranchers - 'The Friends' - who got together once a month for Sunday dinner, rotating round their homes. It was a longstanding companionship of four families who had mutually gone through all the difficulties of converting virgin bush into ranching country after the First World War: Dar and Edith Winchester with their daughter Libby; Frannie Houghton-Framlyn and his tiresome mother known as Mumps; Frank and Madge Cooper with little Lew and, of course, Glory Halleluiah. Three of their ranches joined, but Glory Halleluiah's was further east. 'The Friends' formed a close-knit set of people, ever supportive yet never interfering with each other, Libby and Lew secure within this group. Frannie was also a child of the valley but a full ten years older than Libby; grown up and running Venture Ranch since his father died.

It had been called the five-year 'itch' in the Backlands. Five years after Frank and Mumps brought their infant Frannie to the Backlands, Madge produced the twins, Sally and John, then, five years later Edith had Libby (after a very long time of waiting – Dar and Edith had almost given up the idea of a family) and, after yet another five years, unexpectedly Madge had Lewis – an afterthought.

Everyone felt that Lewis was a blessing for the Coopers after Sally, at a buxom fifteen, was brutally raped and murdered near

Chemchem Club. Her twin, John, was sent to South Africa to get over this – and now would not come back. Sensitive little Lew somehow understood that his parents were not yet over the tragedy and never seemed to mind that he was often overlooked, not exactly neglected but not really in the forefront of his parents' thoughts – a blessing not yet appreciated.

Dar Winchester was the senior rancher, running The Loop, the biggest ranch that was encircled by a great bend in the Chemchem river. At the west end of the valley, near where the road came down the escarpment, abutting The Loop was Venture Ranch, home of Frannie and Mumps. Tucked under the escarpment was the smaller ranch of Frank and Madge and further east lay the considerable spread belonging to Glory Halleluiah.

No one ever asked Glory Halelluiah how she came by her unusual nickname, nor ever asked how it was that an elderly, aristocratic and very wealthy Scottish lady should be ranching quietly on her own in this, the remotest part of colonial Kenya. She just was. That was enough. She was loved and admired and the one to whom all turned in times of trouble, knowing that her calm wisdom would give balm and help.

Libby, Lew and the eagle could see the elephants on Frannie's ranch, just across the river from the picnic site. It was a small family, apparently strolling but, in reality, moving very fast, probably making for the 'elephant gap' in the Littet Hills on The Loop ranch. Both Libby and Lew knew that Frannie longed to go to war like all the other young men, but, because of his foot, he was not allowed; he had to stay farming. All he could do was look after the ranch of the Twybitt brothers, near Glory Halleluiah, whilst they were away and, once a month, go up the Chemchem escarpment to help the wife of a friend of his, Piet, also in uniform, cope with the end of month business. Frannie was a very private person, instinctively liked by Libby and Lew, and admired by the other Friends because of the way he coped with his disability and his difficult, always complaining mother, Mumps.

Somehow, much as they were liked by everyone, the Twybitt brothers – Corn and West, whose ranch, like that of the Coopers', was under the escarpment, and also dear Mario and Maria, who farmed beyond Glory Halleluiah, were never quite in the magic circle of The Friends.

Maria, who only ever spoke Italian and Swahili, was in the kitchen tent now, preparing an Italian dish full of flavour for lunch whilst the elder five of the six children of Mario's manager – all look-alike boys – would be creating mayhem, running everywhere and getting into mischief. These children were apart, somehow – forming a group all by themselves and spending as much time in Mario's house as in their own. Mario – ebullient and extrovert, an American/Italian - loved the noise, the squabbles, and the excitement that made up for the fact that he and Maria had no children. Though how Mario's manager and his wife – both equally insipid – had produced almost identical strong, vivacious boys Libby could never understand.

The Twybitt brothers were missed for their dreadful humour, but everyone knew that they were doing their best, fighting for Britain in this terrible war. Yet at the Neighbourhood Picnic war seemed far away. Farmers came, not just from the Backlands but from the Chemchem area up above, driving down the beautiful but treacherous escarpment road, all ready to have a happy time. Even the Greys and Thomas Bell, anti-social people whose ranches were between The Loop and Glory Halleluiah's land were there. Mr. Grey was an incompetent, lazy farmer and Thomas Bell a part-time one, disappearing for months on end, his only attribute being that he was the star performer at the Chemchem Rifle Club.

4

Between the long kopje and the river on The Loop the tents were always placed. Lunch was always Maria's concern – and always marvellous. After a break some activity was arranged. This time Frannie had organised a game of cricket; likely to be gloriously chaotic but no-one would mind. Then Dar would provide dinner: a young steer that was barbecued, spit-roasted slowly over a whole day or more. Finally Frank Cooper would entertain the crowd with something.

Up on the kopje Lew suddenly said, 'I'm starving, Libs, let's go!' and they scampered down the rock, half slipping, scattering basking lizards and landed, breathless, by the big fig tree whose roots hugged the kopje.

In the food tent Libby found Maria, bottle feeding the latest of the manager's boys. Mario was standing behind her, looking very proud, and the picture suddenly exploded in Libby's mind. Mario! The children! They all look like him! Surely they are HIS?! Maria could not have children! Could this be true?

Libby ran off to find her mother who was sitting by Glory Halleluiah. The latter, planted squat and square on a camp chair with her springy grey hair just showing under the man's pork-pie hat she habitually wore and clad, as usual, in a shapeless pair of old slacks and a faded aertex blouse, was placidly eating her lunch. Edith Winchester found Libby at her side, longing for a private talk and she went to a corner of the bar tent with her daughter.

'Mum, I've just been looking at Maria and Mario and the latest baby. Mum, are they all HIS – Mario's? They look just like him! Do you think so?'

Edith Winchester was amused. At last Libby had spotted the 'joke' that all in the Backlands had enjoyed for years. Of course the children were Mario's. That weed of a manager could never have sired such a vibrant bunch.

'Shh, darling. We don't know but, I agree, they DO look like Mario. Not a word – look, here comes Mumps.' That was enough to move Libby. Mumps would be complaining about something whilst Frannie would be helping in the bar very likely. Libby skipped off delighted at her 'revelation'.

Libby had more fun when the cricket started. There was no pitch and no boundaries – a six if a ball gets into the river and a four if a tent is hit, declared Frannie. Crates of beer were behind each wicket and the standard of dress was not quite up to Lords' (so one old gentleman commented). This year, to her delight, Libby was included. Frannie could bat but not run and asked her to run for him. The serious young man turned into a demon hitting balls everywhere and, her long pigtail flying behind her, Libby ran faster than anyone and the pair made the most runs, their side winning easily.

'Well done, Libs! As from to-day you can be my little sister – all right? I will call you Sis.'

Libby saluted Frannie's great height and said 'Fine, Bro!' and they both laughed. This was wonderful, previously Frannie had hardly noticed Libby; now he was her big brother!

Darkness came quickly, stars looked down benevolently and the luscious meat from the barbecue was eaten. The gathering formed a large circle around the big camp fire and Libby, for the first time, was allowed to stay up for the entertainment, Lew having been put to bed in the Coopers' car.

Frank Cooper, a good looking man in repose, had an India-rubber face and was a great mimic. Always he performed something at the picnic, this time miming the window-cleaner who came upon something interesting through a bedroom window but who never saw the end of it because he'd called so many friends up the ladder to see the fun that the ladder broke – just at the important moment!

Libby laughed as much as everyone else; as a farm child she understood it all. Edith was pleased. She and Dar had kept Libby too naïve for years, she knew, but childhood is a lovely thing. Now Libby was on the threshold of becoming an adult, an exciting and specially important time, her very first period just finished.

Eventually the party ended, everything left to be cleared the next day, goodbyes and thank-yous called out and the site left for the animals whose place it was. The timid herd of resident impala came back to the riverine forest and a hyena smelt the remnants of the food and came padding, bent on finding it.

Driving home with her parents Libby heard the arresting sound of a lion as it roared its supremacy, somehow underlining that she was vividly alive, having enjoyed the very best picnic. Suddenly she was more conscious of everything. It was as if she had just appeared on the stage of life. Now she was growing up – and not just physically; she'd become Frannie's sister, had spotted Mario's 'secret' and she'd stayed up for the entertainment. Nearly adult! She tumbled into bed unwashed, not at all tired, with a myriad of thoughts chasing her mind.

What was life going to be for her? What will she do? Who will she marry? She was not in the least bit afraid of the future but, for the very first time, was thinking about it.

Suddenly, with no warning, happy sleep overtook her.

1952 – 1958

CHAPTER 1

When a boat train was due in Nairobi from Mombasa the railway station was usually chaotic. It was something of a social occasion. Ready to meet friends or family, people kept arriving, spreading up and down the platform despite the early hour.

In the midst of the bustle, like a lighthouse in a buffeting storm, stood Frannie, a rock amongst the waves. He wasn't going anywhere other than by the entrance. No doubt Libby's luggage would be at the back of the train where porters were waiting with trollies. With his great height and his crew-cut hair – that did nothing for his looks – hat in hand, he was automatically left alone. There was something remote about him.

A little late, the train had reached the Athi plains and Libby, together with Miss Benson, were looking out for animals and were rewarded by the sight of an ostrich, looking a bit like Margot Fonteyn, with a retinue of at least fifteen chicks that were scuttling after their mother. Miss Benson and Libby shared one of the train's first class sleeping compartments, just as they'd shared a cabin on the boat from England. Despite their considerable difference in age, and lives, they had formed a very pleasant friendship.

Not far away a Forest Officer was sharing a compartment with an elderly gentleman who was relating the days when he'd shot lion from horseback on the Athi plains many years ago. The Forest Officer was half listening, being a bit more pre-occupied with how he could arrange to see Libby Winchester again. On the ship several young men had chased Libby, who danced with them all and was adept at keeping them at a distance. The Forest Officer was older, decidedly a sticker and had come into the race only after the ship had passed Cape Guardafui. He'd been attracted to the quite amazingly beautiful Libby Winchester from the time the ship left London Docks but, because of a girl in Nairobi, he'd hesitated. At the Cape he'd given up the inner struggle and made his intentions obvious. Libby was always very nice but slightly separate somehow. They'd danced together, swam together, played Scrabble together (at which she was hopeless) yet he'd never got very far. Not even a chaste kiss had he managed.

When he'd offered to help her when they reached Nairobi she'd said, 'Oh, thanks a lot but Frannie's coming. He's a next-door neighbour – Venture Ranch. Dad can't come. Mother's not well. But I'll be fine, thanks.'

'Frannie? Married?' he couldn't help asking. This seemed to amuse her.

'Francis Houghton-Framlyn. No, not married, never will be, not Frannie' and she laughed.

With a bluster of smoke and steam the train finally arrived, scattering the waiting people back from the edge of the platform to the safety of the walls of the station. Frannie remained impervious to any of this and waited calmly for all the passengers and people meeting them to sort themselves out.

In the melle at the luggage van the Forest Officer nearly lost Libby; held up as he was by his innate courtesy to the old gentleman.

Lots of people seemed to be helping her. The she suddenly saw someone up the platform and waved. By the station entrance a tall, youngish man waved back. He looked very serious. Then the Forest Officer noticed that he had a bad club foot. Remembering Libby's laughter he wondered if she was as nice a girl as he had thought. There was still the girl in town ...

Frannie put his hat on to take it off again to greet Libby as she arrived, apparently with half the ship's male passengers in tow. Libby had no inhibitions and gave his cheek a big kiss. 'Bro – you've not changed one bit – it is good to be back! How are you?'

'Fine, Sis, you look good – come on let's get your gear into my vehicle.' Frannie was not going to admit how much Libby had changed since he last saw her as a still gawky eighteen year old – a late developer, so everyone said.

The entourage melted away, Libby said a genuinely nice goodbye to Miss Benson who was met by the Nairobi Secretary to the Church Missionary Society, and Frannie, having piled her considerable luggage into the back of his Land Rover, drove her up Government Road into the centre of town.

'Sis, I've got to collect some farm things – Hartz and Bell and so on – if I drop you at Torr's – until – noon – will that do, then an early lunch and on to Nakuru?'

This delighted Libby. She wanted to walk round Nairobi a bit – enjoy it – as she had Mombasa. When the ship finally docked she nearly cried with joy at the smell of Mombasa – so evocative! It was a mixture of sea, rotting fruit, fish, coffee, urine, spices and sweat – indescribable but so very much Mombasa.

Nairobi was different – much newer, but its own place. There were settlers walking around shopping; the men in baggy shorts, knee stockings, shirts and wide-brimmed felt hats, the women in unfashionable cotton frocks, straw hats and short white gloves. There were colourful Indians; the women like butterflies in bright saris, the men in dhotis or tall Sikhs with marvellous beards and pristine white turbans. There were a few Africans; a Masai or two lolloping along with their special lifting stride and wearing red shukas, and a few little Kikuyu mamas wearing their leather, one-shouldered aprons, bearing great loads of vegetables in closely woven sisal bags on their backs, supported by a strap on the forehead.

The Standard Clock showed the time. Lord Delamere's statue still stood resolute. Oleanders were flowering, jacarandas were towering over them; Libby was nearly home.

Frannie found lunch quite an experience at Torr's Hotel. The hotel was busy but most of the clients were looking at Libby. Her looks were causing quite a stir; who was she - a new girl in Kenya? What was she doing with the odd looking fellow with the crew cut and a club foot? Then someone realised that it was that chap from the Backlands and wasn't the Winchester girl due home now? Once that was decided most of the speculation was over.

Lunch finished, Frannie explained that they'd stay with friends of his in Nakuru that night, reaching the Backlands the next day. It was all magic to Libby; magic to go along Sclater's Road again, the only long tarmac road out of town, built by Italian prisoners-of-war; magic to reach the dramatic escarpment down the Rift Valley at the bottom of which the prisoners-of-war had built a lovely little chapel as thanksgiving; magic to see the extinct (everyone hoped) volcano of Longonot rising in the floor of the Rift Valley; magic to glimpse Lake Naivasha and then Lake Nakuru with its eyelids of bright pink flamingos. She was going home.

She chatted all the way, about her time with her uncle and aunt in Shropshire, about the boat voyage, about Miss Benson.

'Did you know there are wealthy Missionaries? People who work for the mission voluntarily – Miss Benson isn't paid at all – she funds herself.'

'No reason why Christians shouldn't come in all shapes and sizes, Sis.'

'Miss Benson's doing Women's Work – whatever that is – in the hills above Fort Hall. And, guess what, she's a niece of old Col. Foster!'

Col. Foster was an irascible Indian Army man who'd retired to Chemchem, it being, he said, the furthest away he could get from civilisation.

'She's built a retirement cottage on a plot next door to him.'

All the time Libby was absorbing the scenery avidly, soaking it in.

The ship, the journey and England were starting to recede in her mind as they passed giraffe, gazelle, and eland not far from Mt. Longonot. Libby was starting to think of the Backlands.

'Glory Halleluiah? Is she all right?'

'Fine – so's everyone else – Madge broke a wrist a few months ago but she's better. All's well. And you know about Mario's boys? They've all got Italian names now.'

'Yes, Mum wrote and told me. So I have to remember Roberto, Luigi, Marco and so on. Frannie – however did the Rich's agree to disappear and leave the boys?'

'Big money, I would think. Mario can afford a lot and when he'd got the family he wanted he simply paid them off and kept the boys – it's some time ago now.'

'How could any woman abandon her children?'

'Money, money, money – Libs – lots of people will do anything for it!'

'Chemchem?'

'All well – growing – more settlers. There's a Little Theatre started and the golf course at the Club's been enlarged to the full eighteen holes. Oh, and the Lecher is still as lecherous as ever. No wife yet but after every female who sets foot in the place and gets no-where.'

'He's dreadful! – Oh, and what about Corn and West - have they been up to anything?'

Frannie laughed.

'As usual! The best was last year. The Copeland girl got married to an army chap. You know the Copelands?'

'Pretty awful people, yes.'

'That's what we all thought when we got the wedding invitation. It was vulgar in the extreme. Can you believe it – there was a list of shops where the girl – Suzanne – was leaving a catologue of possible wedding presents – so we were expected to buy what she wanted!'

'Oh, Frannie, that's done in England these days – the latest thing. I suppose it stops the bride getting twelve sets of plated tea knives that the local shop wants to get rid of!'

'It seemed pretty awful to us – we give what we want to give. Anyway that wasn't the worst. On the invitation it was added that Suzanne's favourite colour was PINK! What were we supposed to do – give her pink sheets, pink towels, pink plates, pink everything? There was a lot of talk.'

14

'I can imagine.'

'Came the day and at the church Corn and West had asked Glory Halleluiah to save them seats up front because they were going to be late. So she did. People arrived. More people arrived, the church was getting full. It was a big do. Eventually the church was packed – extra seats around the sides – you know. Glory Halleluiah had a job keeping two seats for those rapscallions. Time went on. The bridegroom and best man stood up waiting. It was all quiet because we assumed the bride was coming. Oh no – up the aisle came Corn and West – dressed in suits made of some awful shiny, bright pink material – they looked like a couple of over-ripe strawberries! Everyone collapsed. Giggles everywhere. Of course they were frightfully gracious – do you remember how they could do that – incredibly polite, smiling regally and not giving anything away. They walked very slowly up the aisle – it was hilarious. They were actually bowing to people right and left. Glory Halleluiah could have slaughtered the rogues when they went to sit with her.'

'Wonderful. I wish I'd been there.'

'Where they got those dreadful suits made I don't know. They were appalling. And at the line-up – reception – they were SO naughty. 'We've put them on specially for YOU, dear Suzanne' – and we all know that Corn and West can't stand the Copelands.'

'What a pair!'

'I tell you – it made the wedding for all of us – we were dreading it to be honest. They went through the reception being deeply gracious to everyone with dead-pan faces. It was marvellous.'

The Twybitt brothers! Libby felt gloriously back where she belonged.

Nakuru, their stopping place, was the centre of the farming

community in Kenya with agricultural suppliers, machinery workshops and a huge Kenya Farmers Association shop with lots of stores for coffee, wool, pyrethrum, and silos for wheat and barley. The Kenya Co-operative Creameries had a big centre there. There were flour mills and everything else that the surrounding agriculture needed. A big Agricultural Showground housed the Kenya Milk Recording Offices and the Stud Book records. It was a farmers' town, practical yet not without charm. The place had developed because between the volcanic hill of Menangai and close to the lake shore there was an area of bubbling springs of water that had been a mecca for the early caravan traders travelling between Mombasa and the hinterland in search of cattle, ivory and anything else for trading.

Frannie drove to a pleasant residential area up on the slopes of Menangai that had a splendid view of the lake below. Libby did not know Frannie's friends at Nakuru and was suddenly tired so she went to bed early, leaving Frannie to talk with his old school friend, Rob, and his wife.

'Whew, Frannie, what a looker she is!'

'Very, very different from when I last saw her! She was eighteen but still a hoyden – lanky, still pigtailed at eighteen, no figure at all. She was dreadfully spoilt as a child – best pony – all that. She was nice, though. Of course she was an 'only' and they'd waited years for a child. Dar and Edith sent her to some finishing courses in England and she didn't get back until she was twenty-one. There was a huge party at the Chemchem club for her twenty-first. I was away for several months – on a course down south – so I missed all the fun. But I heard about it. She knocked everyone for six – including her parents, I think. Changed so much.'

Rob's wife smiled, 'It's odd – when girls develop late they often do that – caterpillar into butterfly – more than those who develop young, I think. Amazing she isn't married already!'

'Ah – there's a story about that – and yes, more soda this time, Rob. She's bespoken – if that's the right word – already – but not engaged. I'll tell you.'

Frannie sipped his drink and stretched his long legs.

'There's a good farmer at Chemchem called Alec Dacre, wife from Jo'burg, Stella, one son, Bobby, just a few months older than Libby. A good looking lad, I suppose (this was said slightly grudgingly) – fair, bubbly hair, plays polo, strong, thinks a lot of himself, bit of a swank but works hard on the farm, I hear. Of course he was invited to the 'do' – took one look at Libby – and she at him – and it was all over!'

'Not surprised.'

'It's not a bad match really. Dar and Edith were quite happy and so were Alec and Stella Dacre but, and there's a big BUT – Bobby has a stinking rich grandmother in Jo'burg who has directed in her Will that he gets the lot provided – provided that he doesn't get engaged, married, anything like that before he's twenty five; probably sensible with a lad like that.'

'Go on.'

'So it was a question of waiting a few years. No one was going to let them miss out on a fortune! Dar and Edith, assessing Bobby correctly, I'd say, decided that the pair wouldn't last years without something happening. So they sent Libby back to England to her uncle and aunt – the aunt is her mother's twin – in Shropshire somewhere. They farm. She became a spare daughter as they don't have children – ran the farm office, cooked a lot, looked after her uncle's hunters – and rode them a lot, I gather – she chatted all the way here. She and Bobby wrote to each other all the time and Bobby behaved at Chemchem, I'm told. It was all quite happy apparently.'

'And now she's back.'

Frannie nodded, 'Yes, she's back – only a few months until Bobby reaches twenty-five and everyone felt that was fair. So that'll be Libby settled.'

'Lucky chap, it seems. I think I've heard that the Winchesters are quite well off themselves?'

'Yes, they are. Libby stands to inherit well – and probably from her aunt and uncle, too.'

'Sounds like they're in for an easy life – money, looks and farms. Not bad!'

'Yes – well the Winchesters will give her a great wedding, no doubt at all. That'll liven us all up in the Backlands.'

Driving north-west the next day Libby had the childish excitement she used to have coming home from school. In those days it had been train to Nakuru and then on by road. It was this road section that was so enchanting for her. They drove through some hilly but richly productive mixed farming land with cattle, and some tea and even coffee higher up. The road then went through a long forest, the surface treacherously muddy during the rainy seasons. The country rose and opened up into a wide expanse of open ranching land. This was a long section that ended when a different forest was entered, greener, lusher and with colobus monkeys in the trees and green parrots screeching. As this was a favourite bit Frannie drove slowly so that they could see the monkeys and also catch sight of the huge black and white hornbills that lived in the forest. Sometimes elephant might be seen but not on that day.

The forest became sparser and quite soon, coming to the brow of a low rise, the chequerboard of the Chemchem area came into sight. It was a patchwork of farms on gently rolling land, well watered, with distant hills on either side. This was the most remote of the farming land in Kenya where Europeans had settled and had proved a rich area. But even more isolated was the Backlands, reached by going down the famous – or infamous – tricky escarpment road north of the Chemchem farms.

Libby was almost tense with excitement; she was nearer and nearer home – and Bobby. Because Dar was looking after Edith at the ranch it had been arranged that Frannie would take Libby to the Chemchem Club where Bobby would be waiting. He would take her home, giving them time together.

Edith had occasional asthmatic attacks that Libby seemed to have missed inheriting. In fact Libby was strong, sturdy and very like her father in that way but had inherited more of the personality of her mother. Libby had honey coloured hair, waving nicely, a wonderful figure and a face that possibly could have launched proverbial ships. Luckily she seemed totally unaware of her physical perfection, parents and uncle and aunt being careful never to mention anything. She was, it seemed, fairly naïve still. Frannie didn't want to tease her in any way about Bobby so he calmly said that he's leave her at the Club – which, in fact, she knew already. 'Bobby', she was thinking, 'only a few miles and I'll see you!'

It had been a hard parting after her twenty-first party and the short time after that but she did understand her parents' misgivings; Bobby had been pretty pushy and, though she'd have married him with nothing, her parents had talked to her very seriously. Bobby! He'll be at the Club and we'll have the long drive down to the Backlands together. She was more and more thrilled. She was picturing him, open, smiling face, hair all curly and with his head slightly bent to the left (he said it was to do with riding too much – nonsense, of course). His voice came to her vividly – a very slight Africaans accent – but always spoken with loudness. He had dominated her when they met at the ball. She felt swamped by him – and loved it. They'd be married very soon after his twenty-fifth, she knew, and then live at the new farm that Alec Dacre had just bought next door to his original farm. Lovely – not too far from her parents and, Bobby had told her, with a good house that she could do up. It was just marvellous to be back.

Frannie swung his Land Rover into the Club grounds to find very few vehicles parked, certainly not Bobby's. He said, 'Wait a bit Libs, I'll go and see if there's a message. Maybe he's had a puncture – anything.'

There was a message for Libby from Bobby:

Come straight to the Cottage Hospital. Your Mother's got a bad attack. Dar's there. See you there, Bobby.

Neither Frannie nor Libby was unduly concerned. A few times before Edith's attacks had landed her in the Cottage Hospital, Bobby may not have known that. But when they reached the hospital, only a few minutes away, Bobby was waiting for them very anxiously. He hardly greeted Frannie, gave Libby a quick peck on the cheek and said, 'It's not good – come on.'

Edith Winchester opened her eyes. Whether she actually recognised Libby or not is open to question. She died a few minutes later. Libby collapsed, first onto Dar, then Bobby took her while Dar dealt with the hospital.

It was not the homecoming Libby had expected.

CHAPTER 2

The pall of gloom over the Backlands, caused by Edith's death, was lifted considerably by Bobby whose rather insensitive boisterousness was a blessing in the following weeks. His father allowed him either Saturday or Sunday off – but not both, and he saw Libby then. If there was polo then Libby went to watch him, if not, then he came down to The Loop. Libby had automatically taken over the running of the house and went to Chemchem for shopping every Thursday, staying on to play tennis at the Club, then spending the night at the Club. Bobby was not a tennis player but he joined her for dinner at the Club.

Dar was very shaken by his wife's death but, at the same time, happy to have Libby home – even if it would only be for a few months. Having Bobby around was certainly a great change. Bobby was a big talker and prattled on about anything except the sadness Dar was feeling; it all helped. He was duly invited to the monthly Sunday dinner parties that the friends enjoyed. These evenings rotated around the ranches, Mumps, Madge, Glory Halleluiah and now Libby, taking it in turns to be hostess. They were evenings of general chat and laughter. Guests were welcome and Bobby certainly changed the flow of conversation.

Quite soon after Edith's death Madge and Glory Halleluiah got together.

'He'll need help over the wedding now that Edith's gone don't you....?' Often Madge could not end a sentence.

'You go to him. You do it, but, of course I'll help – just tell me,' offered Glory Halleluiah, knowing full well that Madge had always looked forward to Sally's wedding – a hope that had been wiped out so cruelly. Madge was a romantic and would love to help Dar with Libby's wedding.

'Dar, Glory Halleluiah and me – we've been thinking about.... you and Edith had been quietly arranging Libby's wedding – well – now she's gone, can we help? We'll do as much as you....'

'Madge – how kind - I was going to ask you – thanks. Yes, we'd had many thoughts, but until we know the actual day one can't really do much.'

'Chemchem church, I suppose, and reception ....?'

'We'd thought of the Picnic Site instead of the Club. Libby loves that place and everyone knows it.'

'Oh, very nice and about catering do you.....?'

'Edith suggested we ask the Club to deal with it – probably easier than us trying to cope with that sort of thing.'

Madge agreed heartily. More detail could be dealt with after the wedding date was fixed – in fact it was a delicate situation; no-one wanted to pre-empt the reality. She promised Dar that she and Glory Halleluiah would help Libby as much as possible; both doubting that Mumps would want to become involved.

Thinking as she was of Mumps, it was ironic that Frannie should walk in to see Dar at that minute. 'I'll leave you two togeth.......' and she left a relieved Dar who had wanted to ask both Madge and Glory Halleluiah and had not known which to tackle first.

'Come in, come in Frannie – a drink?' Frannie could rely on a good whisky with Dar and he often needed it when Mumps had been more than usually difficult.

'Very kindly Madge came over to offer to help over the wedding – you know because of Edith.'

'That's great of her …..I came on a similar errand, in a way – at least an offer of help. You've no manager again?'

'Very sad – young Dent was doing very well and I liked him a lot but he said it's just too far from anywhere being here. Well ….it is, if you are young and want a bit of life. That's the third manager I've lost since I decided I needed help. Perhaps I should try for much older men, I don't know.'

'Dar – it was a manager for you that I've been thinking about.'

'Oh? You know someone?'

'You obviously don't know that young Lew has come back home – he arrived a few days ago.'

'Lew – I thought he was working at Makuyu – what's happened?'

'The ranch was sold and the new owner has his own staff so Lew's out of work.'

'He should have gone to college. Bright chap, Lew. Can't think why Frank didn't send him!'

'Mmm – well, Dar – why don't you take him on? At least he wouldn't complain about being too far from anywhere. And you need someone. Libs will be away quite soon and it'll be very lonely. Anyway you really do need a younger chap to deal with the ranch now – I'm not being rude but you're not getting younger.'

'Don't I know it!'

'And it would be an act of charity, I think.'

'An act of charity? Whatever do you mean?'

'Dar – you're a great chap but not the most observant. You haven't noticed the Coopers cutting down, being careful, not buying bulls – I think they're strapped for cash. That's why Lew never went to College. Haven't you noticed?'

'Good Lord, no! Is this true, Frannie? Why?'

'I don't know – but if you took on Lew, you might find out'

Dar went to see Glory Halleluiah and told her what Frannie had thought.

'I have noticed a few things – nothing major but curtains that need replacing, a lovely old mirror disappeared and I wondered why. They never said anything. Not that Madge is house-proud – she's like me. At least she's not like Mumps who'd die if a speck of dust showed. Of course if they are short of money it wouldn't show in the house for a long time – good curtains and chair-covers and things like that last for ages – but they are shabby now, I know. I wonder if this has been going on for some years.'

'Lew? Not going to College?'

'Now that was very odd, I grant you. He was very bright at school – certain of a place at University or wherever. Anyway Dar, are you going to take on Lew?'

'Haven't seen him yet, but he is a good lad and would suit me fine, I think. I'm going over to the Coopers to-morrow – and I'll have a look round. What does worry me is that Frannie said Frank hadn't been buying bulls lately – now that is bad.'

'Yes, it is. But, you know, we are all such friends, surely they'd have told us if they were in serious trouble? It must be something temporary and very private: if it's that then I feel that it is none of our business.'

Dar was not so sure. Frank was the type to die rather than ask for help.

Driving back to The Loop Dar's strong social conscience was troubling him. Why hadn't he noticed anything wrong? But he knew the answer to that; Edith had always told him that he never noticed anything outside his immediate life. He must do something.

Dar was greeted by the Coopers with their normal warm welcome and hospitality. He was given coffee in the sitting room of their very attractive cedar slab house, tucked under the escarpment. Quietly he looked around. It was true; there was an air of things decidedly worn, patched, and even a feeling of space. Some furniture was not there, he suddenly recalled. Frank and Madge had a few antique items that were not now on show.

'I hear you've got Lew back.'

'Yes, he's out doing the salt run at the moment. That ranch at Makuyu was sold, fresh people were brought in so Lew lost that job – he loved it, too.'

'Well – I'm looking for a manager – would he come to me do you think?'

'Dar – we never thought of you – he'd jump at it I think – oh great.'

'Send him over to see me to-morrow morning and I'll have a look at him. He's been away - what – nearly two years? He'll have changed a bit.'

'Yes, but not grown any more!'

Lew was five foot six, by a long way the shortest in the Backlands, an area that seemed to attract tall people. Only Glory Halleluiah was also short; Madge was a well built, motherly figure, Mumps was tall and thin, and even Edith had been on the tall side. The men, apart from Lew, were big chaps, tough and towering. It was this factor that was in Dar's mind. Was Lew really big enough to cope with the physical work of ranching?

Lew arrived at The Loop next day very neatly dressed in well laundered shorts and shirt but Dar, now looking for things, noticed that the shorts were patched. Lew was a bit subdued. He'd known Dar all his life but there was a difference in seeing Dar as a friend and as a prospective boss. He'd certainly grown since Dar had last seen him, not upwards but outwards; he was now stocky, muscular and looked strong. Dar was relieved. He stood straight until Dar got him to sit and they talked ranching, Dar listening to Lew's experience at Makuru. Lew spoke well, rather diffidently, and always politely. He hadn't changed much, Dar thought, always a good lad, under-appreciated by Frank and Madge.

Lew would have what was called the guest cottage, all meals, laundry and the salary offered was good, better than at Makuyu. Lew suddenly said 'Dar, please would you put my salary into Dad's account – direct?' There were other things to discuss, Dar insisting on a proper contract, to be signed after three months, and Lew went home extremely happy.

But as he left Dar was thinking deeply. Lew was certainly old enough to have his own bank account. There must be something wrong with the Cooper family.

'Frank, how long have we known each other? Since you bought this place?' and Dar lowered his heavy weight into a chair in the Cooper's depleted sitting room. 'That's a long time – and you're in trouble and you haven't come to me!'

'Oh damn Lew!'

'No, not Lew – he never said a word. I've been drawing conclusions. Come out with it, we're friends.'

Frank hesitated. There was quite a silence.

'Come on man.'

'John.'

'Yes?'

'We've told everyone that he doesn't want to come back from South Africa. You know. When we sent him there – we thought it'd help him get over Sally's death. They were so close.'

'Yes.'

'Well it isn't that he doesn't want to come back – although that is also true – fact is – he's in prison and has been for some years.'

'Frank! What rotten luck!'

'No, not rotten luck – he's turned rotten, I'm ashamed to tell you. He's in for two long consecutive sentences – embezzlement. Serious stuff.'

'Frank!'

'My cousin couldn't handle him so he's been going his own way for a very long time. Eventually the South African police caught up with him – he's done a lot of different things – mainly insurance frauds – adding up to a lot of money – and what he did with the money no-one can get out of him. When we were told, it was terrible. Anyway we felt that we must pay the money back. We used our savings, life insurance, Madge's jewellery, everything we could think of – but it wasn't enough so we had to take a loan. I'm paying it back slowly but the interest on the loan is crippling. I will clear it – but it'll take years.

It's been so hard on Madge and Lew – no college for Lew – we could hardly finish his schooling. He's been wonderful about it, though he can hardly remember John. He remembers Sally all right – she was such a special.....' and Frank was having difficulty going on, almost choking; Sally had been his joy. 'I'm being as careful as possible. Well – that's how it is.'

Dar shook his head.

'Oh, Frank, if only you'd told me – Glory Halleluiah and me – we'd both have helped you – you know that!'

'How could I? I was so ashamed that a son of mine was a criminal. And I'd have been beholden to you for years – I couldn't do it.'

Dar understood that. 'Well, Frank, I'll look after Lew – that's one problem solved. But I am really worried that you haven't bought fresh bulls recently – that's very bad for the stock.'

'Beggars can't be choosers – bulls cost money. I'm coping – somehow.' Frank seemed to have shrunk a little. 'Dar – keep all this between us, eh? I've tried to keep it very quiet, though I thought it might come out some day.'

'You been amazing to keep it under your skin for so long, but – Frannie guesses, I think, and Glory Halleluiah sees something – not the detail, of course,' Dar hesitated. 'Can I ask – how much?'

'You mean the original repayment?' and Frank told him. It made Dar, a wealthy man, blink very hard. 'Whew, Frank, I don't know what to say. I don't know how you are doing it.' Dar felt he'd gone too far. 'Just leave Lew with me – that's something I can do – help over him.'

The first day Lew arrived Libby settled him into a room in the guest cottage with – luxury – its own bathroom, and sent him to Dar who was at the stockyards.

'Come here, Lew, let's see what sort of judge you are of bulls.'

Dar had got about fifty Boran bulls quietly together in a big boma. 'Now, Lew, can you pick out the good ones?'

They were sitting on the fence together and, as Dar well knew, there were six very good bulls amongst the mob. With no hesitation at all Lew picked them out and Dar called to a man to put them aside in the next boma. After that it was not so easy but Lew quietly went on, this time walking amongst them. 'This one and that white one over there.' Lew went on selecting a few more until Dar stopped him.

'Well done, Lew, you've got a good eye for cattle; that's what's needed here.'

The next day Dar went to Chemchem and arranged a Movement Permit to shift the bulls that Lew had selected over to Frank.

'I've got too many bulls this year, Frank. These'll help you a bit.'

Frank was not fooled; the bulls were young but just ready for serving and they were all good.

'Gratitude is so bloody difficult,' he said to Madge later.

Lew settled very quickly; he knew that Dar trusted him and his confidence grew rapidly so that he found living so much with Dar and Libby no problem at all. The fact that Dar had the two of them around – and Bobby so often - was a great help in his sadness. The Loop was a lively place again. Lew was good with the African staff, firm yet could also make them laugh (always a winner with Africans) and he was certainly stronger than his size suggested. Dar felt that, when Libby left him, he would have a good companion.

The other uplift the Backlands enjoyed was a very simple tease

Corn and West played on Mr. and Mrs. Grey, Dar's next-door neighbours. This happened because West had come back from Chemchem with the news that the secretary in the Town Clerk's office had suddenly left Kenya; a family problem meant that she'd not be able to come back. Mrs. Devrade was a very buxom, friendly widow in early middle age who had seemed a juicy possibility to several of the men in the district but had remained inviolate.

Mr. Grey was incredibly lazy, never getting up before nine in the morning and leaving his ranch to its own devices a lot of the time; Mrs. Grey's claim to fame was that she was an inveterate listener-in on the Backlands telephone party line. Everyone knew this so anything private was handled before ten in the morning, after that time the tell-tale click on the line would suggest that someone was listening in and messages were brief.

Corn and West laid a plan, alerted Frank, and Corn went to use Glory Halleluiah's phone – 3Y5, theirs being 3Y2 – on the pretext that their own was out of order. As usual Glory Halleluiah fell for the ruse and left Corn to make his calls. At exactly eleven in the morning. Corn rang his own home number, West answered and very quickly Frank joined in, just to listen quietly. The brothers spoke to each other until they heard the click for which they were waiting. Immediately Corn went into a South African accent.

'Crikey West, man, I missed you last night eh!'

'Had to leave early. Sorry.'

'You missed something good, man.'

'Tell me.'

'That chap Grey – farms near you eh?'

'Just up the road, lazy bugger.'

'It's all over Chemchem, man, he's been trying to get into bed with Mrs. Devrade.'

'No!'

'Lekker! – seems he got quite far.'

'Didn't think he'd got a prick at all!'

'Christ man, that's the problem – she says he hasn't!'

'Indeed he has – and he most certainly has not.........' but Mrs. Grey was wasting her breath, Corn and West had rung off.

However childish that episode was, the Backlands enjoyed it and hoped that Mrs. Grey might have learnt a lesson.

'Talk about schoolboy humour – those two!' Glory Halleluiah was talking to Madge.

'Oh yes – and the Greys will never talk to West again will......?'

'They never do anyway, so that's no change.'

'Perhaps the Twybitts got stuck at the age of twelve?'

'No, more likely eight or nine. Oh dear. So often I could kill the pair of them.' Glory Halleluiah was very, very fond of Corn and West.

Bobby's twenty-fifth birthday was approaching; Libby was happier and happier. Frank and Madge could afford very little in the way of a wedding present but Madge hit on a suitable present. She had a small glass-topped table that was really a little cabinet. In the past she'd kept some small silver treasures in it – now all sold – but the cabinet remained. It would make a good present. Mumps and Frannie had decided on their gift – a joint one – but Libby had teased Frannie, 'I'll give you a list!' 'Don't you dare, Sis, Mumps'd have a fit – even if it is sensible!' Glory Halleluiah had made her choice during a visit to Nairobi and even Corn and West were ready for the event. There was a gentle air of excitement hanging over the Backlands. This would be the very first wedding that the Backlands had ever enjoyed and Glory Halleluiah and Madge quietly made several decisions about what they'd suggest to Dar. They both enjoyed planning, especially since they knew that Dar could afford the very best for his daughter.

The twenty-fifth birthday coincided with a Sunday dinner get together that was scheduled to be held at Venture but Mumps surprised everyone by quickly suggesting that it should be moved to The Loop. Obviously Bobby would be there and Dar specially invited Alec and Stella Dacre. He assumed that Bobby would propose during the day and the evening would be a huge celebration. Plenty of champagne had been bought.

Dar's house at The Loop was a fairly pretentious affair built of dressed stone with steps in front leading to a verandah. There were big main rooms inside, the family rooms to one side and three guest rooms and a bathroom on the other side. There was a wide back verandah and the usual kitchen outside, but Edith had made a small kitchen for herself inside and Libby often used this; baking cakes or other specialities in the afternoon. Glory Halleluiah's home was also of stone, but a more modest place, and the other houses in the Backlands were made of cedar slabs, so easy to get from the escarpment forest. Only Madge had good forest soil and had a charming garden; the other ranch houses had very little around them but Mumps got Frannie to bring her loads of manure from the old cattle bomas and managed to run a vegetable garden with a fair degree of success.

The Loop also boasted the only Lister engine and a generator in the Backlands - although Mario kept saying he'd get one - and so had electricity to provide lights. Paraffin lamps were more normal. The Loop also had water-borne sanitation; everyone else relied on long-drops, delicately housed in little huts away from the houses and quite often giving homes to snakes. It wasn't always straight-forward, living in the Backlands.

Only three weeks! Libby was hugging herself with joy. Only three weeks!

Then Bobby arrived full of annoyance and apologies. An old school friend of his mother's and her child, from Jo'burg, were suddenly coming to stay and wanted to go to the coast. Stella Dacre had decided that Bobby should drive them; accompany them on this trip. He'd be away for his birthday! Stella had thought this a minor problem – 'You'll be back a week after – don't fuss.' But both Bobby and Libby were devastated. 'I'll phone – Libby, I'll phone from the coast on the day – it's the best I can do!'

A proposal by telephone was not what she would have liked but that was that. Then Alec Dacre said that, because Stella would be away, he would not come to the Backlands dinner. The affair was shrinking and Libby felt a touch of despair. Madge tried to cheer her up, 'Libby, things like this just…... It'll be all right. Stella didn't know these people were coming. It's just bad …... Don't worry. Bad start, good finish – you ….'

Bobby took his mother to Nairobi where they met the two from Jo'burg and went on to the coast. Before he left he'd told Libby that they simply must not let this change in the arrangements matter. Libby felt a lot better after that.

Despite Bobby's absence the ladies at the dinner party made a great effort; special dresses were brought out and Glory Halleluiah wore a remarkable sun-burst diamond brooch that seldom left her safe. The men got out dinner jackets, Lew wore his new blazer (Libby had bought it for him and it made him look taller somehow) but the star of the show was Libby who looked radiant in a new dress; she wore earrings and a pretty necklace of small emeralds and seed pearls that she had been given by her parents on her twenty-first birthday. Even Mumps had made an effort; she was a handsome woman when she tried but the effect was so often ruined by her discontented expression.

Dar had put champagne in the 'fridge and Libby had made the very big dining table festive with sprigs of bougainvillea; ordinary flowers would not grow at The Loop. The best silver, the best china, glassware, napery – all were in use. The shining table glistened with the candles, the silver and the glass. Libby put out the electric lights; the effect was lovely, everything dancing in the candle flames.

Dinner was usually at eight and after a slight delay Dar said that they would start; 'phoning from the coast wasn't easy, he knew; they wouldn't wait. It was a good meal and everyone was in joyous mood yet carefully saying nothing about Bobby until it was a fait accompli, but the undercurrent of happiness was very clear. Libby simply glowed; she was caught up in a happy cocoon of expectation and the loving atmosphere around her.

Coffee had been served in the big sitting room when the telephone rang. Everyone relaxed as Libby dashed out of the room to take the call in the hallway. Now they could talk about it. Madge was flushed with happiness; this was a delight for her soft heart. Dar couldn't help wishing that Edith was alive to enjoy this moment, but he was bolstered by his friends who were obviously so pleased for him and Libby. He looked round the room, conscious of the warmth of them all; the Backlands had some good people, he always felt.

It was Glory Halleluiah who said, after a bit, 'Well – we expected a long call – it certainly is!'

After a few minutes Lew suddenly said, 'Can't hear anything.' A call in the hall could usually be heard as faint twittering in the sitting room. They stopped talking. Silence. It was odd. With dreadful foreboding Glory Halleluiah said, 'I'll go.'

She was away several minutes. Everyone sat quietly apprehensive.

Glory Halleluiah came back, grim faced.

'That was not Bobby - it was Stella Dacre to tell Libby that Bobby has just got engaged to the eighteen year old daughter of her friend – no child that! She felt that Libby ought to know.'

'The bloody bastard!'

'*Frannie!*'

But that was nothing to what the others were thinking.

'Leave her, Dar, there's nothing you can do....... I think we'd all best be going.'

Dar suddenly felt very old.

CHAPTER 3

'How could he do it? How could he! She's only just lost her mother and now....'

Glory Halleluiah shook her head at Madge, 'Goodness only knows.' She and Madge were holding a post-mortem over coffee at Glory Halleluiah's ranch. All the friends were shaken by the event. When Mario and his family heard they went into Italian excesses and Corn and West produced some extremely coarse expletives about Bobby.

'Libby's a marvellous catch for any man! Look at her – she's a really nice girl, beautiful, wealthy, healthy – everything and....... to give her up for a chit of eighteen? Madness! How stupid can one..... poor Libby.'

'We can't do anything, Madge, just wait.'

'She'll come to you when she wants to talk won't she?' Everyone went to Glory Halleluiah when they had problems.

'Perhaps, but Dar says she won't talk about it at all – understandable.'

Lew decided to say nothing to Libby – not even sorry about Bobby. This was because she looked so awful – vacant, really – that he feared if he said anything it would make matters worse. 'She'll get over it in time,' his father had said.

Life at The Loop went on, but at a false level; everyone spoke about necessary things only – to do with the ranch, the house and the staff. It was acting a charade, yet Lew couldn't see that they could do otherwise, at least for a while until Libby was better.

Dar, grimly furious at Bobby, got on with ranching. There was plenty to do and he and Lew were always busy. He couldn't talk to Libby, couldn't reach her at all. She ran the house as an automaton but asked Dar if she could do more on the ranch – help over dipping, for example. He'd have agreed to anything she wanted at this stage and, in fact, she was a help. Dipping over six thousand head of cattle every week was a major job and was always done on Monday, Tuesday and Wednesday mornings. Dar divided the dips between the three of them and so there was more control, more overseeing and a tighter look at the cattle. Libby had not been a farm child for nothing; she could spot when animals were ill or when a herdsman was not looking after his cattle properly. Her work on the farm was definitely an asset and Lew could talk to her about the cattle if nothing else.

Libby continued her shopping trips every Thursday but stopped playing tennis; she simply could not face the people at the Club. During the previous months when she had been playing tennis and away for the night Frannie had started calling on Dar on that evening, often staying for dinner. It had turned into a ritual, so now on Thursday evenings there were four of them to chat but Libby hardly said a word. She went dead.

'It's so understandable, Dar. Give her time. She'll get over it.'

Whilst Libby was in this strange state of suspended animation Lew was developing fast. He and Dar had achieved a good working relationship; he was suggesting more and even taking more control. To begin with he'd hardly been a manager because Dar did so much, but Dar could safely leave much of the ranch in Lew's hands now. Lew quietly left the selling of the stock and the office work in Dar's hands while he was organising the cattle. There was a lot to do – the breeding stock had to be carefully selected and calving was vital; at weaning the calves were branded and left in a boma for a couple of days away from their mothers and then let out to a new life of growing adulthood. Rationing the grazing was always a problem because most herdsmen would be lazy and leave their cattle in one spot too long. Dar had never fenced his ranch, the river being the boundary, except where it looped in the north and his land went up and over the Littet hills. The hills were of little value to the ranches so why they had been included was never clear. To divide the ranch into large 'fields' he had used a system of roads so that an area enclosed by roads was given a name – the 'red boma', the 'zebra boma', the 'long boma' and so on. The staff knew the limits and grazing was rotated around these areas. It was a great saving on fencing and required good staff to make it work, but the network of roads helped as fire breaks; in the dry season grass fires were always a problem to be avoided if possible.

When he started the ranch Dar had decided that he would use plunge dips. These were more expensive than spray races, but he felt more effective. There were not many but dotted about the ranch, Dar always saying that he'd build more. Ticks were dangerous; carriers of dreadful cattle diseases; dipping was vital to kill the ticks. Buffalo, being related to cattle, were carriers of diseases to which they were immune, and they were not wanted on the ranch and were shot with no mercy (the staff loving the meat provided). Added to Lew's contentment at work he was finding Frannie becoming more of a friend. With fifteen years between them he'd hardly known Frannie when he was growing up but now he was adult the gap in years was diminishing. They were talking more on Thursday evenings and Frannie invited Lew over to Venture.

Frannie would never have admitted to loneliness or lack of friends – he loved his ranch so much – he felt it was all he needed. But the propinquity of Lew was suddenly great. Frannie was an excellent rifle shot and Lew would have to do a lot of shooting on The Loop. Dar asked if Frannie could give Lew some tips, Lew having shot as a lad, but never after big game. It would be necessary for Lew to shoot buffalo – the most dangerous of all game – and lion when they took to cattle eating (usually they were left alone if they stuck to wild animals as their prey). Dar was well aware that Frannie was a better shot than he was; Frannie could teach Lew more than he could.

Frannie was an expert at both target and game shooting and he taught Lew a great deal; together they went after problem animals, to the enjoyment of both. Lew was a natural. They were usually accompanied by Nzioka, Frannie's personal tracker and gun-bearer (he filled both roles) who was a small, wiry Mkamba. He was a splendid African who almost worshipped the Bwana Chopi (the lame one). Quickly he approved of Bwana Fupi (the short Bwana - Lew) and made it quietly obvious to the amusement of Frannie. In fact he started to be protective of Lew when Frannie shouted at him if he made a mistake. Lew was loving every minute. As well as a necessity the shooting was a relaxation, the only problem being the need for suitable firearms. Dar had a well-equipped armoury and so did Frannie, but the guns had stocks made for tall people; they were far too long for Lew; however they were all that were available. Lew took no notice at all and shot well with these unsuitable firearms.

Frannie had been persuaded by an old school friend – now a Professional Hunter - to join the East African Professional Hunters' Association and take out a full professional licence. After a short apprenticeship (during which his prowess with a rifle and knowledge of game was obvious) he had done this, not to become a full-time Professional Hunter, but to be able to help his friend, George Geddes, on the odd safari when George needed another hunter. A hunter was allowed only two clients; any more on a safari required another hunter so occasionally Frannie was called to help, Frannie having built up a store of tentage and other equipment necessary.

Now, with Lew, he could do some private hunting safaris north of the Littet hills. They did not have to go far, nor be away more than a night at a time, but there was plenty of game and they were both natural bush men.. Nzioka accompanied them when he could be spared from his work at Venture where he was a jack-of-all-trades, often standing in for herders on leave.

The route north of the Littet hills went through the invisible 'Elephant Gap' on Dar's ranch. North of the loop of the river on the ranch was an angled gap in the hills, so placed that it could not be seen when looking at the hills. When professional hunters wanted to go into the Littet country they usually asked Dar's permission to go through the gap. It was a narrow gap and elephants – and other game - used it so anyone travelling through did so warily. From Venture Frannie crossed the private bridge that joined his ranch with The Loop, drove up on The Loop's many tracks and was across the river, by a ford, and into the gap very quickly. Yet it was a different, wild country through the gap, undulating, dropping gently, dotted with small forests, very sparsely inhabited by the Littet people, nomadic cattle-men. It was watered by the Chemchem river that travelled east through the Backlands valley for a long way and then curved back at the end of the

Littet hills and became a wide, shallow flow north. The country went lower and lower, the river water was warmer and crocodiles abounded.

Lew was very happy; he had a job he loved, camping and hunting with Frannie and he was close enough to see his parents often. If he was constrained by lack of cash, he never said so. He was content.

Dar had no worries over Lew, but Libby was a great concern to him. She was still not normal, far from it; in fact she seemed to be going downhill at a greater rate. She did everything perfectly well but as if in a dream. As the months went by Dar's concern grew. She refused any invitations and Dar went alone to events. It was not right. She looked a bit better, not so ill, but she simply could not pull herself together.

Dar knew that Bobby was to go to South Africa soon to marry the young girl – there had been a delay of several months for this event – for no apparent reason – and he kept this knowledge from Libby, but failed when an invitation for the Kenya reception appeared at The Loop. It invited F.G. Winchester,Esq. and Miss E.M. Winchester to the reception that was to be held on the Dacre farm. Libby saw it before he could hide it; she rushed away, leaving him helpless. As with any problem in the Backlands he turned to Glory Halleluiah.

'How crass of the Dacres to send an invitation!' said Glory Halleluiah, 'Awful. Well, Dar, I'd better do something – I'll come over to-morrow evening – give me dinner?'

Libby was better with Glory Halleluiah than with anyone else and listened to the proposition.

'I'm exhausted, Libby, haven't been away for far too long. (In fact she'd been to Britain the year before.) So I'm off to Malindi to stay at the Sindbad – at least three weeks. Pinto'll cope. Libby, will you join me? And if Dar will allow it I want to annex Lew as well – as driver because my fellow is away on long leave. Let's us three go – you, me and Lew. Do us all good.'

Libby was not fooled; she realised that Glory Halleluiah was offering her an escape from Bobby's reception – to which she wouldn't go anyway. It was all artificial, but she agreed. Lew was surprised at his inclusion but also delighted; he'd not been to the lovely Kenya coast for a very long time. Glory Halleluiah wanted Lew to dilute time with Libby and take Libby out of herself. If Lew was with them Libby would not talk too much about Bobby – if at all. Lew was a good foil, young, disinterested in Libby's problem – although sorry, and he would certainly help if he would drive Glory Halleluiah's saloon car. It was a long way – a three-day drive with night stops at Nakuru and Voi. Glory Halleluiah had it all worked out.

A few days before they left for their holiday Madge came back from shopping at Chemchem with the news that Bobby's 'child bride' (the district had chosen to call her that) was an heiress of monstrously huge expectations. It made Libby's future inheritance look puny. Madge decided to tell Glory Halleluiah, no-one else, but such news spreads quickly and it reached Dar and Libby.

Libby made no comment whatsoever.

Dar thought, 'Stella Dacre – she's pushed Bobby into it – no doubt'. Not that it made him think any better of Bobby, but it explained things somewhat.

None of this helped Libby except that when she entered Glory Halleluiah's car for the coast holiday she was heartily sick of everything and glad to be going away for a bit.

The holiday turned out much better than Glory Halleluiah hoped. Lew opened up and Libby, if not her normal self, certainly took part in everything and appeared to enjoy things quietly. Apart from swimming, fishing, goggling and local visits the most amazing feature was nightly dancing. The Sindbad Hotel was far from busy so the pretty outside 'Moon Garden' was left to the three of them on most nights and piped music was always playing. There was a tiny dance floor, romantically lit, and after the first night of sitting there quietly, Libby suggested that Lew should dance; she would teach him, being a very good dancer. Lew had never tried and was not at all musical but game to try anything. It was the first sign of initiative that Libby had made and Glory Halleluiah was deeply pleased. They were an odd couple, Libby very well built (especially her bosom) and Lew so much shorter but Lew was in the mood for fun and ready to laugh over his hopeless footwork and lack of rhythm. But he improved. They even danced when another couple came to the Moon Garden for a couple of nights, pleasant people who took Libby and Lew for sister and brother; no-one disabused them. Lew knew he'd never remember the steps or what dance went with what music but he found it fun and Libby was extremely nice to him, even joining in his laughter.

After serious deliberation Dar decided to go to the Dacre reception, having politely refused for Libby. Apart from Glory Halleluiah no-one else in the Backlands received an invitation. Dar went for two reasons; the first was his social sense that meant whatever the undercurrents, politeness must be maintained; the second was sheer curiosity – he wanted to see the girl who had usurped Libby.

A surprising number of people were at the reception considering the general opinion that Bobby had behaved very badly over Libby, but most people came in the spirit of Dar's secondary reason – they were just plain itching to see this heiress.

No-one was particularly impressed. The 'girl-wife' was average height, slender, very pale and no great beauty but equally not plain. She looked insipid. With pale hair and a very white skin, she had a completely blank expression, doll-like. Only when she tugged Bobby's arm and he bent down to talk with her did she show any life at all. It was the only animation that was obvious. But Bobby appeared fully confident and spoke very well. Stella Dacre was beautifully dressed – all the Chemchem ladies agreed about that - and Alec Dacre managed to find Dar in the crowd. 'Good of you to come,' he said and wandered away. Dar felt that at least he had tried.

Dar left early; he'd had enough. The girl was a sickly chit, he thought; as much use as a cotton vest in Siberia. He drove back to The Loop and poured himself a large drink.

Madge was seated at her pre-war hand Singer sewing machine, laboriously sewing sheets sides to middle. A few towels were waiting to have frayed edges trimmed and new hems added, others would be cut smaller to be used as flannels or, even more ignominiously, as kitchen cloths. When she and Frank had first faced their financial problem she had offered, unhesitatingly, to sell all her jewellery, some of their precious antique furniture (so carefully brought from Britain) and to cut down on everything as much as possible. It had been a challenge, none the less exciting because it was necessary. They'd sat together, estimating what they could save each month, a decision made difficult by the arbitrary way ranching went, sometimes good prices for beef, at other times low returns. The budget for Madge's grocery bill was to be reduced to a third of her normal monthly expenditure. Frank knew it was asking a great deal, but she had kissed him and bravely said that she would manage. She had, but not without considerable privation for both of them.

As the years went on the feeling of the challenge was wearing thin; Madge felt bowed as she turned the handle of the machine. But she was glad that the Backlands friends now knew their position; at least the charade was over; not that anyone said anything but they had all acted in their own fashion. For Madge it was Glory Halleluiah's kindness that was the greatest help. Every week, not necessarily on the same day, Glory Halleluiah went shopping at Chemchem and started to call on the Coopers for a cup of tea when she was returning home. Always, when she left, Madge would find a contribution on the hall table or floor – a crate of beer, packets of expensive coffee, a bottle of whisky, a tin of sweets, once a huge packet of detergent, often tea or sugar in quantity; it was an enormous help. Madge thanked her in the only way she could; flowers from Madge's garden often gracing Glory Halleluiah's big sitting room.

Inevitably Frank took the fact that the Backlanders knew their situation far harder than Madge. In one sense he was also relieved, but the relief was largely overtaken by embarrassment. He and Madge had married young and enjoyed a great marriage; he could always rely on her to back him to the hilt but when it came to her having to sell the engagement ring he'd given her – sapphires and diamonds – it hit him hard. Yes, the money helped but oh, he wished that it hadn't been necessary. He should be providing for her comfortably by now, but it wasn't like that. Though he'd never tell her, he was often near despair. And for all this to happen on top of Sally's dreadful death was too much. There were times when he was out on the ranch when he called upwards, 'What are you doing to us, God? Where's your famous mercy? Come on do something to help!'

Madge had similar thoughts but they were constrained by the fact that other Chemchem girls had been murdered since Sally's death. (Madge was always the first to reach the bereaved parents.) Looking round the Backlands, she knew that life is never smooth for anyone – look at Frannie's foot! And now there's Libby been jilted most unexpectedly. She finished the last hem, folded the linen and took it to the cupboard. At least dinner would be different from the usual farm beef because Corn and West had called and left a leg of pork for them. She couldn't help it; Madge cried a little.

After hot and humid days the evenings at Malindi were spectacular. Fruit bats that hung in the trees at the hotel car park flew about at night like enormous moths and often there were shooting stars in the sky. The air was balmy and the three mostly had the Moon Garden to themselves. Libby looked better; she tanned easily and had swum a lot but left the fishing to Lew. He'd had a wonderful time, aided and abetted by Glory Halleluiah who handed out largesse on a grand scale. It was easy to accept it from her. After all he was doing her a favour in handling all the driving, at least that was what he persuaded himself. Glory Halleluiah was very wealthy. He caught a very good Black Marlin and a good Sailfish and plenty of other fry. The sea suited him. He balanced easily in open boats, joked with the African boat boys and seemed impervious to rough seas. Having unaccustomed money in his pocket he carefully looked at all the wares Malindi had on offer and to Glory Halelluiah's delight he made a few special purchases of very good items: two beautiful Lamu copper trays, an equally lovely copper coffee pot and, best of all, a camphor wood Arab writing desk (actually a long box with delicate carving, divided into compartments inside – Glory Halleluiah thought it might well be a collector's item in the future). Lew was showing unexpected perception. Libby bought some new kikois but little else and Glory Halleluiah simply bought sprays to ease insect bites.

It had been a very pleasant holiday, all three were relaxed by it and Libby was certainly a lot better; Glory Halleluiah felt very pleased as they drove. Now the reception was over; life would start again. Libby would be all right.

But it was not like that.

For all Libby's relaxation at the coast she retreated once more into her puppet-like state, worse if anything. Days, weeks, months went by and Dar became very worried indeed.

'Surely, Glory Halleluiah, she'd be better off away – Nairobi – or anywhere. But she flat refuses to go!'

'Her security is home, I expect. And, although we all think that a change of scene suits everyone it may not; it can aggravate the problem. Just leave her, Dar. Time will sort it out.'

'But it's nearly a year now!'

Glory Halleluiah was thinking of her personal experience a long time ago. 'Dar – it may take several years.'

That was no comfort for Dar at all.

Lew's twenty-first birthday created a change for everyone. Glory Halleluiah offered to entertain for him and he elected to have a lunch party to which the normal Backlands friends, Mario, Maria and the boys, Corn and West, and Piet and Rena Coetzee from Chemchem, came. There were no friends of Lew's age, except Mario's boys; they did not exist. This was partly because of working in the Backlands, partly his poverty and partly because his school friends had gone off to University or College and had left him behind. Lew did not seem to mind.

His birthday presents were interesting. His parents gave him a watch; it wasn't much improvement on the one he'd had to start secondary school but he appreciated it. Mario and Maria and the boys gave him a lovely tooled leather cartridge belt. 'Italian leather – besta in de worlda!' Then, to his delight, Glory Halleluiah produced a very nice .22 rifle for him – just what would be so useful. Frannie followed this by lifting from behind a sofa a short-stocked, beautifully balanced shotgun made by Coggeswell and Harrison. Lew was almost speechless with joy. Then Dar produced the chef d'oeuvre; the same sofa had hidden a magnificent Holland and Holland .375 – worth, as Lew knew, a great deal of money.

'Well, you're not twenty-one every year and you can count it as your year's bonus as well.'

This time Lew really was speechless. When Corn and West and then Piet and Rena gave their gifts – leather gun slips and boxes of ammunition – it was obvious that the whole event had been organised cleverly. Frank and Madge were ignorant of this plan but Frank knew that the friends were doing what he would have liked to have done, had he had the cash – except, perhaps the Holland and Holland – that was very extravagant! But he was immensely grateful to Dar for that exceptional gift. Lew was sitting with the firearms across his knee, stroking them gently as if he had a cat on his knee. That Dar should have given him such an amazing gift was beyond belief; but it had happened. And Glory Halleluiah and Frannie – their gifts!

'Those'll start you own armoury, Lew, look after them (as if he wouldn't! he thought); there's room in the gun safe at The Loop and we'll change your T.P.P. for a proper licence; that won't be difficult.'

Lew was overwhelmed, especially by Dar showing such appreciation of him. In fact Dar had been very impressed by Lew; apart from his hard work and general competence Lew was the first manager he'd had who asked for packed lunches so that he could get on with work on the ranch and not waste time coming miles back for lunch. This had happened quite often and it was a considerable saving on petrol for the Land Rover.

With his own firearms Lew shot very well indeed and spent

hours looking after these special items. The only thing he did not have was a set of cleaning rods and gun oil, but Dar told him to use those kept in the armoury. They were over-used! Lew was expanding in personality and even Dar, who was notorious for missing things, noticed this.

If only Libby would do the same!

CHAPTER 4

The Mau Mau rebellion that affected central Kenya by-passed the Backlands and Chemchem; they were too far away. It was true that some of the Kikuyu tribe were employed in the area and they were valued employees. They were hard working, intelligent, small Africans who were excellent at growing things; Dar commented that they'd grow potatoes in a quarry, but they were not good with cattle. On the farms they were clerks, storemen, tractor drivers or mechanics. Dar employed three and told them, very severely, that they would not be allowed home whilst the Mau Mau problem was going on; he didn't want them contaminated. They would find it very difficult to remain outside the problem and probably be indoctrinated into the loathsome oathing. Most of the farmers did the same. They also refused to tell the authorities about their Kikuyu staff; otherwise they would have been taken away for screening – and some would disappear.

So the Kikuyu staff remained; Libby was grateful. The house cook was a Kikuyu, an older man with spindly legs and a genius at producing meals out of nothing if necessary. He had been at The Loop ever since she could remember and was a constant, stable factor and she felt she simply couldn't face the idea of training anyone else if he were to leave; she was still existing, not living.

Another year went by, another Neighbourhood Picnic took place, another Boran Show and Sale - this time at Machakos. Dar's bull got Reserve Champion, the Championship going to a bull belonging to Mr. Curry of Rumuruti. Another Hospital Ball took place (without Libby), another journey north for cattle buying and the monthly dinners went on as usual. In fact everything went on normally, except Libby.

'It's over two years, Glory Halleluiah, what on earth can I do with her?'

'Nothing, Dar, I keep telling you – she needs time.'

But if Glory Halleluiah thought that nothing could be done, Frannie thought otherwise. He decided it was time for action.

'Libs,' he called her on the telephone. She hated being called Libs – preferred Libby – 'Come and meet me, Picnic Site – this afternoon – tea time. I need to talk, Sis.'

Frannie was looking anything but happy as he sat on a log when she arrived in her Land Rover. He was worried about what he was going to say. It could easily go very wrong. He sat, facing the river with the big, long kopje behind him. There was a bit of shade, not really adequate, but enough. Frannie never wore shorts, as most other farmers did, because of his foot, but the long trousers emphasised his long legs and great height. He looked incongruous sitting on the low log, crew-cut hair, long legs and with a worried expression.

Libby, knowing him so well, noticed nothing.

'Come and sit here, Sis.'

He had a thermos of tea and offered her some. She declined so he helped himself. Libby said nothing, just waited. He went straight to the point; Frannie would always do that.

'Sis, we're all worried about you. It's well over two years since Bobby did the dirt on you – high time you got over it and start to live again.'

Libby was obviously affronted. Through her time of misery no-one had said a word to her – and now Frannie of all people!

'You can't know what I feel!'

'No, I'm sure I can't but however deep the hurt, Sis, you've got to realise that your – your refusal to pull yourself together affects all of us. We've had a pretty miserable time while you've been like this. Please, Libs, try!'

'I do try! I do everything I can – ask Dar – I run the house, help with the cattle – I do my bit.'

'I don't mean like that. How can I put this? Libs – bring back your personality – you've killed it over Bobby and it's doing neither you nor any of the rest of us any good at all.'

He was beginning to speak very firmly, louder than normal.

'Frannie, you have no right to speak to me like this!' Libby was becoming heated. This did not help Frannie.

'Someone has to say this to you! Please, Libs, remember the world is not at an end. You'll meet other chaps. You must. You've got to marry'

'Why should I?' This was said very defiantly.

'Oh Libs, come on, you know. There's The Loop – when Dar goes there must be another generation ready.'

'It doesn't matter.' This was a childish reaction, she knew, but could not produce anything else.

'Of course it does – if only you knew how worried Dar is over you.'

'No, he's not.'

'Indeed he is – only he won't tell you. He's waiting patiently for you to get over this but it's been a long time – too long.'

'Frannie – it is no business of yours at all.' Libby was now really angry.

'Well – whose is it? Do you want us all to be miserable seeing you wallow in self-pity? You're being very selfish.'

'I'm NOT!' Libby was horrified at that accusation – she was doing all she could in the house and farm – selfish?

'You are! We all understand a certain period but this – this behaviour can't go on for ever!' Both had raised voices. Frannie had a very set expression; Libby was now flushed.

How dare Frannie talk to her like this. What did he know of love?

'I don't want to hear anything else, Frannie, *SHUT UP!*' Libby was totally unable to cope.

'No, I won't,' Frannie was also losing his cool; how can he deal with her? 'You're wasting your life, hurting others and it is high time you stopped. Libs – *BEHAVE!*'

'How dare you talk like this,' she was shouting now. 'You have no business at all – it is *NO* concern of yours what I do!' Libby jumped up in rage, facing him. He stood up opposite her with a deeply serious face.

'No concern except that I love you! *No concern of mine?*'

There was an instant silence and stillness. The world stopped spinning. What had he said? Libby was stunned. Frannie suddenly spoke.

'No, no, I don't mean it like that – I mean I love you as a sister – you're my sister – of course I care for you! *Of course* I love my sister.'

But Libby thought he does mean i!t Oh my God, Frannie! She was so taken aback that she had no words. They were both silent staring at each other. Frannie recovered first.

'Come on, sit down, Sis.'

They both sat down, now sobered. Frannie was swallowing hard.

'Now listen. What you felt for Bobby was infatuation as much as love – that's why you've reacted so strongly. Infatuation is all the superficial here and now feeling; love is deep, patient, calm – quite different. I promise you, Libs, you'll find that with some man. But you've got to try. Libs, I'm trying to help you – understand?'

She nodded, close to tears.

'Whatever you need – help – I'll do it. I promise you – whatever...'

She nodded again, looking at harvester ants on the ground in front of her. She was very shaken.

'Libs – go back to tennis – you're good at that – please, Libs.'

In a voice that was barely audible she managed to say, 'I'll try.'

'Put on a brave face and be more cheerful – it'll help us all.' His voice was more normal now, but almost pleading.

'All right.'

'Everyone will help. Go out – go shopping in Nairobi – visit friends – meet people.'

'All right.' She couldn't think of anything else to say, she was bewildered.

'Go and buy some clothes – that's what girls do?'

'Yes,' she whispered.

'Accept invitations – it's hard for Dar on his own.'

'Yes,' she couldn't look up.

'Show the world you're above such problems as Bobby!'

It was Libby's turn to swallow and she murmured, 'Yes.'

'Head up, walk straight. You are beautiful, Libs, but you haven't been recently – you've been a two dimensional person instead of the lively person you really are. Just try to *LIVE*.'

'I'll try.'

'Good girl.'

Frannie was sweating. He'd lost the cool he expected to keep, said what he shouldn't, but covered up well, he hoped; he was almost shaking. Libby was calmer now. She was still looking down, but she was a better colour. He moved slightly, adjusted his long legs.

'Libs, I promise you – whatever you need – I'll do it. I promise – whatever will help.'

'Thanks, Frannie.'

She managed to look at him and face him.

'I'll try, Frannie, I'll try.' He got up, put out his hand to help her off the log, and they walked back to their respective vehicles in silence.

'Off you go, Sis, you'll be fine.'

But it wasn't Frannie who helped Libby next; it was the other way round.

Libby got back home with a jumble of thoughts – mainly 'poor Frannie'. Everyone knew he couldn't marry; Mumps had brought him up to see the impossibility of that. But he'd slipped out that he loved her. Did he? She wasn't entirely sure – he'd followed it up so well. Did he really mean it? It could be true – just could be true. Poor, poor Frannie. And for a long time she thought of him more than herself – a distinct improvement on her thoughts for the last couple of years.

That was on a Tuesday. There was a wedding invitation on the over-mantle for Saturday. Dar, she knew, would go. He'd already refused for her. Chemchem was used to this by now but politely included Libby in invitations.

'Dar, I think I'll come with you on Saturday,' she said casually at dinner.

He was amazed and delighted but was deliberately trying not to show his feelings. 'Oh, good. I refused for you but that won't matter – it's the Davidson's do. Big wedding. We're not to go to the Church – just the reception on the farm.'

'Yes, O.K.,' and dinner passed off a bit easier than on most nights.

For the Davidson wedding Libby dressed with special care. She had a very pretty sky-blue frock that she'd bought in England and never worn – she'd been keeping it for the honeymoon - a white lacy straw hat, short white gloves and white strappy sandals. As Dar promised it was a big affair – weddings in Chemchem tended to be like this because it was always difficult to leave people out in a small community. Dar was cheerful. Even over the last few days he'd seen an improvement; she'd joined conversations – even laughed at a few things. Glory Halleluiah had been right; time was working. He felt relieved and proud to take his beautiful daughter to the wedding; she'd see people there, get back into the swing of things.

Libby braced herself with the thought that Bobby and his child wife might be at the wedding – it was very likely – yet she felt she could now cope. There were enough people. If she spotted Bobby she could melt into the mass. She was surprised at the number of people who greeted her, 'Hi, Libby, haven't seen you for ages.'

Dar immediately met a fellow rancher from the Nakuru side of Chemchem who sometimes bought bulls from him. Libby offered to fetch beers for them and fought her way to the bar tent; it was a fight, too; there were far too many people for the bartenders to cope. There was Frannie helping at one end of the bar with three African barmen trying to deal with the rest. Libby knew he was sometimes asked to help at occasions like this; reliable Frannie would do the right thing. There were so many people that Frannie did not see Libby. She finally got the beers, spilling one slightly over the Lecher who seemed so surprised to see Libby that he said nothing, just nodded at her apology, but having handed them over she went back to the bar, slipped round the back, threw her hat, bag and gloves onto a beer crate and joined in as a barmaid between two of the Africans who greeted her nicely. They could hardly keep up with the demand. It was fairly straightforward but the Africans helped her over some drinks – they were experts borrowed from the Club. Frannie then saw her; he was so busy that all he could do was smile and nod his thanks. Libby received a lot of ribbing from the guests; that was nice, warming and she felt back in life more. No-one else bothered to come and help and the crowd was getting thicker and thicker.

Some of the men, having got their drinks, stayed by the counter, thoroughly getting in the way. The African barmen would not have said anything but Libby yelled at them 'Hey – Bruce – take your pals away – let other dogs catch the rabbit!' which shout Frannie certainly heard and smiled broadly. She was doing it; she was trying. Thank God. It was a great relief.

The surge subsided when the crowd was called away for the speeches.

'Thanks a million, Libs, go on – go and listen.'

'No, I think I'd rather sit here – what a scrum!'

Frannie sat on an upturned beer crate, hot and glad to have a rest.

'I'll send the men off for a bit. They need a break.'

'Frannie, why isn't anyone else helping?'

'Should be Charlie Soames and Dickie Tait but they've probably found birds somewhere. It's always like this.'

'That's mean of them. How long do you go on?'

'As long as the party goes on or the beer runs out whichever is first!'

'That'll be hours and hours!'

'Someone has to do it,' he answered wryly.

'Look – I bet you've not eaten? I'll go and see what's left in the way of food.'

Companionably they sat on upturned beer crates, eating remnants with their fingers. Laughter and clapping reached them from the crowd, but they were peaceful.

'Sis – keep your shoes on – broken glass and bottle tops!'

'O – golly – I've got the wrong shoes on for this game. Oh well.'

Speeches over the bar was busy again but less hectic and Libby had enough time to slip out. She hunted out the missing barmen and Frannie had been right – they'd got a couple of birds in tow. Ignoring that she told them in no uncertain terms that they ought to be helping Frannie. A bit taken aback at her onslaught they said they would, 'Coming, coming,' and turned to the girls again. (In fact they did arrive half an hour later.)

With less pressure on the bar there was a lot of social chit chat and Libby was very touched when Lilian, the wife of the major Garage owner in Chemchem said, 'Libby! We've missed you so much – please come back to tennis. There are lots of people but very few good like you – do come and play again!' Lilian was a very good player herself and, although Libby had only played for a few months before the Bobby fracas, she knew that Libby was not just good but outstanding; there wasn't another lady player up to her standard. And she was needed, not just for her tennis but because she was a pleasant person to have around. Libby was never a gossip, catty or lost her temper when games went wrong; she could be relied upon to be a good partner in behaviour. That mattered at the Club. Lilian was so warm that Libby agreed to go to tennis again. Frannie half heard the chatter and sighed with relief. Whatever the talk at the picnic site had taken out of him – and it had worried him a lot - Libby was responding. Frannie was delighted. She really was trying hard; a great change-about. His mind tried to find a quotation from Shakespeare. He couldn't remember it all but the words, 'reformation in a flood' seemed apposite.

There was a great load lifted from all in the Backlands now that Libby was back to normal. No-one said anything but life took on an easier tone. Dar felt the house becoming sunnier and Lew started to tease her a bit, to which she replied, giving as good as she got. Libby was even able to take bad news amazingly well.

The bad news was that Mau Mau had murdered Miss Benson, Libby's boat companion. Miss Benson was working in the heart of the Mau Mau activities but Libby had always assumed that, because she was helping the Africans, she would be immune to the troubles. This was proving false, not just in the Fort Hall area but also elsewhere. Libby genuinely grieved over this death; Miss Benson had something that she admired, perhaps the fact that her faith took over her whole life, it seemed. Libby wrote to the Church Missionary Society headquarters in Nairobi, and then quietly got over this sadness. Frannie was pleased that she had managed so well. 'As she's a Christian, Libs, death is no problem at all – just a move to be with God.' Libby partially understood this and, later, thought more about it. What Frannie said was becoming important; he seemed to know things.

With Libby back to her liveliness and her weekly night at the Club following tennis, everything seemed to be going swimmingly in the Backlands – except for Corn and West.

They suddenly faced unexpected expenses. Everything happened at once – two vehicles needed major repairs that could not be delayed, their only borehole also needed repair – very serious - and their paraffin 'fridge accidentally burnt into a shell. None of the cattle were quite ready for sale. Urgent action was needed - to be handled in true Twybitt fashion.

CHAPTER 5

The Standard Bank of South Africa branch in Chemchem needed a new manager. The previous incumbent, who had known the farmers and their needs well, had suffered a slight stroke and retired early. Mr. Stillwater was sent from Nairobi to run the Chemchem bank.

A serious, quiet young man, Mr. Stillwater had trained with the Westminster Bank in Birmingham back in England and had proved a competent trainee. The Westminster, a first class bank, known to train carefully and expect excellent service from their employees, assessed him adequately and he climbed the banking ladder rapidly being sent as Manager to the Birmingham suburb of Hall Green when he was unusually young for such a post. This was fortuitous because he could live with his mother. Still unmarried – he'd put the thought of marriage aside for the time being, not being ready to admit that he found girls rather frightening – he was happy to be relieved of the expense of finding a home and having to cook for himself.

He was undoubtedly a success at Hall Green, but, in reality, Hall Green was no challenge for an ambitious man, and Mr. Stillwater saw himself as that. The place was a middle-class residential area with a handful of small businesses. There were few problems; he did not have to make major decisions. Carefully mannered with staff and clients he found it all quite straightforward – too straightforward. It was clear that he might be at Hall Green for the rest of his banking career. In fact he had a growing suspicion that perhaps the powers-that-be at the Head Office didn't see him quite as able as he thought himself. Equally he had a suspicion that the lady employees, whom he treated with great courtesy, did not see him as the strong, powerful, efficient man that he felt he was. There was a degree of flippancy about them that he did not understand.

When he learnt that the Standard Bank of South Africa – another excellent bank - was expanding in East Africa, he felt ready to apply. Africa! That would be the sort of challenge he could face; nothing like Hall Green anyway. At Nairobi his experience back in Britain was considered very useful and he had hardly settled in when the sudden problem at Chemchem arose and he was sent to fill the gap.

It was pointed out that he must learn about farming and farming finance quickly in order to be of use to the bank, which thought gave him some hesitation. He knew absolutely nothing about farming and was aware of it. But, he thought, I must learn.

The Chemchem farming community were used to a bank manager who understood their needs. Many settlers were still developing their farms and overdrafts were necessary. Also, because of a climate that gave two rainy seasons each year, there were two crops annually – though not on the same ground as the growing periods overlapped – and this brought some financial problems. Help was needed to plant one crop when the previous one had not yet been harvested. The farmers were absolutely straight but inclined to call a spade a bloody shovel and they saw the bank as a convenience for themselves. Mr. Stillwater had rather different views.

Politely the Chemchem people left him a few days to find his feet before they would bother him with any problems; at least most people did this – except for Corn Twybitt.

Corn came to the bank the day after Mr. Stillwater arrived and asked to see the manager. Mr. Stillwater was correctly dressed in a lightweight suit, tie and beautifully polished shoes; his training had been faultless. Corn had come straight from dipping in a checked shirt, baggy shorts, knee socks and boots that hadn't seen a shine for months. He carried his hat – whose brim had a bullet hole in it.

'An overdraft Mr. Twybitt? But from our records you and your brother already have an overdraft – a substantial one.'

Corn took this very calmly and promptly asked to increase the existing overdraft.

'Mr. Twybitt, I am very sorry but the bank cannot offer such a thing – you are already at the limit. You must understand that. Naturally I'd help you if I could.' Mr. Stillwater prided himself on his helpfulness.

Corn explained that the need was only temporary. 'We've got a good lot of cattle almost ready for sale. It'll only take a couple of months to finish them and they'll sell well. We can repay immediately then.'

'I'm so sorry Mr. Twybitt, but with your existing overdraft at its limit I cannot possibly offer more.'

Corn seemed to make up his mind.

'All right, Mr. Stillwater. Yes. At least we can be neighbourly. You won't have had time to visit a farm yet? I thought not. Right, I'll collect you on Sunday morning – I know the bank house – and you come and have lunch with me and my brother. You'll see a bit of the country and have a look at the cattle, too.'

'Well, er, thank you. But you do understand the bank's position – I have made it clear?'

'Yes, yes. But we'll be neighbourly anyway. Just come and enjoy lunch – and the cattle are worth seeing.' (Corn was quite sure that Mr. Stillwater would hardly know a cow from a steer.) 'I'll fetch you at

11.30 and get you back after lunch.'

Mr. Stillwater rather grudgingly agreed. After all he would be seeing something of the district and might learn a bit about farming.

Corn left, all politeness, leaving a faint smell of dip chemical behind in the bank's pristine office.

The house that Corn and West had built for themselves was made of cedar slabs like that of the Coopers, but the difference was that the Coopers' house was cleverly shaped and had a graceful roof of cedar shingles and was surrounded by a garden full of flower beds, colourful shrubs and feathery trees; it was a very attractive home. Corn and West's house had a utilitarian corrugated iron roof, a dull outline and no garden. It was bleak; they knew it and lived with it.

The only common areas of the house were the veranda, hallway and dining room. On either side each brother had his own sitting room, bedroom and bathroom. A small guest cottage was separate. The brothers met for meals, although not always, and exchanged news then.

The Backlanders had prophesised that their mode of work would not work, but it did. They split responsibilities and changed month by month. One was dealing with the outside jobs – the cattle, dipping, fencing, vehicles etc whilst the other ran the office, organised the house and the food and did the shopping – farm or domestic – in Chemchem. Next month they changed over. Each carried a little notebook entitled 'Tell West' and 'Tell Corn' and at meals the notebooks were opened and they told each other exactly what was happening. Incredibly the system worked, apparently without acrimony.

Big men, they looked shorter than they were because of their broad width; they were strong, solid chaps each with a thick thatch of prematurely greying hair. Despite the two years between them they looked so alike that they were usually taken for identical twins; they spoke alike, and seemed to think alike.

When anyone asked them how they got their unusual names they invariably said, 'Oh, it took our parents two years to get from Cornwall to Westmorland,' from which baffling reply everyone had to work it out. They cherished Glory Halleluiah, despite teasing her unmercifully, shot lions for her, kept an eye on her vehicles and managed to pop in to see her every week. They were also deeply indebted to Frannie who had run their farm during the war when they were away fighting (both were mentioned in despatches and never told anyone) but their only indication of this was to strictly ignore Mumps when they visited Venture and kept the conversation flowing Frannie's way all the time. Mumps found them infuriating – their terrible sense of humour! – so low - so childish – Frannie how can you like them? Perhaps oddly the brothers were not on very close terms with Mario and Maria, although living quite near them. It wasn't that there was anything wrong with the Italian family; the Backlanders guessed that it was because the Twybitt humour was not understandable to the Latin temperament. In so many ways Mario and Maria, especially Maria, were far more sophisticated and cultured than the Twybitts although the size and quality of the libraries in each of the brothers' sitting rooms might have surprised their Italian neighbours.

On Sunday, Corn was not only prompt collecting Mr. Stillwater, but also very neatly dressed; clean shorts, white shirt and almost shiny boots. Mr. Stillwater had tried to think what he should wear for a visit to a farm and felt himself very over-dressed. He was given a Cook's tour through the mixed farming country to reach the escarpment road, Corn describing every farm and the owners and being very nice about them all. At the viewpoint near the top of the escarpment he stopped to let Mr. Stillwater enjoy the scene, which he did with suitable enthusiasm. He'd hardly seen such a vast expanse of country before. This was **AFRICA**!

Reaching the bottom of the escarpment – and that trip alone put the fear of God into Mr. Stillwater's heart, it seemed so dangerous with an earth road and a precipitous drop on one side - they were fortunate to see a few reticulated giraffe on Frannie's land near the road and, better still, a small family herd of elephant crossing from the Coopers' ranch to The Loop. Mr. Stillwater was amazed and couldn't get over the way Corn took this so casually. Sensing this Corn started to tell the bank manager the game problems they encountered and the way they shot lions quite regularly. Mr. Stillwater certainly felt out of his sphere and suddenly noticed what he assumed were leather gun cases on the back seat. Was he in the Wild West now?

Passing the Coopers' ranch some cattle could be seen – odd shapes, odd colours, not at all like British cattle, Mr. Stillwater thought, and when they passed another herd on Bell's land he felt the animals very strange indeed, a motley lot with funny humps and something dangling under their necks.

The space seemed tremendous, the country very rugged in parts with scattered bush and the forested escarpment on their right. This was very different to the neatly laid out fields of the farming country at the top of the escarpment; it could be a different world.

'A G and T or a pink gin?' Mr. Stillwater was asked when they reached the ranch and he met West (what peculiar names these men had – must be nicknames). He hesitated for a fraction, beer being more to his liking.

'Tradition – Sunday drink – gin – with whatever you fancy,' said

West firmly.

Since he'd never had a pink gin – whatever that was – he settled for a gin and tonic. The three sat on the verandah with a wide view over Glory Halleluiah's land and across to the Littet hills beyond. Mr. Stillwater had certainly never seen so far before; his eyes being used to the confinement of urban views and annual glimpses of British farms from a train when he went for his holidays at the seaside (he was fond of Exmouth). The sky was enormous; somehow much bigger than in Britain.

Corn and West carried on a conversation in antiphonal responses – about Kenya, the wild life, the geology, the roads, the trees, the distances, the tribes – everything, in fact, except their need for a bigger overdraft and their cattle. Mr. Stillwater's glass was quietly kept topped up. Fortuitously a lion roared - quite a distance away but it was impressive. Mr. Stillwater felt a trifle nervous sitting so openly. 'Have to get him if he starts on the cattle. I'll 'phone Glory Halleluiah later and warn her – he's not very far from her house.' Glory Halleluiah? Is the man mad? Mr. Stillwater wondered what was going on. He was wondering about several things as they sat but his mind seemed unable to deal with anything coherently. The effect of at least four – or was it five? – gins were making their mark. The double act of Corn and West, who were carefully nursing their drinks, was beginning to seem very funny now. They were imitating some long dead relatives of pukkah Indian Army background. Mr. Stillwater was very amused, lolled back in his chair, and felt that this is the life! Hall Green had never been like this. Really.

Helped from his chair and steered to a much-needed visit to the loo Mr. Stillwater found that lunch was now served. It was 3 o'clock in the afternoon, but he didn't know – or care. The curry made him sweat so the brothers gave him more to drink – what it was he didn't ask – and a pleasant fruit salad cooled it down a bit. It was a very

69

convivial lunch, each brother seeming to spark off the next on a series of jokes, some of them very risqué.

By 4 o'clock there was coffee and liqueurs on the veranda. Van der Hum? Very good. South African. You must try. The fact that the brothers had none escaped Mr. Stillwater who was, by now, feeling extremely benign. Yes, he'd had plenty to drink, but he could take it. At 4.30 one of the servants came to talk to Corn in Swahili. Swahili – must learn the language I suppose.

'Oh good, the herd I wanted you to see - not too far from the house. Get the Land Rover, West, eh?'

Again a strong arm steered the totally inebriated Mr. Stillwater into the vehicle where he sat, thoroughly bemused. They crossed the main Backlands road and Corn then drove straight through the bush (he did not need to do this – they were now on Glory Halleluiah's land and she had good tracks) frightening Mr. Stillwater as he negotiated rocks and bushes with aplomb. It was certainly more exciting than any roller-coaster trip.

Suddenly, round a big patch of bush they stopped. There in front was a splendid sight. A magnificent herd of beautifully matched animals was spread out facing the vehicle. The cattle were all glaring at the vehicle. They lifted their heads – in unison – as if sniffing the air, suddenly turned and retreated a few yards, stopped again and turned back to face the Land Rover. It was like facing a regiment of cavalry.

The fact that it was a mixed herd of bulls, cows, heifers and calves completely by-passed Mr. Stillwater. All he could see was an expanse of black animals with the most wonderful horns that curved down, outwards and up; huge beasts. The calves were not black but a reddish brown, very attractive. The line seemed to go on for ever.

'There you are – five hundred (this was naughty of Corn as he and West could count any herd with complete accuracy; in fact there were two hundred and eighty – still a great herd) – and, as you see – so close to being finished!'

Mr. Stillwater had no idea what being finished meant but supposed, in a haze, that it meant ready for sale.

It was deeply impressive. The animals just stood. They were massive. Now these were proper cattle, Mr. Stillwater could see – no funny shapes and odd colours; these were all the same, solid, proper beasts. A lot of meat on the bone, Mr. Stillwater thought, trying to think as a butcher might – but he was having difficulty thinking of the word 'butcher'. In fact he was having difficulty thinking at all. All he could grasp was that he had never seen so many cattle in his life before. From the train, en route to Exmouth, he remembered seeing cattle in fields – maybe twenty? Thirty? Surely not more – this was – was – was…. He gave up.

'So,' said Corn casually, 'An extra bit for three months only? Now you've seen some of the collateral – this is only one herd - we run about three thousand altogether. You can judge for yourself the value!'

Three thousand! The value? Mr. Stillwater had no idea what an animal was worth. But three thousand like these? A combination of alcohol, extreme novelty, ignorance and the good manners of a guest took over. 'Well, yes, I see. Three months – limit – that suit you?'

West answered as Corn was turning the vehicle, 'Oh, yes, we'll start selling in two months, get rid of them all in three. Fine. Corn'll come in to-morrow morning to sort it out. `Spect you'd like to get home now. We'll leave Corn at home and I'll take you back.'

The journey back was definitely taken in more than a slight fog

71

by Mr. Stillwater. He didn't even recognise the fantastic good luck they had in seeing a leopard in the classic pose draped over an horizontal branch of a tree. He was re-living the day – those cattle! That was special, he knew. An increased overdraft? No problem.

Corn was having a much more difficult time that West. The herd had been on Glory Halleluiah's land for a few days, they all knew, and it was time to try to move them back up into the escarpment forest where they belonged. He rounded up some of the labour, used his gun to fire over the heads of the beasts and the men had to drive them, shouting and screaming - quite a dangerous thing to attempt – but the shots did their trick. Had there been only two or three old bull buffaloes Corn would never have attempted such a performance – almost suicidal - but a herd was easier to handle. It took a long time, but it was done. Glory Halleluiah would NOT appreciate that herd on her ranch. He'd `phoned and told her she'd hear shots and not to worry and, by the way, there was a lion near her. She cautiously asked Corn what they'd been up to as her staff had intimated that something was going on. 'Oh, nothing, Glory Halleluiah, just a gentle drive on your ranch with a visitor; we knew you'd not mind.' Glory Halleluiah grunted – just what was the latest tease? At least it hadn't involved her too much.

Next morning Mr. Stillwater was decidedly piano. Yes, he had drunk more than usual. But he could take it! Could he? Could he? A thumping head suggested several cups of coffee and some aspirin but before the effects of these had numbed the hammer beating the inside of his skull Corn Twybitt arrived – remarkably early and very cheerfully. He told Mr. Stillwater how much they had enjoyed his visit, that he must come again. It was great to find someone who knows about cattle. Sign here? Thank you. Yes, we'll be selling very soon. Good morning – and thank you very much.

Know about cattle? Oh yes, they were very fine.

'I must write to mother about that,' thought Stilllwater, I'm certainly getting to know the farming around here. Such good cattle. I wonder what they do with those enormous horns? Never asked. Another coffee? Good idea. 'No visitors to-day, please Mrs. Saunders. They can make appointments for to-morrow.' Oh, yes, I know about cattle now.

It was only about six months later that Mr. Stillwater was moved from Chemchem – at his own request. He found the settlers too much, but wouldn't admit it. He asked for a transfer to a Nairobi branch where things were better but not very many months later he resigned and returned to England; yet another European beaten by Africa.

CHAPTER 6

Libby's life re-entered her old steady pattern. On Thursdays she drove to Chemchem to order the weekly shopping for the house and any farm items that Dar or Lew wanted. Then, after a quick cup of tea at the Club she played tennis.

She'd been welcomed back into the tennis group enthusiastically, firstly because, most unusually, there was a shortage of lady players, secondly because she was an outstandingly good player and, thirdly, because they all liked her.

Always there was a gathering at the Club's main bar after the games then most players went home but Libby stayed the night at the Club, collecting the shopping next morning and driving home in time for Friday lunch. It was a weekly break that Dar encouraged and it was obviously good for her.

Very quickly Libby found herself in the Club's Tennis Team so she played singles, ladies and mixed doubles against other clubs. This meant some week-ends away – happy times with a group of pleasant people. Libby felt herself expand, playing better tennis and often being on the winning side. She knew that she owed this to Frannie for whom she felt a mixture of emotions, mainly gentle sadness, but Frannie never seemed to change; he was always himself. Neither of them ever mentioned their extraordinary meeting and with Frannie so normal it was easy for Libby to try to forget it but that was one thing she could not manage. Poor Frannie, always hiding his inner self.

Coming back to The Loop one Friday she handed over the post to

Dar as usual but he gave one letter back to her. She had not noticed that an official looking letter – it had a typed address - was for her. It looked business-like. To her amazement it came from the Nairobi Secretary of the Church Missionary Society who'd met Miss Benson when the boat train reached Nairobi. He'd been introduced to her, a small, neat man with impeccable manners and a charming crinkly-eyed smile.

Dear Miss Winchester,

As Executor to the estate of the late Miss Ursula Benson I must inform you that in her Will she left to you a Freehold property at Chemchem of approximately one acre on which stands a cottage and some servants quarters (L.R. No. 1277/03). The keys are with Col. Benson who lives next door to the property in Wood Avenue. I have told Col. Benson that you are now the rightful owner. By separate registered post the Title Deed will be sent to you.

On Miss Benson's last visit to Nairobi, before her tragic death, she particularly mentioned this cottage to me. You may be aware that the majority of Missionaries return to Britain for their retirement but Miss Benson had decided on Chemchem, Col. Benson being her last remaining relative. She felt that should anything happen to her (she was fully aware of the Mau Mau dangers) she would like the cottage to go to you as you were her only acquaintance in the area and Col. Benson is already well provided for.

Perhaps you would be good enough to acknowledge receipt of this letter and of the Title Deed.

Yours etc,

In Christ,

S. Goodman (C.M.S. Secretary, Nairobi)

'Dar, read this!'

'Well – good heavens! It's probably a nice little property – Wood

Avenue's a good area. Worth a bit. You could sell it well. Funny that she didn't leave it to the Mission.'

'I expect she left them all her money. I *must* see it quickly. How very nice of Miss Benson. She was a really *good* lady, Dar, and not at all stuffy or pi – you know what I mean. She laughed a lot and seemed so tolerant of everything – so easy to be with.'

The letter arrived just before one of the Backlands' monthly dinners so Libby's new acquisition was great news. Both Glory Halleluiah and Madge were especially interested, Madge thinking that she knew the cottage, having been down Wood Avenue not long ago to see a friend. There was no holding them so Libby agreed that the three of them would go into Chemchem the very next day after dipping and investigate her new property. Libby was deeply excited. Dar was delighted.

It was indeed a very pretty cottage. A single story building of pink brick between wooden frames, it was like a Tudor cottage with its many-paned windows. There was an enclosed porch on the left of the front with a tangle of jasmine on one side and a healthy bush of Cecile Brunner roses on the other side. The roof was made of steeply pitched cedar shingles. There was no proper garden, just grass – somewhat over-grown.

'Go on, Libby! Open up.'

From the porch a sizeable living room was entered. There was no furniture except for a small round dining table in a corner. A door led to the only bedroom that was large and had off it, at the back, a reasonable linen cupboard and a big bathroom. From the sitting room a kitchen was reached with a big storeroom and, as a big lean-to further back, there was a wide veranda with a cupboard at each end and a double dhobi sink. The sitting room and bedroom made the main part of the house with windows at the front. Everything else was behind these rooms. It was neat and far from pretentious; the feel was of a genuine cosy cottage.

'It's lovely!' said Madge.

'Absolutely,' agreed Glory Halleluiah, 'Oh, Libby, you can't sell this!'

'Oh, I won't – I love it! I can stay here instead of at the Club – for tennis – a private place – a hideaway!'

'Not a hideaway – it's charming - it's the Gingerbread House!' declared Glory Halleluiah.

Libby was enchanted with her cottage. If she wasn't busy at The Loop, or playing tennis at Chemchem or away, she was furnishing the Gingerbread House. Instinctively she knew that she wanted it cottage-style and she did it well, combing the second-hand shops in Nakuru or Nairobi for odd furniture and fittings. Glory Halleluiah and Madge often visited the cottage when they went shopping in Chemchem to see the latest developments. Libby's large, smiling African servant, Anna, let them in and made them coffee. Pretty floral prints appeared as curtains and Glory Halleluiah found some old brass items that added to the feel of the place. Occasionally Dar visited and approved heartily and even Frannie and Lew found their way there but Mumps stayed away. She thought it immoral that Libby, who had so much, should have been given even more.

Libby was absolutely fine again, blossoming happily and finding life good.

It became even better when Libby met Christopher Norrris during a tennis tournament held at Parklands Club, Nairobi. They were playing opposite each other in the Mixed Doubles and were immediately attracted. Chris was a medium sized young man with a canny tennis serve, a wicked backhand and a habit of tossing a few lobs that few returned well. Libby enjoyed his play and reacted with clever tennis of accuracy that was her strong point. They managed to be together for drinks after the games.

Chris was fair-headed, rather stocky, with an open, cleanly-scrubbed look and he spoke very well. Libby assessed a British Public school background (she was right) as he was clearly not a Kenyan young man – he was far too polite! She sensed that he would always behave with decorum; he had that air. It was a pleasant change from the perfectly friendly, but often rather rough, manners of the Kenya young men. They had a very short time for chatter but he managed to ask her to let him know when she would be in Nairobi next and they exchanged addresses. The Chemchem team all saw this but, knowing well Libby's upset over Bobby, they tactfully pretended not to notice and said nothing on the long drive back home. Libby was definitely happy; he was a very nice young man indeed, she thought.

Back at The Loop she mentioned Chris to Dar who was delighted at this turn of events – someone she liked! 'He works for Shell eh? Very good company – *very* good company. Invite him up here, chick.'

'Dar – give me time! I've only just met him. He may turn out to be awful!' but she didn't think so. The next few weeks were happy because Chris wrote to her immediately; a nice friendly letter, and she replied in kind. He was obviously very well brought up. She resolved to get back to Nairobi as soon as she could.

When she did get to Nairobi Chris had obviously made plans but was diffident about asking if she would like to do this or that. She was delighted. They went to an excellent amateur production at the National Theatre (Nairobi having outstanding amateur theatre – well up to British professional standards), they dined at Lavorinis (excellent food, romantic setting) and had tea out at the Brackenhurst Hotel, in the cool tea growing hill country about twenty miles out of Nairobi. It was all very easy; they simply chatted, telling each other about their respective lives. They definitely warmed to each other, Libby being grateful that he was obviously going to take it slowly. Bobby had bulldozed her, she thought, though at the time she thought it was so romantic and great. (What he'd actually done was to say to her during their third dance at her twenty-first birthday party 'Right – Libby – you're *my* girl now – don't you let any other bastards near you!')

Chris was definitely not of the type to say anything like that at all – nor would he even swear, she guessed. He gently let her know that he'd been at Oxford, read History, tried reading law (his father was a Barrister), didn't like that so went into commerce, two years with a Merchant bank, and now with Shell where he was very content.

Libby returned to The Loop very happy, thinking a lot about Chris whom she had invited to visit the Backlands when he could get enough time off. There was no doubt that he would come, he had been delighted at the invitation.

The weekend he chose coincided with a fifth Sunday in the month. That meant that the Chemchem chaplain was free to take a service at the Backlands. This was always held at Glory Halleluiah's house because she had a piano and played for the hymns. After the service the chaplain, Mr. Ironside, stayed for lunch with everyone. Libby had no fears that a church service would faze Chris; he had been properly brought up. What she hadn't realised was that Mr. Ironside was away for two months leave and a substitute chaplain had taken over.

The substitute was an elderly bachelor called Mr. Lightwood – who wanted to be called Father Lightwood but the Chemchem residents were not having that. Any High Church leanings were severely squashed by the farming community – many of whom were Christians but of a plain, simple sort to whom bells, candles and incense were anathema.

Libby was ignorant of a substitute chaplain but the Twybitt brothers were not.

They invited Glory Halleluiah to drinks a few days before the service and asked, casually, 'What hymns have you got for us on Sunday?' because she always chose them. Her choice was inevitably simple, the Backlanders being, on the whole, decidedly unmusical.

Glory Halleluiah should have known better but, as usual, she fell into the trap. 'Do we know the hymns?'

'Of course you do' – 'Stand up, stand up for Jesus' – 'Onward Christian Soldiers' – 'When morning gilds the skies' – 'I've forgotten the other two but you know them perfectly well!'

They did.

Chris Norris made an instant good impression on Dar by calling him 'Sir'. Dar thought that in this modern world of the nineteen fifties young men had forgotten that politeness. The visit went on being good. Dar liked Chris more and more; he came from a good background and had the bearing and quiet confidence of a proper person. Although he knew that it was premature, Dar kept assessing Chris as a future son-in-law and felt many plusses. If only he was a farmer! But Dar joined Libby in taking Chris round the farm on one trip and found him deeply interested in the ranch – would he make a farmer in time? Dar had a lot to consider.

Lew liked him, too. So did everyone else when they met for the service at Glory Halleluiah's house. Even Mumps was gracious. In fact it was difficult not to like him.

Mr. Lightwood put on some rather fancy vestments - far too fancy they all thought for the Backlands - everyone sat down and the service began. The first hymn was the rousing 'Onward Christian Soldiers' and, immediately, Corn and West stretched their hymn books in front of them, squinting as if unable to read the words properly and did the schoolboy trick of singing quite different words. 'Onward British sailors, onward to the sea...' and so on.

Mr. Lightwood gave no indication that he'd heard anything, Lew was having an awful time trying not to giggle and Frank was bellowing in the hope of drowning out the two brothers. It was with difficulty that they finished the hymn. From the piano stool Glory Halleluiah glared at the miscreants who were simply gazing with deep, innocent interest at Mr. Lightwood and his words.

The second hymn was 'When morning gilds the skies' which they interpreted as 'When pawning saves our lives' – and so on. This was too much for Glory Halleluiah. At the end of the hymn she left the piano, quietly excused herself to Mr. Lightwood and advanced on the brothers. With a hiss she said, 'Out! Both of you - this minute!' at which they immediately cringed like little boys being caught out in some wickedness and Corn said, 'We'll behave – promise!' and that was that.

Chris had heard of the settlers. Now he was seeing them in action! He couldn't help being amused, especially as Mr. Lightwood seemed totally oblivious of it all, so absorbed, as he seemed to be, with himself.

Later, on another drive round the ranch with Libby he was told more about the Twybitts – no pretension ever got beyond them and she regaled him with some of their childish humour. Then he changed the mood entirely by asking her about the Chemchem murders.

'You've heard? I suppose all Kenya knows. It's awful. So far four girls have been killed – all teenagers. Frank and Madge – you met them at the service – their daughter, Sally, was the first. She was only fifteen but was buxom – looked older. It's always been near the Club area or on farms nearby. Anyway no-one knows who the murderer is. The police have grilled lots and lots of men – it must be a man because the girls have been raped and then killed. Frannie was suspected – so were Corn and West. It's difficult for farmers to come up with alibis – they're out on the farms – hard to prove.'

'So it's thought to be a bachelor?'

'At first those were the men the police went for but now they're looking at anyone, I think. There's a man at Chemchem known as the Lecher – and he is lecherous – the police went for him. And then we've got a chap here in the Backlands – Bell – whose wife left him years ago – they looked at him, too. It's all been very upsetting and uncomfortable for everyone.'

'Weren't you afraid as a teenager?'

'Oh, all girls are warned – there are notices at the Club and everyone tells visitors – be careful - all that. But I think I was sent to England to be out of the way for a bit. I never was approached by anyone – lucky for me!'

'Awful to think that someone is a murderer in the district! At least one supposes he must live in the area?'

'Yes, the police assume that because Chemchem is so far from anywhere else. But the murders are well spaced – about three years between each so someone could come into the district and not be seen

– but very unlikely.'

'Why the Club area – is it someone who lives near the Club?'

'The police are always on to the farmers near the Club – poor chaps - but it could be anyone – and, of course, the Club is where the girls meet. Luckily for Frannie and for Corn and West – all three had unbreakable alibis for the second murder so they're clear.'

'What an awful thing to hang over a district!'

'Yes – though – and it sounds terrible to say it – we're all used to the idea. Girls just have to be careful with men!'

That evening the Twybitts went round to Glory Halleluiah with a peace-offering of a very good bottle of single malt whisky. They got an earful and ended up having dinner with her. She couldn't resist them.

Libby managed two more Nairobi visits, each time meeting Chris and enjoying time with him, pleasant, easy togetherness. He was obviously taking his time but kept telling her more and more about his life, hopes and aspirations.

'If possible I want to stay with Shell. It's a very good company. They expect a lot but pay well and look after you if you do well. Of course I could be sent anywhere – but that's good – travel the world. And when there are children, then boarding school is the answer and Shell understand all that.'

Libby knew exactly why she was being told. He was extremely careful, yet easy and there was no pressure. Just friends, he seemed to say, but implied something more. It was such a great contrast to Bobby; Libby found it comforting and a quiet happiness.

At Venture Mumps was in a blacker than usual mood. Frannie had gone off with George Geddes – can't think what they see in each other – on another safari, this time a long way away south of Narok in Masai country. Marco was helping on the ranch but kept evading Mumps when she needed anything; he'd laugh cheerfully and disappear to the cattle. Really how could Frannnie leave her like this? And it was happening more and more. He should look after her much better than he did; she was his mother!

Not telling her husband, she'd planned a large family in the midst of which she'd be the controlling, dominant figure. She'd seen children as satellites of herself - the sun - in the centre; the matriarchal figure with adoring children ready to do her bidding. It had been her dream since she'd been a teenager, and Frank Houghton-Framlyn seemed a suitable man to provide her with what she wanted; he was well off, well bred and quite quiet. They'd hardly known each other – it had been an arranged marriage because their families lived either end of a village and had been the main families. Determined to become pregnant as soon as possible she was happy during her pregnancy, probably happier than she'd ever been. And then Frannie had arrived and had shattered her dream. A nurse was employed and the nurse and Frank reared the child. The move out of England was an attempt to cheer her up. She hadn't bargained for coming to Kenya but had to accept the change grudgingly, being mollified by the plentiful supply of servants, a breed fast disappearing in Britain.

Now grown up, Frannie was prepared to leave her on her own for long periods – and so often. How could he? His job was to look after her! She was rehearsing these thoughts – as she often did – when she was shopping in Chemchem and was surprised by a greeting from that young man, Chris Norris, that Libby seemed to have acquired. He'd recognised her from the Service at Glory Halleluiah's house and was all politeness. So it was Mumps who knew first that Chris was arriving for an unexpected visit to The Loop. He said he was on his way to see Dar. That suggested something serious. Mumps was annoyed; Frannie wasn't around for her to tell the news. Typical, she thought.

Libby was amazed when Chris arrived at The Loop. He explained that the telephones from Nairobi to Nakuru were out of action so he couldn't warn them, but he wanted to see Dar. Libby was surprised but knew that he hadn't come to ask Dar's permission for a marriage; she and Chris hadn't got that far at all!

In fact that was exactly what he was doing, and with an urgent reason. A car accident had taken the lives of two Shell men in Singapore; Chris was to be moved there in two weeks. Everything had to be quick. Singapore! thought Dar, but he gave his permission, liking Chris for asking it; Libby was well over the age when she needed parental consent.

Later, on the ranch, Chris extremely nicely but without any pressure told Libby that he loved her, that he was being moved and would she marry him. It was all sudden, he knew, but he *had* to ask.

It was *sudden*, too sudden for Libby. She hesitated. What could she say?

'Libby, think it over – tell me to-morrow morning. I've got to go early – but *please* – you know how I feel.' He gave her a gentle kiss that Libby took without responding; she was too surprised to react at all.

After Chris left in the morning Libby went straight to Dar.

'Oh, Dad, I'm so sorry. I just couldn't! He's so nice but – well – I don't really love him. I spent all night asking myself if I loved him enough to go to Singapore with him. But I don't,' Libby shed a few tears. Dar, with mixed feelings, hugged her and said nothing.

Glory Halleluiah comforted Dar.

'I expect he was *too* nice – in a way – too polite. Every girl needs a bit of dominance in her man – a bit of roughage, perhaps. Don't worry, Dar, she's meeting people now. The right man *will* appear.'

CHAPTER 7

It was after tennis. Libby finished her shower and was changing in the shower cubicle. She could hear other Club members – ladies – around, going to the loo, washing their hands. Eventually two were left.

This was only a few weeks after Libby had called Frannie and asked him to meet her at the Picnic Site.

'Hi, Libs, can I help?' Frannie was cheerful but geared to deal with some problem of Libby's life.

'Yes Frannie – you said you'd help me in any way?'

'I meant it – what can I do?'

'Grow your hair!'

Frannie roared with laughter. 'Oh, Libs, come on!'

'No, I mean it. That crew cut is awful. Please. Remember you said my behaviour was hurting others – well your hair makes us all wince – so, please, grow it!'

Frannie laughed again.

'There was I – arriving like St. George to slay whatever dragon problem you'd got and it turns out to be my hair! Libs, you're nuts.'

'I expect so. But you promised. Please!'

'Oh, all right – it'll drive me mad I expect so you can prepare a straight-jacket for me – that'll be your job!'

Then they'd chatted about odd things. Frannie asked about Chris and listened carefully to her side of the story, feeling sorry for the fellow who was so obviously a nice, harmless chap. But he was relieved that she had turned him down. Frannie didn't want to delve into his own feelings too much but quite often they surfaced strongly. This was one of the times. He was pleased, though, that Libby had dealt with it all well and seemed to have no second thoughts. He was even pleased that she'd spoken about his hair! They parted cheerfully.

Libby was thinking of Frannie's hair when she was in the shower. He was growing it. She'd noticed but no-one else had - yet. Then voices of the two other women in the ladies' cloakroom took over ...

'Yes, I heard it from Barbara Fish. Really! Of course it's not surprising about that chap Houghton-Framlyn but he's obviously twisted that young lad – the Cooper boy.'

'Well –I *am* surprised. I'd no idea. Not very savoury is it? Houghton-Framlyn and young Cooper always going off camping together – and *more* than camping. Oh, I hate that. Can't take it. I know some of them are charming men but it gives me shivers up my spine. Horrible.'

'I agree. Oh well. Do you need a lift – I'm going your way.....' and the voices disappeared.

Libby was frozen in horror. She recognised one of the voices, but the name Barbara Fish told her a great deal. Mrs. Fish's husband was a big cheese at the Chemchem Rifle Club.

The Rifle Club.

Thomas Bell.

Thomas Bell (never known as Tom) had always loathed Frannie.

It was a long time before Libby felt safe to leave the Ladies' changing room and go to her vehicle. She certainly couldn't go back to the bar for her usual drink. This Thursday was totally different.

What could she do?

Not for an instant did she give credence to the suggestion. Of course neither Frannie nor Lew were homosexual! The thought that this rumour – produced as fact – was going round Chemchem troubled Libby.

She drove straight to the Gingerbread House where Anna had lit a fire and laid the table for Libby's usual Thursday night light supper. But Libby sat in a chair by the fire and thought – deeply. It was up to her. *She* had to do something. It was no good just telling the tennis crowd that the rumour was false; they all knew that the Backlanders stick together and some would not believe her. She poured herself a drink, nursed it, looked into the fire for inspiration and inspiration came, simply by looking at the shapes made by the log fire.

This time she didn't want to call Frannie to the Picnic Site. That would make it obvious; she wanted to catch him casually, play it very gently and make it appear off the cuff. She was rewarded after a few days by Frannie coming over to talk to Dar about the next trip up north for cattle buying. Dar was out but Frannie said he'd wait. It was evening so Libby gave him a drink and they talked about farm things. Lew was over with his parents for the evening. Libby prayed that her father would be held outdoors a bit longer.

She casually dropped into the conversation, 'Frannie, you know these little camping trips you do with Lew? I know you take Nzioka sometimes, but not always. Do you think I could come as well?' Her effort to be casual was good but not good enough to deceive Frannie; he caught an undercurrent.

'Yes, of course you can. Of course you can. Anyway why? Why do you suddenly ask?'

'No special reason, Frannie, I'd just like to come. I wouldn't be in your way or anything – I'll cook if you like.'

'Well that would help – Lew's as bad as I am. We only ever barbecue something simple.'

Libby turned the conversation onto Lew and the subject was dropped for a few minutes but Frannie, the terrier, came back to it.

'Libs, there's something about this camping bit isn't there. Of course you're welcome but, come on, tell me.'

'No, no, nothing special. I'd just like to come.'

'Libs ....!'

She said nothing. They both sipped their drinks.

'Come on, Libs. What is it?'

He was far too intelligent and discerning, she knew that really. She had to confess.

'At the Club. Two women gossiping in the Ladies room and didn't know I was there. They suggested that you and Lew...........' and she couldn't go on.

'Oh my God!' Frannie was utterly shattered.

'Of course it's not true. But they said you and Lew always went camping together – so I thought that I could casually mention to them - next time I saw them – that when you go camping I go as well – that'd stop it?'

Libby was anxious. Frannie was almost white with anger, yet listening to her carefully.

There was a pause.

'Libs, bless you. Of course you can come. Come next time. And,

Libs, who were the women?'

'I'd rather not tell you but it was dropped that the rumour came from Barbara Fish.'

'Aaah,' Frannie understood completely. 'I'm so angry I could kill that bugger, Bell. It'll be him. He hates my guts.'

'We know. But why? What have you done to him?'

'Nothing. He just can't take my – disability – my foot. It offends him.'

'Frannie, no. It can't be that. No-one does that!'

'They do, Libs – look at Mumps. To some people any oddity is an offence to mankind. That's me to Thomas Bell. He's obsessed.'

'He's dangerous!' flashed Libby.

'That too.'

Libby felt desperately aware of Frannie – so blazingly angry – and male – beside her. It was as if she'd never seen him before. Even in his anger he was totally in control – that was clear. She felt helpless whilst he sat so she took his glass and poured another drink, saying nothing.

'Thanks, Libs,' he said gently and with a wry attempt at a smile, 'and thanks for your help over this – rumour.' He leant forward and kissed her cheek. 'Quite a bloody good little sister I've got! And, Libs, not a word to Lew. Between us we'll handle this. You do as you suggest; come camping and let them all know and I'll deal with Bell.'

Later, as he went to bed Frannie said to himself, 'And to hell with turning the other cheek. Bell, I'll diminish you, you bastard!'

It took time, but Frannie was good at patience, good at planning and good at practicing.

Libby went with the two men on their next camping trip and thoroughly enjoyed it. They did not go far beyond the Elephant Gap, driving to a place where there was a small wooded rise of land quite close to the Chemchem River – now a wide, shallow stretch split with sandbanks on which crocodiles basked. Three tents were put up in a neat row, Frannie's was the largest with Lew's a small bivouac and Libby's in between them.

The men went off shooting Vulturine Guinea Fowl and Yellow-necked Spurfowl, the former for their beautiful blue capes as much as for food – the capes were used for making fishing flies – and the latter were excellent eating with white flesh like a chicken. Libby stayed in the camp, tidying it up (how could men make such a mess?) and enjoying the bird life. She'd been careful not to overdo it but had come prepared with some special toasties to have with drinks and she'd even made puddings – a luxury in camp. The main food would be the barbecued meat of the Yellow-necks. It was very easy, and Frannie and Lew seemed happy to have her although Lew had had reservations before the event. Now, with better food and someone to clean up, wash up and generally spoil them he was glad. She was not the boss's daughter here; she was a friend. And, Libby found, that although they were only one night in camp – a short time snatched from work - it seemed much longer; the place was close to The Loop yet a different world, the camp was put up quickly and there was time to do nothing and relax fully.

Lew was in the middle of gutting and plucking the birds 'Why do I always get to deal with the birds eh, Frannie – come and help!!'

Frannie stretched his long legs out from his camp chair, nursed his drink and said, 'I simply love seeing you work, Lew. It's well known that you do absolutely nothing at The Loop. Libs does it all, don't you, Sis?'

But Frannie had plans for Lew. Although by now Lew was an excellent marksman and had shot several buffaloes, one leopard, some lions, and plenty of plains game (the latter for the pot), Frannie had decided to extend Lew's shooting.

'What – target shooting? A bit dull – all that stuff?' asked Lew.

'Not when you really get into it. It's a tremendous discipline. Anyway it's time you started doing more serious things – different ranges – and so on.'

There was a shooting range on Venture that Frannie's father had made years ago from a natural sandbank. Frannie had been taught by his father there and, in turn, Frannie had started off Lew there. The range was to be revived. After a few goes at different distances Lew began to enjoy himself but still thought it not up to facing a buffalo. 'Dead right, Lew, but this is a different thing altogether – and you're good.'

'Nowhere near you!'

'So much is in breathing and relaxing – try again.'

Frannie was slowly extending the distances and Lew tried again, and again, and again, suddenly realising the challenge of it all. Most evenings they'd have a session at the range, frightening all the game around with the noise. Frannie was very pleased; Lew was such a natural. But Frannie was also doing a lot of practice, more and more and more. He was well aware that if one wants something badly then one must work for it.

When the notice went up about the Rifle Club's Annual Championship, Frannie sent for the application forms. Because he and Lew were not members of the club, they could only enter for the big Open event that comprised of a certain number of shots at four different distances, two being very serious lengths.

Back at Venture, Frannie altered things so that greater lengths could be tackled on his range and practices became even more serious. Libby was often with them – at Frannie's request; she earned her place by changing the targets and scoring for them. She knew exactly what Frannie was after, and he knew that she knew. She took them thermoses of coffee or tea, fed them sandwiches and it was fun as well as having an underlying seriousness that Lew did not feel. Dar, however, wondered why there was this sudden rush to marksmanship and complained to Libby that she and Lew were off the ranch too much in the evenings. Libby soothed him by telling him about the Club championship.

'Frannie's never attempted it and Lew is so good he thought he also try, too – good for them both.' Dar was partially mollified so Libby persuaded him to come and watch one evening and he caught the fever, even having a go himself (once a good marksman he had let it slip and Libby laughed at his attempts – so did Dar himself).

The Championships were held over two days, shooting in the morning and evening, leaving the heat of the day when targets would shimmer in the heat. Quite a gathering came to enjoy the event so Frannie and Lew were not over-conspicuous. They were constantly attended by Libby, much to Frannie's amusement – and gratitude. He knew exactly what she was doing. On the first morning Libby saw Mrs. Fish, a perfectly nice woman she had always thought, and felt a bit sorry for her – it was too easy to pass on a spicy snippet of gossip. The Open Class was on the second evening, the last event, but Frannie and Lew were watching all the classes carefully. There were a large number of classes – for all ages, distances and combinations of the two.

It was clear that Thomas Bell was the star performer. He'd been outright Champion for many years and easily won the classes he entered. He was fiercely proud of his ability, very self-assured and self-satisfied. Disliked by the Club's members, nevertheless his ability was acknowledged. Frannie watched him shooting very carefully and saw extreme concentration, excellent breathing and outstanding shooting. If Bell saw Frannie he made no sign at all. Looking at Bell shooting, Frannie thought if Lew can relax a bit he could beat him – and I'll damn well try!

The Backlands contingent to see the Open Class was considerable. News had got around that Frannie and Lew were competing and the men, especially, were out in strength. Dar and Frank were there to back Frannie and Lew but Corn and West were there to look at the shooting. They were not target-shooting men but were deeply interested in any use of firearms. From nowhere Mario and three of his boys arrived, mainly out of curiosity. Mario had to shoot and so did his sons, but like so many things, they took it as fun, but even they were careful when handling guns. Glory Halleluiah had hoped to attend but a ranch problem had prevented it.

The draw for the Open put Thomas Bell amongst the first few competitors at each distance with Lew a little later and poor Frannie right at the end. They followed this order at each distance, the farthest being at the end.

There was no doubt at all that Thomas Bell was good, very good indeed but, to his surprise and delight Lew matched his score on the first two distances, and so did Frannie. Backlands supporters were now on edge, Libby not even wanting to watch but magnetically drawn to it. She was murmering to herself 'Bell – you fiend – bloody well miss!' and at the third distance he did not do so well, perhaps annoyed at the competition from the Backlands. He was overtaken by both Lew and Frannie. At the end of this third distance, Lew was elated, Frannie calm, Bell furious. His fury did no good for his shooting and at the last distance he showed it. Lew overtook him and it was left to Frannie to perform with apparent ease and overtake Lew's score by a margin. Out of the possible 1,000 score Bell had 982 – a very creditable score, Lew 987 and Frannie 991 to the cheers of the Club's crowd.

Frannie accepted the Cup gracefully and Lew was flushed with success. Many of the Club's members congratulated them and not a few whispered, 'Bell's got his come-uppance – about time.' In the bar later Frannie and Lew were approached and invited to join the Rifle Club. This was in the hearing of Bell who turned his back but the malevolence emanating from him was so strong that anyone could clutch it. Frannie made a grateful but non-committal reply and Lew followed that lead. Mario appeared and asked Frannie to teach Roberto and Luigi – and maybe some of his other sons – which Frannie was happy to undertake, knowing full well that after a few goes at the range they would be bored with the whole thing. Frank came to congratulate Frannie and clap his son on the shoulder and suddenly the whole of the Backlands contingent was together. Corn and West were discussing it very seriously, recognising Lew's calmness and good breathing; Libby was simply delighted. But how, she wondered, was any of this going to stop Bell being beastly to Frannie? Surely it would have the opposite effect?

She missed the exchange.

Frannie caught Bell just as he was getting into his car at the end of it all. 'Bell, get one thing straight. If you do not correct the rumours about Lew and me, we *will* join the Club. And put your nose right out of joint. Clear? Tell everyone you've made a mistake – and it is a mistake – a bloody great one! Put it straight and we'll leave the Club alone. But if that rumour – that lie – is not corrected – we're in. Understand?'

Bell stood absolutely still while Frannie talked, looking at his car. He made no sign of hearing, and when Frannie finished, he said nothing, got into his car and drove off.

'What did you say to Bell?' asked Libby who'd just come out of the clubhouse.

'I wished him the complements of the season – nearly Christmas, you know,' Libby laughed.

It was indeed nearly Christmas. Two events happened in Chemchem that upset the season of good will and happiness for many people. The first was that Bobby's wife went down to South Africa to have a baby. She had a very bad time over the actual birth as she had over the whole pregnancy and the child, a girl, was a very sickly baby. It was not sure that the child would survive – or the mother. Eventually the mother did survive but the baby died. The young mother was told that she should never have another child. This was a disaster for the Dacre family who needed sons to carry on the farms – as with all farmers. Then, when Bobby came back to Kenya after the event, his wife did not accompany him. She would be following later so it was said. But Chemchem wondered.

The other event was even more serious. Another teenage girl was raped and murdered. She was a visitor, staying with friends, and she had been warned – but it happened. This put a pall over Christmas for the whole community and, especially, for the Louch family on whose farm the body was found. Mr. and Mrs. Louch, whose farm abutted the Club and who had had enough trials over the previous murders, had two pretty daughters of eleven and thirteen for whom the community had great feeling. Mrs. Louch was a gentle lady who worked diligently for the Women's League and the Horticultural

Society and every week gave some time to the local African orphanage. Poor Mr. Louch had been grilled by the police after every previous murder and now – the body was on his own land. They had a great deal of sympathy but it did not improve their Christmas. The police started yet another investigation and Chemchem bore a gloomy face.

Yet again, despite exhaustive enquiries, the murderer was not found. Now, over a period of fourteen years, five girls had been murdered.

CHAPTER 8

Lew was having a drink with Frannie in the office at Venture– a small building tucked well out of earshot of Mumps – prior to getting back to The Loop for dinner.

'I'm exhausted, Frannie, with Grey and his bloody cattle! Night after night he's back – pushing his stock our side of the river to graze on our land. The Askari over there has to walk for over an hour to tell me, so I then round up some men to go and push the cattle back and it's the early hours of the morning before we ever get any sleep. I'm knackered! On and on, never stops. Always in these dry seasons when he's short of grass.....'

'And pinches your's because you look after your grazing and don't overstock as he does.'

It was a perennial problem, they both knew.

'Every time Dar goes to see Grey about it he denies any knowledge and blames his men.'

Frannie was pensive. There was no doubt that, young and fit though Lew was, he was tired. Several nights in a row without sleep took its toll.

'Of course at full moon?'

'Of course. It'll stop in a few days – too difficult for Grey's men to round up the cattle in the dark.'

Lew was slumped in a chair rather than sitting; this was unusual for him, he was always upright and firm.

'Well, Lew, we'd better find a way to stop him – permanently.'

'You'd get a Nobel prize if you could!'

Between the ordinary ranching jobs – dipping, weaning, branding, selling and a myriad other things – Frannie put his mind to the problem of Grey and his stealing of grazing from The Loop. It had been going on ever since Grey bought his ranch but it was obviously getting worse. Dar had been too nice about it – should have taken Grey to court. Frannie thought and then started organising – and a very good organiser he was.

The dry season continued and the moon was nearly full again. It shone on a neat line of Land Rovers parked behind a small kopje on the east of Dar's land, not far from the river. A camp table was set up and in absolute silence Madge and Libby were dispensing mugs of soup and meat rolls to the group: Frannie, Lew, Frank, Glory Halleluiah, Corn, West, Mario, Marco, Luigi, Roberto and Franco. They had collected some time before and were waiting patiently. Lew estimated that they'd probably have to wait another half hour before anything would happen. No-one minded. It was a lark, but a serious one this time.

It hadn't been easy. Lew had to persuade Dar to let him move all the stock out of that particular area, Frannie wanted a clean run. Dar trusted Lew's judgment over the grazing but was hesitating this time, *especially* because if The Loop cattle moved then Grey's cattle would come in. But, in the end, he allowed Lew to do what he wanted. Frannie cocked his head at Lew and Roberto who, again, silently climbed up the kopje to look beyond it. The moon made the river a brilliant gently moving shiny ribbon on the right. With binoculars Lew and Roberto could see absolute detail at the place where the Grey cattle usually crossed. They slithered down again for more food. It was going to be a long night.

In turn Corn, West, Luigi and even Frank climbed the kopje for a look and stayed a few minutes. Frannie was studying the stars and Mario was doing the same. Glory Halleluiah sat in her Land Rover for a while and Madge and Libby cleared away most of the food but left the drink. In the end it was Corn and Luigi who saw the cattle coming. They signalled down and excitement grew.

In his briefing Frannie had warned everyone that when the cattle crossed it might be a lot of luck and a long wait before action. They all knew. They were ready.

Being the most agile, it was Luigi who kept going up and down the kopje to whisper progress. The chance of talk reaching the two Africans who had brought the cattle was very small, the noise of the animals and the river combined would blanket most sounds, but Frannie was taking no chances. It was a herd of about two hundred and thirty with the herders pushing them from behind, with that eerie whistle that the Africans use and the cattle know so well. Grey's beasts, half starved on an over-stocked ranch in dry weather, had heads down straight away as soon as the reached The Loop's land.

The ruse worked! Luigi rushed down to tell everyone that the two men had found the remnants of a fire and a discarded, battered cardboard carton – so artfully put in place by Frannie and Lew that morning – as if someone had been looking at the crossing area. The fire had been difficult to fudge so they had actually lit one, hoping that it was not visible across the river. Yes, the herders were rummaging in the cardboard carton, throwing out some old newspaper. Then, yes, they've found it, reported Luigi.

Losing no time the herders opened the large bottle and were taking it in turns to have large draughts. ('Waste of good Scotch' said Frank)

'They're drinking it very fast.' Luigi told everyone. The cattle were roaming as they liked, the herders concentrating on this magical bottle – a gift from the Gods! Then Luigi reported that they'd finished the drink and seemed to be arguing as to who would take the empty bottle home. Frannie expected this and just said, 'Wait.'

This was the tedious bit, the waiting. It was becoming cool, even cold now. Madge and Libby offered coffee to those who wanted it and Mario added a big dash of brandy to all the mugs. He was in his element, itching with fun, longing for action. After what seemed an age Lew came down the kopje.

'I think it's O.K. Roberto and I'll go and have a look.'

'Careful!' but they needed no warning. They were not away very long but came back talking openly.

'Dead to the world, those men, come on.'

Now the organisation, about which Frannie had carefully thought, came alive. The men walked to the place where the two herders lay in an alcoholic haze. Half a big bottle of whisky would not put out a hardened drinker but these men were not of that sort. They were out, totally. Glory Halleluiah, driving her own Land Rover for a change, brought Madge up to the place and Corn and West with Mario's sons, helped lift the unconscious Africans into the back of the vehicle. Glory Halleluiah's conscience had caused her to put mattresses for them to lie on; the others thought that totally unnecessary. Once they were loaded Glory Halleluiah and Madge drove off into the night.

The European men spread out and, quietly behind the now scattered cattle, gathered the herd together. Corn and West each carried long stock whips but were not using them at this point. The sound of a crack of a stock whip would travel a long way. Finding all the steers –

it was a herd of young steers – took some doing and Libby was helping but when it was decided that they had all of the cattle together she went back to collect her vehicle. Using no lights she slowly drove up to the men and the herd.

Now the cattle had to be moved. It was a slow business but the steers were going well. Walking through the bush at night, even with a good moon, was not easy but all the men were tough. They were driving the cattle due north, heading for the topmost part of the loop of the river, near the Littet Hills where the good ford made crossing easy. To get to the Elephant Gap everyone crossed there. It was wide and safe at night. There were other crossings but Frannie was chancing nothing.

When Frannie judged that they were safely out of hearing of any of Grey's bomas he started the half whistle, half hiss that soothed the cattle. The other men joined in, some calling, some even singing (Mario and his 'boys'). Corn and West were using their whips to move the cattle but not cracking them yet. They were all trying to keep the herd together in a tight group, not an easy task.

They trudged on. It was a big distance that they had to cover. The cattle became stroppy; they wanted to graze, not move; there was lovely dry grass under their feet. The men worked hard. Every now and again Libby leapt out of her Land Rover to help the men when cattle were being obstreperous but she also had to be helped when she drove a wheel into a wild-pig hole. It all took time.

At last the herd reached the river and Libby drove over first, parked the vehicle on one side and got out to help guide the cattle in the right direction. The men turned the cattle east, towards Grey's fence line where it joined the Littet Hills. Now they were nearer their objective the men pushed the animals faster. Reaching the fence the cattle were pushed through a wide gap in the fence that Lew had laboriously cut the previous morning. The animals were back on Grey's land.

The really difficult bit came next. The cattle instinctively wanted to turn south back towards their boma but the men closed together to push them north again up the Littet Hills. It was very hard forcing the cattle to go in a direction that they felt was wrong, and in difficult country but the men pushed. Now the stock whips got going and were a great help. The hillside was rocky in places, filled with scrubby bush and very uneven. Mario and Frank were both sweating heavily and often stumbling but kept going. Even the younger men found it tough but with determination they went on.

Suddenly they got there. Hidden in the hills was a small cwm – perhaps of five acres and the cattle were pushed down into this bowl, going willingly now because they smelt water and food. Dotted about were several half drums of water (it had cost Frannie and Lew a lot of effort to manage this. They did it from the other side of the hills, getting tractors and trailers as high as they could and then using pipes to gravity-feed water into the half drums from big containers they had put on the trailers) and a lot of lucerne and ordinary hay (that cost a lot. 'It'll be worth it,' said Frannie.). The cattle immediately started feeding.

'Should keep them going two days – that'll be enough,' said a very tired Frannie.

It had worked. They'd done it. The cattle were out of sight but on Grey's land. The men watched for a few minutes to make sure that the cattle would stay and then, very tired and often tripping, half falling, made their way back to the bottom of the hill where Libby had to make two lampless journeys to get them all back to their assorted vehicles.

As a young lad Frannie had found that cwm when he explored

the Littet Hills. There was a similar one in the hills on his own property, though not as large. He'd explored thoroughly then but got Lew to go and check his memory. This had made Lew decide that, when he had time, he'd very carefully get to know the part of the hills on The Loop as well. Who knew what one might find?

Frannie had been very careful in his planning. He'd been to discuss the problem with the O.C.P.D. a few days before. The O.C.P.D. was amused and assured Frannie that as long as the cattle were returned to Grey's land, and the fence repaired, there was no illegality. Frannie carefully said nothing about the herders and what was to be their fate.

'I wish you luck! That man's a menace. I've had complaints from Dar Winchester, from Thomas Bell and even from the Coopers. He's hopeless, shouldn't be ranching. Let's see what happens.'

In fact the O.C.P.D., a very experienced man and used to the ways of the settlers, thought it all a splendid idea – if it worked it might stop a problem. It all depended on Grey's reaction. But react he did and in the hoped-for way.

As the sun rose next morning one of Grey's herders, who had been spirited away by Glory Halleluiah and Madge, woke up lying in grass with heavy dew. He had no idea where he was at all. Certainly he was not in the boma on the Bwana Grey's ranch. Covering him was an ex-army greatcoat that he found quite heavy as he moved slowly – as fast as a bad hangover would allow. Beside him was a sack, bulging with something. He cautiously opened it and found two packets of posho, a packet of tea, some sugar, and a wonderful tin of cooking fat. Treasure indeed! It was chilly so he slowly put on the greatcoat that was much too big for him but he found, in a pocket, a brown envelope – recognisable to him as all farmers used these as pay envelopes. He opened it and found more money than he'd ever seen in his life before! (Glory Halleluiah had insisted on this and dealt with it.) Whatever had happened overnight was not clear but he was rich! Looking around he saw that he was at the entrance to a farm; there was a road in front and a farm track on his right with a stand for milk churns. This was not the Backlands; this must be up in the Chemchem area. He waited, not knowing what to do. A farm tractor came down the track bringing fifteen milk churns to wait for the milk lorry on the stand. The tractor driver told him where he was – only a mile from the town. If he could hitch a lift with the milk lorry he could be home in half a day with all this wonderful bounty!

Exactly a quarter of a mile from that place the other herder was slower to rise and find his equal delights, but find them he did. He was also at the entrance to another farm and, after thinking about everything as much as he could with a not very clear head, he walked up the farm track, meeting a trailer with milk en route, and managed to land a job as a milker starting that very day. It was a much better position than he'd held with Grey and even if he wasn't a very efficient milker, he soon improved. His problem was to hide his enormous wealth from the other staff!

It was much later that morning when the O.C.P.D. accompanied Mr. Grey to The Loop. Mr. Grey had peremptorily summoned the police because of a massive cattle theft – 230 steers were missing! Being a very lazy man he'd risen well after sunrise and therefore heard of the disappearance of the stock late, and, as usual, was blaming everyone but himself. He was convinced that Dar Winchester had stolen his animals. He hadn't even been to the cattle boma to get the first-hand news; his headman reported to him. By the time the O.C.P.D. – who was determined to come himself – arrived Mr. Grey was in a very bad temper indeed.

'A whole herd gone! They must have strayed overnight onto Winchester's place. He's taken them. Stolen them! You'll see. I'll have him for this!'

The O.C.P.D. took all this calmly, too calmly for Mr. Grey, but insisted on going to the Boma from which the cattle had 'strayed'. The Policeman's command of Swahili was a lot better than that of Mr. Grey and the Africans recognised his uniform and his authority so he had no difficulty at all in discovering that it was by Mr. Grey's orders that the cattle were sent over the river. He kept this fact to himself. But it was odd that the herders had not appeared back in the Boma. Mr. Grey was hardly listening, he was so angry. The O.C.P.D. asked if Mr. Grey had 'phoned The Loop. Of course this had not happened, so the Policeman put Mr. Grey into his own Land Rover and together they drove to see Dar Winchester.

Dar was surprised to see them, innocent as he was of the night's activities, but before the O.C.P.D. could stop him Grey went for Dar.

'Winchester – you've stolen my cattle. I demand you return them NOW!'

'Just wait a minute, Mr. Grey. Good Morning, Mr. Winchester. Sorry to trouble you but Mr. Grey says that a herd of his cattle strayed onto your land last night and have not returned. Do you know of a stray herd on your land?' Dar nearly said that Grey's cattle were always on his land in the dry weather, but controlled himself. 'No, no-one reported any cattle but you're very welcome to look – I'll get my manager – just wait.'

Dar was angry. Served Grey right if his cattle hadn't got back – but that meant they were still feeding on his land – and bringing goodness only knows what diseases. Odd that they hadn't got back but that was typical of the man – no control – nothing. He sent for Lew who was in his cottage with his feet up, resting and waiting for this moment that they'd all hoped would happen.

'Lew, that damn'd Grey fellow's here. His cattle came on again last night and didn't get back. That dreadful man says we've stolen them! The O.C.P.D. is here too. Take them round and find their wretched cattle.'

Lew met the O.C.P.D. and Mr.Grey with both interest and a deceptive air of innocence.

'Your cattle here? Oh no. Our staff would have reported that. It's nonsense.' (Dar would not have been so strong but Lew felt he could say what he liked.)

'You've stolen them – don't deny it!'

'Absolute rubbish,' said Lew, now roused and looking taller than he was, 'Why should we do such a thing? Take your miserable animals when we've got good stock here! Mr. Grey, you don't know what you're talking about!' Dar was surprised that Lew could be so vehement – good for him, he thought.

'You – Winchester – you – Cooper – you've stolen them!'

The O.C.P.D. had let this exchange take place but now intervened.

'Can Mr. Grey and I look over your ranch, Mr. Winchester?'

'Of course, I have nothing to hide – Lew - take them everywhere. My brand is TL and all the stock are branded except the calves running with their mothers. And I don't want to see your cattle here again, Grey!'

It was going exactly as Frannie had hoped and planned. Everyone knew Grey and knew his extravagant claims; nothing was ever his fault and now he'd really been found out about his illegal grazing he had to make the biggest blame possible. Frannie had guessed this; the O.C.P.D. had said that it was likely, too. In fact the O.C.P.D. was quietly enjoying himself.

Several hours later when Lew had driven the two older men all over the east of the ranch, and then, at Mr. Grey's request, almost everywhere else, they returned to the house with no news of Grey's cattle. Lew had been careful not to take them too close to the ford where telltale footprints might show easily, but, from a distance, it was clear that there were no cattle near. Lew couldn't go close to the fence, either, he just hoped that The Loop's small fence team had done a good repair job that morning. He'd check later. As they drove round they saw several of The Loop's herds and at each group, Lew let Mr. Grey ask The Loop's men if they'd seen any of his cattle; the answer was always negative. It was a dreary round but Lew was quite cheerful and the O.C.P.D. quite enjoyed his trip round the ranch – better than a day in the office! Grey became more and more morose.

Libby (who'd also been resting after the night's work) was up, ready to give them tea, sandwiches and cake – lunchtime was well over – in fact it was nearly five o'clock. Mr. Grey was quieter, but still simmering with anger. He'd lost 230 head of steers!

'Well, Grey – none of your stock on our land? Don't say we didn't let you look and should we hear anything about them we'll let you know.' This was generous of Dar but what any rancher would have done.

To the O.C.P.D. Lew said 'We'll send Mr. Grey home in one of our vehicles – he came with you? Anyway, thanks for coming. Sorry it's been a waste of your time.'

But the O.C.P.D. wasn't going without saying one thing.

'Before I go, Mr. Grey, I think I must remind you that you have made a statement about Mr. Winchester – and Mr. Cooper – to the effect that they have stolen your cattle. *That* is a slanderous statement, I warn you. Good evening. I hope the cattle turn up.'

Dar had a lot to say about all this after Grey and the O.C.P.D. left and Lew let him get rid of steam and then said 'Frannie's coming over for drinks soon – you'll hear more then.' Dar stopped. Lew suddenly grinned, Libby burst into laughter and, as if on cue, Frannie arrived at that moment.

'Frannie – do you know something about this?'

'About what, Dar?'

'Grey's cattle disappearing – they'd been here again last night!'

'Grey's cattle disappearing? Oh, what a pity,' said Frannie and he laughed. 'Come on, sit down and I'll tell you where they are and what we do about it.'

The very next day one of Mr. Grey's men, working from a tip-off that arrived in a roundabout way, 'found' the herd. Of course Mr. Grey wasn't going to go up into the hills and the men were delighted about that – they wanted to claim those lovely half drums. They were not going to tell Mr. Grey about those, nor about the remnants of the hay, either. The herd was retrieved, none the worse for their adventure – in fact better as they'd all had a good feed. They came down the hill slower than they went up; it was more difficult, but once down, they made for their own area fast. Grey was fuming. How had they got into the hills? Not even Winchester could have done that. The two missing herders? Had they stolen an animal or two? Three counts were made before Grey was satisfied that all were present. The herders? Were they planning to steal the cattle and couldn't get further than the hills? He thought that likely. Anyway the men had gone! Reluctantly he phoned the police to report that the animals were not missing, in fact found on his own property. The message was received by a constable who wrote it down unemotionally, but the O.C.P.D. had asked for any news and when the message was relayed to him he couldn't help smiling.

Dar Winchester phoned Mr. Grey. 'I hear you've found your steers? And on your own land? Right. A letter will be on its way to you very soon.'

The letter for Mr. Grey was a lawyer's letter that said – words to the effect that in the presence of the O.C.P.D. Mr. Grey had made a slanderous statement saying that Mr. Winchester and his manager, Mr. Cooper, were thieves. Considering Messrs Winchester and Cooper's fine reputation in the district and the fact that the O.C.P.D. was witness to this incorrect statement, should Messrs Winchester and Cooper decide to sue for damages it is certain that extremely heavy damages would be awarded to them. Under these circumstances Mr. Grey should re-consider his neighbourly behaviour because Mr. Winchester and Mr. Cooper have decided that, should any more cattle stray from Mr. Grey's land onto The Loop, they will take legal action.

Dar sent a full carton of twelve bottles of Frannie's favourite brand of whisky over to him, Lew being the carrier.

'Here you are – a thank you from Dar!'

'Oh – good of him – he needn't have done it – fun wasn't it? What's he sent? Whisky?'

'No, Frannie – a Nobel prize.'

CHAPTER 9

Mumps phoned The Loop and invited herself to lunch. She'd sounded agitated on the phone but Lew, who took the message, thought nothing of that; she was often in some sort of abnormal state. However when she arrived her news certainly did enliven lunch.

'It's the police. Frannie has had to go into Chemchem for questioning! It's that man Louch's accident! You know. Frannie found the body!'

At The Loop no-one had heard this news and, eventually, a rather incoherent story emerged from Mumps that Frannie, on his way back from a shopping visit to Chemchem, had come across signs that a vehicle had gone over the escarpment – at the treacherous place everyone complained about – and had had to cope with the accident.

'He went to the Coetzee farm to phone the police and then he and Piet Coetzee climbed down the escarpment – they had to go much lower to find a reasonable place – and there was the remains of a car and Mr. Louch – dead – a real mess. Horrible. Of course Frannie got back very late last night and they've called for him this morning to go back for Statements and all that sort of thing.' Mumps had hardly taken a breath. 'It seems he'd seen Louch in the Men's Bar at the Club – though why Louch should be there for lunch I don't know – he lives next door. AND I've so often warned Frannie not to go to the Men's Bar – I know one can get a snack lunch - but it's a den of iniquity! And why Louch should be coming down our escarpment heaven only knows!' which thought had crossed the minds of Dar and Lew. Libby was away, shopping in Nairobi, and so missed all this interesting, though sad, news.

'Awful – poor Mrs. Louch – that's terrible – she has those very nice girls, too – oh sad.'

'And nasty for Frannie, to find everything. That corner really is bad. We really must get something more done about it!'

It was clear that the police also thought it odd that Mr. Louch had been driving so far away from his home but news rapidly reached everyone that Louch had been completely drunk at the time and probably had no idea of what he was doing. This explained why he'd not seen the big notice on the road warning drivers of the treacherous bend. It was, however, extremely unusual for Mr. Louch to drink at all, let alone become totally drunk. Then it became public that Mr. Louch had been in the Men's Bar celebrating a big win on the Irish Sweep. Things became more interesting and gossip rife.

There was enormous sympathy for Mrs. Louch and her pretty daughters. They'd always had sympathy over the Chemchem murders, too; those investigations had been difficult for them – and each time fruitless.

Chemchem was good at help in times of trouble. The combined community spirit made sure that Mrs. Louch was not left alone on the farm for weeks after the event and local farmers kept the farm work going for her. It was a great show of solidarity; everyone helped in some way. After intensive police enquiries into the accident there was a verdict of misadventure and a funeral at which a very large gathering supported Mrs. Louch and her girls.

Of course Mrs. Louch was now the recipient of great wealth – the Irish Sweep – and she was seen as an eligible widow. But give her time to get over her husband's tragic death first, everyone thought. Not so the Lecher who wasted no time in pushing his way into her view.

He was gently and courteously rebuffed.

Chemchem was amused.

Frannie told everyone at The Loop much more when he had time. Libby, having missed the original event, was fascinated.

'Louch was already screechers when I got to the Men's Bar. Amazing – you wouldn't have thought it of him – quiet chap usually. Don't think I've ever seen him in the Men's Bar before. There were a few other chaps there and they told me that he'd won the Irish Sweep and was celebrating. A massive win - £100,000 at least. Lucky for him, we all thought. He was offering drinks all round and shouting nonsense - really a noisy drunk! One wouldn't have thought it of him! Odd how drink takes people differently. It was fairly amusing to us all, in a way. Mind you I thought the barman shouldn't listen to his ranting – a new chap – speaks English – so I sent him off. Eventually Louch left – and I've got a bad conscience about this – I suppose one of us ought to have seen him home – but he lives only a few hundred yards down the road so we never thought of it. I suppose we thought he'd make it home, pissed or not!'

'Did the police ask you why you didn't help?'

'Afraid so – made me feel an awful heel – we might have saved a death! Too late to be sorry! Anyway, after I'd finished my drink and a scrap of food I went round town collecting the usual stuff – took a bit longer than usual – Jaswant Singh was very slow over some welding – and when I got to the escarpment the skid marks on the dirt road were horribly clear so I slammed on anchors, had a look and could see bits of vehicle spread in the bush below. It was pretty obvious no-one could survive that. Someone had been going far too fast to get round the

117

corner safely. Of course I was terrified that it was one of us! I went to Piet's place and called the police and told them that Piet and I would try to get down in case someone was alive and we could help. Rena gave us a First Aid box – ludicrous in retrospect! It was very difficult – rocky, bushes, and we had to go a long way down the road to find a suitable place to start from.'

Frannie made it all alive; everyone at The Loop was listening intently. 'We found the body long before much of the vehicle actually. Obviously Louch. A quick death anyway. He must have been knocked out immediately. What he was doing going along our road no one knows: Piet and I wondered about that! Nothing we could do, so we waited for the police and had to guide them – by the time we finished it was very late and we were blundering in the dark. Poor Mrs. Louch and the girls. Very sad. But at least she's got the money!'

'That won't replace a much loved husband!'

'Of course.'

Between them Frannie and Dar petitioned the Council to put up a barrier at the bad spot. It took time but was done and made the road a bit safer.

Another, much happier, event took the Backlanders' minds off the Louch tragedy. Glory Halleluiah had a Goanese Manager. The charming and gentle Goanese community in Kenya were often found working as chefs, bank tellers or on the railways but hardly ever on farms. How Mr. Pinto came to his position was a mystery but he and Glory Halleluiah had a neatly tailored understanding on the ranch that, though not in the same league as The Loop or Venture, quietly throve.

The event that was greeted with happiness by the Backlanders was that Mr. Pinto got married in Mombasa and brought to the ranch his slender, smiling Rosa with her cascade of shining dark hair. In no time at all Glory Halleluiah let it be known that Rosa was a dressmaker.

Libby pounced on this and after Rosa made her two pretty but practical tennis dresses Libby went mad with clothes (Mumps' opinion). Rosa was very happy to make clothes for Libby who had a perfect figure, was generous about left-over material and always paid Rosa more than she asked. Although Rosa made clothes for other ladies in The Backlands it was for Libby that she did most work, progressing to lovely ball gowns, ready for future Hospital Balls. One was a very special dress – and the most daring Libby had ever tried. It was in a very heavy cream silk, low backed and in front as well, held only by tiny shoulder straps. The skirt was so well cut that at the slightest movement it flared and swirled gracefully. Libby thought it beautiful but noticed that if she lifted her arms up the soft bodice fell open showing her ample bosom. Rosa laughed, pointing out that no-one puts their arms up at a ball.

Libby's wardrobe was bulging and at each Sunday dinner party she wore a new dress, Mumps thinking that the display was extravagant, Madge thinking that the dresses were lovely and Glory Halleluiah thinking that it was high time that Libby branched out into more femininity; Libby's normal day wear being a pair of slacks and a pale green shirt. With Libby looking so pretty and Frannie looking a lot more normal with a head of thick, slightly waving dark hair Glory Halleluiah thought that the dinners were becoming positively distinguished! Rosa's work made all of them try harder to dress well and the effect was good.

But, despite all this interest in clothes, as Dar complained to Frank, Libby was no nearer marriage.

'Frank, she not all that far off thirty! High time she was married.

If only she'd go and live in Nairobi – but she won't.'

Both Frank and Madge appreciated Dar's concern but Glory Halleluiah, curiously, was unworried, 'Oh, Dar, relax. It'll all come right in the end. Just wait.'

Apart from the sadness of Mr. Louch and the happiness wrought by Rosa the year passed in a normal fashion. The annual Boran Bull Show and Sale was held at Nanyuki that year – an easy distance for the best breeder, Mr. Curry of Rumuruti. The Neighbourhood Picnic was its usual success – this year with trips down the river in rubber boats. Frannie and Dar went north on cattle-buying trips and were unexpectedly joined by Corn. Glory Halleluiah's brother came out from Scotland for his annual visit and Frannie took him camping as usual. Mumps went to England for two months to visit some old friends and family - Venture had a relaxed cheerfulness for that time - and the Hospital Ball was a success again, but this time Dar declared that he'd had enough.

'I've been on that Hospital Committee ever since the hospital was built. Time for younger men! Come on, Frannie – take my place. The Backlands must be represented. Meetings every other month and a lot of argy-bargy but not too bad. Always fund-raising but Glory Halleluiah will help every time.'

'Oh – all right – I suppose I'd better be public spirited.' In fact for a long time Frannie had suspected that he'd have to take over certain things from Dar. He didn't mind much; the Cottage Hospital was vital for the community.

After only a few months on the committee Frannie found himself Chairman of the Hospital Board. His intelligence, efficiency and reliability were too obvious for the other Board members to pass by. It put Frannie into a different and closer position vis a vis the hospital where the problems were not so much medical as personal. Staffing the hospital was a difficulty. Because of the size of the place it wasn't possible to employ many European nurses (called 'Sisters' to differentiate them from the African assistant nurses) so they almost always had to work longer hours than normal. Some accepted this, others did not and left. There was a constant change of staff. If the European nurses didn't leave because of the hours of work they quite often got married, women being in short supply around Chemchem. It was an eternal headache for Frannie whose duty it was to employ the staff. The Africans were no trouble at all; Frannie got on with them well, but the Europeans! Equally the matron changed far too often. Frannie wondered why he'd ever taken on the job.

To ease his load he started to employ one of Mario's sons for at least three days a week, often four. This gave him some freedom to get to Chemchem and deal with other things off the ranch and also to enjoy the odd hunting safari with George. Roberto, Marco or Luigi came – it didn't matter which as they all knew the ranch well and were equally willing to help. Mumps was furious at the expense; Frannie obdurate.

The hospital headache seemed to ease when the wife of a retired farmer in Chemchem – a woman much younger than her husband – offered to help. No-one had known that she was a trained nurse but she was very well qualified, experienced and was prepared to come part-time but fill in anywhere. This was a blessing. She was mature, calm and efficient; the very thing Frannie wanted. The only position she refused to tackle was to become the matron. But, for the present, there was a matron.

Then two new nurses arrived. One was a very small, quiet girl called Janet Evans who was an excellent nurse and did not quibble about the hours to be worked. The other was a striking brunette who soon gathered the soubriquet of 'Sexy Sarah' that she did not deny. Fortunately, whatever she did in her private time, her work in the hospital was very good and she did not seem to mind the hours.

However Frannie was a bit concerned about the little nurse. She seemed shy socially although a demon on her job; she could be very firm with patients. On her time off she didn't get away and Frannie decided that he'd ask Libby to try to make friends with her if she could. Sexy Sarah, on the other hand, was a huge social success and was hardly ever in the Nurses' home during her time off. That was fine. Frannie resolved to have a word with Libby. In every other way the hospital seemed to enter a calm period, for which Frannie was grateful.

All was not so calm at Government House, Nairobi. The Mau Mau rebellion was virtually over and the Governor, Sir Peregrine Wix, a tall, very efficient and diplomatic man who had seen through the difficult Mau Mau years, had other matters to concern him now. One was to do with his younger cousin, Charles.

He wanted to speak to his wife about Charles and their only private time together was at breakfast; every other minute of the day being filled.

'Miriam, help needed.'

'Mmmm?' Lady Wix was scanning 'Miranda's Merrier Moments' – the weekly gossip column of the Kenya press. She was looking to see what Miranda had made of her clothes when she visited the Christian Industrial Training Centre at Pumwani where she wanted to look really interested (she wasn't, but was very experienced at producing the correct face and questions). Stylish! That was the only comment. Miranda normally did better than that.

'What?'

'Charles – help needed.'

'What about Charles?'

'The powers that be want him to have experience as a D.C. He'll be up-graded soon.'

'Ouch – above the heads of others – and him a relative of yours? That will not be popular!'

'Yes, but he's the right age even if he did come into the Colonial Service late – and his credentials are impeccable.'

'He should never have quit the academic world – much more his thing!'

'Yes, well, he's to be given six month's experience as a D.C. and then transferred to the Foreign Office.'

At this Lady Wix did take notice.

'Something special, I assume, that's most unusual!'

'Yes – language – to do with his mother – his fluency in Estolitv.'

Charles' mother came from a very small Baltic country near to Estonia that had one distinction – a massive oil reserve.

'There's something odd brewing in Estolitvia – something that's been simmering for months – and someone who is really fluent in the language is needed. Hence Charles. But, Miriam, the Foreign Office insist that he gets married.'

'Charles! Married! The last person! He's a human iceberg. He'd be far better with a dog – not that dogs would take to him. He's utterly cold!'

'Whatever he may be like, the Foreign Office wants him married. He's not a queer, we think, and the Estolitvian people will not take a single man in the top post. A wife has to be seen'.

'Has he been told this?'

'Yes. I can't say that he was enthusiastic but he said he'd do his duty.'

'Do his duty indeed. Ghastly. Oh Peri, I don't like it.'

'I'm not particularly happy either but that's what's got to happen. He's got about six months – or less – to find a wife. The problem is that he's quite likely to make a hopeless choice – he's no good with women, even in the Colonial Office. This is where help is needed. See if you can find a suitable girl – not too young – that'd do.'

'What a job. I'd not want to foist any girl onto Charles. Oh dear. It's a bit hopeless you know. Any girl worth her salt wouldn't have him!'

'Not sure about that. He'll have a K, he's got a private income, a nice house near Bournemouth and some girl might enjoy the entertaining she'll have to do. See what you can find.'

'So – Nairobi girls are in for a vetting!'

'Yes – but there's another problem – the only possible D.C. post that Charles can take is about as far as one can go – Chemchem.'

CHAPTER 10

Coming back from farm shopping one Friday Libby collected the little nurse, Janet Evans, from the Cottage Hospital. She had visited Janet at the hospital and was intrigued by the enormous difference between Janet, the highly competent nurse who dealt with all patients kindly yet with great firmness, and Janet, the girl off duty who seemed very shy. Libby invited her to stay at The Loop for her next days off and Janet had seemed very pleased with the invitation.

Very quickly Libby decided that Janet wasn't shy but – what was the word? Reticent. Certainly Janet never found it necessary to talk for the sake of talking; in this she was peaceful to be with. Libby told her about all the farms they passed and stopped, as everyone did, at the viewpoint near the top of the escarpment. From the height of the viewpoint, the loop of the river could be partially seen, almost all of Venture was visible and quite a lot of The Loop. The Littet Hills were an undulating line and, beyond them, there was a far haze of Africa. Saying very little, Janet absorbed it all, loving it more than she could express. Libby felt this and warmed to her though she realised that they were very different people. Never mind, if she could help Frannie and look after this little nurse a bit, she would.

'Dar, this is Janet Evans from the Cottage Hospital.'

'Very welcome – Libby'll show you everything.'

To Dar she was a very small, apparently rather inarticulate nurse, nothing more, but a guest to be given correct hospitality. Libby would cope.

On the way Libby had discovered that Janet could ride; this was unexpected as nurses were unlikely to know about horses in Libby's limited experience. It was good news and she mounted Janet on the smallest horse at The Loop – a 15 h.h. bay gelding - and it was clear that Janet was perfectly at ease on a horse, in fact a competent rider. Libby was very happy as she now had a companion. Usually she rode with a syce beside her – good but not as pleasant as having someone to chat with during a ride.

'We can't go over to the east of the ranch because there are some lion there – the horses hate that. But it's O.K. this side - we'll go towards the river. There's a lot of game around.'

Janet was entranced.

'Over there – look – oryx – those long horns!'

'Beautiful!'

'Yes, aren't they? We have them here because we're in the north of Kenya – we get different animals from the south – reticulated giraffe, oryx, Grevy zebra, gerenuk – things like that – and in the hills there are some lovely kudu – the greater ones – big curled horns. Elephant come and go. We have to shoot lion of they're a problem – eating the calves or something. And buffalo have to be shot – at least Lew does the shooting – he's the manager. You'll see.'

Later. 'Oh – lucky – that's an aardwolf! Not common. Like a hyaena but thinner, different shape and thin legs.'

All this was heaven for Janet who was hugging everything into herself. This was the Africa she'd wanted to see and, so far, had missed it. Now she was in it. Her eyes showed her happiness and Libby was pleased. This little dark haired nurse had more to her than expected.

At dinner Janet was introduced to Lew. He was a surprise as she expected a much older person as manager. Lew, as far as she could judge, was not much older than herself. He shoots lions, buffaloes and leopards? He was short, strongly muscled, probably tough as nails, she guessed. Like her he said little at dinner, just referring to two bulls who carried their penises so low that they were in danger of being damaged in the bush. This was hardly dinner-time conversation, Libby suddenly remembered, but Janet showed no surprise. She was just pleasant, relaxed, and, thought Libby, perfectly ready to fit into everything. An easy guest.

Janet was told not to get up early – she was glad as she was quite tired – so she missed her first glorious morning at The Loop; another time, she'd been told, mornings are lovely here. At breakfast Lew was slightly put out to be detailed to take Janet with him round the ranch.

'You're doing salt? Take Janet then, show her round a bit and talk to Abdi about that drainage on the punda milia road.'

Much to their mutual surprise Janet and Lew were at ease immediately. This was because Janet wanted to know about the ranch and, so far, she'd only been told about the wildlife. She asked lots of questions that were pertinent and it dawned on Lew that she knew a thing or two about farming.

'I should! I come from a farm. We're in Shropshire – not far from the Welsh border. Dad does beef cattle, a lot of sheep and some crops. Mixed. We've never done dairy except for a house cow or two. Or pigs – never tried that. Poultry for the house. That's it.'

Lew was ignorant of Shropshire and had he known that Libby had spent some years there when she was with her Uncle and Aunt he might have mentioned it. Any connection was lost. He was busy explaining so many things.

'The vital bit is dipping – awful ticks we get here – bring lots of diseases. Once a week most of the year but if it gets very dry we can risk every two weeks – few ticks in the dry. You'll see. You're here Monday? Monday, Tuesday and Wednesday are our dipping days. We all go out to oversee different places – otherwise things go wrong. The Africans can be great nine times out of ten and then, suddenly, they forget something really important.'

'Oh yes, I've seen that at the Hospital. Frightening!'

'Hopeless as bosses. They need white people over them – then they're fine.'

Lew took Janet to see the night bomas where he was leaving salt, pouring it into small troughs. Up to a thousand head of cattle, four herds of approximately two hundred and fifty each, came into the bomas at night, the bomas being divided to accommodate them. A thick line of cut thorn branches made the walls of the place, the thorn facing the outside to discourage lions jumping in (but lions still tried it). More thorn branches made the divisions inside. A small area was cleared of the thorn by day for a doorway. 'In the morning each herdsman calls his cattle – they get up and walk out to graze – the herds never get mixed up!'

'That sounds impossible.'

'The herders are from a special tribe from a long way away – the Orma – wonderful men with cattle – they love them.'

Janet was horrified at the tiny A-frame huts that the men slept in. 'Well – they're just sleeping places and they have to be small and light – we move the bomas every so often to stop the land nearby being over-grazed – let the grass recover.'

Janet understood it all, fascinated by the cattle that were so very different to the heavy, stocky, short legged red Hereford animals her father bred. The animals at home had white faces and curly hair on their heads. These Boran cattle had humps, heavy shoulders, dewlaps and there was a variety of colours, even ones with spots, and not very graceful shapes, she thought ; Janet doubted that they'd produce the good beef that she knew at home.

'We breed a lot here but Dar also buys some up north. There's a scheme that Europeans can go up north at special times each year and the Africans bring their cattle for sale and then the wazungu - that's Europeans – fatten them up and sell them later. We go on great safaris to buy them – and then they're walked here slowly. It's a bit of a risk but worth it, really. I love going on those trips; Frannie comes and Dad used to go but not recently.' Then Lew told Janet about his home under the escarpment; they could see the very place. Now Janet fully understood; here was a young man born and bred on a ranch; no wonder he was so obviously happy in his work.

For two quiet people there was a flood of non-stop conversation. If Lew wasn't explaining then Janet was asking. Both enjoyed it. Lew, bereft of any friends of his own age – not counting Mario's boys because they made a group of their own and seldom needed outsiders – had hardly spoken to girls of his own age and was surprised at how easy it was. Janet was interested in everything and wanted to learn; Lew was knowledgeable and was ready to expound. It was a very pleasant morning and Janet couldn't help feeling that Lew was a very nice young man indeed. Lew found it more agreeable than he expected and thought that she was a nice girl. It was not a bad start for either of them.

The next day was a fifth Sunday – guests always seemed to arrive for those weekends – and Libby asked Janet if she'd like to go to a service with them (Dar always took it for granted). Janet assured Libby that church was normal for her, and, as it happened Janet was the star of the service. She could sing! They all sat in Glory Halelluiah's sitting room as usual. The Twybitts had good voices, Frank was not bad but no-one else had any pretence to being musical at all. Janet, who obviously knew the hymns, sang with the unselfconsciousness of a girl with good Welsh blood. Her clear voice definitely helped the service. Her mother was Welsh and extremely musical, also Janet had a much older sister who was a professional musician but Janet was always reticent about her family so nobody knew. Farming and music were both in her blood.

When everyone filtered out of the room to go to Glory Halleluiah's verandah for drinks before lunch, Janet lingered at the door, looking back towards the grand piano. As Glory Halleluiah reached her Janet said, 'That's a Bluthner, isn't it?'

Glory Halleluiah was amazed, 'How did she know?'

'Bluthners have such a special tone, don't they,' said Janet.

'You play?'

'Yes – and there's no piano at the nurses home.'

'Help yourself – music in that cupboard – I'll call you for lunch. Enjoy yourself.'

Nothing suited Janet better and with a glissade of scales, chords, and arpeggios she got her fingers back into action and then scoured the cupboard for music.

Later when everyone was drinking Glory Halleluiah said, 'Listen! She's gone for one of the most difficult pieces - Lizt – playing it beautifully - far better than I can. My, what an asset to the community. The Little Theatre Club people had better know there's a good pianist around. Ah – there's a piano at the Theatre – not far from the Nurses' Home.' Everyone was polite but few would have known a good pianist from a bad; however they certainly gathered that Janet was in with Glory Halleluiah – and that meant with everyone. Lew was trying not to appear too interested in what Glory Halleluiah was saying, but he was delighted that Janet had made such a big hit. Janet, happily playing, was completely unaware of her acceptance into the Backlands community; she was simply enjoying herself. But when she was called to join everyone for lunch Corn thanked her for the concert; very nice of him, she thought. And Corn meant it. Of the Backlanders, apart from Mario and his family, Corn and West, after Glory Halleluiah, were the most appreciative of music, even if they only sang.

At lunch Mumps and Frannie, Frank and Madge, Corn and West were all nice to her. She'd seen Frannie often at the hospital and he'd seemed much older then but here, totally relaxed, she guessed he was only in his forties (in fact he was in his late thirties). Mumps was especially agreeable, taking a lead from Glory Halleluiah. Janet was thoroughly enjoying her day.

Even better was the fact that at dinner Lew said he'd take Janet out early to see the dipping and when Dar asked who'd take her back to Chemchem in the afternoon Lew was quick to offer. Janet couldn't help feeling very, very happy.

Dar, who normally never noticed anything, said to Libby, 'Well, those two seem to have hit it off!'

'Lew and Janet? They've only just met – but, yes, great if they have. He's very short of friends his own age.'

With Backlands tact everyone managed to be extremely casual and pretend ignorance of the growing friendship between Lew and Janet but made it clear that Janet was adopted into The Friends' group. Only a few weeks later, with the purchase of a second-hand Morris

1000 Janet could drive herself to the Backlands where she was invited whenever she had enough days off – and every week she had a day and a half off – quite enough to get her to the Backlands. Libby gave her an open invitation but Janet also stayed with Glory Halleluiah, who became very fond of this little musical girl. Janet even stayed with Frank and Madge but Madge said that they'd better not overdo it in case it looked as if they were throwing her at Lew.

Behind their backs gossip was spreading. It was discovered that when Lew went to town on farm business he often called at the hospital or the Nurses' Home for a few minutes (in fact they were exchanging books to read).

All the gossips were well ahead of Lew and Janet who were enjoying a perfectly friendly relationship – at least that was what it was superficially. Underneath Janet was fast losing her heart to Lew. He found her very nice indeed and easy to be with; in fact the wife he'd like but, without a single penny to his name, thoughts of marriage had to be thrown aside. This did not stop his hormones working overtime when they were together but he was carefully under control.

Glory Halleluiah, as usual, took things into her own hands in a gentle way. First she gave Lew membership of the Chemchem Club and every month she paid into his account at the Club a sum that would enable Lew to have odd drinks and meals there. Lew was very grateful and took Janet to lunch there if they were both free. This was exactly what Glory Halleluiah hoped; otherwise how could he ever take her anywhere with no money? Secondly she managed to tell Janet, with apparent casualness, Lew's position and the story of his family. Already Chemchem gossip had reached Janet about Sally's death and John's disappearance to South Africa but she did not know of the terrible penury that Lew's parents were facing and the fact that all of

Lew's salary was going to help them. Glory Halleluiah had no qualms about telling Janet these details; she felt that Janet must know. Janet's interest in Lew, and vice versa, was obvious.

This gave Janet a lot to think about, mainly what a very fine young man he was to be helping his parents so much. What was to be done? Nothing, she thought except keep seeing him if he wanted to see her — and he seemed to want that very much indeed.

Despite Glory Halleluiah worrying that Lew couldn't take Janet anywhere with no money, they found a private place in Chemchem where they could meet for a few minutes when he was in town and she was off duty for a few hours. This was at the Chemchem spring. A tremendous bubbling of water at the base of a hill produced the infant river Chemchem. Some of the water was used for the town's supply so the spring and the large trembling pool it produced were fenced off, but visible and a very lovely scene, especially since the Council had set aside about three acres of land around it as a public park. The area was thick with trees, birds and a few flowering shrubs. Paths wound round and a few benches were dotted about. Despite the shady attractiveness of the place few townspeople went there and Lew and Janet made it their own. Lew always told Janet news of the ranch; Janet had to be more careful — she could not tell Lew about patients in the hospital; that was not ethical. Lew appreciated this but knew perfectly well that Sexy Sarah was spreading all the hospital gossip about with careless abandon. He liked Janet for her professionalism, though, and so kept the conversation on things like the Nurses' Home extensions, the iniquity of the Council not putting tarmac on the road and the fact that he'd just seen a Serval cat the other day.

The talk between Lew and Janet was very light but satisfactory for them both. When she stayed at The Loop — Lew always took her round, to the delight of both of them, Libby and Dar apparently expecting it and never saying anything.

On one occasion Lew asked Libby for a packed lunch for the pair of them and he took Janet to the Littet Hills. He told her that he'd always wanted to explore them and they spent the whole day walking the hills, thoroughly enjoying the views back to the ranches and also over to the wild country beyond the hills. Janet obviously loved it all so much that Lew determined to ask Frannie if she could join them on a camping trip some day.

All this was pleasant but not getting anywhere and Janet bit her words and very carefully said nothing in letters home, just once or twice casually mentioning Lew as the manager at The Loop. As time went on Lew was finding it all rather more difficult; he was feeling very frustrated, yet knew he could do nothing at the moment – nor in the foreseeable future. Frannie was aware of his feelings and so was Glory Halleluiah. They could do nothing either except help them to be together as much as possible. So when Lew asked Frannie if Janet could come camping, he readily agreed.

There were two packed Land Rovers setting off through The Loop to the Elephant Gap. Frannie drove one with Nzioka, Lew drove the other with Libby and Janet together. Janet had no idea of the significance of Nzioka being with the party until the tents were set up and Frannie casually said that he, Lew and Nzioka would go and find some of the Littet people to ask about the lion.

'It's a big one – an old male – and it's been causing havoc with their cattle so we've got to have a go.'

A lion! Janet was wildly excited. Libby explained that Frannie was an Honorary Game Warden and was sometimes called out to deal with problem animals if the Chemchem Game Warden was too busy. She also told Janet that Nzioka only went with them if the men were after dangerous game; Nzioka was Frannie's gun bearer, otherwise he worked at Venture with the cattle.

It was dark when the men came back. Libby and Janet had got the fire going and Janet helped Libby with preparations for dinner. Camping was a happiness for Janet; she'd done a lot as a Girl Guide back at home. The two girls chatted and got their tent ready for the night; they were sharing.

'O.K. for the morning – we know roughly where the lion is lying up. It fed this morning so probably won't move at all to-morrow – we'll just have to go and look for him. Lew, will you have a go?'

Janet was deeply thrilled. She wondered if the girls were allowed to go with the men, but thought it unlikely. Frannie, however, who deliberately wanted her see Lew in action, said casually, 'Libs – would you mind staying in camp - let Janet come along?'

Very early next morning – it was surprisingly cold – they set off. Frannie drove with Lew by his side and Janet behind. Nzioka was further back standing up looking out of the hatch that Frannie had at the back of his vehicle. No-one said very much. The gun slips were behind with Nzioka. They drove quite a long distance through the bush, Nzioka seemed to be guiding Frannie, but Janet couldn't understand the Swahili. After well over an hour's drive through the rough bush Nzioka called urgently. Frannie stopped and he and Lew got their binoculars out, looking left. Janet couldn't see anything remotely like a lion.

'Lew, we can drive a bit nearer; I'll go by that clump of bush with the one tall tree – O.K.?'

Janet said nothing. When they finally stopped Lew said to her, 'You see those low rocks – well big stones really – he's lying to the right,' and he gave her his binoculars. Suddenly she saw the lion, wondering how the men could possibly have seen the animal from their first stop. Guns were prepared and finally Lew and Nzioka set off on foot.

'We'll see it all from here,' said Frannie, perfectly conscious of the suppressed excitement of Janet.

Lew led, but certainly did not go in a straight line towards the sleeping lion. Janet knew enough to appreciate his tactics. Frannie and she just sat quietly. It all took time. Lew and Nzioka sometimes disappeared from their view because of bush and rocks but they were steadily getting nearer. Then Frannie spoke. 'They've got to get the lion up – to get a good heart shot is best and that needs him up – if Lew shoots while he's down he might only wound him and then all hell lets loose!' Janet understood that.

Janet couldn't see how they alerted the lion but suddenly its head was up and then, very quickly it stood – a big lion with a huge black mane. In that instant there was a shot and he dropped. Frannie said nothing. Janet could see Lew and Nzioka who stayed exactly where they were. She wondered. After a few minutes Lew threw something at the body of the lion. 'What's he doing?' Janet couldn't help asking. 'He's making sure it's dead. Throwing a stone at it. So often people think they've killed a lion but it's only stunned and they walk up and end up mangled themselves and sometimes dead.'

Lew threw another stone and then he and Nzioka walked to the body. They waved towards the Land Rover and Frannie drove to them. It was a very old lion, badly scarred in the face and body and with broken teeth. Frannie was explaining that the bad teeth were why it had taken to raiding calves for food. Janet was thrilled, she'd never been so close to a lion before. Frannie and Lew were discussing the shot; it was actually in the brain which was why the lion had dropped immediately; with a heart shot animals will run for a short distance before dropping. Had Lew actually aimed there? Yes, he had because the line of vision was best there. 'O.K.,' said Frannie. It was all a bit technical for Janet. She was shown the weapon, a double barrelled rifle and Nzioka showed her the spare gun he was carrying as well.

She wondered what they'd do with the body? Nothing except, in this case, cut off a paw to show the Game Warden that the job's done, and open the stomach for the vultures. Vultures? Janet looked up and, sure enough, there were at least a dozen already circling in the sky. So quick!

Although she said nothing Lew was deeply conscious that Janet was in awe of his shooting. It gave his ego an enormous boost, even if Frannie had said that he probably should have waited for a heart shot.

The camping trip cemented feelings for both Janet and Lew. Back at the Nurses' Home all Janet could do was to pray for a solution. She was not aware that Lew was doing exactly the same thing. Over the last year or so, growing older, Lew had become acutely aware that the hope of marriage was a distant dream. He had no money and, working in The Backlands, how was he ever to meet any girls, let alone one he could love? Now, apparently dropped from Heaven, the very one had been offered to him – and he could do nothing.

CHAPTER 11

Charles Wix took no time in joining the tennis section of Chemchem Club. Automatically every D.C. was made an Honorary member of the Club, some using it extensively, some avoiding it. Tennis was Charles's game and very good he was, having played for Cambridge. The Club was also a possible hunting ground for future brides, he knew, and though he considered the whole idea distasteful he had to go ahead.

His only sexual encounter had been with a striking fellow student at Cambridge. She was immensely vibrant, with dark auburn hair, great self assurance, a brilliant scholar in her year – brains spilling everywhere and a haughty mien to go with it. Girton was hardly big enough for her. Charles was impressive himself, academically, and was taken with the girl and persuaded her to meet him during a vacation at his Aunt's flat in Chelsea.

It was a disaster. He was shattered by her behaviour and her language – she was the daughter of a Judge – and Charles; with his huge academic flair but nil understanding of humanity was hopeless.

'My God – it's like being made love to by a pogo-stick! Bloody hell - no finesse, no excitement – nothing! Hey – I've got a body, you know. That was dreadful – quick – useless. The arctic! Count me out!'

This had a great effect on Charles who had always excelled at everything he tried and assumed the same with sex. It was extremely humiliating. The girl collected a coterie around her for the remaining time at Cambridge – a clever, sophisticated group with her its centre.

Charles was excluded, even if he'd wanted to join – and quite a bit of him felt that he should. Infuriatingly the girl went on to win every possible major academic award; Charles did very well – but not up to her standard. Then, to everyone's surprise, she turned her back on Academia and went to Canada to join a small group who were trying to liaise between all the cultural fields – theatre, art, ballet, music, literature etc. Charles went on for a Doctorate and then settled into a dry, asexual world as a lecturer. He was extremely accurate and extremely dull.

After a couple of years, however, an unsavoury situation arose because a college Fellowship was awarded to an internationally known poet. His international renown may have hidden some odd personal habits. The poet was an homosexual; he also had perverted tastes that he had the good sense to refrain from pursuing with the students; instead he sniffed in Charles someone whose whole being suggested a degree of sexual abnormality. He was wrong. Charles was not in the least bit interested. The poet increased his attentions, to the quiet interest, and, in some cases, enjoyment, of other members of the College. Charles became increasingly annoyed, irritated and his self esteem was deeply injured by the poet's assumption that he was as degraded as he was. Charles moved University. The poet followed. The High Table at the Cambridge College saw this would happen and greeted the event with not-so-delicate titters; they were glad to see the poet go, international renown or not.

Charles gave up, left the academic world and followed the advice of his much older cousin, Peregrine, and joined the Colonial Office; the poet would not follow him, he was sure, and correct. Coming into the service late he was behind younger men but rose   rapidly through D.O. 2, and D.O. 1 in Kenya. His academic mind was concentrated on tribal conflicts, the Mau Mau rebellion (he served for a while at Fort Hall in the centre of the problem) and he learnt to speak perfect Kiswahili – useless though this was up-country where a bastard version was used – and a smattering of other tribal languages. He was efficient, correct, un-enterprising, diligent; the perfect Colonial Officer in a way, except for his extraordinary detachment from his fellow men. Totally self absorbed, he needed no company, was perfectly polite when asked out, an immaculate host when necessary – but always at a great distance. He might have been a Martian dropped into society by accident.

To find a wife was just another academic problem to Charles and he had little hopes in the distinctly earthy, very rural community of Chemchem. There were other Colonial Officers there, though, and it was possible that a daughter or two might be hiding at Chemchem. He had to find out.

The tennis group was very polite to Charles, immaculate as he was in long whites – all the other men wore shorts – and in his very first game of mixed doubles he found himself playing against Libby. Even Charles could not but be interested. She was undoubtedly beautiful and wore, he noticed, no rings! Not only that, she was an extremely good tennis player – more accurate and more adventurous than Charles and she and her partner only lost because her partner was feeling off colour. It had been an excellent game, such as Charles had not enjoyed since Cambridge. But when the tennis players went to the bar for drinks later, Libby was talking animatedly to two other ladies and then left quickly to get to her beloved Gingerbread House. The next two Thursdays enabled him to speak to her a little. She was well bred, no doubt, knew how to behave and was, as he appreciated, extremely good to look at. She'd do. Already he'd made discreet enquiries and found that she was unattached and genuinely liked.

There were no doubts about her.

'Miriam – you'll be astonished to hear that Charles has found what he thinks is a suitable girl already. He wants us to go and vet her.'

'Good heavens. Who is she?'

'Called Elizabeth Winchester – father's a rancher in the Backlands. Late twenties and he says she is presentable.'

'Presentable – what a description - typical Charles.'

'I'll find out more about her,' and Sir Peregrine put an Aide to work.

'Amazing. She is presentable! Father – Frank Winchester from the Staffordshire Winchester family – well heeled, highly respectable, senior rancher, biggest property. He came out after the First World War. She's an only child. Mother – Edith Wharton....'

'Can't be!'

'Of course not – just the same name. She has a twin, Mary, married to Hugh Constable – they farm in Shropshire. There's a much older brother – twenty years ahead of the twins – Lord Craillin of Marchwood – decrepit eighties or thereabouts – also in Shropshire. Apparently the twin girls hardly ever saw their elder brother – no communication now.'

'So her mother's an Hon.?'

'Was – she's dead. Elizabeth, known as Libby, runs the house for her father and helps on the ranch. Good tennis player, rides, all that. Not much education, though – school here and then a few fancy finishing courses in Britain.'

'Speaks French though?'

'No – the courses were cooking and flower arranging and all that twaddle.'

142

'So?'

'I'll arrange a visit to look at ranching up there – needn't be long.'

'And we'll find out why she isn't married already!'

Dar was politely summed to the D.C.s office. He'd already met Charles Wix at a cocktail party (the sort of entertainment Dar hated), when Charles, as D.C., wanted to meet the older settlers. No ladies were invited, a fact that did not go down well in the community. Dar saw what he thought of as a typical senior Colonial Officer; fossilised before time. But D.C.s came and went; Dar was not concerned in any way.

'Good of you to come, Mr. Winchester. I've had a message from the Governor – he's a distant relation of mine, actually. He and Lady Wix would very much like to visit some ranching areas and I think the Backlands would be ideal – possibly better than that ranching area towards Nakuru. Would you be kind enough to host them for a couple of nights?'

'Of course – glad to,' although Dar was surprised.

Together they arranged that the Governor and Lady Wix would arrive at tea-time on a Monday. There would be a quiet dinner that night. Next day they could look at dipping if they wished. After breakfast there would be a short tour of the ranch and then they would go to Glory Halleluiah for lunch (the D.C. knew there was a social obligation to go to her although he had yet to meet Glory Halleluiah). Back to The Loop for tea and then there would be a dinner party in the evening to enable the Governor and his lady to meet local ranchers. They would leave the next day.

'And I'll accompany them....'

'Yes, of course.'

The Backlands was agog over this visit. No previous Governor had ventured so far. It was fairly straight-forward except for the dinner party. Dar and Libs decided the guest list – Sir Peregrine and Lady Wix, Charles Wix, Dar, Libby, Lew, Glory Halleluiah, Frank and Madge, Frannie and Mumps, Corn and West.

'That's thirteen! No good!' said Libby who was not in the least bit superstitious, 'and it's eight men to five women – a bit one-sided.'

Dar immediately said, 'Let's get Janet – it'll help Lew and Frannie can arrange for her to have some time off. We've got room.'

'Good. That makes fourteen - exactly what the table holds with the leaves out.'

Libby was quite excited. Although Dar and Edith had been to Government House entertainments in the past, she had not, nor had she been presented, although eligible, because Dar and Edith thought it unnecessary – it was the twilight years of presentationsthat had finally ceased a few years ago. They saw it unnecessary in modern society.

Libby was delighted that the Governor and Lady Wix would actually be staying at The Loop; she thought that if precedence was strictly observed, they should stay with Glory Haleluiah but the house at The Loop was the biggest in the area and there was plenty of guest accommodation; that was probably the reason.

Rosa offered to supervise the kitchen for the dinner party, an offer very gratefully received by Libby; Rosa was almost as good a cook as a dressmaker. Rosa also suggested the dress that Libby should wear that evening, an extremely discreet slim-line dress in dark green georgette over an under-dress. It fitted Libby beautifully and Rosa declared that it was very lady-like. There was definitely a stir in the Backlands. All the men blew moth-balls off their dinner jackets; Lew would wear his blazer; it would be a long time before he could possibly have a dinner jacket. He didn't mind.

Libby did not disappoint the Governor and his lady when they arrived. She was wearing a particularly attractive Rosa-made dress, had organised a light but good spread for tea and was her normal, friendly self. Having already met Charles there was no problem there – if no warmth either – and the party was at ease. After tea Dar suggested a gentle stroll around the cluster of small paddocks near the ranch house that held the horses, some special bulls and a few sick animals. The Governor showed considerable interest in the bulls and Dar explained why that handful were near the house, all the rest were out on the ranch, some with females, others in a bunch. With a minimum of six thousand head of stock – usually more - and at least three or four thousand breeding females, Dar needed about eighty bulls and kept more, often a hundred. He was very fussy about them, buying bulls carefully and ruthless in getting rid of any that did not come up to expectations.

As they got back to the house Janet arrived, having worked for most of the afternoon. She was still in uniform and went to change immediately, but this gave Lady Wix her conversational opening. Janet knew that she'd been invited to make up numbers; she didn't mind, knowing such problems. She and Lew had not been too much concerned about the Governor's visit; Dar and Libby would do the host and hostess bit; all they had to do was be polite.

With ease Lady Wix spoke with Janet immediately about hospitals in Kenya at which she was an expert – private hospitals, government hospitals, maternity units, private clinics, mission hospitals, leprosaria – she'd seen them all and knew the right words and the correct questions to produce. Janet was not fooled – probably Lady Wix was not in the least bit interested in hospitals but Janet recognised the social ability – admired it – Lady Wix was so good at it – and they got on famously.

At dinner that night Dar was arranging the next day.   The Governor wanted to see the   dipping; his lady would stay in bed. Charles then asked Libby if riding was a possibility instead of dipping.

'Of course. Janet and I often ride early morning – cool then. Leave at seven – back for breakfast about half past eight to nine?'

The obvious inclusion of Janet was not what he'd hoped for but he was civil. Libby was thinking which horse he could have and never noticed his manner.

The morning ride was pleasant for Janet and Libby. Letting Libby and Charles ride ahead Janet stayed with the syce, but Libby was constantly calling back about something; lively conversation was going on. Charles had no idea that this was deliberate because Libby had quickly seen that although he could sit a horse he was far from a good rider and if there was any disturbance from the sudden dart of a dikdik or other animal she doubted he could hold a frightened horse. So it was distant game viewing, but good.   Charles said very little; in fact he was rather put out by the constant chatter, although he knew women were like that.

Breakfast over, Dar took the Governor, Lady Wix and Charles to see over the ranch. Sir Peregrine showed intelligent interest in all aspects – the breeding of the cattle, the weaning, branding, grazing, selling the stock, tick control and diseases. Diseases. There had just been an outbreak of Foot and Mouth disease in U.K. so the Governor asked if it was prevalent in Kenya.

'Yes – very much so. But we don't slaughter the stock – unless the animals are in a very bad way – but we do use vaccinations – there are different strains. When animals get over an attack they remain immune to that particular strain for at least a year or two – maybe more. A lot of the diseases are tick borne – as I said this morning – ECF – that's East Coast Fever, Anaplasmosis, and Heartwater; they're the worst. The trouble is that buffalo carry so many diseases; we have to keep them away if we can. The horses have to be inoculated for horse sickness every year. It's always a battle against diseases here. We're so far out that we have to do our own veterinary work – unless something gets too bad. My manager – Lew – he's good at that – probably should have been a Vet.'

The animals were admired, wildlife absorbed and the attractive countryside assimilated. It had been a good morning.

Charles drove the party over to Glory Halleluiah's house for a rather formal lunch at which the food was a lot better than normal (Glory Halleluiah was never bothered about food) because Rosa had decided the menu for her and prepared some of the dishes. The Governor and Lady Wix were actually slightly in awe of Glory Halleluiah who was at her most formal self; she seemed, as she was, a true Victorian. (Her friends at the Backlands hardly ever saw this side of their beloved Glory Halleluiah.)

Lady Wix was careful not miss an opportunity and slipped out 'Libby Winchester – a charming girl. Amazing that she isn't married already!' To which Glory Halleluiah replied, 'She's had her share of admirers but she was let down badly some time ago and is now very wary – on her guard.' This told Lady Wix what she needed to know but she thought that Charles, of all people, might have a hard job getting through any guard!

The evening dinner party was a success despite Corn and West who appeared very well turned out – they sported cummerbunds (Madge thought this very dashing) – but they affected the most extravagant 'Oxford' drawls, approaching each female with 'My *deaaaah* lady!' Libby, Lew and Janet found it funny, Frannie tried not to, but it was allied to such serious faces that even Dar had a twinkle but he hoped it was the only wickedness they would perpetrate that evening; it was, so all was well. And since the three guests knew no better and thought it their normal talk it passed off.

Charles could not sit by Libby – she was with the Governor and talking happily – he was between Mumps and Frank (not enough ladies present) and saw her very pretty face and manners. The food was not ostentatious but light and very tasty. Rosa was not a Goanese for nothing – taste was all in all. The evening was easier than expected for everyone. There was amusement over the Twybitts for the Backlands people and they all found the Governor and his wife excellent guests who made themselves very amiable. No-one warmed to Charles but that did not matter; it was a good evening.

Despite this Glory Halleluiah, with her ultra-sensitive antennae, felt an odd undercurrent about the evening – somehow emanating from the visitors. She couldn't crystallise it, which annoyed her. The Governor and his wife were socially excellent; the D.C. looked a little like the British politician, Enoch Powell, by virtue of his moustache and, Glory Halleluiah thought, is obviously marking time before a Governorship somewhere. So what was it that was giving odd vibrations? She gave up, unsatisfactory though that was.

On the way back, next morning, Charles asked, 'Well – what do you think?'

'Good looking girl, good hostess, good connections - so far all good. But not very intelligent, badly educated – that may not matter

148

but a pity. She's very parochial – I tried to talk a bit of politicians and she'd hardly heard of Anthony Eden!'

'All Kenya girls are like that, Peri!' Miriam Wix said, 'Why should they be interested in a country four thousand miles away?'

'Because they live in a British Colony, my dear.'

Lady Wix gave up, she knew her husband too well.

'However, Charles, it's amazing that you could find a girl like Elizabeth way out in the bush. I doubt that you'd do better really. I would say – go ahead.'

Charles was pleased. Libby really was most attractive. He had actually been stirred by her. She'd made him cast aside the horrible memory of the Cambridge girl. Libby wouldn't be like that? Surely not. And she would look good by his side. Miriam had already commented on her dress sense – essential in her future as his wife. Libby would be good in public. He was becoming more and more interested. Perhaps marriage wouldn't be so bad, after all, with such an attractive wife.

'The Twybitts – what did you think?'

'Typical eccentric settlers. Wouldn't surprise me if they aren't remittance men – you know - odd people sent out to the colonies with an income to get them away from being a nuisance to their families.'

That was not far off the mark but Corn and West had escaped from their family by coming to Kenya – and with no remittance at all.

'It was worth coming to the Backlands. Lovely country. Spectacular views – but quite tough farming – not easy. Takes special people. Anyway- Charles – over to you and I wish you luck. I would guess she's at an age when she'd be happy to settled down. After all –

you've got a lot to offer. Go to it.'

Miriam Wix thought – if she'll listen! There had been no sign of Libby being in any way interested in Charles during their stay; she'd been uniformly nice to everyone – especially those oddities – the Twybitt brothers. Lady Wix said nothing but was quite concerned for Libby; to her it seemed throwing a nice girl not into a den of lions but into a parody of that – a waxworks.

CHAPTER 12

Fate did not help Charles Wix because Libby went to Nairobi for a few days over the next Thursday, the following tennis night she didn't stay long in the bar and the third night she was annexed by the farming couple who were really friends of Frannie's – Piet and Rena Coetzee. Charles began to feel frustrated and the need for action. However the following Thursday the tennis Captain asked if he and Libby would be the mixed double pair representing the club at a major Tournament to be held at Chemchem in three week's time. Libby, who knew about this annual Tournament expected this to happen and took it very calmly. She and Charles were a very good pair together – he was a very steady and strong player on whom she could rely whilst she was accurate but ready to play unexpected shots. This meant practice together and they played against everyone else at Chemchem, slaughtering the opposition easily.

After their first practice together Charles invited Libby to drinks and they chatted at the bar. It was not exciting talk but perfectly friendly – after all, Libby reminded herself – he was the D.C. She'd much rather drink with other friends, but knew her manners. This was repeated the next time they played together and he invited her to stay for dinner at the club with him, which invitation she charmingly refused (she was longing to get away to have a peaceful evening at the Gingerbread House – a second home that Charles knew nothing about). Charles was in no whit upset by her refusal; she'd been charming and much nicer than any other girl he could remember from his limited experience, he felt that he was quietly winning. Work kept him busy or he would have tried to visit Libby at The Loop; he'd been impressed by Dar Winchester and the lovely home Libby managed. Certainly no other male was giving Libby undue attention at the Club. Confidence was his, he felt.

At a Backlands Sunday dinner held by Mumps and Frannie – Libby mentioned the tournament and that she and the D.C. would represent Chemchem in the Mixed Doubles (she was also playing in the Ladies' Singles and the Ladies' Doubles).

'He's a good player but always predictable! Odd really.'

'I thought he was positively Neolithic at your dinner party!' said Frank, 'The Colonial Office do send out some oddities.'

'He's said to be brainy.'

'Doesn't show it much! Imagine that cocktail party – no ladies invited! Got the backs up of every woman in the district. Silly ass. Should've known better!'

No-one was impressed by the D.C. The settler/administration 'feud' was of long-standing and often more imaginary than real but the settlers all knew, quite vehemently, that *they* were the backbone of Kenya. The administrative officers – who came and went – just ran the superficial bits. It was an uneasy see-saw. Each faction had to get on with other, but grudgingly. Occasionally a good Colonial Officer got through the settler blockade and became part of the community properly – but it wasn't common. Chemchem was probably worse for this division and feeling of settler-superiority than most areas because the settlers managed very well, thank you, despite being so very far from Nairobi. They ran things their way. In fact the Administration did leave the Chemchem settlers alone; there were many pressing matters to do with the local African tribes to occupy them.

The tennis tournament took up a long week-end. Most of the

visiting players were put up at the club or by the Chemchem tennis team members. The Gingerbread House had only one bedroom but Libby offered hospitality and a lady from Nakuru was her guest, Libby sleeping on a camp bed in the pretty sitting room.

The tennis was of a high standard, Nakuru providing no less than two sets of teams – there being two clubs in the town and Eldoret boasted a very strong husband and wife combination. The Nairobi clubs that sent teams had excellent players. It promised to be a good week-end. The draw gave Charles and Libby stiff opposition but they sailed through the first day easily. Libby also did well in the Singles but she and her lady partner were quickly despatched in the Ladies' Doubles in the first round (Libby's partner was very sorry; she knew she was not up to Libby's standard – Libby did not mind in the least). Altogether the first day was good. Everyone was expected to dine at the club and Charles automatically annexed Libby. As his team partner no-one questioned that, although Libby had had enough of his dull company by this time. Oh, for an easier partner, she thought, but she pulled herself together to behave well. Luckily the Eldoret couple, an amusing pair, were seated opposite and helped Libby enjoy her evening. But when the meal finished she quickly collected her guest and left.

Charles was pleased that the tennis had gone well (he was also playing in the Men's Singles but had been knocked out by the current Kenya champion so he was not too displeased by that result). Libby had been impeccable; a most suitable choice, he felt. He'd even tingled with awareness of her very fine body – beautifully proportioned – during the games. Perhaps the auburn-haired girl had taught him something – he hardly dared to consider that.

The next day the opposition was stiffer and the games very good. Libby was enjoying the sort of tennis she rarely met, except at

Tournaments, and she was in good spirits as she and Charles sailed through to the Finals of the Mixed Doubles. She reached the Finals of the Ladies' Singles as well, though not so easily.

Libby had to put up with another dinner with Charles at the club but she had carefully asked the Eldoret couple if they would join them again and all was well. Again she left early, explaining to Charles about her guest. Suddenly Charles realised that she had a property in the town! Good news, he thought.

On the third day there was a lot of time waiting for the Finals and Charles came to sit with Libby, much to her displeasure, although she accepted that he might do that. They talked quietly, mainly about the tennis. She had a good voice, spoke well. All the time Charles was assessing her, Libby quite unaware of this.

Libby lost her Ladies' Singles Final to a newcomer to Nairobi, a strong rather masculine player who won decisively, but Libby enjoyed the game and said so. Charles, who was watching, again approved. Things were getting better.

Charles and Libby won their Mixed Doubles Final in straight sets, having faced stiffer opposition earlier – such was often the case at Tournaments – and were both pleased. Again they sat together, waiting for the Prize-giving and went up together for the Cup – that Libby charmingly received and then gave to Charles. This really pleased him. What a sign! Had he known it was simply that Libby thought that as he was D.C. he ought to have it he might not have been so pleased.

They were together for the third night running at the club but in a smaller gathering as many visitors had started for home. Luckily the Eldoret couple, who had given them the stiffest opposition the previous day, were still in town and supported Libby, the wife recognising 'help' signals from that nice Winchester girl. 'Poor girl,' she'd said to her husband, 'he's a bore if ever there was one.'

Eldoret was home to a large number of Boer South Africans who had trekked up from the south just after the turn of the century and the pair entertained Charles and Libby with stories of their farming exploits. The Boers were tough men, their women wonderful housewives, good cooks, excellent needlewomen – seemingly able to deal with any domestic emergency - all done on the proverbial smell of an oil-rag. Libby was interested, Charles slightly aloof.

Libby's guest had gone home, Charles discovered, and he suggested that he should accompany her to her cottage in Wood Avenue. Libby was astonished and said that she had her own vehicle, thank you, and he had to accept that. Also, she said, she had to get up early to-morrow to get back in time for dipping – so that meant an early night. It was nice of him to offer, she thought, but totally unnecessary. He restrained her by her Land Rover, still talking.

'Well, Libby, thank you for excellent tennis. I hope you've enjoyed it as much as I have.'

'Oh yes, it was very good, thank you – we were lucky to have a fairly easy Finals.'

He ignored this last remark.

'I want to say something. I think we are an excellent couple – I hope you feel the same.'

'Oh, yes,' said Libby, thinking of the tennis. He was the best doubles partner she'd ever had, no doubt about that.

'I'm so glad you agree.' He was smiling broadly. 'That's settled. I won't detain you longer – I'll be in touch as soon as possible.'

All this was unintelligible to Libby but she thought him an ancient fuddy-duddy anyway, who didn't speak her language so was not concerned. She was just glad get to the Gingerbread House and relax.

Had she understood Charles in the slightest she would have been greatly alarmed. He took himself back to his house in high self-satisfaction. He'd got her. Easy to win. What a graceful wife he'd have. So well mannered and sweet – yes, that was the word (a word he hardly ever used) – sweet. He found he'd got the cup, too, and he managed an unusual smile at that. Nothing could have been easier.

Dar was the last to finish breakfast the next morning after dipping and so took the telephone call. Libby had gone out again and did not hear about it until just before lunch.

'The D.C. called – wants you and me to have dinner there to-night. Monday – odd night for a dinner party. Of course I said we'd go.'

'Oh golly – I've had a basin-full of him recently. Apart from tennis he's a dreadful bore. Oh dear – that's four nights in a row for me. Damn. Oh, well, I suppose we have to go. D.C.s – think they rule the District (which they did, in fact). What a pain. I can't really pretend to be ill after tennis do you think?'

'Fraid not – duty to be done, chick. I think he's a stuffed shirt, too. But we'll have to go.'

When Dar and Libby drove into the entrance of the fairly grand D.C.s house at Chemchem there were no other cars in the drive and they were slightly late. Charles came straight out of the house smiling and welcoming, especially helping Libby out of the vehicle. Still Libby had no idea. She was just surprised. Charles was immediately talking to Dar as they walked into the house.

'Of course I should have talked to you first and asked your permission but the ideal opportunity arrived last night so I took it – I'm sure you understand. Your daughter is so lovely. I've got a special celebration bottle waiting - do come in, Libby dearest – sit with me – there.'

This was incomprehensible to both Dar and Libby for a second – and then Libby realised what Charles meant by the 'excellent couple'. She panicked, clutched Dar's arm and said, 'No-no-no – he's got it all wrong!' fled out of the house, burst into tears, wrestled with the door of the vehicle and flung herself into the safety of the Dar's old Ford.

There was silence and stillness in the house – Charles was fixed – like Lot's wife - but holding a bottle of champagne out – Dar was standing bemused. Slowly Charles put thebottle down.

Dar, for once, saw what might have happened.

'Mr. Wix – were you expecting something of Libby?'

Charles nodded, still rather frozen, 'I thought it was clear!'

'I'm sorry Mr. Wix – obviously not to her. Look, we'd better go – forget all about this. Obviously a misunderstanding. So sorry. So sorry,' and Dar took his leave very uncomfortably, blundering out of the house to the waiting car. He got into the driving seat and stretched out a hand to Libby who was still a bit tearful but more angry.

As they drove away, 'That insufferable man!'

Dar hardly knew how to deal with the situation so drove on, patting her arm from time to time.

'How could he *assume* – oh, it's horrible!' and Libby was off crying again.

'Hasn't he said anything? Made advances – you know?'

'Only that we were an excellent pair – but *that* was after we'd won the Doubles – tennis, of course. Stupid idiot – how could he have thought otherwise? Oh, damn him.' Libby was seriously upset.

Her pride was deeply wounded that an inhuman creature like Charles could possibly have assumed her affection. Him! Oh no! She was hurt, humiliated and angry.

Dar understood a lot of her feelings, his fatherly concern was strong for his chick and he was worried to see her so unhappy. It was not easy to placate her at all. The drive home was a misery.

Libby desperately wanted to get it out of her system; she wanted to talk to someone who would understand. She phoned Glory Halleluiah after breakfast the next morning and was invited over. Her story was fully comprehended by Glory Halleluiah and with it all the wounds that Libby was feeling. Libby was beyond tears now, full of resentment and anger and not a little self-pity.

'How could he? Dreadful man. And now, Glory Halleluiah, I can't possibly go to tennis! He's ruined that, too!'

Glory Halleluiah quietened Libby slowly and gently and with much discretion. She was now illuminated by the explanation of the undercurrents at the dinner party. It was all clear. Of this she said nothing to Libby, it would have made it worse. Of course the Governor and his wife had come to vet Libby; they were relations and, no doubt, Charles is ear-marked for higher office. How stupid the whole incident was – and it would hurt Libby for some time, she knew. Other girls might see the funny side of it; Libby might later, but not just yet.

'Libby, dear, you'll get over this in time, of course. I agree that he's a most extraordinary fellow and should never have made the assumption he did. Too confident. Idiot. Knows nothing about women. It's a compliment in a way – back handed, I grant you – but there you are. It'll all heal in time.'

'But my tennis! I can't face him. I simply can't!'

'No. Don't. Don't try. Something will happen, I assure you.'

They both drank more coffee and thought their thoughts. Opening up to Glory Halleluiah was always a relief to Libby (and to everyone else in the Backlands) and she felt a lot better. Glory Halleluiah took it all seriously; others might have laughed over it all.

'You know, Libby, there are times that appear quite dreadful – a sudden disaster or something – but it may be that one is being spurred to something else – to different action. Perhaps you need to *do* something – and only you can decide what. Give it a thought, my dear.'

The very next day Glory Halleluiah made an appointment to see the D.C. She was prompt and appeared in his office in her usual farming outfit – shapeless slacks, aertex shirt – very different from the lunch-time aristocratic hostess he had seen. She gave him a curt greeting and refused to sit down. Her face was stern. With no preamble, with exact diction and a very slight touch of acid in her voice she said, 'Mr. Wix, Libby Winchester, whom I have known since she was born, has confided in me her distress at your assumption. This will go no further than me. It is your – and her – affair only. BUT it will have a practical effect on Libby. She feels she can no longer enjoy her tennis at the Club.' He tried to say something but was brushed aside by the determination and dominance of Glory Halleluiah. 'As a gentleman (here her voice was more than slightly ironic) I would advise you to forget tennis at the Club from now on and leave Libby her enjoyment – I might say her only relaxation. I can only advise. But I do. Good morning.' And she stumped out allowing no word from the D.C.

He was not used to that sort of talk from anybody.

However he did understand that tennis would be an

embarrassment. That evening he sat down to write two personal notes. The first was to his cousin to say that there was no chance of him marrying Elizabeth (no details - but 'Not surprised' said Lady Wix 'but he's got to marry someone!') and the second was to Libby.

Dear Miss Winchester,

    I regret if I embarrassed you over a misunderstanding. Please accept my apology.

    Because of increased duties it will be impossible for me to continue to play tennis at the Club.

Yours,

Charles Wix.

Libby was both relieved and angry to receive the note. Relief that he'd decided to drop out of tennis, but angry at his stupid excuse 'increased duties' – utter nonsense. Despite the note she did not attempt to go to tennis the next Thursday. In any case she had a thin excuse. She learned that it was Janet's birthday and that she was hoping to give Lew a private dinner at the Nurses' Home. That was almost impossible, Libby knew, so she had offered Janet the Gingerbread House. Janet had loved it immediately, and grasped the offer.

'I'll make an early supper – so Lew won't be late back!'

Libby wouldn't have minded how late Lew was but she heard him come back to The Loop at midnight – a male Cinderella.

Despite Glory Halleluiah's tact the story of Libby and Charles filtered round the Backlands. It was Dar who told Frank and Madge and so it went the rounds.

'So,' said Mumps to Frannie, 'Libby's turned down the D.C. Did you know he was after her? Seems a bit quick. Mind you, she'd better stop being so choosy – she's got to marry someone!' Frannie knew nothing about this but kept quiet. His thoughts were strong on the subject.

Madge approved of the refusal. 'Can you imagine – a man like that – all superficial politeness – no heart – no warmth, probably no guts – like being married to a skeleton! No thank you. Poor Libby. Not a pleasant interlude.'

The reaction of Corn and West was simply that it was a pity they hadn't done a better 'tease' on the night of the dinner party – put the bugger off completely.

Glory Halleluiah was not the only one to doubt the reason for the Governor's visit. Frank thought the same and so did Frannie. Frank would never mention it because he saw that Dar thought the visit a feather in his cap. Frannie said nothing because he couldn't see the point.

Libby was again treated with kindness and tact by almost everyone in the Backlands except Corn and West who, one day after a Sunday service, whispered in her ear, 'That chap – Wix – wrongly named – got no wick at all!' and passed on. Libby didn't know whether to laugh or ignore it but laughter took over and Corn and West knew they'd helped.

It took a little time but Libby got over the episode quite well and went back to tennis cheerfully. Someone commented that the D.C. had had to give up tennis because of pressures of work, but that was all. He was not really missed. Libby thought a lot about Glory Halleluiah's advice, and she'd never known her give bad advice. She thought and thought – *do* something! But what?

CHAPTER 13

The monthly dinner was at Frank and Madge's house. Tactfully Dar took a bottle of whisky, Frannie took beer and Glory Halleluiah took wine. Everyone, as usual, pretended not to notice.

Glory Halleluiah was gently grieved. The Cooper's house was shabbier with more visible mending, but Madge had a valiant show of flowers, beautifully arranged, and they all knew the food would be simple and ample. If Glory Halleluiah, Mumps and Libby could offer something more exotic – well, - did it matter? There was immense understanding about it all.

Before Dar and Libby arrived there was news that was quickly mentioned. Bobby's wife had come back to Kenya from South Africa and had, apparently, settled again. She'd been on the Dacre farm just one month. But the latest was that she'd gone again – back to South Africa. 'The whole thing was such a mistake – I feel sorry for the poor girl,' said Madge and, in general, there was agreement. In fact Libby knew – little gossip passed the tennis section at the club

Dar and Libby arrived; the party was complete. Frank was talking to Frannie.

'How did the hunting trip go?' Frannie had been away for five weeks – a long safari.

He'd missed the last monthly dinner during which Mumps had continually moaned about his absence.

'Good – three hunting clients and two wives. They were happy. Got all they wanted. Good trophies,too.'

'American?'

'Yes – from Chicago or near there. Big business. Nice men. One of the wives was a slight pain but not too bad. I enjoyed it very much.'

'Will they come back?' This was always the sure sign of a successful safari.

'Already booked. Plus another couple. Makes it a bit cumbersome.'

'But good business.'

'Very. George is doing well. Mind you he runs a superb show – very efficient, excellent food – everything.'

'You wouldn't ever do it full time – hunting, I mean? Put a manager into Venture?'

'I sincerely hope not,' butted in Mumps, 'his place is on the shamba – he's away far too much as it is!'

Frannie ignored this.

'No, I'd never go full time, but I enjoy the bits I do – and so does Nzioka – feels he's with the big time boys – which he is, of course. Remind me – after dinner – I've got a story to tell that came out during the safari.'

When everyone was settled with coffee Libby reminded Frannie about the story.

'It'll take some time in the telling! In the evenings there was a lot of chat round the camp-fire. The clients were educated, intelligent men – good talkers. We covered a lot of things. One evening somehow the subject of big money came up – Chicago is a rich area I gather. The clients were obviously very wealthy men. They started talking about the Mafia. Did you know that there were a lot of Italians in the

Chicago area – and many of them Mafia? The Chicago Mafia have a lot of the big money in the area and are always thirsting for more. They control businesses, run protection rackets – what they get up to is hardly believable.'

Frank sat back, enjoying Frannie.

'The main client, Chuck, started telling us one story about how the Mafia were beaten years ago. It is so rare that the story is still remembered around Chicago – a sore festering in the Mafia record, I suppose.'

Frannie finished his coffee.

'We move to Italy. Somewhere – roughly in the Milan/Turin area there lived a quiet, very clever man. He was modest, kept himself to himself so no-one ever saw his intelligence. He ran a minor business – it was making fine leather goods – ladies' handbags, purses, belts – things like that. They were sent to high-class shops in Rome and elsewhere and the little business did well – but never got any larger. This fellow had the good sense to understand that often going bigger is no advantage.'

Dar nodded.

'Apparently – and a lot of this is guess-work – he started investing cleverly and certainly made a lot of money. But it was never obvious to the outside world. He and his wife - and there was one daughter – had a small house in a suburban road, one car, yes one maid, but no real show of wealth – very un-Italian. He began buying other small businesses – especially those owned by families that had run into the position of needing an injection of capital. He put in some money, left the families to run them – obviously he was smart at judging men – and left them to run the show. Slowly he built up a minor empire of small businesses – never obvious because he didn't run them himself – bicycle spares, a glove maker, a minor printing works, saddler, small bell foundry – a huge variety. How much he personally made must have been a fair amount – but still there was no show at all. In the end he owned over a hundred small businesses, mainly in the north of Italy but a few in central Italy, too. He'd added hotels, boat building, a jeweller, oh – so many things – but all relatively small – and – the point is – he kept them small. There was no expanding – the businesses just went on as before but now under his guidance. He wasn't after big profits – had the good sense to see that safe, small profits beat risky big ones.'

Again Dar nodded.

'But all the time he was investing very cleverly. Chuck reckoned that he was worth - in American terms – at least several million dollars – and, somehow, in the end the Italian Mafia caught on to him.'

Libby was smiling.

'But they were too late – he'd died!'

'Wow!'

'Yes – and his wife had died only the year before so that left the daughter. This daughter was in her early thirties, not very prepossessing – in fact downright plain, plump, quiet and she'd never worked – just stayed at home with her parents. She did, though, keep an eye on their very own first business – that was just down the road really – the small leather works. And she had a passion for music – not that she played in public or anything but regularly she went to Milan - La Scala.'

This interested Glory Halleluiah.

'She had an old school friend – married – who lived in Milan and so she used to stay with her and they'd go to the opera together. That was about it. She shopped locally, had no real local friends – just polite – again – very un-Italian.'

All the friends were listening carefully.

'Now the money – or at least the bulk of it – was not in Italy – the Mafia soon discovered that – so the guess was that it would be in a Swiss account.'

'One of those numbered, secret things?'

'Probably – at least that was ninety-nine percent likely. The girl had a local account that was healthy but not enough to interest the Mafia. So now the Mafia had to try to persuade the girl to tell them where the money was so that they could pinch the lot.'

'Torture?'

'No – oddly enough the Mafia are quite careful over women. They kill men with no compunction – but women – different. So they came up with a very simple idea. One of their men had to marry the girl!'

'Lovely!' said Madge.

'Yes, but they had discovered that the girl was no fool so it all to be done cleverly. They thought that any Italian would be a bit too obvious – so they had the idea of importing an American Italian from the Mafia in Chicago!'

'Hmm,' this was from Frank.

'A suitable young man was found – very good looking, extrovert, lively, strong body, even liked music, too, and he was sent to Italy – no doubt with a huge bribe. There was a pause here because no-one knows how this happened but he got a job in the small leather works down the road from the girl – the very works that she visited from time to time. The Mafia know how to wait. But the pair obviously met and she certainly noticed him because they were seen having coffee at a local café more than once.'

Libby was entranced by the story.

'He'd got his entrée all right. But he was bright enough to go slowly. After all he was just one of the workmen, apparently. And this had been done cleverly because the girl had a soft spot for the underdog, it was known. Anyway he visited her at her home several times – this is known from the maid. What went on is not known, of course. Then the girl went off to Milan for her opera session. Normally she left in a morning – she didn't take the car but went on a train. Usually she came back the following afternoon, but this time when she reached Milan she phoned the maid to say that she'd be staying an extra night so would be back on the afternoon train the day after the next.'

Frannie paused.

'But she never came back. She had a small overnight bag and her handbag - nothing more. The maid said nothing until the day after she was due back because on one previous occasion she'd missed the train and stayed another night. So by the time an alarm went out she'd been away a good three to four days. There was panic. She had a lawyer who thought that she'd been kidnapped and the police went into serious action. But then the lawyer – with the maid – discovered that certain papers were missing from the house – she'd left everything, including the car and most of her clothes – even some jewellery – but her passport, bank papers and other things were missing. Then ideas changed. Had she gone deliberately?'

Madge was delighted with the story.

'Then it was found at the leather works that the American Italian chap had been off sick for a few days. The maid said things and everyone started to be very suspicious. The Mafia were furious because they thought the fellow had decided to grab her money for himself – but the maid had another theory –she said that the chap had actually fallen for the girl – really in love with her! The Mafia thought this very unlikely as she was most unattractive – everyone agreed about that. But the maid insisted – all this being told to the police, of course, not the Mafia who, naturally, heard every bit of it!'

All were listening intently.

'So not only the police but the Mafia were after the couple. Where had they gone? She'd taken a fair bit out of her bank account – enough to get them oversees - that was discovered. But what about the real wealth? Of course there was a gap of at least three days when she could have done anything but the chances were that she'd gone to Zurich. But there were no traces anywhere – nothing at borders and so on. Equally the fellow left no trace as he'd disappeared the same day. He spoke English and Italian, she spoke only Italian and a smattering of schoolgirl French. So where do you go if you want to run away from the Mafia?'

'South America,' said Lew promptly.

'Yes – that was the first bet. Despite the Mafia being there it is so huge that almost all criminals aim for it, don't they, if they are on the run. Not that these two were really criminals.'

'Pretty obvious.'

'So we move to Brazil – to begin with. It seems that a bank account had been opened in her name at a place called Belem.'

'Mouth of the Amazon,' said Lew efficiently.

'Yes. The amount was reasonable but not huge – about the equivalent of to-day's fifty thousand pounds – a tempting carrot if not the main money. Of course how the bank let this news out is anyone's guess – Mafia again probably. Anyway the hunt was on and Mafia agents were sent to Belem, only to discover that the money had been moved to a bank in a place called Salvador. So the chase moved there.

Yes, you can guess – by the time the bloodhounds had got there the money had been moved to Rio de Janiero and then on to Porto Alegre.'

'She was playing games!'

'Yes, clever lady, because she'd got them all on the hop and everyone was concentrated on Brazil.'

'That meant they were no-where near Brazil at all!'

'Undoubtedly – especially since the money in those bank accounts had finally been moved back to Europe – to the account of a small convent in France that ran a tiny orphanage. And that was the end of that money! It'd all been carefully thought out and instructions given.'

'All the time the pair of them could have been anywhere!'

'Yes – passports are not a problem – if one has money and they certainly had that – so they could have gone anywhere. But, because the probable starting point was Zurich the chase had almost certainly looked west instead of east.'

Frannie was smiling, changed his voice slightly. 'What if they had come slowly east – probably by car – though not necessarily – and filtered through Austria, Jugoslavia, Albania to Greece, Turkey, down the Levant coast, across to Africa?'

'Almost easy.'

'Frannie – when did this happen?'

'That was my first question. Chuck thought late twenties to early thirties.'

'Italy had territories in Africa then.'

'Yes, and they had to avoid anything Italian didn't they?'

'You didn't say anything about what you thought?'

'No – I was very careful – but I was thinking exactly what you

170

are thinking now. It is an incredible coincidence, isn't it?'

'They are very careful – hardly ever go out of Chemchem – never go to church. As far as I know they've never taken a holiday. The boys go to the coast – but with friends from school. And, did you know, those boys all keep their British Birth Certificates and British names – there is no legal contact with Mario and Maria at all!'

'Well, if it's true – I can only say that the maid was right – they do love each other! Mario is besotted with Maria and the other way round,' Madge pointed out.

'Yes – it all fits, doesn't it?'

'Frannie – we've got to be very careful with this story – think of what might happen if they were found!'

'Agreed – we must keep this entirely to ourselves – but I thought you'd like to hear the story.'

'Absolutely fascinating!'

'So they beat the Mafia – not many can claim that!'

'Did George react to the story?'

'No, he's heard of Mario and Maria but really doesn't know them, he'd not make a connection. And I was careful to disguise my interest. Chuck stopped the story when the 'scent' – if I can call it that – reached the convent. He told it all very well so there were some speculations about where they might be and I was very careful to say nothing except that they probably were in South America.'

Madge was smiling, 'I love a good romance and this is a corker, isn't it?'

'Yes – if it's true. We'll never know, will we?'

'Left in the air! The best stories are like that!'

CHAPTER 14

Initially there was no indication that anything too serious was happening. Glory Halleluiah had phoned Corn and West to say that she'd got a bush fire on her place; annoyingly having jumped the fence from Bell's ranch where he never kept his fire- breaks in good condition. Corn felt the wind coming up in strength and asked Glory Halleluiah to phone everyone else for help. West was away in Nakuru on a farm shopping trip.

From next door Mario and his three eldest sons, Marco, Luigi and Roberto, arrived quickly with some men. Frank came next with as many staff as he could get into his vehicle. Dar and Lew set off in two Land Rovers each crammed with Africans and, lastly, Frannie arrived, also laden with men.

They knew the form. Bush fires were not uncommon; sometimes one could burn back and stop the fire, sometimes a tractor was needed to make quick fire-breaks, but always the men spread out to beat the fire with branches they'd collect en route. It was very hot and exhausting work.

The fire was still near the boundary with Bell's place but Corn was correct; a fairly strong wind was blowing it towards the centre of Glory Halleluiah's property in the direction of Mario's ranch – quite a long way away but the wind was increasing.

Back home Libby knew what to do. She was left with a skeleton staff and got into action in the kitchen. The men would all be dehydrated when they got back. If they got the fire under control quickly lots of hot tea with plenty of sugar would be enough but, if the fight went on a long time, a proper meal would be needed. Libby looked at the state of the wind and she went to the outside cool room (made of double walled chicken wire filled with charcoal on which water dripped – inside remaining quite cold) and took out a lot of meat. She phoned Madge to compare notes.

'Yes, it looks bad. The men from a boma up the hill say they can see it all and it's spreading. Oh dear. Started on Bell's. It'll be a long day. Oh dear. I'll let you know what more the men tell me.'

At The Loop Libby organised a vast meaty soup as well as huge sufurias to be ready for tea; charcoal jikos being used in the yard near the back kitchen. Libby collected as many vegetables as she could – onions, carrots and anything else she could find. She left Kariuki, the cook, in charge and went to sort out first aid requirements – burn dressings and salves and bandages. She got everything she could think of; she'd done this before; and just hoped that it wouldn't be a really bad fire. But the wind was strong.

Mumps and Madge were both doing the same; experienced as they were. Madge, having got as much ready as she could, drove over to Corn and West's ranch to see the cook there. But he had already got food going; he knew the form; they all did; it was routine. For the women it was now a question of waiting. Madge, with men up the escarpment, had the advantage and could report, but she got the men to look at all the ranches, not just where the main trouble was. In very dry weather and certain conditions, just a broken piece of glass could start a fire anywhere. If one started, others might. Libby remembered a fire that had gone on for two days and prayed that this one would be stopped quickly. Madge phoned her.

'The men say it's spreading – going due east – quite fast,' Libby was worried. The usual Backlands wind was from the east but if it ever came from the west then it was strong, serious. Rain from the west was always heavier than that from the east; they called it the Uganda rain.

As the day wore on the women became more worried. Madge kept calm and, as always when something was serious, she finished all her sentences. The news was not encouraging. The fire had spread to the centre of Glory Halleluiah's ranch, heading for Mario's boundary.

'The men say it's going very fast. The wind!'

Libby tried to cheer her up.

'It should stop at Mario's boundary. Glory Halleluiah's fire-breaks at the fence-line are good and so are his – but imagine what this is doing to Glory Halleluiah's ranch!'

The men fighting the fire were spread out in grim groups. Their efforts were puny compared to the force of the wind and they all saw that they were unlikely to hold the fire until it reached the wide, double firebreak at the boundary fence. Corn went round to Mario's ranch and borrowed his tractor and a disc-harrow. He collected some more men, broke the boundary fence and started to enlarge the fire-break on Glory Halleluiah's side. The men were cutting bush as much as they could and Corn was slowly moving the harrow. If only the others could hold the fire in a band coming from the west to the east and not let it spread north or south then it could be contained at this boundary. With a grim expression and not yelling at the men, as he usually did, they all worked as fast as they could. Corn could see the smoke easily as it was advancing towards him. Mario's three youngest sons arrived on motor bikes, Maria having tried to stop them, and they went off to join the other fire-fighters. It was like trying to push back the Indian Ocean with a tooth-comb.

175

Now split into two groups, roughly north and south, the battle was going on with fierce determination; they all felt the wind. Loud cracks and leaping flares of trees going up in flames went on around them but, in fact, the wind was such that most trees were spared – the fire was travelling too fast, but bush and grass were blazing. Often a patch that was black would flare up again as the wind sometimes circled an area. The crackling noise was deafening and the sky was alive with birds flying into the smutted smoke to catch escaping insects. On the ground small animals were running away, some to be caught in another place. The cattle were all moved as fast as the herders could manage and gates were left open and fences broken to help them. The men were beating, beating and trying to keep at least the sides of this fire from spreading.

Although the men knew where the fire was heading it was no simple job; the ground was undulating, in places rocky or with wooded dells and with bush dotted about. It was easy to lose one's sense of direction temporarily. Up a rise and it was clear again. As the fire was moving fast so did the men, although they knew this was not always the best action as there was a danger of the fire reviving behind them. Lew thought it was like the falling nightmare. With great effort on either flank the men were managing to save a big spread north and south but they could never stop the main burn, romping ahead with incredible noise. Frannie had never seen such a quick moving fire before. He did not know that Corn was already enlarging the fire-break ahead but was cursing himself for not thinking of it. There was no hope of the wind dying down now before early evening. They were in for a long day and the men were already tired.

The African men worked doggedly, knowing very well the serious nature of a fire; some were in a small group with a European, others were in African groups, but they were now all spaced out quite well –

or as well as possible. Dar was feeling his age. He looked at his watch – one o'clock. He knew they had got a very long time to go – until dark most likely. He'd been through fires before and knew the scene only too well. Bloody Bell, he thought as he was beating and beating. He wasn't anywhere near his ranch; he was often away.

Mr. Pinto had a big group of men on the south of the belt of fire. Rosa had never experienced a fire before so he'd rapidly told her what to prepare and went off to do what he could. Glory Halleluiah could do nothing except drive to the areas she could and encourage the men. She took water for them, which they drank quickly; most wouldn't stop for a drink. After a while she went round to Mario's ranch, using the main Backlands road, and found Maria with a few of her staff ready to keep the fire off the house – there were buckets of water, hosepipes and axes all ready. Glory Halleluiah told her what she had seen, and Maria was able to tell her that Corn had got the tractor and the harrow in action. That was good news.

At four in the afternoon the fire was about a mile from the boundary fence, not quite going at the furious rate it was earlier but still making progress. Corn could see it easily now and was desperately keeping the harrow going. He'd sent a man for more diesel and prayed that the tractor would keep going on the fuel it had for a bit longer. He'd started at what he hoped was the north end of the fire and was working south along the fence firebreak, almost doubling the width. That, together with the firebreak on Mario's side, should stop it even with a strong wind – should – but there was never a guarantee.

Frank was with three Africans on the north of the fire, working furiously but feeling it all on his hands; he knew he'd end up with massive blisters. Lew had got rather more men with him also on the north. Dar with a group and Frannie with a couple were still on the

177

south side, worried about Glory Halleluiah's house that was on that side. Mario and his family were each doing the best they could. They were now all spread out, the groups hardly seeing each other, and often not at all, but they knew what they must do. At odd moments a swirl of wind caused havoc when a 'dead' bit flared up again, but, on the whole, those patches were left alone as they would die out themselves.

At five thirty the wind suddenly lost its force, almost died, and the men knew that the fire would move slower now. They redoubled their efforts in order to catch up with it; they might even be able to get it under control before it reached the firebreak. That was a desolate hope as the fire was almost there but when advance tongues of fire reached the firebreak they stopped; Corn had done his job well. With any luck the fence itself would be saved. The side sections were still burning and the work went on; weary men nearly dropping with fatigue.

Madge reported to Libby that the worst was over; Libby reported to Mumps.

Seven o'clock came, eight o'clock, nine o'clock as well. It was extremely late and the women were all very worried. In the dark the men at the Cooper's house said that there were plenty of glows but the worst had stopped some time ago. There would be some men watching that it didn't flare up again – but where were the rest of them? Why were they so late?

Finally, at nearly ten o'clock Frannie drove up to The Loop in an overloaded Land Rover from which he decanted some of The Loop's men.

'Libs – I've brought some of your chaps – Lew and Dar are behind.'

'A drink ? Why are you so late?'

'Beer, please.'

Frannie downed a pint in a few seconds. 'Any tea?' and Libby produced a mug of sweet tea. He was almost unrecognisable, blackened face, red-eyed, sweating, hair awry, filthy clothes and smelling strongly of the smoke and dirt.

'Libs – it's been the worst. I tell you – the worst. Look – Dar's had it – give him drinks and into bed quickly – to hell with washing. Lew'll tell you all about it. I must get my lot back.'

'They're getting something here.'

'Yes, thanks but I'll have to get them back – all the watu have been wonderful. Libs – just look after Dar – I'm off.'

After another ten minutes Lew drove Dar with the rest of The Loop's crew crushed into Lew's Land Rover. There wasn't time to ask about the other Land Rover – Frannie was right, Dar was in a terrible state – hardly able to get out of the vehicle and every bit as filthy as Frannie. Lew took the men off for sustenance.

'Come on, Dad (she hardly ever called him Dad), into bed – I'll bring drinks and things; Lew's looking after the staff.'

'Must wash – oh, Libby – let Lew tell you. I'm all right – just. It was terrible, terrible. Bell needs crucifying.'

Libby made him drink some tea and as much soup as she could get into him. Then after a perfunctory wash Dar fell into bed

Lew was with the men at the back; they were all quiet. He was sitting with them sharing the tea and the soupy stew. None had washed and the sight – and smell - was awful. The usually chattering men were abnormally silent; they were very subdued. More tea. More soup. Some men needed first aid and when Libby arrived to check she took them off to deal with their cuts and burns. They never grumbled; accepting the vicissitudes of life in the way that only Africans can.

When Lew felt that the men were reviving he went to find Libby who was just putting on the last burn dressing.

'Dar?'

'In bed – absolutely flaked.'

'Libby – it was the worst ever – did he tell you?'

'No - he was too tired.'

'Luigi's dead. Burnt. Couldn't get out of a bad place. Awful. We didn't know until the worst of the fire was over – then he wasn't there so we had to look. Roberto found him. Terrible. You can imagine.'

'Oh, Lew, no!'

'Frannie said he'd be dead of the fumes before the flames reached him – hope so. But the body !' He suddenly thought he'd better not tell Libby.

'Luigi – the nicest!'

'And we've lost two Land Rovers and one motor bike – couldn't get back to them and the fire went round. One's Dar's, the other's Mario's and the motor bike is Fabio's.'

'Oh, Lew.' It was all too much. Libby pulled herself together. 'Lew – drinks – food – there's everything.'

'Beer then – I had tea with the men and the stew stuff – that was fine. The men are shattered; tough guys, though. The Africans are really great in an emergency like this. But when Luigi was found they went dead quiet – sorry – wrong words – it was eerie. We all had to go to Mario's place – Maria in a state of course. But it was very late so none of us stayed – just to say sorry and be with them all for a bit. What else could we do?'

'Dreadful.'

'All of them in tears. But Mario said they'd bury Luigi to-morrow. We've got to go. Twelve noon. No priest – nothing – just a burial – if Dar will be O.K. by then? He was absolutely beaten – almost couldn't walk at the end. West arrived from Nakuru. He's going to do night patrol at Glory Halleluiah's place in case it flares up again – it may not but could get going in the morning if we don't watch out. Dad's looking a funny colour but he's quite tough really. And did Dar tell you about Frannie saving his life? No? He'd better tell you. Libby, the death toll might have been much higher – six more. I must get a bath and go to bed – a million things to organise in the morning. I've given some more burn dressings out – O.K? Oh, and Glory Halleluiah's distraught, poor soul. I must go.'

Libby looked at the dining table, ready for a proper meal. She nibbled at a piece of cheese, went to the kitchen to put things away, had a much needed cup of tea and went to bed.

Dar slept until dawn, woke up, drank tea that Libby produced and slept again until ten when he felt a lot better, had a bath and got dressed for a very late breakfast.

'But for Frannie, I wouldn't be here! I was with a couple of the watu when the fire broke out again behind us. One of the men called and then Frannie with two more chaps came running – they'd seen the same thing. The wind had jinx'd so the fire was coming fast in front and behind and on one side. The other side was a rock precipice – we were really trapped. Frannie immediately got us beating the grass down to make a wide path towards the main fire. He was really fierce with us – so we did – about fifteen feet wide and we were going towards the fire that was coming at us fast. Beat, beat, flatten the grass – it was long. Then Frannie said when the fire met our beaten track we were to wait just a second – he'd lead and we were to run through the path. It sounded madness. But when the fire got there – oh, it was hot – the flattened grass really did hold it a bit. Frannie grabbed one of the men, pulled him and ran – so we all followed – I got another – one of the older chaps – we were right in the flames – scorching. We all got burnt and then Frannie made us go on running – the ground was still sizzling – until we got to a few trees where the fire had missed a bit. We all collapsed. Libby – we'd be dead. No-one could say anything for quite a while. We had to wait for the land round us to cool a bit. Then Frannie casually got up and said we'd better get on with fire-fighting! But – Luigi!'

Frannie was concerned about a burial without a priest; it had been assumed that Mario and Maria were Roman Catholics; the boys had gone to Catholic schools in Nairobi. He thought again; the nearest Catholic priest was at Nakuru – and was an Italian. If what they all thought about them was correct then Mario and Maria would avoid all Italians; interesting, but not conclusive. Frannie carried his prayer book and had a word with Dar when they got to the house where everyone was gathering quietly.

A grave had been dug in the garden – or the patch of land in front of the house that served as a garden – and a quickly made coffin was resting on two chairs on the verandah. Dar spoke with Mario and Maria. When everyone was there they stood round the grave and Mario and the five remaining boys carried the coffin and lowered it on ropes into the grave. Dar, with a rather choked voice, then read the burial service from the Anglican prayer book – 'I am the resurrection and the life .....' Mario was translating into Italian for Maria so Dar went slowly and kept stopping. 'We brought nothing into the world and it is certain we can carry nothing out.....'

Dar chose Psalm 39, 'I said, I will take heed to my ways.......'

He read the whole of 1 Corinthians Ch. 15 verses 20 to 58. Here Mario hesitated a bit in his translation but Maria was obviously desperate to hear. It was very hot. Madge and Libby were both crying and even Glory Halleluiah was wiping tears. When it was over Mario stepped forward to throw some earth onto the coffin and everyone else followed. At the end Maria called in Swahili – 'He's gone – come and have food.' And, apart from Corn and West who were filling in the grave properly, they went into the house where food revived them. Glory Halleluiah was insistent that she'd replace the lost vehicles and the motor bike as soon as possible. 'Insurance!' said Dar. 'Yes, but that'll take time and work has to go on.'

Someone mentioned Bell. It was like throwing a grenade into the party. Invective was hurled unimaginably strongly but seemed to relieve the tension. 'When does he get back?' No-one knew.

'Glory Halleluiah, when he gets back – don't you tackle him – you know what he's like about women. I'll deal with him – leave it to me.' Dar knew that he must shoulder that burden.

It was several weeks before Bell came back, during which time Glory Halleluiah provided the wages, rations for his men, dip chemicals and salt for the ranch. He had evidently not intended to be away for so long and had not left adequate provision. Whether he had heard of the disaster or not, no-one knew, but someone had to keep the place going. The African staff on the ranch were visibly shaken by the result of the fire, knowing perfectly well that their bwana was bad about keeping his firebreaks in order – he was bad over other things, too. There was sympathy with the men and Glory Halleluiah certainly did not hold them responsible; she made that clear. Bell finally returned. Glory Halleluiah sent him a precise account of the money she'd spent – no other mention of anything – and a cheque came to her by return.

But Dar decided on other action. He wrote a strong letter, pointing out that it was a legal requirement in Kenya to keep fire-breaks in good order and because of Bell's negligence a life had been lost, vehicles had been destroyed, valuable grazing ruined, etc and he then added a detailed valuation of all the items – pointing out that he could never put a price on a man's life. But it included everything, the men's wages for the day, the cost of the vehicles, and of renting grazing that Glory Halleluiah was obliged to do to save her cattle (some of her cattle were on Mario's place, some on Corn and West's and others on a ranch further east; no-one was charging her any fees). Dar even estimated the cost of first aid to the men, of food, overtime – everything he could accumulate. The final figure was enormous. He sent the letter to Bell with a copy to his own lawyer, with whom he'd had a word. The last sentence was pretty strong:

A case of manslaughter is being considered. You will hear more about this soon.

In fact the lawyer said there was no chance of a case of manslaughter being upheld but the negligence over the firebreaks could be taken to court and, because of the consequences, the fine would be very heavy. Bell would understand this and realise that if the negligence case went to court it might possibly lead to the more serious charge. Together with the account Dar sent, his possible financial outlay would be huge. 'All for the loss of a horseshoe nail ....' someone pointed out.

Dar gave Bell a month to pay his debts. There was no response but a letter arrived that was copied to all the Backlands residents. It came from the firm of Muter and Oswald – auctioneers and estate agents – saying that Mr. Bell's property was for sale and neighbours were being alerted in case they would like to purchase the land to add to their existing properties. Glory Halleluiah thought about it, but only briefly. It was sold to a Nairobi investment company who put in a manager. The poor manager faced a big job getting the place back in order. Bell simply disappeared. Nobody was sorry.

'Libby – when you were a little girl your mother and I were at Muthaiga Club and a new settler out from Britain got into conversation. We told him that we were ranching. He said, 'Oh – that's the easy farming, isn't it?''

CHAPTER 15

'I can't imagine why you should be invited!'

Mumps emphasised the 'you' heavily. Frannie took no notice, threw his overnight bag into his Land Rover and said a cheerful, 'I'll be back in the morning,' and drove off.

In fact he didn't know why he had been invited either. An invitation had arrived from the Chemchem O.C.P.D. for Frannie to have dinner with him and stay the night, an invitation Frannie had no intention of passing up.

The O.C.P.D., Roger Tarrant, a solid, slightly older man than normal for an up-country posting, was very interested in Frannie. Over the affair of the cattle from the Grey's ranch Frannie had shown himself to be intelligent, daring - in fact audacious - and ready to use unconventional methods to solve problems, and he had come to the O.C.P.D. to ask the legality of it all beforehand. This had been quite impressive. (Frannie never mentioned the fate of the two herders or Mr. Tarrant might have revised his opinion somewhat.) Mr. Tarrant, with long service in the police, knew well that it is not always the Law that has the best answer for problems and in the case of the illegal grazing Frannie had managed what the police never could. That Frannie could raise help from so many people was never in doubt; he had a natural air of command. And, to add extra spice, the whole affair had a great deal of humour about it. The O.C.P.D. had admired it all.

Now quite a different issue had arisen and Mr. Tarrant thought that Frannie, on another occasion, *might* have seen fit to use his audacity, courage and intelligence – but not humour; this was a very serious matter indeed. Mr. Tarrant had to find out.

At Chemchem the O.C.P.D. was housed in typical Government housing, a solid stone rectangle with a neat space at the front and a verandah and garden at the rear. It was in a   block of official housing, all bungalows, well spaced and separated from each other with dark green hedges of Kei Apple. Frannie arrived just at dusk to find no other cars in the short drive.

Roger Tarrant came out to meet him. 'We're alone this evening – hope you don't mind. My wife's gone to Nairobi. I wanted to have a chat with you. Come in, man. Put your kag in this room – bathroom opposite, loo next door. Then come out and have a drink – back garden.'

In the surprisingly large back garden drinks were on a table under an Erythrina tree with camp chairs either side. A few more trees and bushes spattered the lawn; unimaginative but pleasant and peaceful. The sky was rapidly darkening and pinpricks of stars were appearing. It was a very mild night; the garden was heavy with the scent of Yesterday, To-day and To-morrow bushes and the house glowed with yellow light bulbs used to keep insects at bay. Other houses were distant glimpses of light. It was very still and balmy, cooler than down the escarpment; an easy, relaxing temperature. Frannie thought how different it was from the Backlands; the thousand feet upwards changed everything.

To begin with Roger Tarrant made superficial conversation, asking about people in the Backlands and, especially, the aftermath of the Grey episode.

'I heard from Mr. Winchester that Grey had been no-where near the place since then.'

'Yes. No sign of Grey's cattle. It seems to have worked. I must say we all enjoyed it!'

'So I gathered. I hear you even had Glory Halleluiah on the job.'

'Absolutely – she's got a great sense of humour and wasn't going to be left out.'

'Well – I'm glad it worked. None of the warnings we've given Grey ever got anywhere!'

It was easy and pleasant but Frannie wondered if this was all. Suddenly the O.C.P.D. changed the direction of the conversation.

'We'll be quite safe here; no-one can overhear us and what I want us to talk about is not for anyone else's ears.'

Frannie stiffened slightly at this surprising statement but said nothing.

'Frannie – I wanted to have a very private talk with you; absolutely confidential. Understand?'

Frannie nodded, sipping his drink.

'Nothing that is said in this garden will go any further, I promise you. I've asked you here because of curiosity. I am a policeman – but I'm also human. Later on I want to ask some questions that I'd be grateful if you'd answer. I can't force you to answer, I can only ask. But I feel I must ask. Privately. Confidentially. O.K.?'

Again Frannie nodded, slightly tense.

'You'll remember the death of that fellow Louch – about a year ago – went over the escarpment?'

'I found him!'

'Yes. Did you know that one of the murdered girls was found on his farm? Next to the Club. In fact they were all found – almost in a circle – on farmland round the Club – and one in the Club grounds.'

Frannie nodded cautiously; he now had the drift of the conversation.

'Whoever is the murderer has given us police an incredible headache for years. It's not far off twenty years since it all started.' Mr. Tarrant leant back a bit, nursing his glass.

'That the Club has been central to it all never surprised us – after all it's the meeting place – if you want to find a girl go to the Club.'

Again Frannie nodded gently.

'I was in Chemchem for the first murder – that Backlands girl – then I was moved but I've been back off and on – whenever there's been a choice I've chosen Chemchem. It's a good posting for me but I admit I've always wanted to be here. I've felt very strongly over this Chemchem murderer. It's niggled me. Why haven't we got any further with it? Why has the bugger got away with it so often. Goodness knows we've tried hard enough.' There was a slight pause. Frannie said nothing. Mr. Tarrant smiled.

'Of course most police think I'm mad to want this posting – too far from Nairobi – but I've hankered after finding the murderer before I retire – next year! These murders! When there are murders combined with rape we always look for the men who are out on a limb – you know – the bachelors, the divorced men, widowers, or any male oddities...'

'You certainly had a go at me when Sally Cooper was murdered – I got really angry – I'd known her since she was born – a great friend!'

'Ah yes, but you were not the only one, you know – we had to look into every one in the district – but mainly the type I've mentioned. And for the next murder you were easily cleared ...'

'By the grace of God I was at the dentist in Nairobi and then stayed the night with an old school friend – now a lawyer with Kaplan and Stratton – thank goodness.'

'Yes. You were clear. And though we have to consider the possibility of someone different murdering the second time – a copycat murder – it isn't often the case. It was much more likely to be the same chap – and events have shown that to be ninety nine percent true.' Roger Tarrant took another sip. Frannie did not move.

'Of course we had to look deeply at all the farmers around the Club including that fellow Louch – not popular we were – Louch – very quiet fellow and that good wife and lovely kiddies. But we had to do it. And when cases drag on like this one has we have to look at everyone – not just the obvious. So we've looked at the happily married – everyone. Every single male in this district who is old enough to have murdered Sally Cooper now has a file. You may not know but we've had plain-clothes chaps up here off and on for years – delving, looking. The trouble is that alibis are difficult for farmers. You ask any of them what they were doing last Tuesday afternoon and they'll say they were out on the farm. And true, no doubt. But how do you prove it? The farms are big, the watu will say they saw the bwana but have no idea of the time – anything could happen. Roads are empty, no-one need see anything.'

Frannie shifted slightly in his seat, still saying nothing.

'We've learnt a lot over the years. There are about 900 farms within Chemchem and the Backlands – most up here, of course. With owners, managers, the business people in town and so on we've had to comb a lot of men. You'd be surprised what we've found. No less than two men are living here under false names! Why, we have to ask – but looking into them they are quite honest citizens – maybe they came to

Kenya for a new start. Who knows? But I wish they hadn't as it's cost us police a lot of time and effort to trace it all. And we've got an ex-convict in our midst. How he got here without the Colonial Office knowing is a big query. But he's quite straight here. And there's another oddity who gets up at midnight every full moon, dresses in women's clothes, goes to the river, strips, swims, dresses again and walks back to his house. No-one sees him – but my men did. He's quite harmless and it's obviously a mild case of lunacy. Otherwise he's fine. There's only one homosexual up here – I expect you know about him, everybody does, but he's not going to rape and murder a girl. There are some other odd things, bound to crop up in a community like this, but we still haven't been able to pinpoint the murderer. All we can go on is that it's a male and someone that the girls seem able to trust – and my goodness they've been warned enough. So........'

There was another pause. Frannie was listening carefully with a serious face.

'Frannie, I've got you here to talk about the day Louch died.'

'Yes,' said Frannie quietly.

'All of you in the Men's Bar said that Louch was celebrating his big win and was shouting his mouth off.'

'Yes, It was all a load of nonsense. He was very drunk. He'd won all that money and gone bananas. We'd never seen him like that – quiet fellow normally – not often in the Men's Bar. But he was screechers all right.'

'Right. Now – according to the reports you decided to send the barman away because – so the report says – you didn't want him to hear all the drivel Louch was spouting?'

'Yes, he was a new fellow – on trial, I think, Mission schooled, spoke English. Not good for him to hear Louch, I decided. We'd all got drinks anyway and those who wanted had got food so I sent him out of the Bar. Of course if he'd been one of the old barmen he'd probably not have gone but his chap was raw, thank God.'

'Now. Listen to this. There is an interesting sequel to that lad leaving the Bar. You are right, he was on trial and yes, Mission schooled and yes again, he spoke English. When you sent him off he went back to the kitchen area of the Club but on his way he had a fit of coughing and he coughed up blood. Mrs. Fellows – you know, the housekeeper woman – saw him and yanked him straight to the Government Hospital that minute. The long and the short is that he was diagnosed with Tuberculosis. That put him straight out of the Club and back to the Reserve with drugs and an order to rest for a year. So he disappeared. Whether he'll ever come back to the Club or not I have no idea. In any case we, the police, were not interested in him. He was out of the picture some time before Louch left the bar and, in any case, Mrs. Fellows can vouch for him; so can the Government Hospital. He was nowhere near the escarpment.'

Frannie was looking at the indigo sky sparkling with multiplying stars. Distant hills were becoming black, sharply outlining night's canopy. He said nothing. The O.C.P.D. had another drink and continued.

'As chance would have it my gardener here comes from the same location as that lad. He's just come back from his annual leave, my gardener. He's a garrulous old boy and went on to me the other day about the lad from the Club and what he said about Louch. According to this lad Louch kept on about being rich and how he would be able to have lots and lots of girls now he's got all this money. Of course when an African comes into money he usually pays another bride price and takes a second or third wife – you know all about that. This lad didn't know if Europeans did the same but when Louch went on about it he wondered if Europeans did the same. So my gardener asked me.'

Frannie murmured, 'Mmmm.'

'I wasn't going into details like bigamy so all I said was that it does happen in a few cases. That was that.'

Frannie repeated, 'Mmmm.' There was quite a long pause. Venus shone clearly, with infant stars now crowding the sky.

'To me the interesting thing is that none of you mentioned what Louch was banging on about. All you witnesses said that he was talking wildly as many a drunk will. It is interesting that this lad picked up that particular thing.'

'He said a lot of foolish things – all nonsense.' Frannie sounded quite casual, but did not take his eyes off the stars.

'No doubt. But I cannot ignore what the lad says. It struck me that Louch may not have been thinking about wives or even prostitutes – but something else.........'

'Yes?' replied Frannie guardedly.

'Frannie, you're no fool so will have got the drift of my mind. Louch's death was odd – there were plenty of question marks. As police we are bound to wonder. At the same time we are bound by rules and evidence comes strongly into our rules – and there was no evidence other than Louch's death was accidental. You found him but you were nowhere near when he went over the edge; you were vouched for in town for a couple of hours after he left the club and, in any case that fellow, Haines, saw Louch drive past his place and wondered where he was going – so that gave us a time. You understand?' But Roger

Tarrant wasn't waiting for Frannie's response, he was looking very serious now. 'I want to ask you a few questions, as I've said. I'd be grateful if you'd answer – strictly confidential. And it strikes me that it must remain confidential because there is a good woman and her children involved.' Roger Tarrant glimpsed at Frannie who shifted in his chair again. The moon started to glow as it began its quick rise in the east. The stars were overtaken.

'Why me? I'm just one of the men in the bar at the time.'

'There were five of you, apart from Louch, and you arrived last. It was you who sent the lad out of the bar. It is possible that you saw into Louch's ravings what I have seen. You may have realised the consequences of it all. Frannie – I've seen your ability over that fun with Grey's cattle. You are known to be intelligent, quick-witted, sensible, far- sighted – you are the one with the ability to recognise something and act. So I am asking you.'

Frannie sighed, took another sip and nodded. He had often wondered if the true story might come out eventually; better with Roger Tarrant than anyone else. A nightjar called.

'All right. Go ahead.'

There was a long silence while Mr. Tarrant considered his words.

'In all seriousness, Frannie, do you think the Chemchem murderer will ever strike again?'

There was the suspicion of a smile on Frannie's face. After yet another pause he took another sip and spoke to the far hills, now a black silhouette. Frannie knew it had to come out.

'I think you can take it as certain that the Chemchem murderer will never strike again.'

The O.C.P.D. was looking at Frannie who suddenly returned his looked, raised his glass as if in a toast. The policemen smiled.

'Aaaah. Thank you. Thank you very much. Thank you very much indeed. I hoped that might be the answer. It solves a lot of problems. You know when one questions witnesses – like all of you in the bar – there are always some discrepancies in each person's story. As it happened I didn't do the questioning but I saw the reports later and noticed what no other officer had spotted. All the accounts were remarkably similar. It was as if someone had rehearsed them in what to say.'

'Really?' said Frannie but he was smiling. He'd had to be so quick to tell them their story. They'd been so horrified, so shaken by what Louch had been saying that they took Frannie's lead easily.

'Louch must have made it pretty clear in his rantings?'

'I'm afraid he did – he even named one girl.'

'Oh, dreadful. But you wouldn't come straight to me?'

'I think you know why.'

'Yes – one very good woman and her daughters.'

'The law can't solve everything.'

'Don't I know that. Law is fine but not necessarily human.'

They sat differently now, in companionship.

'Another question – how on earth did you get Louch to go down that escarpment road?'

Frannie smiled at the memory. 'I told him that Libby Winchester had fallen for him.'

'*What* a risk!'

'No, I knew that Libby was in Nairobi.'

196

'But if Louch hadn't gone over the escarpment – and I know that for a really drunk chap to negotiate that road safely is unlikely – but if he'd managed it?'

'Then he'd have got to The Loop, found Libby not there, but Dar Winchester or Lew Cooper would have seen his drunkenness and got him home.'

'And ....'

'And I would have had to report to you what happened.'

'And Mrs. Louch and the girls would have been finished for ever.'

'Yes.'

'Whew, Frannie, of course I can't say that what you did was right – the Law being the Law, but, personally, I can only say that I'm glad you did it. I don't think I'd have had the guts or the quick-thinking to deal with it.'

Each sat with his own thoughts. Frannie was quite glad that it had come out – it would be safe with Roger Tarrant. Mr. Tarrant was amazed at this second and far more serious example of Frannie's audacity.

'The file on Louch was closed on the verdict of accidental death so that's that. The Chemchem murder file is still very much open. I'd like to close it but I can't. It's a pity – lots of girls will go on being careful near the Club – or maybe that's not a bad thing. The whole district would be happier if it was tidied up – but we can't do that. Time will sort it out. I shouldn't have told you so much but I had to – and you'll guess that there are a lot of things in police work that never seem to come to an obvious end – but they do, quietly. If there are no more murders it will be assumed – eventually – that the murderer has either moved, died or something. Have another drink.'

'Thanks – two is my limit. Dad introduced me to whisky when I was twenty one and I took to it immediately – but I restrict myself – two only – but thanks.'

'Yes,' thought Roger Tarrant, 'Frannie is immensely self-controlled. What a chap!'

'I'll call for dinner. It may be a bit simple, Sally being away, but there's usually plenty.'

He walked into the house leaving Frannie surveying the now moonlit sky with its edge of mysterious hills. He has certainly relieved, he knew. One special load off his mind. Tarrant had taken it extremely well; Frannie knew perfectly clearly that he had disobeyed the Law; Tarrant, thank God, knew why.

'Dinner in a few minutes.'

'Thanks. Did you know Tarrant, that Mrs. Louch is selling the farm, feels she can't carry on?'

'Yes, I'd heard that. She'll be missed. And did you know that Baccup had a run for her?' (Baccup being the Lecher.)

Frannie laughed, 'I think all Chemchem knows that. Apparently she dealt with him very firmly. He really is a hopeless case. The ladies down in the Backlands reckon that if he'd stop trying he'd find a nice women eventually but he's far too blatant. Mrs. Louch is well out of it.'

'There's Mwangi. Come and have some grub. And our conversation is entirely forgotten.'

'Thanks,' said Frannie, knowing that he really could trust the O.C.P.D.

'I think it is the other way round. I should be thanking you. All over. Finish....Dinner now.'

Frannie left next morning after a fairly early morning breakfast during which the men found a lot to admire in each other. But after Frannie drove away Roger Tarrant thought 'Hmmm – what a cool, audacious customer. I would not like to be his adversary, but I can't help liking the chap.'

CHAPTER 16

Glory Halleluiah went to Nairobi in a gentle air of anticipation. She had been very aware of Dar's kindliness but total misunderstanding of Janet. Dar was so often like that. Janet was to him a little nurse from the Cottage Hospital and a suitable girl friend for Lew – that was all. The rest of the Backlands had spotted that she probably came from a higher class family than Dar had guessed. Her pronunciation gave her away – as it does always in society - and Glory Halleluiah was amused by Dar's polite ignorance. Dar thought that Glory Halleluiah liked the girl because she was musical – and this was true, but Glory Halleluiah and Janet were perfectly at ease with each other, whereas the likes of Sexy Sarah would have found Glory Halleluiah impossible. In one of their rare moments when they dared discuss the possibility of Lew and Janet getting together, both Glory Halleluiah and Madge had seen Dar's lack of perception. It amused them slightly, fond as they were of Dar.

Now Glory Halleluiah was going to meet Janet's parents who were coming to Kenya for a month's holiday. No-one else was free to meet them, Janet was working; Glory Halleluiah volunteered. In fact Janet only had three weeks holiday so it had been arranged that for the first week her parents would stay at the Backlands – a few days at The Loop and the rest with Glory Halleluiah. After that Janet was to drive them to the coast in her little car.

Glory Halleluiah was watching the passengers walk from the big plane across the tarmac at Nairobi's Eastleigh Airport. There was no doubting Mr. and Mrs. Evans. They were both below average height but had a complete air of assurance and Janet looked very like them. Confidently they walked towards the airport building; people in control, successful, obviously in the upper echelon of the middle class – not at all what Dar might expect. Glory Halleluiah smiled to herself.

She took the couple to the Norfolk Hotel for lunch, all her thoughts being underlined. They were very pleasant people. Mr. Evans was what Glory Halleluiah called 'a nut brown' man – clearly a successful farmer with a great air of command. He insisted on paying for lunch and dealt with the Goanese major domo with firm good manners. Mrs. Evans was thanking Glory Halleluiah for the hospitality she gave to Janet. They were doing all the right things. When Janet stayed with Glory Halleluiah she had been reticent about her family, so Glory Halleluiah had to guess quite a lot. It did not surprise her to learn that the Evans's farm was big – over 900 acres – a considerable property for England. Dar was in for a surprise.

On the journey to the Backlands both Mr. and Mrs. Evans showed a great deal of interest in the farming, although it was clear that Janet had already told them a lot in letters. They stopped at Nakuru for the night, managed to see the flamingos fringing the lake – albeit from a distance - and enjoyed the journey on to Chemchem and the Backlands. Everything was of interest and Mr. Evans took a lot of photographs.

Dar had to make a considerable social adjustment when they arrived at The Loop, Glory Halleluiah seeing it all and smiling. Because Janet said so little about her background to anyone except Lew, Dar was in ignorance of the fact that she came from Shropshire.

'My wife's twin sister and husband farm in Shropshire – Hugh and Mary Constable.'

'Oh, we know them. Hugh helps me on two committees – good

man. Mary and Olwyn get on well, don't you,' said John Evans. 'Oh, yes, we see each other quite often.'

'Libby – my daughter – she was with them for a while some years ago.'

'Oh - Libby – yes, we met her – never clicked that she was the Libby Janet wrote about – how incredible – small world and all that!'

It was a splendid start. Dar noticed that John Evans said that Hugh 'helped him' and found out, slowly, that the Evans' property was considerably larger than the Constable place and that Mr. Evans was a force in the county. Dar was adjusting a lot of thoughts.

When Libby arrived she certainly remembered Mrs. Evans and there was a lot of 'how odd I never connected' and more of the 'small world' until everyone had got the length of each other. The Evanses were totally at home on The Loop from the beginning; their biggest difference to their daughter was that they would talk – and talk they did, Dar enjoying them both very much. The men understood each other easily. They quickly got onto farming problems – the Farmers' Union in each country, marketing problems, inconsistent prices, diseases, abnormal weather, the inability of any Government to understand farming. 'You'd think the Tories would – not a bit of it – almost as bad as Labour.'

Lew came in and was introduced but remained silent during the barrage of talk between the two senior men. He was deeply interested to meet Janet's parents and wondered how much Janet had told her parents in letters – not that there was much to say. Evidently she had been quiet. In fact she'd mentioned Lew as the manager at The Loop once or twice but never gave any detail. Well, there was nothing to be said, was there? The Evanses knew nothing of their friendship. Glory Halleluiah realised this, and expected it. Lew relaxed.

'Lew, I'll take John and Olwyn around to-morrow – you carry on branding. We'll meet you at the straight kopje boma.'

Lew wondered if Janet even liked him at all. He was hopeful she did like him – and more than like – but could not be a hundred percent sure. It was obvious she'd said nothing to her parents. What did that mean – if anything? He was unsure – but liked her parents. They were obviously very straight farming folk.

Everything on the ranch interested Mr. Evans and his wife and they understood it all with intelligence, Dar enjoying their company. When they got to the branding the Evanses were fascinated. 'We don't do that any longer – use ear notching or ear tags – but you couldn't do that here with the numbers you handle!' Lew invited Mr. Evans to have a go at branding – in fact he'd done it in his youth. There was no holding the man, he put on the leather gauntlets and got working, quickly getting the right time and depth. He was a hands-on farmer, no doubt. The smell of scorched hide did not upset Mrs. Evans – she was a true farmer's wife. Janet was very like her, Lew could see. She had a twinkle in her eye that sometimes emerged with Janet, who was usually much quieter than her mother.

They were very easy guests and when the talk turned to the vermin control needed on the ranch Mr. Evans was deeply interested.

'Lew, you shoot lions?'

Lew explained the problem and said, 'You'll be a rifle shot, Mr. Evans?'

'Only after small stuff – rabbits, foxes – nothing big. I've done some deer stalking but that was years ago. I have to keep the pigeons down and there's good pheasant shooting in Shropshire – properly organised - and I get a good bit of that so, yes, I keep a .22 and a shotgun – that's all.'

Lew took him to see the armoury at The Loop where both Dar's and Lew's guns were neatly racked. Mr. Evans was fascinated by all the guns, especially the heavy rifles. Lew gave him his own .375 to handle and Mr. Evans opened it, inspected the barrels and greatly admired it. 'I'd love to use this!'

'Why not – we've got a bad lion around – he's taking calves. We'll put up a bait and try and get him. I'll ask Dar.' Mr. Evans was pleased beyond speech at this idea.

Dar was happy with Lew's suggestion and they went out that evening to shoot a zebra to put up as bait. To assess Mr. Evans' ability they got him to take the zebra and he made no mistake about that. He could shoot. He was most interested in the way they opened up the stomach of the animal, dragged it behind the Land Rover for quite a distance to lay a scent and then, with the help of more ranch staff, it was hoisted below a branch of a big tree – just off the ground so that the lion would have to reach up for it.

'It's unlikely to come to-night but we'll try to-morrow – all right?'

Dar left Lew and Mr. Evans to deal with this alone. A small hide that was made of hessian supported by four light poles had been left in position. When the pair entered the hide the following night Lew had already been told that the lion was around, not far away – the staff had heard him. The two men waited, Lew warned Mr. Evans that they might be in for a long, hard session. He'd told Mr. Evans where to shoot – it was great that a man like Mr. Evans understood the anatomy of animals – and Lew said that he'd cover him. The wait was not as long as expected. Mr. Evans felt a tingle of excitement when the lion padded very quietly past them, just in front of the hide it seemed (though further than he thought) and sniffed up and then reached up to get at the carcase. Lew told him to wait for the lion to get into a good position but both men had their rifles ready aimed. The lion dropped with some meat, chewed, reached up again and this time he was sideways on to Mr. Evans who made a heart shot that dropped the lion to the ground and Lew instantly followed with another shot trying to get the brain. The lion lay, twitching. Lew whispered – 'You've got him – but we've got to wait.' Eventually when the convulsions stopped Lew threw a stone, as usual, and the men went to the lion. It was another very old lion – 'So sad that they end this way but probably better than them starving to death,' said Lew. In fact it had taken both shots to kill the animal but Lew was careful to let Mr. Evans think that it was his shot alone that had done the deed.

It was a very proud John Evans who went back to the house that night. It wasn't everyone who had shot a lion! Dar was delighted and thought it most fortunate that a very old lion happened to be around during their visit. Often they would go months without lion problems. Dar said that if they wanted the skin he could get Zimmerman's in Nairobi to deal with it, but they decided against that. What would they do with a lion skin in a farmhouse in Shropshire, they wondered? John had friends who filled their homes with hunting trophies, but he felt that not very good taste.

The next day there was a report of a wounded oryx on the ranch so Lew took Mr. Evans off after that, too – an act of mercy. They talked a lot about necessary shooting, as opposed to blood-lust shooting. John Evans was pleased that Lew saw it all as he did. Lew spoke about the most dangerous animal – the buffalo. 'Why are they the worst?' asked Mr. Evans.

'They are utterly unpredictable. You shoot, think you've got them, maybe a heart shot so they'll run a short way – then you find they've got round your back. Elephants will do that, too. A wounded elephant will come round and get behind you. We try not to shoot elephant but buffalo carry too many diseases. Dad – that's his ranch over there – under the escarpment – he's constantly having a go at buffalo. They're up in the forest and always trying to come down for Dad's grazing.'

This was news to Mr. Evans. He had not realised that Lew was a local young man, son of another rancher. It was no wonder that he was so much at home at The Loop. Interesting. A good lad.

The few days at The Loop were a great happiness for the Evanses and also for Dar who had genuinely enjoyed talking with John Evans over drinks each evening. Dar was certainly hoping that Lew and Janet would get together some day; it would be a good match. Dar was invited to visit the Shropshire farm, an invitation that he gratefully received but set aside for the time being; he'd temporarily given up the idea of travel after Edith died.

John and Olwyn Evans were quite sorry to move on to stay with Glory Halleluiah, much as they'd liked her on the journey from Nairobi. As they guessed there was less action for them on her ranch but they were taken round, met the Pintos and also Corn and West who came to dinner one night and behaved themselves ('Now – no tricks – Janet's parents – wouldn't be fair.').

There was plenty of talk with Glory Halleluiah and John Evans casually asked her how it was that Lew was working at The Loop rather than helping his own father.

'There's a tale to tell – a tale and a half. It's no secret now. I'll tell you.' Glory Halleluiah told the whole story of the Chemchem murderer, the tragic death of Sally, John's sojourn in South Africa and his criminal activities there, the desperate attempts of Frank and Madge to repay the stolen money, and Lew's lack of College.

'He's a great chap.   Every single penny he earns goes to his parents – every penny.   Mind you, we all help a bit – he's not short of things.   Dar houses, feeds, clothes him – so that's all right. And Frannie – you haven't met him yet? He gives Lew good Christmas and birthday presents – a gun – a radio – things like that.   I pay for him to be a member of the Club and Corn and West, bless them, keep him stocked with books – he's a voracious reader. So he's fine except for no personal cash at all – but, of course, if things do not work out he may never inherit his father's ranch!'

Both Mr. and Mrs. Evans were interested.   'Quite a young man! Very good of him to help his parents. What a sad story.'

'Frank and Madge – a dear couple – you'd like them. Of course they refuse to accept help from anyone else – and who would, in their position?   But it's so hard.   We all feel that John might have been perfectly all right if Sally had not been killed. It must have tipped him over an edge. Twins – very close and Sally such a great character – she was the dominant one.'

Did the Evanses know that Janet and Lew were such friends? Glory Halleluiah was longing to know but couldn't ask.

At tea time one day Glory Halleluiah asked, 'How did Janet decide to come to Kenya?'

Mr. and Mrs. Evans exchanged looks.

'Olwyn, if you're going to tell that story, I'm off for a walk!' and he left.

'You see it's his fault really.' But Mrs. Evans was smiling. 'He didn't mean it at all! We've got an elder daughter – Steffie – Stephanie

– she's eight years older than Janet – like two single children really. Right from a child she was musical – picked out tunes on the piano as a toddler. Never interested in anything else. She went to the Royal College – did well – started on piano and switched to oboe. Played with the London Philharmonic. Then she married – Paul Zwenk.'

'The flautist! My word!'

'Yes, he goes all over the world – concerts – so she's reverted to piano and sometimes accompanies him if there's no orchestra.'

'No wonder Janet is musical.'

'Not bad but no-where near Steffie. The problem is the farm. I'm an only and so is John. We badly needed a son but had no luck. So when Steffie went into music so deeply John hoped that Janet might marry a farmer who could take over. She's always been more interested in the farm than her sister.'

Glory Halleluiah was listening carefully.

'You know about Young Farmers' Clubs? We invite the local group to the farm every year – a farm walk-about. John didn't mean it but he must have said something about having no son and it leaked into the district that the farm was up for the taking for any lad who'd marry Janet.'

'Oh dear, poor Janet.'

'Of course John didn't mean it to come out like that! Janet was absolutely furious. She finished her training and came to Kenya.'

'Not surprising.'

'She's always been John's favourite. Things between them are fine again now, they write good letters to each other – he's been very careful to make it up. But he won't apologise.'

'No, I don't think men can!'

'And he keeps saying he never meant it – but he must have said something unwise – and, of course, it makes sense!'

'Anyway, Janet seems happy here.'

'She loves it, that's clear, so it is all right. But the future of the farm does worry John. You'll understand.'

'Clearly.'

In the normal course of events Glory Halleluiah would not have gone further, but with Mr. and Mrs. Evans's concern about their farm she felt herself justified. Later, that evening, at coffee, she asked, 'Does Janet ever mention Lew in letters home?'

Mrs. Evans picked this up very quickly. 'What do you mean, is there something there?'

'Very probably.'

'She's told us she spends a lot of time at The Loop and is obviously happy there. She mentions riding with Libby and she's been camping with Libby and others. We thought the friendship was with Libby.'

'I can only tell you that whenever she goes to The Loop she goes round the ranch with Lew – every time. She is friendly with Libby, of course, but she spends most of her time with Lew. She does ride with Libby but that's about all, I think.'

'Ah ha. Interesting. No, she's never mentioned more than the manager's name is Lew – Lewis, a good Welsh name, I add.'

'Lew calls at the hospital when he's in town, takes her to lunch at the Club sometimes. In fact they're together a lot but never show anything more than friendship. But we all think that's because Lew simply hasn't got a penny and he's the honourable sort who'd never say anything to a girl unless he had something behind him. And, sadly, even if his parents clear their enormous debt, it'll be years before he catches up with other young men – financially, I mean.'

Both Mr. and Mrs. Evans were fascinated by this.

'Hm. That's given us something to think about, hasn't it, Olwyn?'

Glory Halleluiah was a bit concerned that she'd gone too far. 'Please be discreet, won't you? They haven't ever shown anything that suggests a lot more – so we are all guessing.'

'After the fiasco of the Young farmers I'll zip John's lips tightly, I promise!' at which even John laughed. 'We'll be careful. Janet's a special lass to us. But it's a bit of a fix, isn't it? Gives us something to think about. A lot to think about, in fact. Although you say you're guessing, you wouldn't have told us unless it was a pretty good guess?'

Glory Halleluiah had to admit that she really thought that Lew and Janet were very fond of each other. 'Frankly, I think it is serious.'

'I can see that he'd be Janet's type – that's pretty clear. She'll not say a word to us. Olwyn – we've got to think a bit – how we might help – IF they come into the open – IF.'

They certainly learnt nothing at all from Janet during their weeks at the coast. Janet and her mother had a happy time swimming and goggling and Mr. Evans went deep-sea fishing. He was not as successful as Lew nor was he quite so happy in small boats but he caught a small shark and some other fish. Mr. Evans felt he'd far rather have spent all the time at The Loop with Dar and Lew, especially with Lew now he had such an interest in him. He and Olwyn hardly mentioned their time at The Loop except how much they'd enjoyed it and how the lion shoot would go down well back home. Janet was relieved, being in no position to say anything to her parents about Lew but she realised that he was not only liked but also admired. That was enough for her. Mr. Evans was very sorry that he hadn't known the situation whilst they were at The Loop but Olwyn said 'No, you'd have put your great Hereford bull hoof in it and wrecked the whole thing – you - tact? Forget it. What you can do is put some cash aside for Janet – that might be useful!' He decided he would.

The Kenya holiday had been not just an enormous success, but a deeply interesting enlightenment for them both. On reaching the Shropshire farm they made some decisions, opening a special Savings Account into which they quietly put money aside for Janet.

'Even if Janet doesn't marry Lew, this will still help her.'

CHAPTER 17

It was Janet who mentioned it to Lew, quite casually, one day. 'You know Miss Cattermole, the new Matron? She's making an awful fool of herself over Frannie. Every time he comes to the Hospital she's all over him, rushes around with coffee and cakes, positively paws him.'

Lew was astonished.

'Does Frannie notice?'

'He must,' said Janet. 'But he can't do much about it – after all he's virtually running the Hospital so he has to see a lot of her. Pretty difficult. She's fairly ancient – in her fifties – should know better.'

It had never struck Lew that any woman would look at Frannie. The whole of the Backlands knew that he could never marry. The eternal bachelor, Frannie. Everyone knew.

'She's probably thinking it's her last chance,' said Janet who didn't care for the Matron very much although acknowledging that she was a very good nurse. 'She's much older than Frannie. It's very awkward. The staff are all finding it amusing but I bet Frannie isn't!'

This gave Lew some thought. Poor Frannie, giving so much of his time to the hospital to have this problem! But Frannie was so level headed, so mature, surely he could cope with that embarrassment?

In fact Frannie was finding it extremely difficult. He had to talk over many matters with the Matron – and she was a good matron – but he'd soon realised that she was setting her cap at him, and far too obviously. He didn't like it but had to be polite. Rigidly he stuck to

213

business, clamming up when she tried to make matters personal. It was a damned awkward tightrope he was walking, he felt. Worse was that the Matron's behaviour was so blatant in front of the European Sisters and the African staff. He trusted the good sense of the European part-timer and of Janet but feared the rest were probably having a good giggle behind his back. It was inevitable, he knew, and bloody uncomfortable for him. This distraction was not helping the good running of the hospital. He needed to be utterly professional, no side issues at all.

For a while Lew and Janet said nothing but, as will always happen in a small community, it became gossip at the Club and so leaked to the Backlands. Janet quickly told Libby, thinking that she'd better know before the tennis set started laughing about it. Eventually everyone heard about it, except for Dar who never heard gossip. Chemchem was finding it quietly entertaining. Everyone liked Frannie but a joke is a joke and if he was the butt of it – then tough luck! Visitors to the hospital increased slightly; visiting the sick became a bit of a game to catch the Matron running after Frannie.

Frannie battled on with a commitment that had turned somewhat sour. If only she'd been a bad matron he could have sacked her but, as he knew, any matron was difficult to find, let alone a good one. He rued the day he'd taken on the hospital work.

Apart from the Matron Frannie had other hospital worries that year. The annual Hospital Ball had to be put forward – because of the Nairobi band's engagements – a bit too close to the last one. This meant quick preparation and advertising and the possibility that people might not want to contribute to another Ball so quickly. It was a headache. The Ball was necessary; a great fund-raiser that the hospital relied upon each year; the place was not self-supporting. For several years one of the Hospital Board members had run the Ball but this year he could not offer his help. No-one else came forward; Frannie was left to deal with it. He found himself groping through a very complicated maze, he felt, having no idea of all the detail that such an event entails.

Altogether Frannie was feeling the load an uneasy one. Then help came from Piet Coetzee, who had heard the gossip about the Matron and also knew that Frannie had a deep problem handling the Ball. Piet offered to look after the big auction that was a major part of the Ball every year. Someone had to find interesting items – anything from a couple of nights for two at the Blue Marlin, Malindi, to a croquet set – that would raise big bids. Auction items had to be wheedled out of friends, businesses, anyone – and Piet very kindly took over that job. Frannie was very grateful. That was one load lifted.

Frannie's next problem – that even he had overlooked – was that the Matron fully expected Frannie to be her partner at the Ball. She never said so, but it was obvious. Frannie felt he couldn't face that – duty or not. He thought of telling her that he couldn't dance – and this was partially true as his foot held him back; he could shuffle along in slow music – but he realised that she wouldn't mind that. There were some difficult days for Frannie.

'Libby – the Matron! Now she's expecting Frannie to be her partner at the Ball. So embarrassing. He's always polite to her but we can all see. She's making such a spectacle of herself!'

'Running the Ball Frannie's hardly got time to be anyone's partner – you know – there's so many things to look after. When Richard Medcombe did it we hardly saw him during the event!'

'She'd not worry about that. She just wants him caught on her hook. She really is impossible. But, I admit she was marvellous with

215

Mrs. Stringfield – she diagnosed the problem when the Doctor was stumped and she did a lot of the nursing. It's just that she's a real idiot over Frannie!'

After some thought Libby took action.

'Dar, darling. The Hospital Ball. Would you be an absolute saint and ask the Matron to be your partner? She hasn't got anyone at Chemchem – she's too new – and she must go. After all you're part of the Hospital after all the years you were on the Board!'

'What about you, chick?' For the last few years Dar had taken his daughter.

'No problem. I'll go with Frannie. Of course he'll be busy but I'll be fine, don't worry.'

The stratagem worked. Without any qualms, Dar most courteously asked the Matron to be his partner when he next visited Chemchem. She was surprised, taken aback, but, despite her annoyance at the turn of events, she had to accept. Part of her was pleased; his name had been connected with the Hospital, she knew. Beyond that she'd heard nothing about him, but he was a very upright man, distinguished looking, she thought.

For years Frannie had taken his mother to the Ball, not that either of them danced much, but to support the affair. Since Frannie became Chairman of the Hospital Board, Mump's interest in the hospital waned. It was part of her automatic switch-off from anything that involved Frannie. All Backlands could foresee what would happen. The very fact that he had to run the Ball was enough for her to decide not to attend.

Libby called Frannie to meet her at the picnic-site one afternoon.

'Frannie – help needed!'

'Sis, what can I do?'

'Take me to the Hospital Ball, please!'

'What about Dar? Isn't he going?'

'Libby's face was alive with something, he could see.'

'Wait for it, Frannie – he's taking the Matron – that Miss Cattermole!'

'*What?*'

'How's that, Frannie?'

'Did you arrange that, Sis?' Frannie had never mentioned his problem but assumed everyone would know.

'Since you ask – yes. In fact I'm trying to save you from being lured by the hospital siren onto the rocks! Dar won't even notice what she's like, bless him. Is that O.K.?'

Frannie had to smile.

'Sis, yes, of course. That woman is a pain in the arse but a good matron.'

'Yes, we know. Can I come with you then?'

'Of course, but I'll be busy most of the evening – checking up on things – you know.'

'No problem. I'll get lots of dancing anyway.' As a good dancer Libby was never short of partners. 'And I thought that if the Cattermole saw you with me she might be put off a bit. She doesn't know what goes on in the Backlands, does she?'

Frannie got the message quickly.

'It's a thought. O.K. fine, Sis.'

'So I'll be an adoring female, yes? And I thought that if I told

Lew and Janet what we're doing – you know spread it around Chemchem a bit – some people would play up; make the right remarks about us being together - it might get you off the hook completely.'

Frannie was a bit startled by how far Libby was going but admitted the sense in it.

'Everyone would enjoy the tease, even if not Twybitt inspired, wouldn't they?'

It was a bit too public, Frannie thought immediately, but if Chemchem knew the ruse, he'd play along with the idea. He saw Libby's concern for him; this time she was trying to solve problems; usually that was his prerogative.

'Sis, you're a star. Alright. We'll do the loving act, when we can but I will be busy.'

News of this ploy swept round Chemchem with great speed and added another dimension to the Ball. Some people, who had thought it too close to the last event, dashed to buy tickets. The Ball was assured of success.

On the evening of the Ball Frannie had to go early to the Club to supervise things so Dar took Libby, left her at the Club and went off to collect Miss Cattermole. The Cottage Hospital was not very far from the Club and the Matron's cottage was in the grounds. The Matron had dressed well with a good evening skirt and a pretty top, that much Dar acknowledged and he gallantly told her how well she looked. When they arrived at the Club Chemchem was agog. Libby's planning had gone further. She'd persuaded Dar to take Miss Cattermole to join other, older members of the Hospital Board at one big table. She annexed a smaller table for Frannie and herself, Piet and Rena and a pleasant couple from the tennis set. Frannie couldn't help being amused. Miss Cattermole was slightly put out to be put with the elderly. Then she saw that Frannie was obviously booked at a table containing a stunningly beautiful girl whom, it appeared, he was escorting.

She turned to Dar Winchester. 'Who's that girl with Mr. Houghton-Framlyn?' To which the reply, 'That's my daughter, Libby,' was no comfort.

'They're very close?'

'Oh yes,' was all Dar replied, quite innocent of the imputation.

Miss Cattermole was much put out by this. Dar Winchester's daughter was not only lovely but wearing a sensational gown, quite daring really, and it was soon obvious that she was an excellent dancer, popular with everyone. It was also obvious that Frannie, in his dinner jacket, was younger than she'd thought. She was feeling rather let down, miffed, but couldn't show it.

Janet was on duty at the hospital, Lew was not going to the ball - he was spending the evening with his parents – but, suddenly, Corn and West decided to go. They couldn't resist any fun. Glory Halleluiah always went and never minded being solo. She wore the same dress every year, a dreadful, old-fashioned creation in velvet, entirely inappropriate, and contributed hugely to the financial success of the Ball. She was at Dar's table, quite unconcerned about anything, or, apparently so. Corn and West, turned out immaculately, chose to sit at the end of the bar where they could see into the actual ballroom. They could, but didn't, dance.

Libby wore the cream ball gown that Rosa had so lovingly made. It was so cut that from the hip the skirt flared out like curling waves when she danced. It was spectacular. Cut very low at the back she couldn't wear a bra and her lightly tanned skin glowed against the dress. Her shining hair was lovely; she looked really beautiful.

The Ball went into action rapidly. Dar did his stuff properly and danced with Miss Cattermole , who was not a bad dancer, and so did all the other males at the table. Glory Haleluiah sat, amused at everything. Frannie was often being asked about things and was on the move a lot. He realised that he should be a better prepared for next year's Ball, but hoped that someone else might take it on. He was near the Bar when he heard slow music so he went to claim Libby. Frannie really walked around but Libby was used to this. They tried the loving act by gazing at each other with soulful expressions and she once stroked his cheek. Chemchem loved it.

The whole place came alive when the Lecher approached Miss Cattermole for a dance. This was something! Obviously the Matron knew nothing of his reputation; other ladies avoided him. When they took the floor Frannie was with the Club Secretary talking over a detail but when he returned he felt the atmosphere.

'Frannie – look at that!'

The Lecher and Miss Cattermole were together for three dances in a row, after which he took her back to her table and went to the Bar where, Miss Cattermole presumed, he must have left his wife. Good, thought the district, collectively, having seen the prolonged dancing.

The evening was now interrupted for the Auction. Piet had got a very entertaining younger man to be the auctioneer and he made a very good job of it. The smallest item almost made the most money. It was a Victorian thimble. Glory Halleluiah bid for it and it was soon obvious that Corn and West had connived with her; they kept raising the bids until a huge figure was reached and then they left Glory Halleluiah with her lot. No-one was surprised.

Dancing began again and Miss Cattermole's thoughts were reviving because Dar had told her, most politely, more of his connection with the Cottage Hospital. He'd been the original instigator, he was the founding father of it all and had been on the Board for a very long time. She then discovered that Frannie lived next door to the Winchesters. So was Dar Winchester's daughter with Frannie because of the Hospital connection? Were they close in the neighbourly sense? Her hopes rose. Her evening became even more interesting when she asked Dar about Mr. Baccup and his wife. 'No wife. He farms not far from town. Breand's Bridge way. Maize, sunflower and grass-seed. No livestock. A bachelor.' Dar nearly added that he was known as the Lecher but thought better of it. A bachelor? And he'd danced with her three times! But Frannie was still more interesting to her. She'd have loved to ask Frannie's age; one question she couldn't ask.

At midnight the Club served breakfast – actually a full meal – and many people moved to the dining room long before this, especially the older members of the community. Dar asked Miss Cattermole if she'd like to come but the Lecher arrived at that moment to claim her for a dance so she excused herself and told Dar to go ahead. He took Glory Halleluiah to the Dining room where they joined other friends.

Frannie came back to his table for a rest quickly to be disturbed by one of the staff – a problem in the kitchen. When he came back Rena asked him what had happened.

'One of the waiters went berserk – attacking everyone in the kitchen with a carving knife.'

'Drunk?'

'No – just gone off his rocker.'

'What did you do?'

'Knocked him out. The others'll look after him when he comes round. I'll see the Club Secretary in the morning. He'll be sacked. Damn nuisance, though. The kitchen was frantic with everyone coming for food before they were ready!'

'Knocked him out!'

'I had to – no other quick method.'

The ballroom was thinning out with so many people either in the bar or the Dining room. Less people were dancing. Slow music started; Frannie saw the opportunity.

'Come on, Sis, now's our time!'

Those in the ballroom were looking at Frannie and Libby; this was a good moment. There were few on the dance floor but Miss Cattermole and the Lecher continued. Frannie and Libby repeated their loving looks for a while. Libby smiled, and slipped her arms up round his neck while he held her waist with both hands, showing no reaction to the splendid view she'd given him of her marvellous breasts. After a minute like this he held her tighter and they were cheek to cheek, Frannie carefully watching the Cattermole and the Lecher.

'Libs, a kiss.'

To the delight of all in the ballroom he and Libs stopped dancing, just swayed to the music while they kissed, a very gentle kiss that seemed to go on for a very long time, broken only when the music stopped. It was all that Chemchem could do not to applaud.

Frannie walked Libby back to the table. Rena was laughing.

'The minute you kissed, that Matron grabbed the Lecher and almost dragged him away. They've gone – went out the reception way.

He's got a willing victim this time! Piet's gone to see where they are.'

Piet came back, also laughing. 'Straight into the Lecher's car and away. Frannie, man, you're safe!'

Officially the Ball ended at 1.0 a.m., farming communities usually going to bed early, but if enough people wanted to carry on the party would extend for one hour, Frannie having to pay the band for the time from his own pocket, he knew. At half past twelve Dar said he was leaving, Miss Cattermole having disappeared completely, to his surprise. Frannie said he'd bring Libby back later and the dancing continued, Libby being claimed by many partners. Frannie was busy again; he was finding the whole enterprise more delicate than he'd expected. There were upset people to calm down, barmen to harry and a quick quest for a cleaner when a whole table was upset in the dining room. He was hardly still for a second. Glory Halleluiah punctiliously caught him to say good-night and thank him for the evening. She was not going home but had booked a room at the Club. She thought he looked unusually taut; normally he could take a lot of problems with ease. But, she reminded herself, it was his first time in control of the Ball.

One o'clock. Last waltz. Good-night (although it should be morning) and the event closed. Hangers on hung on. The Bar was still busy and Frannie and Libby joined the group there. Corn and West were continuing to behave perfectly. Frannie was deeply suspicious.

It was very late when Frannie finally collected Libby to drive her home. Both were tired but also stimulated by the Ball and its success; a queer mixture of feelings.

'Bro – it's all right. The Lecher's taken over. You can relax!'

'Thank God – and thank you, Libs, too. What a night!' and Frannie went quiet. They continued silently until they reached the viewpoint when he stopped the vehicle.

'I must have a pee. Won't be a moment.'

'Me, too.' They parted and came back to stand looking down at the view together. The moon, though not full, was enough to make the view ethereal, the river showing in parts like a broken silver necklace.

They stood, soaking in the beauty. Suddenly Frannie pulled her to him, pulled down her left dress strap, exposing her breast, kissed her savagely whilst fondling her nipple that immediately lengthened and became hard. He'd got her mouth open and she could feel his body – hard, hard. It was richly erotic, wildly emotional and Libby was filled with the jagged lightning of sexual power and need. It seemed to go on for a long time.

Suddenly, just as quickly as he'd grabbed her, he threw her away and said in a strange voice, very harshly indeed 'Go back to the car.'

It was an order. Bewildered, Libs put her dress straight and faltered back to the car. She sat, getting her breath back. Frannie was away several minutes, it seemed. When he got into the driving seat he said 'Sorry, Libs. Sorry. Sorry. I've had far too much to drink. Animal lust took over. Sorry. Did I hurt you?'

'No, no.' She looked at him but he was busy with the car key. 'It's perfectly all right.'

But it wasn't.

They continued the journey in silence. When they reached The Loop Frannie jumped out of the vehicle to open her door and said, 'I've got to get back to the Club quickly. Good night and thanks.'

'You're going *back*?'

'A mass of things to do – sort the money, everything.'

'Frannie! I could have come home with Dar!'

'It's O.K. I promised to bring you. I must go. 'Night.' He drove away quickly.

Libby had no need for a torch in a house she knew so well. Perfunctorily she washed her face, slipped off her clothes and flung them over a chair, threw herself totally naked onto her bed – and wept.

CHAPTER 18

Both Dar and Libby were late getting up on Sunday morning. Lew was dealing with the ranch whilst they had a very light breakfast.

'Frannie did well, didn't he? The Ball will have made a lot of money. Funny woman that Matron. She just disappeared – might have said something. Not very polite. Enjoy yourself, chick?'

'Thanks, yes,' was all that Libby could reply.

They parted, Libby to deal with the kitchen and Dar went to the office. Wasn't he getting a bit old for affairs like last night? Glory Haleluiah still managed it, not that she danced; a Ball without her would be a strange, empty event, he thought. Suddenly he remembered evenings with Edith and had to get his head into accounts rapidly.

Quite late in the morning a telephone call came from Don Craill, one of the Cooper's representatives who regularly came to the Backlands ranches, gathering orders for cattle dip chemicals, cattle dawas and introducing new medicines. It had always been a joke in the Backlands that Frank and Madge had the same surname as the big agricultural chemical firm for whom Don was a traveller. He'd had problems, had to re-organise his schedule, could he come to The Loop to-day? Sorry it was a Sunday.

Cooper's reps always brought news around the farms and the ranches, always welcome, always efficient, good men. Don had an extra virtue – he was never a nasty gossip. Dar promptly asked him to come for lunch. Where was he? Oh, at the Club? Come straight down.

'Dar, Libby – good of you to have me. I had the clutch go – luckily near Nakuru – but it set me back. Otherwise I'd have got to the Hospital Ball. Just too late. Stayed at the Curtis place last night.'

Don was welcomed cheerfully; it was assumed that he'd stay the night and do the rounds of the Backlands ranches to-morrow.

'The Club was buzzing with the Ball. Huge success, I gather. You should see the bar – Frannie's still there in his dinner jacket – never got to bed and he's pissed as a newt. High as a kite. Absolutely stotious. Never seen him like that before. Mind you, he's a good drunk – not nasty - but telling stories that'd make your hair curl! Risque. I've never heard the half of them. I said I'd bring him down to Venture but Piet Coetzee arrived and thought he'd better take him to his home so that Rena and he could sober up Frannie before he reached that mother of his!'

Dar was shocked. Frannie!

Libby was distressed. Frannie!

Dar suggested that Don and he might do their business together quickly in the office before lunch and they left Libby with a roundabout of thoughts.

The next Sunday was a Friends' dinner party, this time at Glory Halleluiah's house where the food had taken a major turn for the better, Rosa being behind the scenes. The Ball was discussed again. Neither Dar nor Libby had seen Frannie since the Ball, nor had they alluded to Frannie's drunken bout; it had been hurtful to both of them. But Frannie was at the dinner looking just as usual, he was giving nothing away.

'You did a good job, Frannie, what did the Ball make?'

He told them. It was a record sum, in fact.

'Jolly good,' said Frank. 'I hear the Twybitts were there. What did they do?'

'Amazingly, nothing – behaved beautifully.'

'Not quite,' said Lew.

Everyone turned to Lew. He hadn't even been to the Ball. Lew was smiling, he'd been waiting for a suitable moment.

'Actually Sexy Sarah saw them come to the Cottage Hospital – just after you drove out with the Matron, Dar. They dashed into the Matron's Office and slap in the middle of her desk they put a packet of condoms!'

'Whew! They are so wicked, those two! I thought they'd do *something*.' Everybody was laughing, except for Mumps who had pinched lips. She was looking at Lew – usually such a *nice* boy who'd never mention condoms.

'They are a pair – goodness only know what they were like as youngsters – holy terrors, I should think,' Frank was smiling.

'Pity they never married.' Everyone turned to Glory Halleluiah.

'Yes, I mean it. Of course they're dreadful teases but, underneath, they're really caring, you know.' Since a lot of the teases were played on Glory Halleluiah this was very kind of her, the friends felt.

'Perhaps they can't afford to marry?'

'Perhaps – but really I think they are such a good pair together that anyone tipping the balance would ruin everything for them. Sad.'

Frannie had to go to the Cottage Hospital soon after the Ball – to deal with a staff problem. Miss Cattermole had been polite, efficient and not over-friendly. Frannie was deeply relieved and continued the conversation in a brisk business-like way. The Ball was only mentioned once, Frannie simply telling her the final figures of the cash it would provide for the Hospital.

Chemchem, having enjoyed the Frannie and the Matron episode, was settling expectantly, now waiting for different news – this time of the Matron and the Lecher. Frannie was in the clear.

It was not very long after the Hospital Ball that Frannie had a phone call from Libby, whom he'd hardly seen since the Ball.

'Frannie! Help needed!'

'What can I do?'

'Meet me at the Picnic site this afternoon – 2.30. O.K.?'

'Yes, of course,' Frannie had no idea what was coming to him.

'Now what's the matter?' he asked as he arrived. Libby was already sitting on the log.

'Frannie - I'm not sure how to say this. I'm – I'm not sure of myself.' Libby found it hard.

'What do you mean, Sis?'

'Frannie – listen – I'm nearly twenty-nine – and still a virgin. Isn't that a bit – well – strange? I mean most girls of my age aren't like me, are they?'

This was something Frannie had not expected. He was stumbling, unable to answer.

'Libs, I don't know – I mean – how would I know?' Libby cut in quickly.

'You see I never felt I wanted to with Bobby – and we were getting married anyway so the thought was put off, I suppose - and since then – well, some men have wanted me to but I've never felt like it. I've never really felt anything. Am I *normal*? That's what's worrying me.'

Frannie was definitely floundering. This was nothing he could cope with, he felt.

'I'm sure you're fine. You're bound to be!'

'Not necessarily!'

'Look, Libs, I think you have to talk to women about this – or a doctor – not me!'

'Ah, but I want to talk to you about it. You can help. Frannie – I want you to make love to me so that I *can* find out.'

'*What?! Libs!*'

'Yes, I mean it. I've got to find out if I'm O.K. and I *think* I could – with *you*.' Frannie instantly thought of their session on the viewpoint after the Ball. My God, what have I done?

'Libs, I don't think that.... well, I feel you should...' he was stumped.

There was a moment's quiet when he stopped looking at her but surveyed the ground.

'Frannie – if you feel you can't, don't want to - whatever. It's all right really. I can go to the Lecher.'

'*Absolutely not!*' Frannie was horrified.

Frannie was now sweating slightly, beads appearing on his upper lip and temples, his hands feeling clammy.

'Look, Libs .....' and she stood up in front of him, eminently desirable, wonderful figure. How many times, hundreds, even thousands probably, had he dreamt of taking Libby to bed? Here she was – on offer.

'Please, Frannie!'

This was too much. He knew he'd have an erection any minute.

'Libs, when, where?'

'Now – it's a safe time. I've brought a blanket. In the shade of the Fig Tree?' She put her hand out, he took it, got up and was led away.

Libby stripped quite unselfconsciously, Frannie wishing she'd let him undress her. Her glorious figure was displayed. Quickly Frannie dropped his clothes and gently took her in his arms, not kissing her but holding her and feeling for her breast again – her nipples stiffened and lengthened immediately with desire.

'Come on – down.'

He took her as slowly as he could, but faster than he intended, Libby responding with tremendous strength, her finger nails biting into his back. It was glorious; they came to their climax together and Libby called out 'Oh' and then laughed. He stayed in her for a short while and then slid off lying on his back beside her. She moved over putting her head on his chest. He slipped his arm round her and they lay, quiet. He could smell the shampoo on her freshly washed hair and he turned and kissed her hair, smiling at himself. They lay, both deeply happy.

After a while Frannie broke the silence.

'I'm afraid a few ants want to join the act. I'll have to move.'

Libby laughed again, 'They're coming my way, too.'

They stood up and he held her again, kissing her hair.

'Libs, you're fine, very fine!' She was smiling at him.

'You're not bad, either.' They both laughed, hugging each other.

Regretfully he said, 'Libs, I'm afraid I've got a ranch to run. Can't stay. And this – strictly between us two?'

'Of course. Absolutely private.' They dressed quickly.

'I must go.' Libby got into her Land Rover quickly and started the engine. Frannie was at the driver's door.

'So, Libs, what would you like? A certificate to say you're a real sex kitten?'

Libby laughed. 'No – but I know what I need now. I need a lover. Tomorrow – same place, same time, Frannie.'

There was a surge of dust and gravel enveloping the departing vehicle as she drove off quickly, leaving Frannie fixed to the ground in amazement. What on earth had he done?

My God, he thought, as he got into his own vehicle.

That evening Frannie was so thoughtful that even Mumps noticed it. 'I've asked you to pass the gravy twice, what's wrong with you?'

'Sorry. Usual things, the ranch and all that.'

'I wish you'd share more with me, you never do.'

Frannie thought, wryly, that today's effort was one thing he certainly wasn't going to share with her. As for the ranch – on the many occasions he had told her some of the problems she had said, firmly, that it was his job to run the ranch and not to bother her. Typical.

That night he relived every moment with Libs, she was *so* special to him. He knew well the depth of his love for her but, to his very real regret, he knew they must not carry on. He could not possibly meet her to-morrow. It would be easy. He'd not argue. He'd simply not turn up.

The Dacre family had been in a stalemate over Bobby's marriage for some time. It had been natural that Estelle (the 'child bride') should want to have the baby in South Africa after her very uncomfortable pregnancy, equally natural that she should have stayed to get over the difficult birth and the tragic death of the baby. Bobby came back to

Kenya quickly after the birth of the child to get on with farming. Estelle said she would join him as soon as possible. A long period went by and when she finally came back to stay barely a month it was more than clear that the marriage was not going to prosper.

Stella Dacre was keen for Bobby to hang on in the hope that time would settle everything (because of all the lovely money at stake). Bobby accepted this initially and went to South Africa several times to try to persuade Estelle to come back. At first it seemed possible but after the third visit he could see that it was hopeless. Bobby spoke to his parents about divorce. Stella was against it, Alec for it; obviously the ground would be desertion by Estelle. All of Chemchem saw their plight and assumed that divorce would be the answer but the Dacres kept very quiet.

In Johannesburg, to Estelle's own surprise, let alone that of her mother and grandmother, to whom she was especially attached, a very eligible older man started showing an interest in her, insipid though she was. He was wealthy and, in truth, was lured by Estelle's future riches but he was much calmer, kinder and more gentle than Bobby; an experienced businessman, he knew how to play the game.

Estelle had been submerged by Bobby at eighteen; now she was older she wanted something very different and the older man was a prop she could lean upon. Her grandmother, in particular, was horrified at the idea of a divorce in which Estelle would be named the guilty party. In fact the Dacres had not yet broached the subject with them, but it was thought that they might do so. Estelle's family took legal advice. Would Bobby agree to a divorce in which Estelle was not a guilty party? The family were only too well aware that Bobby stood to gain a great deal, financially, from holding out against a divorce. Legal discussions were intense.

The lawyers finally recommended that Bobby be bought off – with a huge settlement – to make him agree to a divorce on the grounds of incompatibility – a nebulous, splendidly vague reason but one that would not put blame on anyone. Cautious letters were sent to Kenya. Alec and Bobby were prepared to accept the idea; Stella prevaricated at first, then agreed. Bobby was relieved that the impetus had come from South Africa; Stella saw that the Dacre family were in a strong bargaining position. A lot of arguing went on about the finances. The ground for divorce was dubious; the lawyers determined to make a huge profit; it was going to take a long time.

Throughout these proceedings Bobby, and, he would have been surprised to know, his parents also, had Libby in mind. All carefully avoided mentioning her.

When Libby arrived at the Picnic Site next day Frannie was already there, waiting. She leapt out of her vehicle into his arms totally unaware of the battle he'd had with himself, a battle that had been decided at four in the morning. In the end he'd persuaded himself that Libby needed him but he knew damned well that he needed her, too. Frannie hugged her, said nothing, but this time he led her off to the big fig tree. He was taking charge and started to undress her. Libby laughed and returned the compliment.

'Down, girl! – Sounds like I'm talking to a dog!' This time he prepared her and Libby did everything she could to please him. The sex was stupendous. After a rest they chatted. It was light, inconsequential talk, meaning very little but happy and relaxing. They had more time and Frannie, in particular, wanted the time and the chat as well as the sex. Everything seemed right.

'To-morrow's fine. After that we'll have to stop for a bit. I'll tell you when we can again.'

'You are being careful, Libs? We can't have a mistake!'

'Of course. I promise. Lucky I'm regular.'

'And Libs, this is not the best place. Anyone can come here.'

'What do you suggest?'

'On my place. I know exactly where everyone is – more than you do here.'

'All right. Where tomorrow?'

Frannie had it worked out.

'Meet me at the bridge. We'll drop your vehicle out of sight there and I'll take you on. O.K.?'

The next day, a Wednesday, Frannie took her to a small copse on the far west of his ranch, an undeveloped spot. The sex was just as successful but Frannie spoke seriously at the end.

'Libs, this is great for both of us. I'm well aware that in the normal course you'd have been safely married by now – so that must still happen. Libs – you must find a chap to marry. You know that, don't you?'

'Yes, I do, Frannie.'

'Libs, I'll keep you happy for as long as you want but it can't be forever. And we'll be found out eventually if we're not careful. Disaster that'd be!'

'Oh, Frannie, I know all that. Yes. But we're as safe as possible here, aren't we?'

'Yes. No-one wanders round here unexpectedly as Lew and Dar might do on your place. I always know where the watu are. Yes, as safe as possible. But Libs, you know this is only a temporary solution for you?'

'Yes. I know. You're marvellous Frannie, thanks for everything. Now – tomorrow I'm off to town and tennis and you'll be with Dar for the evening. Can you cope?'

'I'd better! Don't worry, Libs, I'll be fine. Dar, for all that he's a great chap, wouldn't notice if the Queen rode past him stark naked on a zebra!' Libby laughed.

Because life always throws a joker on the table when one needs it least Dar chatted with Frannie almost exclusively about Libby.

'She's getting on. If only she'd move to Nairobi – somewhere – even overseas – she'd meet men. Here, who does she see? The D.C.! No good at all and a terrible upset for her. Of course I want her to marry a farmer but *anyone* would be better than no-one. What can I do about it?' he asked Frannie who could come up with no useful reply. This sort of conversation did not help his conscience as he dug deeper into Dar's excellent whisky.

The only event that enlivened Christmas that year was the decision by Glory Halleluiah to have a quiet Christmas on her own.

'You can't do that!' said everyone.

'Oh yes I can,' she countered, 'and it will solve the eternal problem of getting a turkey!'

Towards Christmas Glory Halleluiah started to regret her decision. Always she had either entertained or been entertained by some of the Backlanders. Why she suddenly wanted to be a hermit she could not explain. She told the cook she'd be alone on Christmas day and would simply have roast chicken.

On Christmas morning she opened the few presents she had received – from her brother, Dar and Libby and Frank and Madge. After breakfast the cook called her.

'Memsahib, the chicken won't go into the oven!'

Oh dear, she thought, he's probably got a hang-over. She gave the staff a Christmas party on Christmas Eve. They had a whole steer to cut up and share, packets of tea, sugar and a bonus. It often rebounded on Christmas day with sore heads.

She stumped off to the kitchen.

There, almost overflowing the kitchen table was the biggest possible fowl anyone could imagine, beautifully plucked, drawn and prepared, with the legs tucked correctly. An *ostrich*! The cook and the other house staff were peeking through the door to see the Memsahib's reaction. She walked all round it, laughing.

'Do you eat Mbuni?' she asked the cook.

'Yes, Memsahib.'

'Take this, cut it up and share it with the other staff. Now where is my chicken?'

'Gone, Memsahib!'

'Gone?'

'Yes, Memsahib. Here's the letter.'

Glory Halleluiah opened the envelope. The message was short.

A fair swap? We've taken your chicken. You can eat it with us tonight. See you about six thirty. Corn and West.

When she joined them it was a full-blown Christmas dinner with turkey (her chicken was never mentioned), all the trimmings, Christmas pudding, brandy butter, crackers with dreadful mottoes and silly hats (that they wore) and a never ending supply of alcohol. Glory Halleluiah enjoyed herself enormously and later had to be escorted home by West. It was very late. The next day, after she'd had enough aspirin, she thought it had been an especially lovely Christmas.

'I had dinner with a man called Roddy Southwell after tennis at the Club.' Libby told Frannie when they next met. 'He's in town for a while. Civil engineer. New bridges – three – at the Kilpel area.'

'Was he nice?' asked Frannie, sounding quite cool.

'Yes, he was actually. Anyway he's asked me to have dinner again next week. So I will. I am trying, Frannie, honestly!'

He wished she wasn't.

'I hear you're a teacher now.'

Libby laughed. 'Tennis, you mean? We all thought it would help if lessons were offered; not everyone learns tennis at school. I do one Thursday every month – start people off on the tennis wall and then play different strokes to them on the old court – that sort of thing.'

'News at the Men's Bar is that you're the star teacher.'

'Nonsense. But I quite like it. Meet different people and some carry on and join the proper tennis set.'

Frannie knew. A very talkative young man who had come to Chemchem to run the maize store of the K.F.A. had asked about Libby at the Bar. He'd said how good she was at teaching but, he said, 'She's an elusive girl.'

Other men at the Bar told him to ask Frannie – next-door neighbour.

'I don't know about elusive; careful, I'd say,' and that was all he'd offer, but it gave him something else to consider about Libby.

Frannie and Libby continued to meet, sometimes a few days in a row, sometimes after a gap of a week or so. It was not easy for them to fit in the right times. They were paired to the great contentment of each, both aware of the situation and the limitation. Over the weeks they became more confident in each other. No-one seemed to suspect what was going on; Libby's afternoons were always her own, neither Dar nor Lew ever questioned her; Frannie was his own master. Libby mentioned to Frannie a few friendships with men she'd met at the Club but every time it fizzled into nothing. Half of him was relieved, half worried. Why didn't she take to these men?

CHAPTER 19

One lunch-time at the men's Bar of the Club, Frannie heard the news. It had leaked out. Bobby was definitely going for a divorce. There were complications, he heard, regarding the finance but proceedings were going ahead. Along with many other people in Chemchem, Frannie had often wondered if this would happen; now it was clear. Had Libby been waiting for this? Delicately he felt he simply couldn't ask her, but it explained why she had so steadfastly turned her back on so many suitors. Bobby! He was not someone that Frannie could respect at all, someone Frannie could not like, but she had fallen for him so deeply all those years ago. Bobby! Frannie didn't want to think about him but he consoled himself with the thought that divorce – especially with complications - takes time.

The news released Frannie in a curious way; he felt he was the stop-gap Libby needed and she would be safely married in the end. There was no more suspense, Frannie now understood her reluctance with others; no doubt Libby had clung on to the hope that Bobby might eventually be divorced. Frannie felt secure keeping Libby warm for Bobby; it made his time with her oddly easier; he became more abandoned with her.

'No, Libs, no bra – just forget the bloody thing when you come to me – awful things – hide the best parts. I'm definitely a tits man!'

Libby laughed and left off her bra, not that it was at all comfortable, but she did it.

Frannie and Libby found one place that they specially liked. It

241

was a small ledge with a rocky lip only about twenty feet up on the Littet Hills. After an easy walk they could lie hidden or, when standing, could see the whole extent of Frannie's ranch. They called the place The Hammock.

After a session at The Hammock one day Libby suddenly said, 'Frannie – you know when I asked you to make love to me because I wasn't sure of myself. Well – I may not have been experienced but you certainly were. You knew exactly what you were doing. Come on – tell!'

Frannie laughed and laughed. 'I wondered whether you'd ever ask!' He rolled on his side, smiling broadly.

'It was when I was at College. Did you know? I did two years - agriculture. There was a girl - much older than us students - probably late twenties, I'd guess, who had the reputation of sleeping with the students. Her name was Rosy. She helped in the kitchens.' Frannie was enjoying the memory. 'We were lads of eighteen or nineteen - all randy - you can imagine. Rosy was said to be a nymphomaniac and would sleep with anyone. Of course one after another the chaps claimed to have slept with her. It was a bit of a joke, I thought. Mind you, I'd longed to have a go at her - but with my foot? No. I realised that.'

Libby was entranced with this story.

'In my second year... it was a Saturday afternoon - there was a big rugger match on. Naturally I couldn't play. Sometimes I watched but quite often I used the time to get some work done - at least the hostel was quiet then. Who should come knocking at m door but Rosy! I was absolutely astonished, pleased, embarrassed... everything. To cut a long story short Rosy taught me a thing or two that afternoon. And she came again. So we met twice. She was quite a girl and, yes, I think she probably was a nympho.' Frannie smiled even deeper at the memory. 'So there - Libs, my introduction to sex!'

'And since then?'

'Nothing. Oh Libs, don't think I haven't wanted it – but with my foot? You know I can't marry. So until a certain Miss Winchester came along for help I've had a pretty arid time.'

'What a story. Rosy! I suppose she did go to all the students?'

'I think so. She said to me she saw it as her duty to educate the students in life. She didn't think the College covered that!'

Libby was smiling. 'Oh great. It's a lovely story, Frannie. Actually she was doing a public service.'

'Yes... and free as well!'

With his different attitude to his time with Libby, Franny recognised in himself a new energy, new power that he gained from his time with her. He was living as a normal man; it changed him. His perception seemed greater, his inner self more confident, his physical strength enhanced and he had the intelligence to see it all and revel in it. Whatever limited time he would have with Libby he was going to get the best out of it. To Frannie life seemed easier than all the rest of his ranching years. Problems came that he found easier to solve or at least to accept. Halcyon days, he knew, and he treasured every moment. It had to have an ending. Not only was the ranch thriving financially but after years of selective breeding, he'd got two exceptionally good bulls ready for the Boran Show and Sale that in 1958 would be held at Chemchem. The timing could not have been better. Frannie drank every drop of happiness he could. Carpe diem? He did.

Frannie had to go to a K.F.A. dinner at Nakuru and took out his dinner jacket and the rest of his clothing. When he was getting ready at Nakuru he found his dress shirt tight around the neck, definitely tight. When had he last worn it? Had it shrunk in the dhobi? No. He suddenly looked at himself in the mirror and laughed. 'Bloody bull, that's what you are now!' A bit late, he thought to himself, but I've got there. The following day he bought some bigger dress shirts in Nakuru.

The next Sunday dinner party was at The Loop; everyone was there including Janet who had a few days off and whose presence always helped the conversation move away from the eternal ranching problems. It was a normal gathering until Libby gave Dar the wine to pour out.

'What's this?'

'Rose. I bought it for Frannie. He likes it.' Libby replied. Frannie, who never gave anything away, was suddenly caught, his face showing a curious emotion for a fraction of a second. Glory Halleluiah saw the fleeting expression, didn't understand it but quickly said, 'I like Rose too, Libby dear, a nice change,' and the moment passed.

Glory Halleluiah, ever ultra-sensitive, was curious about Frannie's expression but thought it nice of Libby to provide something he liked. Frannie was all too often taken for granted.

Frannie and Libby were up at The Hammock.

'Mumps. I'd better tell you, Libs. After I was born she wouldn't sleep with Dad again.'

'That's awful!'

'Yes, end of marriage. And they'd only been married a year when I arrived so Dad had a very raw deal indeed. He told me that it was understood in the village where they lived that he and Mumps would marry... they lived at opposite ends of the village – the two big houses. So marry they did. But they never really knew each other. Tragic for

Dad and, in a way, for Mumps also. Dad couldn't leave her because of me and she was determined to keep all the benefits of a so-called marriage - you know - she was provided for, had a nice house, looked after, had servants - the things she wanted - so she wouldn't leave Dad but she wouldn't look after me.'

'Frannie, I'm so sad for your father - awful.'

'I'm sure that's why he died young - that heart attack. He told me this not long before he died. And he left Venture to me - never mentioned Mumps in his Will. She has money of her own so it wasn't necessary - but it said a lot.'

'I'd no idea – but it does explain things. Is she afraid that you'd ever turn her out of the house?'

'I don't think it would ever cross her mind. She feels she has a right to be there - and, I suppose, I agree. But after Dad died and the Will was read she never spoke to me about it - just carried on. I was expected to accept that - which I did, of course. Whatever she's like, she's my mother.'

'How do you manage, Frannie?'

'I'm out on the ranch almost all the time – that's great. I love it. We meet for meals – not always. In the evenings sometimes we sit together but if she'd being especially painful I go to my room or to the farm office. She always wants more of my time but I can't do it. Perhaps I'm very cruel. It's fine really. I love the ranch so much and I'm out so much. It's become a small niggle now. Where I draw the line is when she expects me to take her places, escort her to Nairobi – to the theatre and so on. I like the cultural world but I'm damned if I'm going to take her. She doesn't like me one scrap but is prepared to make use of me if it suits her. I stop there.'

There was a silence while Libby digested this. She'd half known some of Frannie's difficulties with Mumps, but not all.

The Dacres were unaware how far the news of Bobby's pending divorce had spread. But Dar Winchester had not heard the news and one day in town Alec Dacre met Dar. They always punctiliously avoided the subject of Bobby and Libby after the fiasco but this time Alec said: 'I think I'd better tell you that Bobby is petitioning for a divorce. Thought you'd better know.' Alec Dacre walked away quickly. When Dar got back to The Loop he phoned Glory Halleluiah and invited himself to drinks.

'But, Dar, do you want her to marry a divorced man? He let her down so badly those years ago.'

'I know. But she was so much in love with him. Glory Halleluiah, I think she's been waiting for him, all the time.'

'Possible, of course. But Dar, there's no guarantee that he'll look at her again once he's divorced, is there? He's grown, changed. Things alter.'

This was no particular consolation to Dar but he had other thoughts.

'I think he will. I am pretty sure he'll come straight to Libs.' Otherwise, thought Dar, why would Alec Dacre tell him so especially about the divorce if not preparing him for Bobby coming to Libby again?

Part of the pleasure of Frannie and Libby's sessions together was the chat time. Often it was about very silly things, sometimes about deeper issues but both Frannie and Libs enjoyed it. Libby realised that, even though Frannie saw a lot of Lew, they couldn't talk together as she and Frannie could.

'Frannie, you said we aren't intellectuals in the Backlands... true enough, but don't we have a bit of intelligence?'

'Being intelligent and being an intellectual are two different things. Not that any of us on the ranches are particularly bright, we're certainly not, but had we been intellectuals the chances are that we'd have hot-footed it to Europe – for the culture, the stimulation. But ranching is a business so one has to be fairly intelligent to make it pay. Look at Grey – hopelessly stupid and what a mess he makes of his place!'

'Libs, can you imagine living in a city where all one sees is concrete or stone. One needs a lot of intellectual furniture in the mind to cope with that, I think. We've got all this' and he pointed to the land below them, 'so we are very, very fortunate. Do you know, Libs, I once had to travel in a tube train in London. It was a revelation. Everyone got on, sat or stood with completely blank faces. No-one said any greetings. It was inhuman. Eerie. I don't think mankind is meant to live in huge cities; small towns, villages, hamlets are fine, but in cities man loses Nature, loses God, I think. Am I talking rubbish?'

'Not to me. It makes sense but really I suppose we see it that way because we have all this.'

'Libs, did you know that years ago when a baby was born on a British ship in the middle of the ocean it was impossible to put latitude this and longitude that on the birth certificate so all babies born at sea were said to be born, I think, in Wigan! Miles from the sea. Someone in authority had a sense of humour!'

'Is that true?'

'Not sure – but a good story.'

'Frannie you're an awful fraud!'

'Libs, death doesn't matter – if you're a Christian. It's just a transference. One is moving to be with God. That can't be bad! Of course in that sense it matters hugely.'

'Frannie, you mean going to Heaven?'

'Whatever that is. But we are promised we'll be with God and things will be better than we can ever imagine.'

'Yes.' Libby found Frannie way ahead of her in thinking; but it made her think, too, she knew. She was aware that her education had been sketchy.

'But, Frannie, as Christians we shouldn't be doing this, should we?'

'Strictly speaking, no. Either married or celibate. In the normal course you'd have been married already and I can't marry so we just hope that Mungu sees us in an unusual category. I don't know. Neither of us is a natural celibate. Can't think about it too much. God gave us sex to enjoy and it should be enjoyed within marriage, we both know that. But here we are.....' Frannie looked at her. 'If you're worried about it we must stop, Libs.'

'No, I'm not worried really. We're not hurting anyone else – or each other, are we?'

'No – and in that case, Miss Winchester, kindly turn over.'

There was a fifth Sunday in the month and the friends were at Glory Halleluiah's house for the Service. If possible they always tried to get Janet to come; her voice made a big difference and she would play the piano, giving Glory Halleluiah a break. The manager of Thomas Bell's old ranch had been invited but reacted by retreating as if someone had offered him strychnine. Already the Friends knew he just didn't want to be social; it was a pity, they thought, but left him to get on with ranching, a job he did far better than Bell.

During lunch after the Service Madge suddenly said, 'Frannie, you've put on weight haven't …..?'

Frannie smiled. 'Yes, I have, a bit. I'm getting on. Not far off forty.'

'You mustn't get fat!' That was Mumps looking angry.

'It suits you,' continued Madge, ignoring Mumps, 'Your face has filled out more. Frannie – I never knew you were so good looking!'

'Not me, Madge!' Frannie laughed. But it was true. Over the months with Libby his whole being had changed and he looked a happier man. Although the conversation then moved to other topics everyone looked at Frannie and all noticed the difference. When they got home Dar commented: 'Madge is right. Frannie has put on weight. About time. He's always been too thin. He looks better. Don't you think so, Chick?' To which Libby, who had been well aware of Frannie's development, could only agree.

'Frannie, I read a book the other day – can't remember it very well – by a chap called Lewis. Anyway he said, roughly, that a friend was bellyaching about a dreadful woman in the village. She was frightful, a bitch, everything nasty and, the friend said, she calls herself a Christian! The author - this Lewis man - replied, 'You don't know how much worse she might be if she wasn't a Christian!'

Frannie laughed. 'That cheers me up! And glad you're reading C.S. Lewis. Did Glory Halleluiah put you on to him? I thought so. I admit to being a very bad Christian, I'm afraid. I try – but I don't win very often.'

'Isn't that what Christianity is about – forgiving our sins?'

'Yes – and trying to make us little Christs and glorifying God, I believe. Do you know what the Presbyterians say about Christianity and their duty – to glorify God and enjoy Him for ever. Pretty good, isn't it? To enjoy Him for ever – that means His creation, everything He has given us as well as all the promises – everything. We don't show the enjoyment enough, I suppose.'

'Did you know that the great readers are Corn and West? They lend books to Lew by the dozen!'

'Yes, I knew that. Where do they get books from – Nairobi?'

'Some, perhaps, but they order from England. They take the Times Literary Supplement and other things and then order. It's where all their money goes!'

'Frannie, thinking about Corn and West and their reading. We're not really much of a cultured lot here on the ranches, are we?'

'No, not much, I agree. Glory Halleluiah likes music, The Twybitts read a lot, so do I and Lew as well. Madge does lovely artistic embroidery, but basically, no, we're not. How can we be, really? Miles from theatres, concert halls, art galleries and all that. But we have Nature and that fills most of our needs, I suppose – well it does for me.'

'Libs, did you know that Marmite is made from Carrots?'

'No, is it? Not that I mind. Is that true? I love the stuff.'

'So do I. No, I'm not sure but it's a good non-fact, isn't it, Libs?'

'Franny, you are utterly mad.'

'You know, Libs, Britain can't really afford this Welfare State, marvellous idea though it is.'

'Explain, professor.'

'Well, imagine the cost of the last war and all the money that Britain had to borrow. How can a very expensive idea be put into operation before Britain is out of that debt?'

'Yes. But it is a great idea, isn't it?'

'An idea started long before the war – after the great depression. Well, not quite like it has been put into operation now, but social help for people in need was on the cards. Anyway that plan was put aside because of Hitler and possible problems ahead then.'

'So why was it started just after the war – so quickly.'

'A good political move. New government. Make oneself popular – all that. And it is a good thing – but not really all the idea of the new government. The problem is cost – finance. That's at the back of most things. I tell you, Libs, if ever the Africans in Kenya get self-government, it won't be because of Mau Mau or any great ideals about giving the Africans their own sway – it'll be because the British Government can't afford to fund their Colonies any longer, you bet!'

'Libs, one of your most marvellous points with me is that you never use perfume, do you?'

'No. Funny. I just don't. Mother did, very seldom, but Dar never liked it.'

'Neither do I. Odd, isn't it. But when you've washed your hair I quite like the shampoo smell.'

'Frannie, you're mad.'

'Frannie, why did Churchill lose the election after the war? He'd done so well – it seemed awful!'

'Agreed. Politics – funny thing. During the war the Tories closed down their political offices because all energies, they felt, should go to the war effort but the Labour party didn't do that and they worked hard on the forces, I think. And you know there was that very nasty rumour that Churchill was a war-monger. Not true at all, but it had a bad effect. Anyway he came back to office... when was it? About 1952. But I think it is sad he didn't have a chance to put Britain back on its feet immediately after the war because I don't think the Labour party thought of that enough. Churchill always said that the problem was not winning the war but winning the peace – and he meant not just in Germany but in Britain as well. But a change in politics is helpful; any party going on too long may not be a good thing. One needs a balance of ideas.'

Libby hardly thought anything about politics but listened intently and decided to ask Dar his ideas.

'Libs, have you read 'Winnie the Pooh' and those books?'

'Oh, yes, lovely!'

'Arthur Ransome?'

'I've got them all, I think!'

' Wind in the Willows ?'

'Yes – super.'

'O.K. you pass. You'll do!'

'Frannie you get worse.'

'No, I don't – I just have high standards.' Libby hit him quite hard.

'Libs have you ever eaten tripe and onions?'

'Yes, we have it at home, you must have been with us sometime when we're eating it.'

'No, didn't know you liked it. I do. Mumps won't have it. You'll have to do a 'Rose' on me someday when I come over!'

'No problem. I'll let you know when we've killed a steer.'

'I can provide the tripe just as easily.'

'But do you blanch it properly?'

'Ouch. Now I'm in deep water – don't know about that!'

One Thursday evening Libby went to her Gingerbread House after tennis and was relaxing before her usual light supper when she heard a vehicle arrive. It was Frannie, most unexpected.

'Libs, I've had to bring a chap into the Government Hospital. I've booked into the Club for the night but I've come to scrounge a drink and a meal off you.'

'Great. It's only soup and scrambled egg – but come in.'

Instantly Libby felt something amiss with Frannie but gave him a beer (she didn't keep whisky) and told Anna to prepare the meal. Frannie chatted about the man whom he'd taken to hospital.

'Trampled by a cow. He was just plain stupid. She'd just calved – naturally she was kali. He's a bit of a mess but will be O.K. in time.'

After the meal Anna left and Frannie said, 'Any good tonight?'

Libby smiled. 'Yes – O.K.,' and took him to her bedroom where her single bed stood forlorn in the middle of a big room.

They stripped and this time he entered her quickly with no preliminaries. It was rather fast, a bit brutal and when it was over they lay, very tightly on the small bed. Libby stroked his forehead and whispered gently, 'What's wrong, Frannie?'

'Yes, that wasn't the best. Sorry, Libs.' He turned slightly to hold her better and spoke into her hair.

'I've just had a flaming row with Mumps.'

'What about?'

'Money. This year, in fact for the last eighteen months, the cattle have been doing well, growing well, less disease, selling well. It's been a good period. I suppose Mumps sees this. This morning a cattle buyer came and I negotiated a very good price and took him to have coffee in the house. Mumps joined us. Unfortunately this fellow talked about the good price I'd got. He went and I thought no more. But later she suddenly said that it was high time I gave her an allowance – part of the ranch earnings. I saw red. I pay all the household bills and all the accounts around Chemchem; I bought her car and pay for all the upkeep and the fuel – everything. The ranch is mine. The house is mine and she is very well off in her own right but all she ever pays for are her own clothes and when she has her hair done. I just flared up. Couldn't cope. So she told me how selfish I am and I said the same to her. Not good. Most of the time I can cope but not to-day. I used the accident as an excuse to get away for the night – I could have sent a driver with the chap. Libs – I'm not giving in.'

'I'm so sorry. Horrible for you.'

'In one sense I know I should look after her but it's a one way ticket – everything she wants. To her I am despicable but useful!'

'Frannie!'

'Sorry Libs. I've taken it out on you. And I must get to the Club. If I stay here longer tongues will start wagging. Libs, thanks and sorry.' He dressed very quickly and left.

Libby stayed awake a long time. At least he had come to her for comfort. Where else could he go?

CHAPTER 20

Madge Cooper arrived at Glory Halleluiah's house in a state, red eyed from tears.

'Come away in!' Glory Halleluiah reverted to Scotticisms sometimes. 'Tell me what's happened, but coffee first.'

Seated with coffee in front of her, Madge produced a folded piece of paper and gave it to Glory Halleluiah.

'I never go into Frank's desk but he's away and baboons got into the veg garden. He used to keep one .22 bullet out of the ammo safe somewhere in his desk. I've got the gun safe key but not the ammo key. Frank keeps them separate for safety. So I went to find the bullet and saw this – in fact it was open – on top of all his papers.' Madge was finishing sentences so Glory Halleluiah knew it was bad; she read the paper quickly.

It was a short, simple arrangement for the writer and Frank to meet. But it was also, very obviously, a love letter and it was clear that there had been previous assignations. There were three initials as signature: J.O.E.

'Frank has to go to Nairobi from time to time – to do with the repayment of the loan – usually twice a year, but recently – for about six months, he's been going every month. Of course I never thought anything about it. He's handled the finances, why should I think? But this – oh, Glory Halleluiah!' She burst into tears.

Grim faced, Glory Halleluiah read the letter again, leaving Madge to get over her spate of weeping. The curious thing was that Glory

Halleluiah knew exactly the identity of J.O.E. It had been several months ago when she was in Nairobi and had lunch at Muthaiga Club with some Scottish friends. Seated not far from their table was a group that included a young lady who was, to Glory Halleluiah at least, quite striking. She was slender, pale faced, not conventionally beautiful but with large, dark eyes and dark heavy hair that curled on her shoulders. She held herself well, looked as if she came from good stock and seemed to be curiously separate from the group with whom she was having lunch. What invited attention was not her physical looks but her air - an incredible mixture of serenity and insecurity. Yet those things do not go together, thought Glory Halleluiah. She had asked her hosts about the girl. She was Joanna Orde-Ewart, a Scottish name that Glory Halleluiah easily placed; a well known family from Perthshire. Joanna was an horticulturalist, she learned, working with the excellent Closeburn Nursery on the outskirts of Nairobi, specialising in garden design and propagation of plants. Apparently she'd been in Kenya about two years and had gained a remarkable reputation in that time; people were queueing for her help. The group she was with were clients. At the time Glory Halleluiah thought no more but the girl's impression had stayed with her. There was an interesting personality there.

'Madge, I'm so sorry. I wonder if you are mistaken; this is so unlike Frank?' but Glory Halleluiah knew there was no mistake; the letter was quite clear. Frank was undoubtedly being unfaithful to Madge. Glory Halleluiah hardly knew what to say.

Madge managed to talk again, 'Of course he's with her now! He went yesterday. I found this just after breakfast. Oh, what am I to do! Frank – after all these years! I can't believe it!'

'No more can I, Madge. Just let me think a bit. Give me a few minutes.'

'Madge, I think, I think this has nothing to do with your marriage...' and Glory Halleluiah was instantly interrupted by Madge.

'What do you mean? It has *everything* to do with our marriage!'

'Wait, Madge. What I want to say is that the last few years have been an incredible strain for both of you what with the loss of Sally, then John and all the financial worries – everything. But, in fact, although you may not recognise it you are stronger than Frank. You've carried on with your life, your work, quietly, doggedly – we've all admired you. Frank has covered his worries with a veneer of great humour so often, hasn't he? But the more he does that, the worse his troubles underneath may be. Laugh Punchinello! Do you understand? Frank probably feels all the problems weighing him down more than you do because he is supposed to be in charge, the bread-winner, the father-figure, the strong male. You see?'

'A bit, but why *this*?'

'Perhaps it is a form of escapism? To forget everything for a while?'

'What about *me*?'

'He probably can't face the realisation of being a failure in front of you – you, especially – not that he is a failure but he may *feel* that he is.' Glory Halleluiah was struggling.

'So he goes for comfort elsewhere?' Fresh tears took over.

'It looks like it but, Madge, very likely it has nothing to do with your marriage. Think of him. He's always been a good husband? Loving, kind, everything. We've always seen you as an ideal partnership.'

'I thought we shared *everything*.'

'Yes. The strain may have got to a pitch where as a man, he felt

257

he wasn't being an adequate husband to you, not able to provide for you as he'd hoped. You see?'

'Not really. But, Glory Halleluiah, what can I do?'

Glory Halleluiah had been very shocked and extremely worried that what she might have said was no help but here was a problem that she could solve.

'Now that is straight-forward. Put the letter back. Did you take the bullet? No? Good. Say nothing at all. Behave as usual. But next time he says he's off to Nairobi you say you'll go with him. Say you need to get away – you'll go mental if you don't have a break – whatever – say that regular trips to Nairobi will help greatly and blow the expense – a bit more debt hardly matters. Go on in that vein. You see?'

'Yes, alright, if I can behave normally for a month!'

'You can and will. Because it will stop this, er, liaison. In Nairobi stick with him like the proverbial limpet. Of course he may very well guess that you know and then it will be up to him to say something – or not. Madge, be ready. You must forgive him. You've got a long marriage behind you and probably a long future ahead. Do you want to ruin it all?'

'But he has!'

'Madge, listen. I'm sure this was not intentional, whatever it is.'

'But how can I trust him now?'

Madge sighed gently, looking worriedly at her friend. Dear Madge, not very intelligent but such a good person. For this to happen to her!

'Yes, your trust is fractured. Has he ever let you down in any way before in over – what is it - thirty-five years – I doubt it. One failure, and I agree a bad one, but only one in all that time is not worth losing your marriage over is it? Is it? Madge, dear, think carefully. You are both under great strain and a crack is likely. In a way you've done amazingly well not to have had a hiccup before!'

'Call this a *hiccup*!'

'Sorry. Inappropriate. But either of you might have given way ages ago. You have had the incredible strength not to; poor Frank has given way. Help him, Madge! He obviously needs it!'

'But I do help him!'

'Yes. Just try to be a little bit more helpful, more loving. Don't overdo it but let him lean on you. It will be all right.' Glory Halleluiah was praying that anything she said might be true. How did she know? But this marriage must be saved at all costs, she knew.

'Madge was quieter, more thoughtful.'

'Stay to lunch. We'll have a drink. Sit in my room. I'll play the piano a bit. Just be quiet for a while.'

Meeting Frank had been such a natural, easy thing for Joe. It was a Saturday morning and, because she'd worked a lot of extra hours doing work for a special garden design, she'd been given the morning off and had been shopping at Slater and Whittaker, the Westlands grocery store close to her flat. Just as she was driving into the small block of flats she had a puncture. The driver of the car behind obviously saw it happen and stopped; a man got out, 'Can I help you?'

He was a tall man, well proportioned with a good looking face that gave no indication of his age – certainly in his fifties, she thought idly as he competently changed the wheel for her. (Frank was in his sixties, in fact.) Automatically, as she thanked him, she said, 'My flat's just here – you'll need a wash,' and he thanked her.

She put on the kettle as soon as she'd shown him her bathroom and offered him coffee. He accepted and they sat in her small, neat sitting room that was enlivened by several clusters of potted plants on different levels. It was a bit like sitting in a conservatory. Joe couldn't help it; plants just grew for her and she felt comfortable amongst them.

Comfort was what she needed.

Frank saw a youngish (early forties, he guessed) lady, no rings, who was not really beautiful but had an unusual effect. To Frank the effect was a mixture of tranquillity and vulnerability, especially the latter. She had charming, slightly diffident manners and had thanked him so delicately for his help. It was rather like being with a shy, emerging debutante, yet she was not really shy. She was extremely restful to be with, different, calming and yet also exciting to him. It had been many years since he'd spoken socially to any ladies other than his Backlands friends and business people in Chemchem. He asked what she was doing in Kenya and she spoke about her work with plants in a direct and simple way. It was extremely soothing to be out of his own world, his own problems, and sit with this gentle girl (he thought her young for her possible years). Another cup of coffee was offered and accepted.

When he felt he must leave her and continue his journey he found that he couldn't help himself. As they stood in her tiny hallway he simply put his arms round her and kissed her very gently. They broke apart and looked at each other; recognition was complete. He took her in his arms again, this time not so gently.

After Madge left, an exhausted and thoughtful Glory Halleluiah rummaged in her personal desk for a letter from her brother that went back a few weeks. They wrote to each other weekly – like at school, they said – usually on Sundays. She found the letter she wanted, read it again carefully and then, checking that no-one was on the party-line, she made a long and very confidential telephone call to the friend with whom she had lunched when Joe had been pointed out. Glory Halleluiah was very worried. Personal problems like this were very distressful – oh, Frank! Poor Madge. They've been through so much!

Glory Halleluiah thought about the telephone call, re-read her brother's letter, and with great care laid plans.

The next time Frank was due to meet Joe he was late; they always met at her flat, never going out together. She had food ready and was anxious. Eventually he phoned her, explaining that he was in Nairobi but, very sorry, couldn't see her this time. It was a very quick call and seemed to lack the tenderness he'd always shown her. She was sad, eating the carefully prepared food by herself. Was he all right?

Another month went by and she received a very short note ending the affair. Frank gave her no explanation. He just wished her well. Joe collected this letter at Closeburn's office where her mail was directed, read it, wrote a quick note to her very nice boss, got in her Volkswagen Beetle and drove home to her flat. It was only when she got into the flat that she gave way and could not stop the tears. *Again!* She'd been let down so often. Was there no happiness for her anywhere?

It had been a previous unhappiness that drove her to Kenya, that and the propinquity of her family. The middle of three sisters she had seen each sister marry happily and she was an aunt five times. The children were all healthy, intelligent, very confident, noisy, boisterous, often unfeeling of anything but themselves and had become a source of pain to Joe. She'd loved them when they arrived but after each sad romance their very earthy ebullience seemed too much for her, driving home her loneliness. She knew her feelings were wrong, being terrified that some of it was jealousy; she was getting older, possible children would be less sure for her. Kenya seemed a good answer. Now this. She'd loved her two years in the country and Frank had seemed heaven-sent. He'd always been reticent about himself; all she knew was that he was a farmer. Frank knew more about her but she never told him about her sadness back home. That was unnecessary; he easily sensed all that. With Frank everything seemed so right, so simple; nothing else mattered. The wonderful sex was filling a huge need in her. All gone. She was alone again and, she was afraid that she had been far too naïve, *far* too naïve.

From Nairobi, Glory Halleluiah's Scottish friend wrote saying that it looked as if Joe was devastated by something. People at the Nursery had noticed her change, though she'd said very little and just got on with her work. But something had happened. Glory Halleluiah was ready to act.

Joe received the phone call at work. She was called from dealing with some special cuttings to find herself invited to have lunch on Saturday or Sunday at the Norfolk Hotel. The invitation was from a lady with very precise diction and a certain air of command. Glory Halleluiah gave her proper name, Joe certainly recognised the family; who didn't know of that ancient family in Scotland?

Glory Halleluiah, typically, wasted no time.

'Miss Orde-Ewart - Joanna, may I? You will know, I am sure, the gardens of Invereth?'

'I've been there often.'

'Good. What you may not know is that the gardens belong to me.' Glory Haleluiah paused. Joe had no reply but showed her surprise.

'What happened was that the owning family – you'll know – the McLevens – suffered many reverses during the war. The old man died. The present Mr. McLeven was away in the forces and the labour at the gardens drastically reduced – everyone went to war. So there was neglect. And, for other reasons, the present Mr. McLeven felt he was unable to put quite so much money into the gardens. You'll realise that, although the gardens are open to the public, that income in no way pays for all the upkeep. At the end of the war it was evident that a great deal of money was needed to get the gardens back in shape. So my brother and I went to the rescue. A company was formed to run the gardens. I am the principal shareholder. Effectively I own the place – not the house and its grounds – just the gardens open to the public.'

Joe's attention was fixed. She could sense what was coming.

'Mr. McLeven wrote to tell my brother and I saying that, although the restoration of the gardens went well after the war, he feels the place is tired, dull, mundane now. It needs total re-organising, planning, changing. I hear that you have done a very good job with two smaller gardens at Kiambu and Limuru (the farthest Joe had ever worked from Nairobi.). Would you care for a much bigger challenge? The finance is there – waiting to be used. There's a pretty Gardener's cottage – not big but adequate – you may recall it - by the entrance to the walled garden. That is available. The salary will be correct for your qualifications and experience. Joanna – would you like to try?'

Joanna was amazed. Had this been God-sent? Come at just the right time?

'Naturally you do not have to answer me immediately. I'll put the offer in writing, terms, conditions etc. But Invereth needs someone with your particular gifts quite soon.'

'Thank you. Thank you very much. I think I'd like to go there. But aren't there plenty of good people available in Scotland?'

'Maybe. But I'm here and you are here. That's the chance of it. And I've heard a lot about your work. Right. I'll get a proper offer sent to you. What notice do you have to give at Closeburn? Three months? Fine. Your air fare will be covered, of course.'

After lunch, when a few more details had been mentioned, they made polite remarks to each other and left, Glory Halleluiah praying that she had done the right thing.

Joe was bemused. Of course it was an answer – a sort of answer anyway and not close to her family. There was a kind of inevitability about it; she knew she would agree. There was deep sadness, yet also acceptance within her.

Frank was in too strange a state to perceive anything in Madge. She'd tried very hard to be normal, extra helpful and loving but he'd scarcely noticed. The last few months had a curious dream-like quality for him; it was hardly real at all. He was living on two entirely different planes: the ranch with Madge and a contrasting, microscopic life with Joe. Nothing fitted at all. He just did it; totally emotionally and physically exhausted on one plane, he found solace on the other. There were moments when he recognised this, but couldn't see another life; a fly caught in a web with no escape.

When Madge suggested that she join him on his next Nairobi visit he capitulated immediately. Here was an answer. Madge would stop what he could not. Frank was relieved in a way and Madge felt this, though not understanding it. Not for a second did Frank think that Madge knew about Joe; that wasn't possible; they'd been far too careful. But he knew that his Joe-life had to end.

In Nairobi he'd been to the Head Office of the Bank and then took Madge to the cinema; a treat neither had enjoyed for many years. Back home he said that he probably didn't need to go to the Bank so often now. Madge was both relieved and also deeply hurt that he couldn't talk to her. Glory Halleluiah just said 'Give it time.' Frank knew that he'd let down Joe and also been unfair to his faithful, loving Madge. What a bloody useless bugger I am, he thought continually, now more mentally exhausted and disturbed than ever.

In far off Scotland Ninian McLeven was walking through the gardens, being noticed by the few visitors there at this time of year. He was trying to imagine some changes that could be made to the whole place. Many years ago his father had said that they should use the high ground and the stream more – make a spectacular water garden that could be a central theme. A lot could be changed, he knew, but it needed a better eye than he possessed. His father had great imagination; could see what a garden would be like many years after it was planted. Ninian knew he had none of this. He was a rather scraggy man, weather beaten and looking older than his years. Coming back to the gardens after the War he'd almost given up and if the company hadn't been set up he would have sold the place and departed south. Yet he had a great love for it.

Now the gardens were financially secure, but he could see clearly that the years of neglect had altered the garden badly, even after such a big effort of restoration. Something fresh was needed. He'd voiced his feelings and Glory Halleluiah's brother came to stay for several days during which they both walked the gardens intensively, spoken to the staff and visitors who were there. Yes, a catharsis was necessary. It seemed drastic but action should be taken. Get rid of it all and start again!

Ninian felt that he, personally, needed exactly the same thing. He was embittered. After a hasty war-time marriage it was almost immediately clear that he had made a mistake. The pair of them were ill-matched and very rapidly any affection had disappeared. She was demanding and never satisfied; he grew soured by it all. His wife simply could not take the thought of constantly living in the North-West of Scotland; too far from anything, she complained. But it was his home. Yes, he could have moved and left the gardens with a manager; probably Edinburgh would have been correct; that was where he had business interests, but, in reality, he knew that his wife didn't want him not just the place where they lived. She'd finally gone, two years ago now, and he was still hurt, not by her leaving – there was no fondness left - but by his own inability to have got things right. He was wounded. This made him irascible at times and the staff at the gardens warned each other when Mr. McLeven was having a bad day. At the same time the gardens were his salvation, desperately in need of renewal as they were. He often thought that whoever could revitalise the gardens could have a go at him, too.

Sitting by the driver on the long journey to the Backlands Glory Halleluiah was meditating all that she had seen of Joe and all that she knew of the current situation of the gardens. Ninian McLeven had a few shares in the company but was also employed to run the gardens. He was perfectly competent but in an unhappy state, so her brother had written. It may be necessary to inject more capital into the place, her brother suggested, and Glory Halleluiah had agreed. But really serious was to find someone to do a pumpkin-into-Cinderella-coach act on the gardens who would also help lift Ninian out of his low spirits. A woman, Glory Halleluiah's brother wondered? But women with suitable experience and of the right upper class type with whom Ninian could agree were rare. Glory Halleluiah said that she'd think about the problem, knowing that an appropriate woman would be impossible to find. Yet, here, in Kenya, she thought she had landed an amazingly suitable fish.

'Meddling old fool,' she said to herself out loud. Luckily her driver only spoke Swahili and Kikuyu.

CHAPTER 21

Libby found a note from Dar at her breakfast place. Evidently Lew had eaten and gone again.

Something wrong at the Coopers. Madge in hysterics. Frank off with a gun threatening suicide. Call G.H. and come if you can. Get Lew.

As she was reading Frannie came in. One look at her face spoke problems. Without a word Libby handed him the note. He reacted quickly.

'You phone Glory Halleluiah. Where's Lew? Out? Do you know where? Hopeless! I'll go straight over. Libs – go to Madge – give her sugar – anything sweet. Just be there. I'm off.'

Madge was indeed hysterical. Before breakfast Frank had suddenly said that he was so useless he'd better end it all – grabbed his .45 Colt and got in the Land Rover before Madge could take it in.

'I don't know where he's gone! Oh Frannie! Dar's gone looking – Oh God – I can't take any more. Frank!'

Libby arrived just at that moment and after hurried words Frannie took off. Vehicle tracks were quite easy to see and Frannie realised that Dar had spotted them as well and would be ahead of him. He prayed that Dar would be in time. The trail led along the lower, flatter country for a while, gates left open, but was heading for the base of the escarpment under the cedar forest. Suddenly Frannie got to where two vehicles were parked. He recognised the place. From this point a footpath led up through the forest to the spring that supplied water to the Cooper's house and a lot of the farm. Frannie had been up that path a few times, especially when he was very young and Frank had been opening up the eye of the spring, building a collecting basin and putting in piping. It was a very beautiful place, a tiny clearing with a thick, cool, forest canopy. Frannie left his Land Rover and started the climb up the narrow path that wound through the trees, mainly cedar but with some olive and quite a few noble Podocarpus as well. The tracks of the men ahead of him were clear. It was quite steep; a major climb for Dar, he thought. He was thinking of what he remembered of the clearing; it had always struck him as a particularly lovely spot; not a place to end a life. Or was it?

It was remarkably quiet; no bird song, no animals; eerie, he thought. Dar had done well to get up here. Suddenly he reached the clearing and found Dar, exhausted from his climb, and Frank, alive, both sitting silent on the concrete lip of the collecting tank. They looked old, limp, bent and incapable of anything. They glanced at Frannie but said nothing. Frannie sat beside Dar who was still breathing heavily. Frank was hunched, now looking at the ground. Behind them the beautiful clear spring water bubbled with hardly a sound. Frannie bent backwards to fish the gun out of the water.

'Good gun. Shouldn't rust. I'll clean it, oil it and all that.' He opened the chamber and removed the bullets, slipped them in his pocket and took out a handkerchief and wiped the small, but surprisingly heavy weapon. The two older men said nothing but Dar was looking at the gun. It was very quiet but somehow right. Frannie looked around the exquisite clearing. Spanish moss depended from some of the trees, splashes of sunlight danced on the ground in front of them. They just sat, Frank even more bent and Dar with a very worried face, but breathing better. It was literally minutes before Frank suddenly spoke to the ground.

'You see. I'm so bloody useless I can't even kill myself!'

'Thank God you didn't. Though why you see yourself as useless I can't imagine!'

Frannie was brisk and decisive. It seemed to stir Dar.

'Frank you've had your problems, God knows, but you're doing the best you can. We all know that. What more can you do?'

Frank did not reply. There was another long silence, this time broken by some small bird-song not far away. It fractured the indefinable suspense. Frannie stood up.

'Come on, let's get down. I'll drive Frank, we'll get his vehicle later. Come on, both of you.' Dar turned to Frank but he was slowly unbending, getting straight and then stood.

In anticlimax and mundanely they walked back down the track, Frannie in the lead, pausing every now and again to make sure the others were following. They were moving like puppets; it was an unreal procession. Dar, very shaken, was walking slowly. He was thinking of the days when he, Frank Houghton-Framlyn and younger Frank Cooper were the first settlers in the area, starting with raw Africa and turning it into ranches, building houses, roads, dips, fences. The three men were very different in character yet united in their mutual concerns. They'd helped each other a lot in those days. Now? Frannie's father – dead. Frank Cooper reduced to this! Dar was horrified that he hadn't seen the measure of Frank's despair – such an old friend!

Libby looked up from the teapot she was wielding to find what looked like a Victorian painting. Everyone seemed to be striking attitudes. Frank and Madge were seated on a sofa looking at each other as if they were total strangers but holding hands tightly. On a chair beside the sofa, Dar was leaning towards Frank in solicitude. Glory Halleluiah was similarly seated the other side near Madge. To complete the picture Frannie was leaning over the back of the sofa looking at Frank. They were all frozen. Libby had a sudden urge of hysterical laughter, quickly stifled. Was this what happened to perfectly decent people who, through no fault of their own, inherit enormous problems? A collapse of rational behaviour? Libby was frightened as well as embarrassed. She had to do something and poured tea, splashing some of it. When she passed tea round it was drunk automatically, no-one noticing that she'd sugared every cup. Still no-one spoke. The cups retrieved, she put them back on the table, the only movement in the room, except that Madge had grasped Frank's hand again.

With sudden decision Frannie straightened. He was taking charge.

'Now you two. I think the time has come for all of us to face something. Frank, Madge, you've had enough. Absolutely enough. You can take no more. You've done incredibly well, we all know, but you can't go on. It's time to accept help – loving help - financial help – from all of us. Let's clear this intolerable debt once and for all and get you back to normal.'

Glory Halleluiah was quick to sit up and with her extremely exact, clear diction said, 'Quite right, Frannie. Frank you'll have to tell us what the remaining debt is. Then we – me, Dar and Frannie…'

Libby quickly added, 'And me.'

To which Glory Halleluiah nodded, 'And Libby – will settle everything. Our gift to you. Our appreciation of how very well you have coped.'

'Oh no…' started Frank.

'Oh yes,' countered Dar. 'It's got to be done. Well done, Frannie. This is what friends are for, for goodness sake!'

'Well – a loan,' said Frank.

'Absolutely not,' said Glory Halleluiah crisply dominating Frank. 'No loan, as a gift. As Frannie said it's got to be settled once and for all. Frank – how much is left to be paid?'

'Frank – you'll have to tell us.' Dar added, concerned about the enormous embarrassment Frank must be going through.

Frank sighed and then, after a couple of false starts when he could hardly talk, he came out with the figure. It was large but far less than Dar was estimating from his original knowledge.

'You've done so well to clear as much as you have. Damned if I could have done it at my place. Frank, leave it to us and we'll cope. Happy to. Need to get you back to proper life again. Glory Halleluiah, Frannie – we'll get together? As quickly as we can.' At this Frank was now bowed and Madge crying softly, their hands held even tighter.

'Yes, not easy to accept help. We know. But we can help and we will.'

No-one heard a vehicle arrive but suddenly Lew burst into the room; he'd found the note that Libs and Frannie dropped on the table at The Loop.

'Dad! Ma ! Are you all right?' he said looking at the whole serious company.

'Lew – oh Lew. Yes, we're quite all right, everything is all right,' said Madge, very bravely, thought Glory Halleluiah who was the only one to know the problem beyond finance.

Much later a very subdued party left Frank, Madge and Lew; Dar having told Lew to stay with his parents that night.

'Will they be all right?' asked Libby, very anxious.

'Yes, Frank's exhausted, lost his will power for a bit. He'll be all right, Libby. What we've got to do is sort out the finance as quickly as possible.'

Early next morning they met at Glory Halleluiah's house, Dar and Libby calling at the Cooper's home en route. All was well there; Frank and Madge were calm though Frank was trembling a bit. Lew had dealt with the early morning work on the ranch, and then left to get back to The Loop. Dar started to take the financial meeting but was easily overtaken by Glory Halleluiah who was determined to make the largest contribution to the repayment. The others knew she could afford it – easily - and so agreed. Dar and Frannie each were to supply a considerable sum and Libby a nominal amount from the bequest she received from her mother. Dar took Frank to Nairobi to discuss this final repayment with the Bank and in the surprisingly short time of one month it was done. Frannie and Dar had to sell some shares, Libby had her amount available in a Savings Account and how Glory Halleluiah got hers no-one asked. It was done. Frank and Madge were free of debt.

A celebration lunch was held at Glory Halleluiah's home with champagne and extravagant food (organised by Rosa). Frank and Madge found it very, very hard to react as they felt they should but it was evident that they were quietly relieved though embarrassed by the situation.

'It's wrong, Libby, to see money as evil,' said Glory Halleluiah a few days later. 'It's the love of money that is wrong – you know – putting it above more important things – the Bible makes that very clear. To amass wealth can be good – but one must use wealth. I did not amass mine – I inherited it.'

Libby was interested, Glory Halleluiah never talked about herself normally.

'Everyone assumes that because one has a title there must be money – that may have been true once but not necessarily to-day. My parents, for all that they lived in a so-called castle – it's a particularly ugly three storied square block of stone that is nothing like a castle at all - north west Sutherland – go any further and you fall off Scotland – where was I? Oh. My parents had very little wealth for their supposed position. Mother couldn't stand the place and spent most of her life in London, coming north once a year so my brother and I were brought up by servants – Father took little notice. Victorian days when I was a child, that was not uncommon. My brother went to school but I didn't – had odd governesses – and they were odd, too, some of them. None stayed long, we were too remote.'

Libby was entranced. At last she was learning something about Glory Halleluiah.

'My brother went to Harrow and there met a lad with whom he made great friends and so the pair of them often came home during the holidays. I'm four years younger than my brother but I'd always been his shadow and spent an enormous amount of time with him out of doors, stalking, shooting, fishing, on the sea – not being the quiet daughter of the house doing needlework! Not me. So when my brother – Ian – and his friend, Gerard, came, I still tacked on. I was the dogsbody. I was made to carry the ammunition, food, rugs, anything, while they had a good time. But I loved it, too! Anything outdoors was better than indoors.'

Glory Halleluiah was launched, nothing would stem this flow now, Libby thought.

'As I grew older I suppose I realised that Gerard was not only very good looking but immensely wealthy. His family owned vast estates in Yorkshire, Northumberland, Durham and industries around Newcastle – including coal mines. And he was the only son of a sick father. His mother had died some time ago. Ian and Gerard went up to University together and I still saw a lot of them during the vacations, although Gerard said that he had to spend more time with the family businesses. It didn't really mean very much to me at my age.'

Glory Halleluiah had a slightly far-away look, memories surging back like a slow, but very strong tide.

'Suddenly I had other problems. It was now King Edward's reign and I had to be presented. You weren't, Libby?'

'No, Dar and mother thought it unnecessary and in, any case, the whole thing was virtually over by the time I reached that age.'

'Yes. Mother insisted that I did a London season. Oh dear. Libby, you will imagine. Me! I have never had any looks or figure; I was gauche, knew nothing of society. It was a disaster. There was no hope for me. At every dance I was a wallflower except when Ian and Gerard came – and, bless them, they came often. By this time Ian was with his regiment; the officers got a lot of time off during the season, and Gerard was dealing with the family business but always joined Ian when he could. They saved my life and, of course, mother was delighted because Gerard was extremely eligible. Not that he'd look at me, but the fact that he danced with me retrieved mother's pride, I think. At the end of the season when many girls had found husbands, of course I hadn't so I simply went back to Scotland and ran the castle for father, now not well, and still saw Ian and Gerard quite often.'

Glory Halleluiah smiled.

'Then things started to happen. Ian married lovely Lydia Shutford – and she was lovely in form and character. I was very fond of her. Not long after that marriage, in January 1914, quite unexpectedly Gerard arrived to stay – alone. Of course we went out onto the grounds – it

276

was freezing cold - and he very quickly proposed to me! I was so surprised I nearly went utterly silent. Inevitably I'd loved him for years yet knew that he'd not look at me. But he did! He had no more time for the social superficialities than I had, it appeared. Libby, I was in heaven. Mother, who was not very well, could hardly believe it. Father, also not well, probably wasn't interested, I fear. Anyway there followed wonderful months when we planned our wedding. It had to be in London - in September. During the planning I was taken to all the estates and businesses and found it fascinating. They were months of pure joy, although during that time Gerard's father died so he inherited everything – a busy time although Gerard had been in command for some years really. Then, suddenly, on the 4th of August war broke out and Gerard had to go. It wasn't going to be a long war, everybody said, so we postponed our wedding for a while. That was the last time I saw him. In early 1915 Gerard was killed.'

Glory Halleluiah paused. Libby could not say anything.

'Gerard left me everything. I had to try to cope with the vast concerns. Of course there were agents and managers but there were major decisions to be made, things to be signed; it was Herculean – so many workmen were away at the war. I learnt a lot in a very short time. In a way it helped me get over Gerard, I suppose. Father died so I spent the war travelling between Sutherland and Newcastle trying to keep everything going. Luckily Ian survived the war and, when he came back, I suggested that he might leave the army and take over. Almost at the same time, Lydia had an awful accident when she drowned – and she was pregnant – so Ian and I had to support each other. Ian decided that he would try to run Gerard's affairs – or, really, mine, and left the Army. He took over. So now he continues to do what I did and travels between both places. He's much better at it than I ever was and we simply split the proceeds. Ian's also been clever over investments so he's helped me a lot. But when he was firmly in the saddle I was left stranded. I knew this would happen. For a considerable time I'd wanted to get right away – away from any memories of Gerard – so I opted for Kenya and here I am. And now Ian has the son of a cousin of ours – he's the heir, in fact - working with him so it's easier these days. Libby – how did I get to tell you all this?'

'We were talking about using wealth.'

'Ah yes. Both Ian and I feel the responsibility of having money. So we give large dollops to charities every year. When he comes out we discuss this so that we do not clash. And he also does a lot of private giving – I know he gives scholarships at certain Scottish schools and one at Harrow - that sort of thing. And I have my own way of helping people and organisations here in Kenya, and sometimes overseas, too. Both Ian and I try to live sensibly, but simply. Mind you, the castle now has central heating! We both feel we are responsible to the memory of Gerard – he was such a good person.'

There was another slight pause. 'I think it's wrong to hoard money, to be a miser; it is to be used. None of the beautiful houses or collections of paintings would ever have been made without big money somewhere. Using it makes it filter down to those who need it, it rotates, keeps people employed.'

Libby nodded.

'Frank and Madge – they've been admirable, haven't they? Never a word of complaint. But you'll see – no more debts and a living income will set them free. Awful though the last few days have been the result will be worth it.'

'Yes, I'm sure you are right. But, Glory Halleluiah, your story!

So tragic!'

'All the major romances end in tragedy – look at Romeo and Juliet! Oh, Libby, I'm fine. One gets over anything in time if one tries. I love my ranch. I have a very contented life here. But, dear, I've never told anyone else my story – please keep it to yourself.'

'Of course I will – I feel privileged to have heard it.'

Lew felt the effects of The Friends' generosity immediately when he was asked to open a bank account with his next month's cheque. He had money of his own! He felt awkward at first and politely told Glory Halleluiah that he could now pay his own Club bill. She agreed but insisted on paying his monthly subscription. Then he told Dar that he felt he ought to be contributing towards his keep, 'Certainly not. In your Contract. Read it. Living provided.' In fact Dar had only added this because of the needs of Frank and Madge but he was happy to continue. One day he'd have to build a proper house for him; he'd put this off so that he and Libby could look after Lew; now he must think again; he'd discuss it with Libby. No hurry but there was Janet to consider, he was sure.

Lew immediately opened a Savings Account and put a considerable amount into that every month. He was good at saving; he was so inured to not spending. But he took Janet to the Club as often as he could and bought her some books. He was carefully watching his savings, knowing that he'd got a long way to go before he could approach Janet properly and even then, where would they live?

Not very long after the debt was completely cleared he went to have dinner with his parents. They had recovered and even looked younger, he noticed. There was a different feel to the evening. No one niggled about second drinks, the food, always wholesome, seemed to taste better. Lew thought that cannot be true but realised that his sense of everything in the house had been quickened. The tightening was starting to relax, the aura was changing; it couldn't happen overnight, for too long Frank and Madge had lived in penury, but there was a gentle relaxation.

Frank looked round the house one evening, at the gaps where good furniture had once stood and where an old mirror and a couple of reasonable paintings had been on the wall. Madge's few bits of silver, her jewellery: all gone.

He said, 'Madge, I suppose we can start again. Get another table over there and a good desk, what do you think?'

She smiled. 'Frank – if these years have taught me anything, it is that we don't need half our possessions. Let them go! Less to fret over. Less to clean, mend, polish! Forget it. Put anything we've got back into the ranch and – Lew. He's the one we should be thinking of now.' This jolted Frank. Lew! Why was it that, somehow, he could never get Lew into the forefront of his mind. Lew, who'd helped all these years. Lew!

Neither Frank nor Madge mentioned Joe. 'It's best, really,' said Glory Halleluiah when talking with Madge one day. 'She's left Kenya. Did you know?'

'Gone? No, I didn't know. That really is episode closed, I suppose. How did you know?'

'Through mutual friends. I hope it makes it a bit easier. All over completely.'

'Mmm. You know, Glory Halleluiah, part of me wants him to tell me all about it – but I see that he won't.'

'Can't, more likely.'

'Oh, why are men like that? We were always able to talk about anything. Now there's one bit we'll never share.'

'No. And better you don't try to. You know there are always parts of life that can never be explained, never settled to our satisfaction, something we want to know but can't – things like that. I simply cannot read Revelations. Odd. But a Presbyterian Minister said to me once that if I can't I must not worry. Just leave it. Put it on the too difficult to handle pile and one day it might come clear or it may not. Unfinished business. Life is like that. It is not like a work of fiction where everything can be tied up neatly. Life has a mass of blurred edges. We all have them. Accept and be done.'

There was a sequel to the end of Frank and Madge's financial problems. A letter arrived from South Africa. It was from John in gaol. He needed money, he said, that would shorten his time in prison considerably. Dad must send a very large sum to a bank account – name, number, address given (the name was obviously that of an African) - as soon as possible. It was a peremptory order rather than a request. Frank gave the letter to Madge to read. 'A bribe?' she asked. 'Obviously.' Frank had a very severe expression. 'No doubt.' He took the letter back and deliberately tore it into careful shreds.

'Madge, he's not our son any longer. He's gone. Gone.'

'But what if he's sorry – if he really is sorry?'

'Does it look like it? Madge, if ever that day comes then, of course, he'll be welcome. Forgiven. But I think that day very, very unlikely. It was you who said just recently that we must concentrate on Lew. We've got to do that.'

CHAPTER 22

Libby came in from the ranch a bit late for breakfast to find the back verandah definitely not as she left it. There was furniture everywhere: a set of dining room chairs, three sofas, two small tables, a pretty glass-fronted cabinet and a pile of paintings. All were old – mainly antique – and seemed vaguely familiar to Libby.

'What's going on?' she asked Lew who was finishing his meal.

Lew was alive with mischief. 'Corn! He wants us to look after that stuff for a few days.'

'What for?'

'Ah, wait for it! Last evening and this morning he's been going to Glory Halleluiah and my folks ferrying furniture – all their good bits. Then he's filling their own house with camping gear.'

'Yes, but what for?' Libby was impatient and Lew was laughing, deliberately keeping her waiting.

'The dreaded Aunt. You know, their Aunt Ina who always threatened to visit them. Well she's coming to-day. No warning! West had to go to Nairobi yesterday to collect her and they want to make it as uncomfortable as possible so she won't stay!'

'Oh, they are so naughty! She must be getting on – seventies?'

'Don't know. But she keeps threatening to disinherit them - she's disgustingly rich – if they won't do this or that. Apparently they came to Kenya to get away from her. She's a battleaxe. Organises everyone, always knows best. She sounds frightful!'

'So what are they going to do with her while she's with them? Inevitably they'll bring her to all of us on visits?'

'Probably, if they can't get rid of her quickly enough. Anyway Corn asked if we could hide that stuff so she won't guess what's going on. I must say I'd love to see their place. Apparently they're putting the bare minimum everywhere, banished the good cutlery, brought out the enamel camping plates, tin mugs, chipped glasses – everything! Oh, and they've found some girlie calendars to put on the walls! Can't you see it? This Aunt Ina will have a fit!'

'She really will disinherit them, won't she?'

'That's exactly what Corn says they want, then she'll leave them alone. It seems she's been writing to them ever since they came out to Kenya telling them what to do on the ranch. How she can possibly understand how to run a ranch from Edinburgh goodness only knows but that's what they've suffered. Actually I'd rather like to meet the old cow!'

'Lew!'

'Well, she must be dreadful. Corn and West always play jokes on people but they never hurt anyone, do they? I mean they're decent chaps so she must be awful.'

This story was watered down slightly for Dar when he finally arrived but he got the drift of it and wasn't sure whether to ignore it or laugh. Lew and Libby were definitely laughing.

It wasn't until the next day that they had news. Glory Halleluiah phoned at tea-time.

'Dar, don't go out to the cattle now. I'm coming round and I need several strong whiskies. Corn and West! I'll tell you.'

This was too good for anyone to go on the evening rounds so

when Glory Halleluiah arrived she found Dar, Libby and Lew waiting to hear her news.

'Yes please Dar. I need it, not too much soda, thanks. Those two rapscallions! I could murder them. Oh dear.'

Glory Halleluiah shook her wiry hair, took a large draught and looked up, half in exasperation, half in resignation.

'The famous Aunt Ina. You know? She gave them no warning that she'd arrived – just phoned from Nairobi so West had to go down in a hurry to collect her from The Norfolk. Corn did the furniture-moving bit – he brought some to you? You should see my store! Oh dear. Then early this morning West phoned me; would I give them lunch? Well of course. But he asked me to keep lunch on the veranda with all my rough furniture and not let the Aunt see my dining room or sitting room. I was to take her to the outside long-drop loo. Oh, they are wicked! A very simple meal please, well that's a normal lunch for me. If it isn't cold left-overs it would be a stew and that's what it was.'

Dar, Libby and Lew were waiting for the denouement.

'They arrived. The Aunt is a large lady – huge bosom, very commanding, booming voice, ultra confident, imperious and condescending. West introduced her and she said, 'My dear soul, Westmorland has told me all about you. How very sad. A dreadful life. I'll certainly do what I can for you. You cannot be expected to run this place and have nothing. A prisoner of the place! Quite awful!'

Corn butted in. 'Of course you must help poor dear Glory Halleluiah if you can. Poor soul. So brave in all her difficulties.' By now I'd got the message – those awful brothers were playing a huge hoax on me – blast them!'

'I couldn't do anything except play along and see what happened.

So I said very little and we had drinks only jungle juice, no alcohol, I'd been told. Eventually lunch came. The Aunt asked me questions all the time. How big was the ranch? How many cattle? Did I have to go out to the cattle every day? It went on and on. An inquisition. It finally emerged – and I'd been groping in the dark all through – that she'd been told that I was a poor orphan, forced to run the ranch on no salary by a wicked distant relative who took all the ranch earnings, and could she do something about it? Well. You should have heard. It went on. She would deal with the situation. She could find me a perfectly good job as a live-in maid to some friends of hers in Edinburgh. I would have a home and a proper wage – the house is big but she could see that I was healthy and strong despite being elderly. Could I cook? They quite like simple food. Poor Glory Halleluiah. Never mind, quite soon I would be relieved of my appalling condition. The Aunt will cope. The Aunt will arrange *everything*!'

The three listeners were full of laughter.

'All the time Corn and West were sycophants and repeating everything she said. Oh yes, Aunt will find a suitable position in Edinburgh. Oh, poor Glory Halleluiah to have been incarcerated on this big ranch all those years. How dreadful. Butter certainly would not have melted in their mouths. Deadpan faces. Stricken with horror at the plight of poor Glory Halleluiah. I could have killed the pair of them.'

'Yes, Dar, and a little more soda water this time.'

'In the end this dreadful woman – who never asked me once what I wanted, I might add – had decided everything and would cope with everything. The only hesitation came when she asked for the name and address of my supposed wicked relative. Corn said he'd send it to her and she could deal direct with him. Oh dear. You could feel her imagining herself on a pure white charger galloping to the rescue and feeling marvellous about it – giving herself a huge boost. Corn and West. They're a couple of rogues, the pair of them. It came out that the Aunt has been told the Backlands is full of people who were either penniless, mentally sub-normal, ex-convicts, alcoholics, drug addicts, roués hiding from their wives – all socially unacceptable – and she must sort them out. Nothing she'd like better, no doubt. I was the first victim. Dar, if they want to bring her here say *no!*'

'What's Dar supposed to be? An ex-convict? Maybe a roué would suit him! Oh Glory Halleluiah – it must have been fun though.'

'Not at the time, Libby. Well, all right. I've got a sense of humour, I hope and I can see those two enjoying themselves enormously but............'

'So the Aunt is as bad as they say?'

'Worse. She thinks she is God and can rule the world. Full stop. I don't think even my brother could deal with her - oh, all right – it is funny!'

In the end they were all laughing, Glory Halleluiah having had enough whisky to soften her feelings.

At lunch next day Lew came in full of news.

'She's gone! The Aunt. Gone. Off last night. Insisted that West take her straight down to Nairobi. I saw Dad; Corn had already been there collecting furniture, full of victory won!'

'Already?' said Dar.

'How did they manage it, Lew?' asked Libby.

'Simple really. Well the night she arrived it was late so she just had a bowl of soup in her room. Next day, yesterday, they sent a tray in for her breakfast. Then it was lunch with Glory Halleluiah. So they pulled it off at dinner last night.'

'*How*?'

'They'd got a camp table as the dining table with pretty rough camp chairs and used all the camping kitchen gear. I told you: tin plates, shoddy cutlery, chipped glasses – all that. They'd got enamel soup plates ready on the table and soup was poured into those. Then they told the Aunt that they save on the washing up and use the same plates for the main course. She was pretty horrified but they said that, of course, they are cleaned between courses – *and then they called their big dogs up to the table to lick the plates!*'

'Oh, aren't they dreadful!'

'The Aunt was totally finished, said that she couldn't possibly live like that and tried to move her plate. It was stuck to the table! End of Aunt. She started to pack. Gave them no end of a wigging, I expect. West actually drove her over-night as far as Nakuru. They'll be in Nairobi now and that is that!'

'Brilliant – and awful, too,' laughed Libby.

'Inheritance lost?' asked Dar.

'That's pretty certain, you bet. But they don't seem to mind. They'd rather lose it than kowtow to that old fiend!'

After tea Corn arrived to remove his furniture from The Loop.

'We hear you did a good job – getting rid of your Aunt,' said Dar.

'Not bad. We simply – very politely – asked her to leave,' said Corn, utterly straight-faced. 'A pity. She'd not even signed our Visitors' Book.'

The Chemchem River descended the escarpment in a series of waterfalls, the lowest, on Frannie's land, being the biggest. As Frannie,

Sally and John, then Libby and Lew were growing up, they all swam in the pool at the bottom of the waterfall. It was a bit too shallow for grown-ups but was beautifully cool and shaded by a wide fringe of trees. Happy picnics were held there.

Frannie took Libby there one day for a splash before making love. It was a lovely place, a cool bowl with the river spilling over a rim to carry on its course. Frannie left his Land Rover well away from the river, dropped the blanket and led Libby to the pool. They stripped, Frannie throwing a stone into the pool first; a precaution to frighten off the big python that was often there. They played in the water, a pair of naked children again, showering each other. When they left Libby grabbed her clothes, put on her shoes and went back to the vehicle through the trees ahead of Frannie. He was slowly putting on his shoes - the one for the deformed foot always took a bit of time - when he noticed movement in the trees across the river. He threw a towel about himself quickly. Onto the opposite bank came a farming family from Chemchem, father, mother and three children complete with towels, bathing things and a huge picnic basket. They waved cheerfully to Frannie who managed to wave back. It was difficult to hear anything because of the waterfall but Frannie sensed what he thought was, 'Caught you having a swim, eh?' and he called back, 'I'm finished – help yourselves. Bye!' He quickly disappeared to find Libby.

'Libs, I can't believe myself. How careless! Of course all Chemchem are welcome to swim here. Ages ago Dad put a Notice at the Club welcoming everybody. He felt it selfish of us to keep such a good place to ourselves. Whew, Libs, we were nearly caught! Come on, we'd better move.'

This shook Frannie. Much more care was needed.

Frannie decided to concentrate on The Hammock – a completely safe place. There they could relax. The next time he and Libby went there he was smiling broadly, 'Safe here. A good harbour and to prove it I've brought something special.' After they stripped he produced two thin ribbons, one green and one red and promptly tied a bow on each of Libby's extended nipples. 'There you are – port and starboard. Ship safely home.'

'Frannie – you are totally idiotic,' laughed Libby, as he entered her. They were both laughing, Frannie quietening as his climax came then suddenly said, 'Oh Libs, I love you!' Libby didn't say anything. She wasn't sure whether it was a cry at the heat of the moment or true. He may not have known that he'd spoken out loud. They lay together longer than usual before chatting. Libby was very thoughtful. She felt that Frannie meant what he said. Oh, Frannie!

Two weeks later, coming back from Chemchem on a Friday morning just before lunch Libby was surprised to see Frannie's Land Rover at The Loop – they were supposed to be meeting that afternoon at The Hammock. Frannie was with Dar having a beer. 'Thought you'd never get back, Libs! I need you. Had a cri de coeur from George. One of his clients wants a lot of Vulturine Guinea-Fowl capes. I don't want to shoot them on my place and I know Dar doesn't like it here so it's a quick camping trip and I have no cook. That's you. Get your camping stuff and we'll go quickly.'

'Lunch first,' said Dar.

'Yes, thanks. Go on, Libs, get cracking!'

Libs was amazed. She off-loaded all the goods she'd brought from Chemchem and got her tent, camp bed and bedding from the camping store. 'What have you brought, Frannie – what about food?'

'Got it all, chop box, cooking gear, table, chairs, lamps, the lot. All you need is your tent, bed and that sort of thing.'

She stowed her items into the back of Frannie's vehicle that looked suspiciously empty; there was no sign of a table or chairs. What was he doing?

'We'll be two nights away – is that all right?' he said to Dar who replied, 'Of course. Have a good time and you might bring me a cape or two. I've got friends who make their own fishing flies.'

Immediately after lunch Frannie took Libby away, Lew being nowhere in sight; Libby knew he'd taken a packed lunch because he was moving a cattle boma, always a major job.

'Frannie! How dare you? We're off on our own!'

'No problem. Dar didn't turn a hair – natural that I'd come to you for help - we've camped enough times together!'

'Do you really need the capes?'

'Yes. That's true. One of George's clients fishes a lot in the States. The blue feathers from the Vulturines are great for fishing flies – Dar knew all about that. I'll get the Guinea-Fowl quickly. The point is that we've got time together, Libs. And the minute we get through the Elephant Gap off comes your bra!'

Libby was laughing. Always with Frannie she seemed to be laughing. He was constantly surprising her. His sex drive, capacity, inventiveness was something special, she thought. It wasn't just exciting sexually – it was enormous fun.

Not far beyond the Elephant Gap Frannie relieved her of her both her blouse and her bra.

'That's better,' he said.

'But it's pretty uncomfortable in a bouncy Land Rover!'

'You drive.'

'That won't help!'

'Oh yes, it will – get in.'

Topless, Libby got into the driving seat and Frannie slipped into the seat behind her, leaned over and firmly held each boob. 'I'm your human bra – drive on. You're fully supported now.' Libby, helpless with laughter, started the vehicle and set off along the indistinct track.

It was too much for her. She stopped. Her nipples were extended fully and solid with longing for sex. He knew. They made love, half dressed, leaning against the vehicle.

Libby was a bit shaken. 'Frannie! Wow! I think you need something to calm you down!' She'd never felt him so recklessly determined. He was grinning.

'Nonsense. I've only just started. You wait, my girl!'

They put up Frannie's tent only and threw their mattresses onto the groundsheet. There was precious little cooking equipment, no table, no chairs and not much food. 'We won't need much. This is a horizontal weekend.'

'I'll just get the Guinea Fowl; you make tea. I'll be back quickly.'

'It'll take time to get the birds – what was it? Twenty?'

'Not this time. Libs, I've spent all my life as a decent, upright, law-abiding citizen. Now I'm having a change. I'm going to shoot a flock on the ground! Get the kettle on. There's a flock just a hundred yards back. I'll be quick.'

He came back in a remarkably short time with twenty two Vulturine Guinea Fowl that he quickly disembowelled. 'I'll deal with the capes later,' he said, flinging the birds into the Land Rover.

'Frannie! And you an Honorary Game Warden!'

'Yes, well – I'd got to get twenty so just this once it isn't going to matter whether I got them on the ground or in the air. Come on, Libs, this is our weekend together, probably the only one we'll ever have. Enjoy it!'

Increasingly Libby was seeing a different Frannie to the view he presented to the rest of the world. He was light-hearted, incredibly energetic, sexually amazing and totally dominant. His more usual persona of the conscientious, reliable, quiet, serious rancher was quite another thing. Libby found it fascinating, stimulating and a special happiness to see the uninhibited Frannie. She couldn't believe that they were to spend two whole nights together.

Frannie had put the tent in a secluded spot; not even a hunting safari would find them. He'd even dragged a tree branch to confuse and remove the tracks of his vehicle. The place was an almost round clearing in a small patch of forest that Frannie obviously knew well. It was set quite a way back from the river but Frannie had two water containers that he'd brought from home and they could walk to the river to wash, always being conscious of the nearness of crocodiles. Food was a secondary thought, sex uppermost – in between sleeping. It was a completely abandoned time, Frannie being more and more extraordinary and adventurous. 'Wow,' she said, 'Lust!' Quietly he murmured, 'No, not that,' and each time he reached his climax he repeated, 'Libs, I love you.' She never said anything, now certain that he had no idea that he was talking out loud, but she felt for him greatly.

There was a lot of idle chatter, Frannie's quirky mind often producing oddments.

'Did you know that Darwin never wrote 'survival of the fittest'?'

'I thought he did.'

'No, what he really wrote was that those most fitted to an environment would survive.'

'Oh, like a nice plump polar bear will survive the ice better than a skinny monkey?'

'Exactly.'

It was a weekend beyond Libby's dreams. Frannie and she were entangled, if not sexually then physically most of the time. They forgot meals, lived on drinks and laughed and laughed. Libby recognised that ever since she and Frannie had been together she had learnt to laugh in a free way.

'So this is a dirty weekend?'

'Good gracious no! I'm perfectly clean and so are you. Whatever next, girl!'

Libby was carefully feeling every vertebra down Frannie's spine, gently tickling him.

'If I was a cat I'd purr,' he said, intent as he was on Libby's left buttock. 'Here you are all lovely and rounded while we men have knobbly muscle – unfair!' They were utterly content with any physical contact – exploring each other, giving each other great pleasure.

'What are you doing now, Frannie?'

'It's called buttock biting.'

'Frannie you are truly mad.'

'Too few people do this, I guess,' said Frannie. 'It's so important. We automatically touch and tickle our cats and dogs but do we do it to people?'

'Well, it is a bit – what's the word – intimate, isn't it?'

Frannie laughed, 'You could say that.'

Finally and reluctantly they packed up quietly, not saying anything at all, slowly winding down. The whole time in camp had held a magical quality that neither could express but both felt deeply. Somehow, with no words, they communicated this feeling to each other. Libby had never before felt so close to Frannie's spirit. Once they were in Frannie's Land Rover and driving back the spell started to collapse.

On the way back Libby sighed, 'I suppose we've got to face reality again.'

'We've just had reality.'

Libby looked at Frannie but he was concentrating on the track ahead. Libby wondered; he was often too deep for her.

They drove quietly. Once through the Elephant Gap, across the ford and onto a better track, Frannie suddenly quoted:

'Then since we mortal lovers are,

Ask not how long our love will last;

But while it does, let us take care

Each minute be with pleasure passed:

Were it not madness to deny

To live because we're sure to die?'

In silence they continued their journey.

Frannie was correct. No-one thought it in the least odd that Libby should have been away with him for two nights. It passed unnoticed.

CHAPTER 23

There were more camping trips including Lew and sometimes also with Nzioka and Janet, times of decorum and great enjoyment. Suddenly another camp became a necessity and Dar agreed to release Lew for a weekend when he should have been on duty. The Chemchem Game Warden asked Frannie to deal with a damaged elephant that was reported to be in the country north of The Loop. Lew had not yet shot an elephant although he held a licence and Frannie felt that this was a good opportunity. Nzioka must be with them and Libby was, again, to be cook; Janet was on duty.

All the Backlanders felt that elephant s were special. They were left alone. In any case elephants were constantly on the move and rarely caused problems beyond breaking fences. Even Frannie rarely shot elephants. He'd been with clients who wanted tusks but it was one bit of hunting that he did not enjoy. Elephants? They were too intelligent, far too special. But Frannie was happy to shoot an animal in pain, beyond recovery, and it was reported that the damaged elephant had a snare on a hind foot and was dragging something.

With both Frannie's and Lew's vehicles this time, they set up camp in their usual place on the slight rise near the river with Nzioka's tent a discreet distance away. He cooked for himself, always doing well on safari when he had rations provided and plenty of meat. Both he and Frannie were somewhat dubious about their chances of finding the animal.

'He's probably thirty miles away by now – even with a bad leg he'll be moving. You know how they travel. We can only try.'

The evening they arrived the men left Libby to sort out the camp after tents were up, and they went on a search. There was no sign of elephants at all, let alone a damaged one. All the elephant dung they saw was days old ('Prehistoric,' said Frannie). With a stride of at least four feet, elephants could appear to be walking slowly whilst covering great distances. Libby made a simple supper; they ate and went to bed early. In camp they were always up by six in the morning when it became light.

Frannie, Lew and Nzioka went out looking for the animal before breakfast, again with no success. They decided, after breakfast, they would drive to the nearest Littet manyatta to see if any of the men there had news of the elephant. Libby would stay in camp; she never minded this, enjoying the bush and the peace.

The men were late getting back for lunch so Libby made herself a cup of coffee and was just lifting it to her mouth when immediately in front of her, but about two hundred yards away, limped a large bull elephant with great tusks. She could see that something was being dragged behind one leg – at a distance it looked like a block of concrete. Despite that, the elephant was managing to walk but flapping its ears and looking very distressed. There he was! And Frannie and Lew were miles away. There was no means of contacting them. It was utterly frustrating.

The elephant stopped from time to time but went on. He was so close! Libby was maddened. Suddenly she thought, why not? She leapt to Lew's Land Rover. No keys, nor were they in his tent. All right. Think again.

She found a cereal box, tore it up and wrote on the blank side, leaving the message prominently on the camp table, wedged with odd forks. What did she need? It was very hot – a hat. Then she grabbed a loo roll, thought for a second and took another and set off.

It was quite all right. Frannie had said the area was singularly empty of big game; he hadn't seen buffalo, lion or rhino about. Well, that happened from time to time. Lucky, thought Libby, who knew the dangers of the bush very well. What she really feared was a lone bull buffalo. She'd avoid thick bush, if she could, where one might be lurking.

Despite the burden on its hind leg, the elephant was keeping a fair pace, even with the occasional stop. He kept shaking his head, Libby saw the agony the poor beast must be feeling. She followed at a respectable distance, tying loo paper onto bushes as she went, each time looking back to be sure that the last piece could be seen. She was laying a trail of white flags, hoping that it would be clear for Frannie. Had the elephant not stopped so often she would have been unable to keep up; tying the loo paper was not always easy and finding the right place was difficult.

Libby disturbed a small herd of beautiful oryx who scattered. Their movement made no difference to the elephant; he was too far away. Libby tried to move faster but the ground was very uneven, full of scattered rocks, odd bush, small kopjes and small forest patches. Away – far ahead – Libby knew there was a very big forest and if the animal reached there she would lose him.

A huge leopard-tortoise was in her path; Libby jumped over it, frightening a family of warthog who ran away, tails erect. There were a few reticulated giraffe on her right, but far enough away not to matter. She knew perfectly well that each animal has its own invisible bubble inside which it feels secure but penetrate that – go too near- and the animal would be frightened and escape.

The going was very rough for a while and it was difficult for her to find reasonable places on which to hang the loo paper. She knew not to put it on the ground but the land was now more open and bush scarce; it meant diverting her path to find somewhere suitable. Even whistling-thorn trees were rare now. The country was opening out; she could see further and the elephant was gaining on her so she tried to move faster.

The land in front dropped gently. Looking back she could see just Africa; the camp had long since disappeared from view. Libby was sweating and feeling the pace, even though she was strong and healthy, and realising the difficulty of what she was attempting. She was very concerned that she'd lose the elephant in the difficulties of fixing the loo paper. Fortunately the elephant kept stopping and Libby managed to keep her distance behind it.

With no path she had to be careful in the parched grass with spreading wiry plants underfoot that could trip her. There were triangular, thorny seeds that got into shoes and were a menace; she stopped several times to remove them. Once she saw a puff adder. Fortunately it was crossing a bare patch of earth, the nest of harvester ants.

On she went. It was about an hour and a quarter into her chase that she saw them – the unexpected. From a patch of bush between the elephant and herself, well to the left, strolled a small pack of wild dog – hunting dog. They started to trot and would cross her path in front of her if they kept going. Libby almost panicked. Wild dog! Killers for the sake of killing! Would they ignore man? She didn't know enough about them, except that they would savage a herd of sheep mercilessly. They were rare at The Loop but she'd heard tales.

On her right was a small kopje, not high, perhaps twenty-five feet. She climbed it. From the top she had a clear view of the elephant and the wild dog. Behind her the far bush eclipsed the scene. Libby was about to go down when the pack of dogs – all nine of them - changed direction and turned towards the kopje.

Frannie and Lew learnt nothing at the manyatta but distributed some tobacco that the Littet men (and sometimes the women) loved. They drove quite slowly back to camp, enjoying the day, the space, the animals and birds of this low country – so very different to the Backlands.

It was Lew who spotted Libby's note.

'Frannie – look! Libby's seen the elephant. She's gone after it – leaving a trail!'

'WHAT – OH, MY GOD, she shouldn't have done that!' Frannie snatched the card but Libby had put no time on it.

'Lew, quick. We'll take my double, your .375 and Nzioka can carry my other gun. The double's really too heavy for you but it might be best. You'll get a hell of a kick from it. You know where the solids are. Water – get as much as you can. Get the first- aid tin. Binoculars. Pangas, axes – everything. Quick. Quick.'

Frannie collected a few items, chivvied Lew and Nzioka and they were off, leaving the camp to look after itself.

There was no track so the going was slow but the loo paper showed better from the height of the vehicle than on the ground and they made progress. Lew was driving Frannie's vehicle – the bigger of the two Land Rovers they used – concentrating on the difficult terrain, Frannie was peering ahead for Libby.

'White – about two o'clock. Yes, by that Selal (a form of Acacia tree) – mind that bloody hole!' Frannie could swear rigorously but used it seldom. Lew knew he was worried about Libby's safety; the swearing was an outlet.

Although they were quicker than Libby nevertheless it was slow going. They lost the trail once and had to get out of the vehicle to find the paper that had fallen from its perch. Eventually they came to the edge where the country dropped and there was a wide sweep of land below them.

'The elephant – look – down there.'

'And Libby – oh, thank God – she's on that rock – go for her, Lew. Go straight now if you can.'

Libby was frozen. She didn't know whether to crouch, lie down, stand up – anything. Would the wild dog find her anyway? She stood, staring at them as they trotted towards her. They stopped – all gathering at something on the ground, seemed to be interested for a moment, then carried on again. Big, handsome dogs, patched dramatically with black, brown, yellow and white, with big ears, they were ruthless killers, often eating their prey before it died. They were a terrifying sight, trotting determinedly towards the kopje. Libby just stood. The world stopped.

'She must hear the Land Rover?'

Libby, they could see, was staring at something beyond their vision. Suddenly she heard the vehicle, turned round, waved and pointed to something in front of her.

'Drive round, Lew, there's something there.'

As they got close to the kopje they saw the wild dogs. The dogs stopped, so did the Land Rover.

'Lew, frighten them off with the vehicle. I'll get Libby – she'll be scared silly.' Frannie went to the kopje as quickly as he could. Libby was frozen in position but crumpled when Frannie was near. 'Frannie, I was so frightened.'

He was very harsh. 'Damn silly of you to go after the elephant. Idiot! Lots of things could have gone wrong. Never wander through the bush like that.' He was shouting. This was a different Frannie, he was almost cruel with his voice. 'Come on. Get into the Land Rover – quick – we've seen the elephant.' He escorted her down but never touched her; Libby had tears welling. She sat in the back of the Land Rover, drying her eyes and feeling very small. No-one had thanked her for following the animal and Frannie had been downright hurtful. The men were ignoring her, concentrating on the elephant. It was still standing, close to the edge of a large patch of bush. Lew was driving to Frannie's instructions.

'Lew, stop now. I'll take the .375. Go for a brain shot if you can – otherwise heart. I'll cover if necessary. No wind. Try from the right – he'll probably go into that bush when he moves. Get as close as you can. Go on.'

Libby felt she might well not have existed. The men went off. From the safety of the vehicle Libby could see them moving with great caution through the bush, using every bit of cover possible. Why hadn't Frannie hugged her – realised her fear – thanked her for following the elephant? Nothing. Libby felt miserable.

Lew, followed by Frannie and Nzioka, was making a semicircle right; he was going apparently slowly but making ground. The elephant was absolutely still but Libby expected him to move at any moment. As the stalk went on her feelings were overtaken by watching the three men, such experts in the bush, Frannie bending, concealing his great height; Lew and Nzioka both short. Lew was moving very well in the bush, very carefully yet not too slow.

The elephant still stood.

Lew got into position. He'd got the elephant sideways on. A brain shot. Aim just behind the eye; between the eye and the ear hole. Hold the rifle steady. Stand firm. Breath gently. Squeeze the trigger. The double gun gave Lew quite a recoil but there was no other shot.

'Well done, Lew. Very good shot. Slap into the brain. Wait a moment just in case he's only concussed. Are you all right? You'll be bruised. Never mind.' (Lew wasn't bruised. Frannie had underestimated Lew's strength and grasp of the heavy gun.)

'O.K. Let's go and have a look at him.'

They walked cautiously to the fallen elephant and saw the awful, open wound on the leg with the wire deeply biting into the flesh; bone was exposed. The wire was attached to a block of concrete like a big building stone.

'It's a steel hawser. Some bastard's done this deliberately. Poor bugger,' said Frannie looking at the elephant. 'Lew, you've got really good tusks – about ninety pounders. Not bad on your very first elephant licence. Worth a bit. Let's get on with it. Tools in the car. Go back and fetch the Land Rover.'

With axes and sharp pangas they started to cut out the tusks, a major job in the hot sun. It seemed to take hours. Libby could do very little but she grabbed a panga and tried to help. 'Cut up there, open that flesh.'

Most fortuitously the elephant had fallen in a position where they could work on both tusks simultaneously although they had to dig into the earth to make space to get at the bottom tusk. Libby joined Nzioka to whom this was a familiar task; Frannie and Lew were working on the more difficult tusk underneath, both having stripped off their shirts and were sweating freely.

Apparently out of no-where half a dozen Littet tribesmen arrived, wearing even less than Frannie and Lew.

Frannie straightened up and spoke to them in their own language. They stood politely watching Lew, Nzioka and Libby working on the carcase. Frannie told them yes, they could have the meat – or most of it – but first help the Bwana Fupi with the lower tusk (the top one was nearly out). The Littet knew all about hunting; they'd often been used as extras on safaris and they knew Bwana Chopi (the lame Bwana) well. They'd only seen Bwana Fupi (the short Bwana) but if he was with Bwana Chopi then he was a proper Bwana. The Africans set to; they were better than Frannie or Lew, Libby could see. The tusks were beautifully curved, long and very heavy.

'They're going to be the devil to carry,' said Frannie.

With the help of the Littet, the tusks, with bloody ends, were put into the Land Rover, sticking out at the back. Thank goodness, thought Frannie, we brought two vehicles; there was no big Bedford hunting lorry to help.

Nzioka cut some meat for himself after the Littet had opened the stomach and then they left the Littet to it. Nzioka had done the time-honoured thing and threaded his bits of meat onto a stick that he'd de-barked. 'We don't need any meat, do we?' Lew asked, but they had brought plenty of food with them.

'We'd better take that hawser with us. Show the Game Warden. Not the concrete – can you untie it?' It took all of Lew's and Nzioka's strength to get the hawser off the block but it was carefully coiled and put into the vehicle. 'Can't leave it here. Some other bugger'd use it as a snare.'

'Let's go. The Littet will get all the meat faster than lightning.'

This time Frannie drove back to camp, very slowly across the uneven land; they arrived just as the first stars were winking. It had been a very long day and all they'd had was water.

Libby had been extremely subdued. In a way she understood why Frannie had ignored her; he had a job to do, but the thought didn't help her. She'd been foolhardy, perhaps, to go after the elephant, frightened stupid by the wild dog, but she did get them the animal in the end, there were a pair of marvellous tusks to show for it and the poor creature was out of pain at last.

Frannie and Lew carefully eased the tusks out of the vehicle.

'Libs – beer, please.' Frannie called and she silently obeyed. Both Frannie and Lew drank the beer straight off and then grinned at each other. 'Well done, Lew,' said Frannie again as he washed his filthy hands in the camp basin.

'I'm going down to the river for a proper wash,' said Lew, grabbing his kit.

The river was only a few yards below them, perfectly visible; Frannie motioned Libs to come with him behind the big Land Rover where he took her in his arms. 'You've been brilliant, Libs – it's all right – but don't do it again.' He held her tightly for a minute and kissed the top of her head, then let her go and smiled at her. 'Pretty brave, you are!' and Libby was happy again.

Comforted, Libby made supper.

Just before midnight Lew woke up needing a pee; he'd had more beers than usual in celebration of his first – and excellent – elephant. Libby's tent was between the two men; not wanting to wake her up Lew moved quietly to unlace his tent – and stopped. Through the crack he saw, in clear moonlight, the backs of Frannie and Libby sitting on a log. Both wore kikois, Libby's as a sarong. Frannie had his arm round Libby and she had her head on his shoulder.

Lew withdrew. Well, well. Actually he thought Frannie had been hard on Libby who'd obviously been very scared but she had followed the elephant – quite a brave act. Was he making up for it now? Or was there something else?

Lew still needed to pee. He quietly lay down again and got up as noisily as he could, knocking a tent pole and saying a quiet, 'Damn.' Then he unlaced the tent as slowly as possible from the bottom up.

Frannie and Libby had disappeared.

Only four weeks after this, the Sunday before the big Boran Cattle Show and Sale for which everyone was preparing feverishly, Frannie and Libby had enjoyed an afternoon together up at The Hammock. It had been an especially successful time; they didn't always reach their climax together but they had then – and Frannie, at his peak, had again said that he loved her, words ignored by Libby as usual. They were later than normal, chatting in a desultory fashion and Frannie was due to visit a boma on his way home so it was after six in the evening when he drove into his yard to find Dar's Land Rover parked there.

Dar was having a drink with Mumps.

'Oh, there you are. Now you can help,' said Mumps.

'Evening, Dar, what's the problem?' said Frannie, helping himself to a drink.

'Libby.'

Frannie froze for a moment. He rather slowly added soda water to his whisky.

'Go on.'

'Bobby came to see me this afternoon – he'd phoned, wanted to see me privately. Libby'd said she'd be out. Bobby wanted to see me without Libby. His divorce has come through and he wanted to ask me if I thought – if I'd mind – with what had gone on before – if he could approach Libby again. It was difficult for him to come out with all that, I must say. Decent of him to come to me, really.'

'Yes.'

'What disturbs me is that for months I thought that Libby was seeing Bobby. She's been out a lot, she's been much happier and I knew his divorce was on the way so I thought they were being together – quietly and so on. But if she's been seeing someone, it hasn't been Bobby! So who?'

Frannie ignored the last bit.

'What did you say to Bobby?'

'That he was welcome to see her as far I'm concerned. I didn't mention what I thought – and perhaps she hasn't got another boy-friend – I don't know. She doesn't say much. If only Edith were alive she would have, I expect.'

'So?'

Mumps interrupted, 'So Dar wonders if you know about a boyfriend – who it is – if it's serious – if Bobby has a chance. You see a lot of Libby. Has she told you? Have you seen her with anyone?'

Frannie stood impassive for a moment. He'd known all along the crunch would come. It had arrived. The end. He'd enjoyed over a year with Libby and hoped for at least another year. This was unexpectedly quick. Bloody hell. Face it.

'Dar,' he said, turning to him. 'I think you needn't worry about Libby. Bobby will, no doubt, do his stuff.'

'But who has she been seeing?' That was Mumps again.

'Libby's an adult. That's her business, not yours.'

'You do know! Frannie, don't be so infuriating – tell Dar.'

Frannie looked at Dar again.

'I can't break Libby's confidence, can I? Dar, it's all right. She's come to no harm. Excuse me, I must wash,' Frannie took his drink out of the room.

'Of course she doesn't have to tell me,' said Dar, rising. 'Well – up to Bobby. Frannie's right, Mumps, she's an adult, can do what she likes.'

Frannie turned on the hot tap of the bath, still holding his whisky. The water was steaming hot. He stared at the heat of it for several seconds, downed his whisky in one gulp and tasted nothing of it.

CHAPTER 24

Frannie spent the night thinking deeply and sadly. It was all over; he knew it had to come but he certainly didn't want it to end. Bobby. The thought of Bobby with Libs almost made him physically sick. He just couldn't understand how Libs could love a chap like that. Libs – of all people – and after what Bobby had done to her! He didn't sleep much, knowing that he'd got to get it over quickly and finally. After the early morning dipping rounds he phoned The Loop and, luckily, got Libby.

'Got to see you, Libs, as soon as possible. Picnic Site.'

'What – now? This morning?'

'Yes please.'

'Give me half an hour and I'll come.'

Frannie had not sounded good. Libby was thoughtful for a moment and then went into the kitchen, gave orders to the staff, collected some items for herself and told Dar that she'd be out for the morning. Dar had just come in for breakfast and Lew was still eating, saying that he'd got to go back to the furthest dip to mend a crush.

Frannie was waiting for her on the log in the shade. He looked exactly how he felt – tired, grim and braced for bad news; at least bad news for himself.

'Libs, come and sit. Must talk.'

'Go on, Frannie,' he hadn't touched her at all. She knew it was bad.

He told her unemotionally, staring at the ground.

'After I left you, I got home to find Dar with Mumps. He'd been looking for me. What's happened is that Bobby went to see him yesterday. He's got his divorce and wanted to ask Dar if he felt he could see you again. Surprisingly Dar has noticed that you've been out a lot and guessed you'd be seeing some chap and assumed it would be Bobby – because the divorce was on the way. Of course Bobby showed him that it wasn't him. So Dar asked if I knew who you've been seeing. Of course I said nothing.'

Libby said nothing as well.

'There you are, Libs, Bobby's heading for you. We both knew we'd got to stop so this is it. Libs, you know you came to me for help but you must know what a huge help it has been for me, too. You've given me my manhood – very special indeed. Thanks a million. Lucky Bobby!'

Still Libby said nothing. He glanced at her. No obvious reaction.

'What I'll do, what I think is best, over your wedding, if you'll tell me the date quickly – I'll arrange to go on a course in South Africa for a few months. I've always wanted to learn about sheep there in case I ever do Merinos here. Anyway, I'll go – course or not. That will save you any embarrassment. And by the time I get back you'll be on Bobby's farm and we'll hardly see each other.'

There was still no reaction from Libby.

'I know how you have always felt about Bobby so, Libs, I wish you the very best and many, many thanks. It's been great.' He put out his hand and held hers.

Still she said nothing.

Suddenly she slipped his hand and got up, walking to her vehicle.

Frannie watched, knowing that she was going out of his life for ever. She was walking with grace, her hair shining. Oh Libs!

But she didn't get into her vehicle. She opened the passenger door and reached for a kikapu, bringing it back to Frannie. She took out a thermos, some mugs, other things.

In a normal voice she said, 'Frannie, I don't think you've had breakfast?' He nodded.

'Coffee, and all I could do in a hurry was bacon sandwiches; that do?'

Again he nodded and she gave him a mug of coffee and a packet of sandwiches and poured a mug for herself.

'Go on. Eat.' She drank her coffee.

They were quiet, Frannie eating mechanically.

Suddenly she sighed.

'Oh, Frannie, if only this could have waited a few weeks more!'

He couldn't answer. She went on. 'I want to say something too. Listen. Do you remember when you gave me that talking to – after Bobby ditched me?'

'Vividly.'

'It was pretty vivid for me, too. No-one had ever spoken to me like that before. I was shattered, but I listened. I suppose that really, underneath, I knew I was being unreasonable. What you said to me was true. Deep down I knew that. And you were genuinely trying to help me. You showed that, didn't you?'

'I hope so.'

'And you've helped a lot ever since. Oh, Frannie, I had a lot of thinking to do! You said what I felt for Bobby was infatuation and one day I'd learn what love was all about – that it didn't snatch, it was patient, deep – not superficial. Remember?'

'Yes.'

'In time – and it took time – I did look at what I really felt about Bobby – and it was infatuation. He'd bowled me over so fast I'd been thrilled – but, to be honest, I didn't really know him. When he walked out on me it hurt – oh, so much – but probably my pride most of all. I did finally see that it would never have worked with Bobby. He was impetuous, a surface person, and only a boy. I wanted someone more manly, properly mature....'

Frannie was staring into his mug.

Libby was looking at his intense face.

'You said that one day I'd learn about love – not quickly but slowly and deeply. Well I did. I found a man I love beyond anything I can say.'

Frannie looked at her briefly and then back at his coffee mug. Libby was serious.

'He's so special to me. But there's a problem.'

Quickly Frannie said, 'He's married already?'

'No, Frannie, nothing like that. He's free. No. His problem is that he's got a mother who's indoctrinated him – brain-washed him since he was a tiny boy – that he can't marry because he has a very minor impediment – a club foot!'

'Libs!' Frannie was so startled that he dropped the mug and gazed at Libby who was facing him with great seriousness.

'I had to think what to do carefully because if I'd come straight out with it you'd have done exactly what you have just done – said no, no, and sent me on to other men. That indoctrination has been far too deep. You've never queried it – and to be honest none of us in the Backlands have done either. It wasn't until I knew I loved you that I saw how ridiculous it is. So – Frannie I had to think of something. You certainly can marry – and should. You need a home, wife, children, like any other man. This indoctrination has been criminally deep for you.'

Frannie was looking at her as if he'd never seen her before.

'I pretended I was unsure of sex to get you to make love to me. But, Frannie, I was cheating on you! Not at first. I wanted to see how you felt about me and I felt – feel – that you do like me.' Libby was cautiously choosing her words. 'I think you do, so I started. I've been trying to get pregnant to show you that I really do love you, am prepared to have your children and give you a proper home and love. Oh, Frannie, I think I've done it but it hasn't been easy – we've not been able to get together at the right times. But I think I'm pregnant now – I need a few more weeks to be sure. Frannie, your foot doesn't matter a bit!'

Frannie was staring at her, unable to take it in. His face was a blank, like a marble bust. Suddenly all was quiet, not even any sounds of nature around them.

'Oh, God, Frannie, I've done absolutely the wrong thing? You don't really want me? I'll go south – Rhodesia – South Africa – have the child and get it adopted. I'm so sorry.'

The words came in a great hurry and tears flooded.

In an instant he bestrode the log, grabbed her into his arms and she sobbed on his shoulder. Tears always came easily to Libby and this time it was as if they were uncontrollable. He found a handkerchief that she couldn't use because he was holding her too tightly.

Suddenly he was talking into her hair, 'Libs, it's all right. It's all right,' with a myriad thoughts racing through his brain.

He started rocking her like a baby, still she wept. All the time he was repeating, 'It's all right. It's all right.'

After a very long time she slowly contained her tears, used the handkerchief but was still. He was holding even more tightly. 'It's all right. It's all right.' Then they were both quiet. He rocked her again very gently.

A Martial eagle soared above them, making a shadow across the ground in front of them. Only Frannie could see it but he looked up. The bird was huge, contemptuous of the world around. A long time passed.

They sat, both exhausted, bemused and bereft of speech.

Eventually Frannie kissed her hair and whispered, 'Are you all right, Libs?' and she nodded.

'Now listen. I've got three serious questions I must ask you. No, don't move, stay where you are. Will you answer?'

Libby nodded apprehensively.

'First – can you make steamed pudding?'

This was not what she expected. She shot up.

'Yes, of course I can!'

'Good. Get back on my shoulder, that's better. Mumps will never have them and I love them. Next question - can you turn collars?'

This time a much happier Libby was ready.

'I do it all the time for Dar. He loves his shirts and frays the collars faster than Stirling Moss can drive!'

'Good – getting better. Now – last question. Miss Winchester –

will you marry me?'

Libby just clung to him in relief. She shed a few tears but, this time, of happiness. He still held her. She looked up and he was smiling.

Suddenly he pulled her and they stood up. He wiped the new tears from her cheeks with his thumbs, then kissed her very gently and they stood together, just hugging each other.

'Oh, Libs, I've loved you for so long.' She kissed his chin, and the whole world shone.

He pulled her to the log again. 'Libs, I've got to do a bit of thinking. This is all a bit sudden. How far are you on with the pregnancy do you think?'

'I've only missed one period – but I'm so regular – so maybe three weeks – but I need a bit longer to be sure. I do feel different – if that means anything.'

'Fine. You're going to have a premature baby. We'll get married as quickly as possible. We'll do it. Don't worry, Libs. Just let me think.'

They sat quietly again with Libby in his arms.

'Libs, what you said about me being brain-washed - it's all true! I can't believe that I accepted it all myself! I hope I'm mildly intelligent but I've simply accepted that I can't marry – all these years! It's been a fact of life for me – I'm different so I can't marry! How could I not have seen through it all? It was Mumps, of course. It's been drummed into me since I was a tiny child – you can't marry, you can't marry. Thinking about it, Dad never said anything and I think Mumps did all this when he wasn't around. Oh, Libs!'

'Frannie look at Russia and the Russians. You can persuade people into anything if you say something often enough! Dangerous isn't it?'

'Lethal.' They were quiet again for a moment.

'Libs, if this isn't the most awful pun, I feel totally liberated now. Free from Mumps. I've always had the feeling that, however she loathes me, I must look after her. Not now! That's gone.'

'I think she might have done this to you so that if anything happened to your father you would be there ready to take care of her.'

'Absolutely right. I can't get over my stupidity in not seeing through it!'

'Millions and millions of Russians are in the same boat!' He smiled and kissed her hair again.

'Libs, if it's a boy he's got to be called Frank.'

'Oh yes. A girl?

'Something simple that can't be shortened easily – Mary, Ann, Ruth, Jane, Jean - a name like that.'

'Fine. Let's wait until we see what comes.'

'I'll leave Mumps in the house and build one for us. We'll get right away from her. It'll take time but we can camp until I've done it. Is that all right?'

'Lovely.'

'Libs, I've loved you for such a time. I can't believe what you've done for me. Thank you. Thank you. We'll be O.K.'

Time passed again. Frannie had a jumble of thoughts now channelling into essentially practical matters.

Eventually he said, 'Libs, I think this is how we handle it......' and he told her at length.

The crush that Lew went to repair turned out to be only a case of loose posts and that was dealt with swiftly. He decided to look at the grass on the north west of the ranch – an area he'd been holding in reserve until other grazing was used up. It was a typical, clear, sunny Backlands day that he loved. This morning he had time; he'd dealt with the bulls that he was preparing for the show earlier. Monday to-day; he thought they'd look very good by the time they went to the Showground on Wednesday, his staff were grooming them hard. It was pleasant not to be rushed. For a change there were no major dramas to be handled. Yes, the grass was coming on but he'd not use it yet.

That decided, he turned south and suddenly though that he had time to do something he'd always wanted. He'd climb the Picnic Site kopje. It didn't look difficult from the north end. The long kopje must offer wonderful views. He'd be able to see way into Venture across the river.

The climb was easy. He disturbed a few Agama lizards basking in the sun and finally reached the highest point. There, below, were Frannie and Libby clasped together in a most amorous embrace. Lew slithered backwards, out of view. He was embarrassed and also fascinated. The picture of Frannie and Libby sitting together at camp was still very fresh. Frannie and Libby! He had to get his mind round that – adjust his thoughts. Frannie and Libby! Back in the Land Rover he said to himself firmly, 'And why not?'

As he drove back to the house he passed the short side track that led to the Picnic Site. Suddenly he realised that they would hear the vehicle passing, know someone might have seen them. He worried. Obviously they wanted to be very private; what should he do?

Frannie and Libby had been together for a full three hours, thrashing out everything, Frannie looking better and better as the time went on. He was gathering strength, Libby could feel it. They were both now calm, happy, thrilled at the certainty of a future together. Of the two Frannie was possibly the most moved and deeply content. At last he'd got what he wanted.

'Do you realise, Libs, in one morning I seem to have acquired – or am about to acquire – one wife and the start of a family! Not bad for a day's work is it?' He was back to being the strong male. 'How about making sure you are pregnant?' and he grinned at her. 'You wait 'til we're married – you'll never have a moment's peace from me.'

'I can guess – the prize bull of Venture!'

'Come on, Libs, the fig tree.'

Libs arrived for lunch very late, just as Lew had finished so he slid away, grateful that he didn't have to face her. He was still embarrassed and thought that she and Frannie must guess that the vehicle that passed them was either his or Dar's. Libby looked perfectly normal, but a bit lighter, somehow. Lew went to his cottage for a while and then decided that he must get on with jobs around the office and yards; the main store where all the spares were kept, the food store (posho for the men and salt for the cattle), the workshop and the veterinary cupboard could all do with checking and tidying up. He got on with it.

It was early evening when Lew arrived at Venture. He saw Mumps who asked him to stay for dinner; not what Lew expected but Mumps was so seldom affable that he agreed.

She told him that Frannie was in the farm office so Lew went to where Frannie had built the room, a discreet distance from anywhere that Mumps frequented.

Frannie was sitting in his office, apparently doing nothing except staring into space with a bottle of whisky in front of him. He seemed very pleased to see Lew.

'You're manna from heaven, Lew, come in and have a drink.'

Lew preferred beer, Frannie knew. 'I'll get some beer – stay to dinner?'

'Mumps asked me.'

'Did she, by Jove – you're favoured.'

Drinks organised Lew said, quickly, to get it over, 'This morning, Frannie, I'd finished jobs and decided to climb the Picnic Site kopje – I'd never done it before – so I did – and you and Libby were on that log below. Well – I thought you'd better know that the vehicle that passed was me – and no one else.'

Lew found it surprisingly difficult to come out with that.

Frannie smiled broadly. He hadn't even heard a vehicle and he was extremely grateful that Lew had not been on the kopje later when he and Libby were under the fig tree below.

'Good of you, Lew. Now you can have a drink and congratulate me – she's going to marry me. How's that?'

For a second Lew was astonished. Frannie! Then he, too, grinned and put out his hand.

'Fantastic, Frannie!' and they shook hands.

'You didn't expect that, Lew did you? It's taken a long time to find out if she'd take me. I'm damned lucky! But, Lew, I need some help…..'

They talked until Mumps sent a servant to call them for dinner and then, at dinner, they were both remarkably well behaved, concentrating on Mumps so that they didn't spill any beans. Unaware of the background, Mumps found a much better atmosphere than normal and was as pleasant as she could be.

Lew `phoned The Loop to say he'd not be back for dinner. Dar and Libby had a companionable meal together, Dar still worried and looking at Libby who looked extremely happy and glowing with health. He longed to ask her but restrained himself. Frannie was right; she was adult and has her own life.

Libby was sitting by him longing to tell him her news but Frannie had other plans. He'd been overflowing with ideas once he started, his brain in racing gear, thinking of the many facets of the short-term problem they had ahead. He'd get them married quickly and, although he didn't mention it to Libby, he knew that he had a cast-iron reason for marrying her in a hurry. At last Bobby could be useful. The fact that he was now after Libby would explain Frannie's haste – or so he hoped.

Libby was deeply asleep when, at midnight, she was woken by a light rattle in her room. It wasn't bats that sometimes flew in; there was a farm cat that had come to her room before now but he'd leap onto her bed so it wasn't the cat. She put on her torch and saw an envelope on the floor that had been tossed through the open window.

The letter explained how it got there.

Lew, wrote Frannie, was au fait with everything and would help and be discreet. Frannie outlined what Lew would do in the next few days. That much was on the page she looked at but there was a second sheet on which she found that Frannie's precise, spidery writing had covered the whole page with one sentence, repeated and repeated. Just three words.

She put the letter under her pillow and knew absolute happiness.

CHAPTER 25

'A *lorry* for Frannie's bulls? He's gone mad – cost a lot for that short distance!'

'He doesn't want to risk anything with them. He's got some really good bulls – two fantastic - and he's after the Championship, that's why. But some will walk,' Lew told Dar.

Between the Cooper's and the Twybitts' ranches there was a stock route up through the escarpment forest; a short cut to Chemchem that cattle used, but not possible for vehicles.

Dar's bulls were to walk that way on Wednesday to the Chemchem showground, ready for the big Boran Bull Show and Sale. Judging would be all day Thursday and also on Friday morning. Prize giving was on Friday afternoon and then the Sale would take place on Saturday, by which time all prospective purchasers would have had good time to study the bulls.

It was Tuesday and the day opened strangely for Mumps when she found a note from Frannie at her breakfast place:

Been called away. Back Wednesday evening if all well. Lew will come over and tell Roberto what to do. F.

'Frannie's had to go away for a couple of days. I promised I'd go over and see to his bulls – O.K.?' Lew asked Dar who agreed absentmindedly, still amazed at Frannie bothering to hire a lorry when the bulls could easily walk.

Lew knew perfectly well that Frannie was spending a lot more money than just on a lorry; he'd hired a small aeroplane for a flight from Chemchem to Nairobi and back – unheard of! But Lew knew why. Lew was enjoying being part of Frannie's plan and was putting himself into it wholeheartedly, extra work or not. He'd managed to say to Libs: 'So glad, Libs – he's a lucky chap,' and had been amazed at her obvious joy; she'd actually kissed him on the cheek!

The Chemchem showground was slightly further out of town than the Club, a well designed place with one big show-ring and several small ones, the smaller even had trees growing in the centre to the delight of Judges who appreciated the shade. The 'stabling' – separate boxes - was in extensive lines with attractive reed thatching. Years before grass was used for thatching but an animal knocked down one end of the boxes and some cows started to eat the thatch. The sisal string holding the thatch killed three cows – blocking the intestines - so reeds were rapidly substituted; reeds could be twisted, needing no string. At all the shows the younger Europeans sometimes slept in unused boxes in order to keep an eye on their charges. Frannie and Lew had often shared a bull box with a pile of hay bales (that gave some privacy). There were long, hostel-like buildings for the Africans.

In 1958 Frank was showing and buying, the first time for years. Glory Halleluiah was only going to buy, Corn and West were showing and buying as were Dar and Frannie. The standard of Boran cattle in the Backlands was high, although Glory Halleluiah never bothered to show. Dar, Frank, Frannie, Corn and West were all good cattle men and Lew was as good as his elders. Selling cattle was their business; it paid to have the best possible animals and make sure that Kenya knew it.

'Frannie's bulls had better be good to warrant a lorry.'

'Wait `til you see them, Dar, they're good – better than anything we've got this year and ours are not a bad lot.'

That was true. Of The Loop's bulls to show and sell, at least six were easily in the very good to outstanding class, Dar well knew. If Frannie had something better than that it would be worth seeing.

Frannie did get back safely on Wednesday evening but declined to tell his mother why he'd disappeared or where he'd gone. 'Business,' he said, laconically, and she could get no more out of him.

The Show opened promptly on Thursday morning. There were a considerable variety of classes for the bulls, mainly on age selection but very limited age ranges so that all the bulls could be studied carefully; potential buyers as well as the Judges were scrutinizing them. It all took time. The two Judges were experienced men, one from Kenya and the other from Southern Rhodesia. They wore white coat overalls and felt hats; they were extremely conscientious and business-like. Each bull was given a really good examination. From the very first class that entered the ring it was obvious that the farmers – excellent judges of cattle themselves – approved the Judges' choice so the main hurdle was over; if the farmers felt the Judges were wrong there was a great deal of grumbling and a bad Show and Sale. The Chemchem Show started well.

Early on two of The Loops's bulls got 1sts, then one of Frannie's – 'Not the best, wait,' hissed Lew to Dar. Odd 2nds and 3rds came the way of the Backlands until the more serious, senior classes came into view, by which time it was Friday morning. When one of Frannie's really good bulls appeared there was a trickle of clapping – never heard of before at a Show. The Judges agreed; the bull was an easy winner. The next of Venture's bulls, the best, produced even better applause and was an equally easy winner of his class. Frannie was obviously delighted.

Glory Halleluiah was watching with Mumps.

'I think he's bred stock carefully for years to get those,' admired Glory Halleluiah.

Mumps was not impressed.

'Spends too much time on the ranch. The house could do with some attention,' meaning that she could.

The Championship class was now to be judged. All the first prize winners were stripped of their rosettes and led into the ring again. It was a brave show; majestic, slow moving power walking steadily round the ring. Frannie's men led his three bulls that had first prizes; they were experts at the showing game, knew how to give the Judges the best view. Frannie himself was watching with Dar, Libby, Madge, Mumps and West. Lew, Frank and Corn were somewhere behind the scenes. The show-ring was now quiet; this was the important time; the Champion and Reserve Champion could expect high prices at the Sale; it was serious business.

This time the judging was more difficult; all the animals were outstandingly good; to decide the Champion was never easy at this stage. The bulls were kept moving round slowly, the Judges watching carefully and conferring from time to time. Then the judges pulled in two bulls – not Frannie's – and then another, also not Frannie's, and they inspected those three carefully. The procession went on. Frannie was clasping his hands, knuckles white, barely breathing, rigid. Libby saw this and could do nothing.

By the entrance to the ring Frank and Lew were equally amazed.

'They *can't* miss them – by far the best!' and just as Lew said that the Judges suddenly called Frannie's two best bulls into the centre, but hardly gave them a glance. The crowd was even quieter, wondering at this turn-around.

A lady helper came into the ring bearing the Champion sash and another for the Reserve Champion. Calmly the senior Judge – the Rhodesian man – went straight to Frannie's best bull with the Champion sash and gave the Reserve to his other bull. The Judges hadn't needed to look at Frannie's bulls again; they had just given the others a careful look-over to please the owners.

Frannie face was wonderful, Libs thought. He turned, suddenly kissed his mother, to her surprise, then Glory Halleluiah, Madge, Libby, and took Dar's offered hand.

'Frannie – you've worked hard for that. They are absolutely splendid. I've never had bulls like those.'

The two bulls, with their shining sashes swaying proudly on their solid bodies, led the winners' parade around the ring and out; the Judges' work was over.

The group from the Backlands were all talking together, delighted that Frannie had come to the fore at last. His father was a good cattleman but never went beyond fair-to- reasonable bulls; he was not interested in the Show-ring. Frannie had always wanted the best. He'd done it. Frannie, smiling, was a Frannie seldom seen.

'He looks so different, happy!' Madge saw.

Knowing Bobby's reason, Alec Dacre agreed that he should have Friday off to go to the Boran Show; the Dacre farms had milk herds, beef farming was for the ranchers. Bobby now wanted Libby so much that he was unable to talk to his parents about it but Alec had overheard his son making the arrangement to see Dar Winchester. For once the Dacre parents were tactful and never mentioned Libby; they both knew she was the right choice now, but were concerned that she might turn him down after what had happened.

For years Bobby had avoided seeing Libby, now he was desperate to do so. He had a variety of feelings; long ago he'd repented marrying Estelle – that had been a disaster from the beginning – and longed for the lovely, healthy, vivacious Libby. Bobby knew how much at fault he'd been, even allowing for his mother's part in his marriage. He secretly wondered if Libby would forgive his stupidity and marry him. Usually over-confident, for once he was unsure; Dar Winchester had been perfectly pleasant, but not over-friendly. Now he must tackle Libby. At the showground this was proving difficult.

He saw Libby early on; she was looking extremely good in her work clothes of slacks and a pale green shirt, helping Lew bring out the correct bulls for the classes. No good.

Bobby wandered off and saw her again with a group of Backlands people watching a class being judged and talking animatedly. No good.

In the long break after judging and before Prize-giving everyone dispersed for food, drink and other things. A bell would summon them ready for prize-giving.

During this break Bobby tried to find her again and glimpsed her in the box where Frannie and Lew were sleeping; she was with the two men and they were eating their lunch on their knees. No good. Later he missed Frannie and Libby disappearing in a vehicle together (they were going to the Gingerbread House to change).

Bobby decided that he must speak to her and would go to her immediately after Prize-giving, even if she was with other people.

Dar sat in a chair near the refreshment tent, chatting with a fellow Boran breeder from Ulu. They both agreed that Frannie's bulls were as near Boran perfection as possible. Dar had done well, and even Frank, not expecting it, had one rosette. Dar was content.

Suddenly, from no-where, he found Libby crouched beside his chair. She'd changed, put on a pretty frock, was wearing a little jewellery, her hair was loose and shining. Libby was smiling – really a mischievous smile, but sincere.

'Dar, darling, quick – I must tell you. Whatever happens to-day I love you and I always will.'

'*Chick* ...' but he guessed, 'Who is it?'

Her smile was even broader.

'You'll see. And you'll be surprised at first, I expect, but then think it the best possible thing to happen.' She went, not allowing anything more, leaving Dar stranded. He stood up. He wanted to know. Oh, Libs, why keep me in suspense?

Dar walked heavily to a place in the shade by the Prize-giving ring and sat. As so often seemed to happen, Glory Halleluiah appeared just at the right moment by his side.

'Libby,' he started, and then stopped.

'She's fine,' replied Glory Halleluiah who was the only one in the melee to have noticed that when Frannie was kissing everyone on the cheek in his delight at getting the Championship, he'd kissed Libby full on the lips and they'd had a special smile. She'd wondered for some time; she was now sure it was happening.

'I hope so,' replied Dar, then pulling himself together he said, 'Frannie's done extremely well, hasn't he?'

'Excellent. Yes, he knows how to wait, how to move at the right time. He's a special man, you know.'

They were interrupted by the arrival of Frank and Madge, Mumps, then Mario and Maria (Mario never showed but sometimes bought bulls) and, finally, Corn and West. Backlands United was going to give Frannie huge applause.

Dar's mind was working a little quicker than usual. If Libby had changed then the man would also have changed – be out of the normal farming wear that everyone used, even at some Shows. He looked round and saw nothing, except for Frannie, patiently standing by the entrance to the ring. Of course Frannie had put on his blazer to receive the main Cup. No-one else seemed at all different. Of Libby there was no sign.

The big silver cup on the table shone, the Judges were ready; a hush fell. The Senior Judge spoke very well, appreciative of the good running of the Show, the hospitality and welcome. Then he spoke about the bulls. The general standard was very high. In many classes it was difficult to judge the winners and several very good bulls had not had rosettes. He felt sure that buyers understood and that this would be reflected in good prices at the Sale to-morrow. But, he went on, in all his years of breeding and judging Borans, he had never seen anything to equal to-day's Champion and Reserve Champion, both belonging to the same owner. Applause. It gave him and his Co-Judge great pleasure to award the Championship to bull number 6702 bred by Mr. Houghton-Framlyn of The Backlands. More cheers and applause.

Frannie, his hair blown a bit, went to shake hands with the Judges and receive the big cup, its shine almost eclipsed by his smile. He lifted it high for the crowd; there was more applause and cheers; everyone liked Frannie and was delighted with his success. Then he stood, obviously waiting to speak. The noise died down.

'I can't tell you what to-day means to me,' he said in a clear, controlled, carrying voice. He meant everyone to hear, 'First I've got this cup – something I've wanted for a very long time and for which many thanks,' he said, turning to the Judges momentarily. 'And, secondly, but really first for me personally, to-day is a day of all days. To my delight – and thinking it would never happen – I have got engaged to be married.'

This was a huge surprise for the crowd, faces showed it, but quickly there was more clapping and cheers. Dar, his face transfixed with delight, stood up – almost jumped up. *Now* he knew. Unbelievable. The one thing he'd never thought of. He clapped as hard as he could as his eyes welled with tears.

'*He can't!*'

'He certainly can,' replied Glory Halleluiah and she clasped Mumps' arm with a strong grip.

'*No…!*'

'Yes, indeed. Mumps be glad for him,' Glory Halleluiah increased her grip.

Frannie was going to say more. Quiet was called.

'I've got a Special Licence in one pocket and an engagement ring in the other and I've put twelve cases of free beer in the bar for those who get there first – so celebrate!'

'Hey, Frannie – *who* is it?' someone called.

Frannie was enjoying himself and smiling very broadly.

'Didn't I tell you? I've only ever had one girl in my life. Where is she? Libs!' he called, turning round and she ran into his arms and they kissed in front of everybody. He slipped the ring on her left hand. The crowd were delighted. The gabble from the Backlanders was indescribable.

Frannie took Libs to the Judges where they shook hands and the two men gallantly gave Libby a kiss on the cheek, then holding the big cup in one hand and with his other around Libby, he steered her to the Backlanders.

Dar couldn't disguise his delight; his tears showed, shining on his smile-filled cheeks.

'Frannie!' and Frannie first clasped his hand and then, most uncharacteristically, they hugged each other.

Frannie turned quickly to Mumps while Libby was being embraced by Madge. 'Here you are, Mumps,' and he put the cup in her lap, 'and don't say that I don't bring you the best daughter-in-law because I do – the very best.'

'Frannie – you can't...' she started but the steely grip of Glory Halleluiah stopped her.

'You simply couldn't have done better, Frannie. Give this old lady a kiss,' which he managed to do despite her grip on Mumps.

Dar was then hugging Libby, both glowing with delight.

'I never guessed, Chick, but you're right – the very best thing to happen.'

'Of course, Dar, I don't really like her. I'm doing this to stop you grizzling about her being on the shelf – that's all.'

'Libby, what a lovely ring. It's old, Victorian?'

'Where did you get that, Frannie?'

'David Lyall's – yes, it is old. Libby didn't want anything new.'

'Hey Libby, give us a kiss!'

'Frannie – you are a sly one. You hid this incredibly well. You old fox!'

'Libs, stop kissing all those blokes! It's me you're going to marry!'

'A jealous husband?'

'Too right. If I go away I'll slap a chastity belt on you!'

'*Frannie!*' Mumps was outraged. The rest of the Backlanders were laughing.

Noise and congratulations surrounded everything.

Suddenly Lew arrived with two African barmen, bearing champagne glasses and several bottles. Frank, Corn and West expertly popped corks.

'Keep a cork for Libby!'

Dar pulled himself together. 'Celebration tonight at the Club?' He and Glory Halleluiah were staying there.

'Dar, darling - please – tonight Frannie and I are going to have a private celebration at the Gingerbread House – Sunday – at home?'

'Yes, Dar, Libs is cooking a steak for me to-night and if she gets that wrong it's all off!'

'Sunday then, *everyone!*'

Only a few people noticed; Lew, Frank and West saw Bobby walk away from the Prize-giving ring as if in a trance. He went alone.

The excitement finally died down and the men went to check on the cattle lines. Mumps had a driver to take her back to Venture, Glory Halleluiah carefully escorting her to the car. Mumps was pale, inwardly furious and mumbling to herself. Glory Halleluiah took no notice until Mumps was seated in the vehicle.

'Enough, Mumps, enough.' Glory Halleluiah repeated, 'Be glad for him!' but she felt she was wasting her words. She watched the vehicle depart, shaking her head slightly and then stumped off to join

Dar at the Club. At least there they would celebrate. She thought it quite likely that Dar would have too much to drink. Did it matter to-night? Definitely not!

'Lew, I'm off to the Gingerbread House. If I don't get back – cover up for me?'

Lew was astonished. For Frannie to say – 'if I don't get back' – oh well. Nothing to do with him what Frannie does.

Later, as he settled himself on the camp bed in the bull box surrounded by hay, he couldn't help thinking about what Frannie and Libby would be doing. And then he thought about Janet. She was both a farm girl and a nurse; she'd be fine. Very fine. He slept, but not until after a time of longing.

CHAPTER 26

When Dar came to the cattle lines next morning he found Lew but not Frannie.

'He's gone to have breakfast with Libby,' said Lew, pleased with his own quick thinking. But, on cue, Frannie and Libby, holding hands, sauntered into the lines.

Libby had had a job getting Frannie out of bed.

'Come on - Frannie – you'll be late for the Sale.'

Frannie, still naked, was admiring patterns on the ceiling above the bed.

'Can't move, Libs. I'm far too happy. Feel like a Turkish whatsit after he's had all his concubines.'

'Well, there's only me!'

'You're a complete dish of concubines!'

'Up, Frannie. I'll start the eggs and they'll be ruined if you're late.'

'My God, nagging already. What am I doing?' and he leapt out of bed, dashed into the kitchen and kissed Libby. 'Give me five minutes and I'll be with you.'

'Frannie – the auction – what bulls are you after? I can't bid against my future son-in-in law, can I?'

'Good heavens, I never thought of that!'

Dar looked at him slightly sideways with a smile. 'Had your mind on other things?'

335

Sitting on hay bales, they compared catalogues to make decisions. Libby was forgotten, but she understood and wandered off to find Glory Halleluiah.

The auction ring was quite small and the crowd round it big. There was a circle of benches; the rest of the prospective purchasers had to stand. The excellent auctioneer, Tom Chettle from Nakuru, was a very experienced man who wasted no time. The farmers were known to him; he'd already spotted where the best buyers were sitting and called for the first lot to come into the ring.

It was brisk. Dar and Frannie sat together, lifting a catalogue for certain bulls. At 10.45. a.m. there was a break for coffee, very necessary for the auctioneer and his assistants. The more valuable lots were coming later.

When the Reserve Champion came into the ring there was great interest – who would bid for this one? Mr. Chettle correctly suggested a high price to start and this was taken up. No-one thought this bull would go cheaply. Frannie sat very still, eyes only looking at the bidders. The bids went up and up and in the end the bull was knocked down to Mr. Brian Curry of Rumuruti. 'That's a great compliment, Frannie.' The Champion was the very last lot. Would Mr. Curry bid again? He did, and so did others. When the bids reached the level of the Reserve Champion the whole ring was tense. Mr. Curry went on, this time against Major Joyce of Machakos. It looked as if Major Joyce was faltering when, suddenly, the Rhodesian Judge raised his catalogue. Excitement now! He and Mr. Curry went on. There was absolute silence. Finally Mr. Curry quit. The bull would go to Rhodesia! And at a huge price. Frannie sat back, stretched himself, full of deep, wonderful achievement. It was a record price. Everyone was congratulating him. 'You've got the price of that ring back, Frannie!'

On Sunday evening all the guests were at The Loop before

Frannie and Mumps arrived. Mario's boys were a sight to admire – all in dinner jackets but with odd string-like black ties (fashion? wondered Madge). Even Glory Halleluiah was in a different dress – Rosa-made and therefore very suitable – and Janet had got time off to be with them. She had bought a new dress and looked very pretty; she'd never be a beauty but she had a charm of her own. Libby added another table to the normal dining table – and that was big – to accommodate everyone. Rosa was behind the scenes helping Libby, enjoying all the excitement. It would be quite a crush in the house with eighteen people.

At breakfast that morning Mumps had immediately attacked Frannie. He was waiting.

'Frannie – yesterday I was so angry, I couldn't talk to you. You know perfectly well you cannot marry. I've told you hundreds of times.'

Frannie just looked at her.

'You cannot do this. You know perfectly well you cannot, not with your foot.'

He replied quietly, 'If Libs doesn't mind it is fine, thank you. There is no problem.'

Mumps was working herself up to something of manic proportions, Frannie could see; her face was incredibly bitter. *'She doesn't know what she is doing. But you do – and it is wrong – wrong!'* she almost spat it out.

It was now or never, Frannie thought. He put his knife and fork down.

'Right. Mumps, now listen,' and his voice was full of power. 'Let's get one thing straight. I am marrying Libs and no-one is going to stop me. Least of all you. And you'd better understand some more. I own this farm. I repeat, I own this farm. It was left to me. You now have a choice. Get out now or stay. You can have this house to live in,

337

Libs and I will build our own home – *but* if you choose to stay, should you upset Libs just once – I'll turn you out.'

'Frannie – you can't speak to me like this! I'm your mother!'

'Yes, and I know full well what the Fifth Commandment says. But when that was written it was assumed that parents would automatically love their children – no need to tell them to honour their children – only the other way round. Well you haven't, have you? You've made me the object of your scorn, of hate, for nearly forty years. That's it. I'm telling you your choice now – and the consequences if you don't behave. I've stuck it ever since Dad died – but it's over now. You understand. *Do you want to stay or go?'*

Mumps was staring at him, 'You can't mean this!'

'I can and I do. You are welcome to stay if you'll behave but I will no longer pay your bills – you've got enough money of your own – plenty – to deal with that. Make up your mind – stay or go.'

'To think that I'd ever be spoken to like this – by my own son!' She was not crying but still defiant in her shock.

'Stay or go?'

'How can you do this?' She was starting to crumble. He meant it – and she knew the house was his.

'Not easily but I've got to do it. I've got a wife and, hopefully, children to think about and I am *not* having their lives spoilt by you. *Stay or go?'*

Mumps was staring at him, unable to believe what was going on. This was a Frannie she didn't know. His power frightened her; she had always been the powerful one, she thought. Then she remembered their recent row when he'd refused to share the ranch profit with her; he'd been strong then – and won that battle. Suddenly she almost cringed; the house, the ranch, everything was his. Tears nearly came, but not quite.

'I repeat. Stay or go? Come on.'

There was a second's pause.

'Stay, of course. Where could I go?'

'If you change your mind there's a new Home in Nairobi opened by the Women's League – do you hear? And if you upset Libs that's where I'll send you. Now – pull yourself together.' Frannie took another bite of food, leaving Mumps gaping at him.

'And you will come to the party tonight. And you will behave well. No moans. No telling everyone that I shouldn't be marrying. That's decided, finished. I don't like saying all this but you've driven me to it.'

One of the servants came into the dining room and the conversation stopped. Frannie finished his meal grimly. He felt terrible at what he'd said but had to conclude it. When the servant was safely out of the room Frannie stood up.

'I've got a lot of work to do before this evening. Before I go I want to hear that you understand everything I have said to you. I repeat – if you stay you will have to behave. Do you understand what that means?'

She looked at him, pulling herself upright. 'I will make my own decision.'

'And you will face the consequences!' he virtually shouted. He left to get on with his work, his feelings released in a way. He was starting to be free of her – at last it was happening.

Frannie and Mumps were late getting to the party. She nearly dropped out but one look at Frannie's extremely serious face made the decision for her. They had eaten lunch together in absolute silence but the atmosphere of strength from Frannie was so strong it was almost touchable. She was slow getting dressed and, in defiance, did not wear one of her better dresses. When she got into the car she was shaking slightly. They were silent on the journey.

Dar and Libby were waiting on the verandah; they had seen the car coming. Libby whispered to Dar 'Look after Mumps,' and she fled round to the driver's side where Frannie unfolded his height, enveloped her in a great hug and then spoke to her quickly and very seriously, Libby nodding. Then he smiled and all was well.

Glory Halleluiah made Corn and West promise to behave and they did; they were just their cheerful selves, always looking a trifle incongruous in dinner jackets below their ruddy faces with greying hair that stuck up in clumps, anachronistic with their definitely upper class pronunciation. Mumps sat down heavily and presented a mutinous face that everyone tried to ignore. Lots of cheerful chat was going on but Mumps refused to join in, refused to answer anything and simply emanated huge disapproval. Glory Halleluiah saw Frannie looking at his mother a few times and decided to act.

'Mumps, you look very tired. I'm going to send you home with my driver. He can come straight back here.' No-one ever said no to Glory Halleluiah. Mumps rose with a venomous look at Frannie; Glory Halleluiah steered her out of the room and saw her off. When she came back she immediately went to Frannie.

'I'm sorry, Frannie, I had to do that. We can relax now. She said you made her come?'

'Mistake, Glory Halleluiah, I hoped she'd behave. Never. Thanks for your help. Let me get you a drink.'

Dar asked for silence and spoke a few words of love and congratulations to Frannie and Libby who were holding each other tightly. Everyone cheered. Then Frannie, thanking him, shocked them all by announcing that the wedding would be the very next Friday, eleven o'clock, Chemchem Church – just all of us. No big ceremony.

'After church you'll come to the tent home I'm putting up for Libby and me and have lunch with us there. That's it!'

This created great talk. The speed of events was amazing. 'I tried to get Mr. Ironside to marry us quicker but next Friday was the first slot he'd got!'

Dar, Madge and Frank wondered about Bobby. Was this Frannie's way of making sure of Libby? Dar, after his initial surprise, saw it that way and smiled. Good for Frannie. Not that it looked as if Libby would look at another man now, she was so happy with Frannie, but one never knew. Mario and Maria obviously approved. Maria said, in Swahili, 'Why wait? – enjoy life!' and Frannie dashed over to give her a hug and a kiss. She loved that – a real Italian gesture.

Glory Halleluiah was deeply happy for the couple. She was looking at them with great benevolence as they stood in front of the empty fireplace, Frannie behind Libby, his arms around her waist, Libby clutching them, both looking so joyous. Frannie caught her look.

'Glory Halleluiah. I do believe that you're not too surprised that Libby and I are together?'

'Not entirely, Frannie. I noticed – some months ago – that you'd stopped calling each other Bro and Sis. Such ugly words, so I was very relieved – but I did wonder!'

Frannie and Libby were both laughing. 'No-one can hide anything from you!'

Madge was concerned at a wedding at such short notice.

'Libby, what will you wear?'

'Oh, just one of my nicer dresses and Frannie will wear his blazer. We don't want a show we just want to get married.'

Glory Halleluiah heard.

'Libby, dear, no. You should be a proper bride. I know! That dress you wore at the Hospital Ball – lovely cream colour – if Rosa could make a jacket or something to go over the top it would look lovely – very suitable.'

There was no point in arguing with Glory Halleluiah so Libby smiled, 'Oh, Glory Halleluiah, all right.'

Dinner was a noisy meal with one great surprise. The pudding – or, rather the puddings, for there were two for that number of people – was a steamed marmalade pudding. Not what many people would have thought was party fare. But when Frannie got up and kissed Libby they understood. At the coffee stage, when they were back in the sitting room, Maria suddenly called out for music.

Mario started. He sang a love song from an Italian opera that no-one knew. Marco translated the words. It was splendidly mawkish – as sentimental as possible – and they all loved it. Then Mario's boys took over and sang modern songs from musicals – *Oklahoma, My Fair Lady, Annie Get Your Gun*, even *Salad Days* and *The Boy Friend*. It was gloriously noisy. Suddenly Maria started; no-one had ever heard her sing before. She sang an aria from an opera that Glory Halleluiah tried to recall – Verdi, she thought. Maria had a clear, pure soprano voice that she used beautifully with power and emotion. There was great applause when she finished. She then spoke to them all in Swahili.

'Now we are together Mario and I must tell you. Marco and

Roberto are leaving us – going to Australia. They will start a business selling motor bikes and scooters in Melbourne – where there are Italians already. We are sad but it is right. They must find girls and marry like Frannie and Libby. Marco – Roberto – sing for us – sing *Torna a Surriento.*'

The two eldest boys sang together; rich tenor voices combining in the one Italian song everyone knew. The friends were not surprised that the family was breaking up; the two singers were already in their late twenties; big changes were in the air; everything was happening at once.

Mario was explaining to Dar that they were going as British young men, using their old names. For Australia, you see, that is best. Dar understood. He looked with affection at the whole family. Mario and Maria! Frannie and Libby would be just as good a couple.

Glory Halleluiah moved to sit by Frannie and Libby.

'Frannie,' she said in her clear diction that, this time, was overlaid with extra caution. Was she entirely sober, Frannie wondered? 'Frannie,' she repeated, 'you must not be afraid of emotion.' Frannie and Libby exchanged glances. 'Never, never become sophisticated – false – that is what that really means.'

'Why me, Glory Halleluiah?' he smiled.

'What was I saying? Oh yes, emotions. Let them go – not all the time – but they are important. Look at Mario, Maria and the boys – such lovely, happy people. Be sentimental sometimes. Listen to sentimental music. Read sentimental books, have sentimental dinners – sometimes.'

Frannie was about to interrupt but was himself interrupted. 'The worst possible thing one can do is to try to be someone else or something else; emotion – even sentiment – stops that. Let go sometimes.'

Libby was smiling broadly at this attack on Frannie. What with his anger this morning, about which he'd told her, and his love for her this evening his emotions were in full swing, she thought. Glory Halleluiah had certainly had a drink too many. Frannie was trying to keep a straight face.

'Yes, Glory Halleluiah, I will,' he said as seriously as he could. Glory Halleluiah got up and stumped off – she never walked – to sit by Maria.

'In vino veritas, Libs. But I know what she means – I've hidden my emotions far too long – but not now!' and he kissed Libby.

Janet knew where the playing cards lived at The Loop and at one end of the room she'd got all Mario's boys, Lew and West on the floor where she was teaching them to play Racing Demon. Mario's boys picked it up immediately and it was like a children's party. Corn couldn't resist and went to join them. There was non-stop shouting. Lew was thrilled that Janet was leading the fun. She was more and more at home in the Backlands, he could see. It was a natural place for her.

Dar's thoughts were slightly sad that he wouldn't be able to give Libby the wedding that he and Edith had planned years ago. What he'd not noticed was Glory Halleluiah and Madge talking together. Madge then came over to him and he smiled agreement; he knew they were a formidable pair when they got together.

On Monday morning, quite early, Glory Halleluiah and Rosa were in Libby's bedroom where Libby was standing in the cream ball gown. Glory Halleluiah brought with her a complete roll of cream lace. Libby looked at it and guessed.

'Something like forty four years old?'

'Yes, dear – it was to be my dress – but it will cover yours.'

Rosa measured, pinned, and took lots of notes and tried draping. Libby stood still, knowing that she'd have no say in the matter at all. Glory Halleluiah and Rosa had taken over. After the dressmaking session Glory Halleluiah joined Madge with Dar.

What they were doing totally by-passed Frannie and Libby who went to see Mr. Ironside. It was his day off but he always gave couples a pre-wedding talk. He offered them lunch, spoke seriously, helpfully, kindly and finally was very funny, never commenting on the speed of events; he was far too wise for that.

On Tuesday Frannie started putting up their home to be. He used his own tentage and also borrowed a big, heavy, mess tent from Dar. It was huge and made their living and dining quarters easily. The site he chose had shade from some trees and was between his old home and the river but nearer the river. Libby was carting furniture, some of it camping things but also some more comfortable items that Dar insisted they should use.

'Libs, I'll get our own home built quickly. Gurdev Singh – I'll call him to speed things up. We'll design it together.' Frannie already knew what he wanted and didn't think that Libby would object because it was roughly modelled on the house at The Loop.

On Wednesday Frannie worked on their tent home and Libby sorted out the kitchen equipment, china, cutlery, bedding and other household items. 'If it pours with rain we can always retreat to the Gingerbread House,' she said.

On Thursday Libby went shopping in Chemchem and had her hair professionally washed and trimmed.

On Friday the wedding took place.

Frannie was almost overcome when Lew arrived for him and he was made to sit in the back seat of the car. It was comical. Lew now had the upper hand and insisted.

The church was the first surprise. Someone had turned it into Chelsea Flower Show; there were flowers everywhere in yellow and white and the scent was overpowering. Also someone was playing the little mobile organ that the church owned. Frannie and Libby had said, 'No music.'

The congregation was already seated. Glory Halleluiah had deliberately brought Mumps – in case she refused to come – and Mr. and Mrs. Pinto who'd been specially invited. Rosa's work on the dress had been excellent. Frank, Madge, Corn, West, Mario,

Maria and all the boys were there. Piet and Rena, both so happy for Frannie, had also been invited and Janet had managed to get a day off work.

The car from The Loop arrived. Frannie, with Lew, both in blazers, stood up. It was now silent. Dar proudly brought his beautiful daughter up the aisle to be claimed by Frannie who quickly kissed her.

'Not in the script!'

'Shh, Frank!'

'Dearly beloved, we are gathered together here in the sight of God, and in the face of this congregation, to join together this Man and this Woman in holy matrimony; which is an honourable estate...'

'Francis James, wilt thou have this Woman to thy wedded wife, to live...'

'Elizabeth Mation, wilt thou have thid Man to thy wedded husband, to live...'

Dar gave Libby to Frannie.

Lew gave the ring to Frannie.

Libby gave the prayer book she was carrying instead of a bouquet to her father – it had been her mother's. There were no bridesmaids.

Frannie and Libby were made man and wife. Immediately just the two of them took Communion and then signed the register in the vestry.

Suddenly it was all noise and commotion when they left the church, rice thrown at them (by Madge and Maria) and photographs taken (by Mario and Roberto). Libby's transformed dress was lovely. Rosa had made a complete over-dress of lace but had looped the lace skirt about eight inches from the hemline of the underdress, the loops held up with tiny bows, the heavy silk showing below. The effect was very pretty.

Frannie finally said, 'Let's get down to camp.' He led Libby to the saloon car that Lew had driven. Lew was at the back door quickly; opened it with a flourish. 'Mr. and Mrs. Houghton-Framlyn, in you get.'

Lew drove away – but not directly to The Backlands. Because they were kissing Frannie and Libs hadn't noticed but when Frannie saw something odd he said, 'Hey, Lew, what's going on?'

'New route to Venture, that's all.' Lew was grinning. His instructions had been to drive them around for ten minutes to give the others a chance to get to Venture first.

'Libs, they're up to something.'

'I hope not!'

'I wondered if we'd get away with it so lightly. Best face it. We'll have to.'

After driving Frannie and Libby all round the area of Chemchem town and down a few side roads Lew decided the time was enough and he took the correct route, past Piet and Rena's farm, towards the escarpment.

'Lew – stop for a bit at the viewpoint, please.'

'Yes. And I've got your first wedding present for you. Here you are.' He handed to Frannie an envelope of an unusual shape. It was longer than foolscap and slightly wider. Frannie immediately knew what was inside. He had an identical envelope at Venture. It was incredible. Libby wanted to know what it was.

'We'll look at it when we get to the viewpoint.'

They stood looking down at the country they loved and then Frannie opened the envelope. Inside were the Title Deeds for The Loop.

'Libs – he's given us The Loop – unbelievable!'

'Marvellous. He's wanted to retire for ages, he kept telling me. Oh!'

'We'll have to do a lot more thinking now – where to put our house, how to run the places as one – whew. We'll leave him in his house, of course. What a gift!'

They talked a little more, slightly dazed and then went back to Lew.

'Lew, can you look after this? It's very precious. Should go in a safe.'

'Yeah, fine.' Lew knew exactly what was in the envelope. Dar had a long talk with him about it on Wednesday.

'And Lew, we all know what a lousy manager you are but when Dar kicks you out will you come and work for me? Half pay, longer hours, no perks, sleep in a tent, no holidays – all that – O.K.'

'O.K. But we'll have to discuss worse terms.'

'Good.' Through the driving mirror the two men grinned at each other; Lew certainly knew. Frannie held Libby tighter. He now had many more things to consider.

A few minutes later Lew said, 'Frannie , since you've been good enough to offer me a lousy job, perhaps I'd better warn you that you're going to have to make a major speech.'

'Ouch. Libs, I'd better think – and maybe I better not tell the whole truth!'

Lew drove them, not to their tent home, but to the Picnic Site where a great crowd of people, marquees, noise, cheers and laughter awaited their arrival.

'Frannie – look at what they've done!'

But Frannie had guessed that Dar wouldn't let his only daughter's wedding go un-noticed.

'It's a full scale reception we're in for. Libs, Dar's doing us proud.'

Lew added, 'You have no idea what has been going on behind your backs. There's a three tier cake, a tent full of presents, enough champagne to drown an elephant – the whole works.'

Frannie and Libby laughed at each other, 'And we were trying to have a quiet wedding.'

CHAPTER 27

'The Loop! Dar do you really mean it? It's tremendous.'

'Of course I do, Frannie. You'll put the two ranches together very well. The Loop would go to Libby when I die anyway and it's time I sat back. I'd like to stay in my house......'

'Naturally.'

'Frannie, if Edith was alive I think I could have continued longer but.... Now you've got Libbby and together you can do it.'

'I don't know how we're ever going to start thanking you...' but Dar brushed him aside.

Frannie's speech was only roughly prepared. He thanked Dar for Libby, thanked all the Backlanders for the reception and thanked everyone who'd come to join them in their happiness. He forgot to use the time-honoured words 'My wife and I,' not surprising thought Glory Halleluiah.

'When one has a foot like mine, approaching girls is not easy,' he said. 'So when I noticed that Libby was ignoring the many men who were after her I thought – all right, I'll try - having loved her for years. But I went very warily, very slowly. After what seemed like a millennium I managed to give her a proper kiss – not the Hospital Ball variety – and the reaction was enormous. Did I get an earful? You should have heard Libs. But it was to ask me why I'd never done it a long time ago!'

Laughter.

'After that things went on quite rapidly.'

Frannie was standing behind Libby's chair, his hands on her shoulders.

'I have to make one confession. I have actually seen my bride stark naked already.'

The crowd was silent.

'I was ten at the time and there was an awful fuss next door about a baby arriving and I was forced to go over and see it. I'd just been given an airgun for my birthday and was only interested in that. Well – there was this baby – initially with some white stuff over her lower half. I tell you – she was red in the face and screaming. They took off the white towelling stuff and she was also very smelly!' Libby was laughing.

'They said she needed changing. I'd have changed her for a tin of airgun pellets immediately. Today? No, I don't think I'll change her, not even for two tins of airgun pellets.' The crowd loved it.

'Have you seen Corn and West?'

'No, where are they?'

'Shadowing Frannie – they're up to something.'

Frannie felt something on his back but as he was talking to the Chaplain he couldn't move. A bit later he asked Libby, 'Have a look, someone's done something to my back!'

Libby was laughing.

'You've got a notice pinned to your blazer. It says *'LATE BEGINNER BUT WILL BE ALL RIGHT ON THE NIGHT. HAS BEEN TAKING LESSONS FROM J. BACCUP.'*

Libby said, 'Don't think you need lessons from the Lecher. Stand still and I'll take it off.'

'No, leave it. Corn and West – their dreadful humour – but at least it's harmless and might amuse some people. Let them have their fun.'

Frannie and Libby were walking round trying to talk to as many people as possible but never letting go of each other. A number of the Chemchem guests commented on how different he looked now he was happy. 'Funny, I'd never have said he was good-looking – but *now*!'

'Have you seen Dar?'

'Yes, sitting by Glory Halleluiah and rocking his chair. A bit gone, I'd say!'

'Too right – and she's pronouncing words very carefully, too.'

'Who's looking after Mumps?' Libby suddenly asked, anxiously.

'You'll never guess – Corn and West – look over there.'

'What are they up to?'

'Giving her too much to drink, I expect. It's what she needs. Anyway you know what they're like – they'll probably take her home and provide the aspirin as well.'

'Libs, let's go. It's time everyone got on with the party without us. Lew's got my Land Rover somewhere.'

Lew and Janet were sitting by Frank and Madge, apparently deciding which party piece Frank should produce later on. The light was already fading, the big camp-fire lit, and Frannie and Libby quietly left.

Chemchem people were good at parties; they really enjoyed them. When they were all round the camp-fire Frank did the piece where letters from a doctor went to the wrong ladies; one to an elderly spinster who suffered from piles and the other to a young married woman who was having difficulty in conceiving. It was a riot.

'Lew, I've got to be back by midnight.'

'Yes, O.K. I'll get the Landy – wait by that bush.'

On the way up the escarpment Janet said, 'Such a lovely wedding. Of course Libby's so beautiful.'

To this Lew replied, with the courage of too much alcohol, 'Oh, do you think so? I prefer smaller girls, dark-haired, half Welsh, nurses.'

There was a fractional pause.

'Anyway, what do you think of Frannie?'

Janet was ready.

'Frannie? Too tall. Gaunt, almost. No, I prefer shorter men, fair, preferably ranch managers.'

There was a short silence.

'Janet, are you smiling?'

'Yes, are you?'

'Yes.' He slid his left arm to hold her hand, both very content. He held her all the way to the Nurses' Home except when a corner needed two hands for the heavy steering.

They said nothing when they got out of the vehicle but Lew escorted her to the porch of the building.

'Janet, I want to say something but I can't just yet. It's difficult...'

'I know, Lew, I know. It's all right. I'll wait. I'll wait. I will. I promise.'

They clasped each other in their very awkward first kiss that, by a gentle manoeuvre, turned into a sensational kiss that might have gone on all night but for the African night-watchman coming round the corner of the building.

Next day Lew had no recollection whatsoever of the drive home but a very clear memory of Janet's lovely smile. She'll wait!

'When we've built our house – say in six months – we'll go on a proper honeymoon, Libs. Where would you like – Malindi, Lamu, Zanzibar, Rhodesia, South Africa?'

Libby was laughing – she seemed to be laughing all the time.

'By the time the house is built I'll be sticking out in front rather a lot. Perhaps not honeymoon time!'

Frannie had to smile.

'Guess I'm not thinking too straight. Maybe we've already had our honeymoon! Let's design our house and get on with that as soon as possible. And, though we said we'd have a quiet first week together, I must do some farming. The ranch has been neglected for the last two weeks.'

'Yes, of course. Anyway I've got no end of thank-you letters to write so I'll be busy. And there's an awful lot to unpack. You must see what Glory Halleluiah has given us.'

'What's that?'

'It's a beautiful canteen of solid silver cutlery – a set for twelve! I know about it. It was part of her dowry that she never used.'

'How typically nice of her. She's spent all her life looking after other people – a saint!'

Dar had been doing some thinking after the wedding. He was so relieved that Frannie was now in charge he could hardly put it into words. He would help Frannie but be free to go to Nairobi, visit friends, go to Britain, have time off. Lew, he thought, such an excellent chap, but he needs the confidence and maturity that marriage brings. (Dar was thinking of himself before his marriage to Edith.) If only Lew and Janet would marry. But there was no sign of that; Dar knew only too well Lew's position. Although he was now earning and saving, Dar knew he'd need a reasonable nest egg before he could marry. And he must have a house. But would he and Janet ever be more than friends?

A letter reached Shropshire that would have answered Dar's question had he known about it.

Dear Mum and Dad,

I've got great news – but don't start rejoicing yet. It's Lew. You liked him didn't you? He wants to ask me to marry him but, financially, he can't just yet – he made that plain. But I said I'd wait for him. He's absolutely perfect...

There followed a long eulogy of the perfections of Lew with which, on the whole, Mr. and Mrs. Evans agreed.

'There you are, John, just what we hoped. Can we speed it up a bit?'

'I'll write to Dar Winchester and see how the land lies.'

For their first real entertaining Frannie and Libby decided to throw a lunch party at their tent home exactly a week after the wedding – the party they intended for their wedding day. Unfortunately it was the birthday of Mario and Maria's youngest son so they could not come; they were holding their own family gathering – another time, they promised.

Glory Halleluiah arrived very early. It was only eleven in the morning.

'I wanted to see you, Frannie, before Mumps arrives.'

'She's not coming. We invited her but she refused.'

'Aaah. She came to see me – you may guess.'

'I can imagine,' said Frannie drily, 'It hasn't been easy.'

Glory Halleluiah vividly recalled Mumps arriving at her house full of temper. She'd waited until after the wedding so her feelings had seethed into deepest anger. Mumps couldn't contain it any longer and had to tell someone; she was furious with Frannie.

'Can you believe it. My own son turning me out of the house. My own home!'

The recital went on and on with Glory Halleluiah saying absolutely nothing.

Eventually Mumps ran out of words.

'But Frannie said he was going to build his own home; we all understood he was going to leave you alone in the old house.'

Mumps was not to be diverted.

'He said I could go to the new Women's League Home in Nairobi!'

'Yes, Harrison House. I've heard about it. Of course if it's run by the League it will be excellent. But you have other alternatives – you could buy or rent a house in Chemchem – or go to Britain. You've got money of your own, I know.'

Mumps chose to ignore this.

'I told him he shouldn't marry – and now look at what is happening. Libby will take over everything. It's my home, my place! Libby - where I should be. It's absolutely wrong!'

Glory Halleluiah, who thought the marriage absolutely right, refrained from pointing out that the house belonged to Frannie; she knew that, but with Mumps' state of mind, it would have been useless. Mumps went on and on, wearing Glory Halleluiah to a standstill. It was impossible to stop the tirade. Literally hours later Glory Halleluiah persuaded Mumps to go home; it had been an extremely upsetting visit.

'What did you say to her?' Glory Halleluiah asked Frannie.

'I snapped. It was just after the Show when I announced our engagement – the Sunday morning. She went into a fantigue about how I must not marry Libs; obviously she wanted me to look after her. I'd had it by then, Glory Halleluiah, and I lost my temper. I told her that we were certainly getting married and that we'd build our own home; she could stay in the house but I told her that if she upset Libs just once I'd turn her out. I gave her a choice – stay in the house and behave or leave. It was an ultimatum. Cruel, no doubt. But I had to do it.'

'I'm very sorry that happened Frannie, but it is understandable.' Glory Halleluiah looked very serious. 'However I've come to tell you that I am sure she will go. Your marriage has shattered her complacency. She realises that she won't be the chatelaine of Venture any longer. Libby will be in what she sees as her place. She can't bear that idea. And, I think she probably knows that in any competition from Libby she would be a non-starter. I suggested that she might rent or buy a house in Chemchem. That idea was not welcome – she would have to look after herself. She was with me a very long time but in the end had talked herself into going to the Women's League Home in Nairobi where she knows she would be very well cared for. But she was determined not to tell you until it suited her. Frannie, I'm sure you need to know, that's why I'm telling you now. You may not need to build another house after all.'

'No, whatever happens, Libs and I will have our own home. I couldn't take Libs there – too full of unhappy things. Glory Halleluiah, thanks for telling me all this. It helps a lot because I need a house for Lew; he'd be O.K. there.'

'Frannie, I am extremely sorry that you had to speak to her like that because I see that she's a very sick woman, but, in the long run, it may be for the best.'

'Oh, I'm very well aware that she is sick but I'm not a psychiatrist and I doubt of any of them could cope with her; I think she's unchangeable.'

'Probably. Frannie – you can start anew – and that is very, very good.'

'With enormous thanks to you!' and he kissed Glory Halleluiah on her leathery cheek.

Everyone sat on camp chairs in the shade of three big trees, Frannie having given them all drinks. No-one commented on the absence of Mumps but Lew was sad that Janet had to work and so was missing this pleasant party. Dar, Frank, Madge, Glory Halleluiah, Corn, West and Lew were all relaxing together.

Frannie was being teased by Frank. 'I hear you've got lion problems? Sitting up all night over lion bait on your honeymoon?'

Frannie laughed. 'Frank – we manage – we manage. Yes, it's a lioness. I've had two nights waiting for her and I'll have to go again tonight. Too many calves are going.'

'I've got the same problem,' said Glory Halleluiah, 'Corn and West are taking it in turns to stay up. Mine's an old male. Canny beast.'

Libby came from the kitchen store tent and sat on the grass in front of Frannie's chair, leaning against his knees. He immediately touched her shoulder, her cheek, her hair, whilst he was talking. He'd started telling everyone his plans for the combined ranches and was in full flow.

'Libs and I think VentureLoop sounds better than LoopVenture – what do you think, Dar? We'll run the two places together but keep the names – important, we think. Even ranches have a history. We'll get cracking very quickly on the smooth running of the two places together – it needn't be difficult. But we've go to do it properly – no nonsense.'

As if Frannie ever allowed anything to be run badly, thought Frank!

Madge suddenly had a vivid impression of Frannie then – a new Frannie – blazingly male, strongly sexual – something she'd never really seen before.

'Maybe four courses of stone and then cedar slabs. That's quick and very attractive. We've done a rough design – Dar – you'll smile – it's very like The Loop house – we'll start as soon as possible. We'll put it nearer the centre of both ranches. Whether we move other things I'm not sure yet. We're very much hoping that Lew will move into my old house (Mumps going? This was news to most of the hearers though they were not surprised.) and we'll get another under-manager over to The Loop next to Dar.'

This was great news for Lew who suddenly saw marriage with Janet a much nearer possibility. The whole party saw this as well and glanced at him. Poor Lew actually blushed slightly. Frannie went on quickly.

Glory Halleluiah was sitting with great contentment. Despite the breach with Mumps, or, perhaps because it, all was well. Frannie and Libby were together; something she'd prayed for and longed for over many years, no-one ever guessing.

'...*better finishing over at The Loop so it would be sensible to put the breeding stock this side and move all the steers and young heifers over to The Loop. Then...*'

Lew was listening intently. This was his new boss – also his friend – but definitely his boss. He was looking at Frannie with new eyes – the strength, the dominance of the man. Lew suddenly felt invigorated, wiser – so this is what marriage can do to a man? And now he can propose to Janet properly – as soon as he is sure of the house. Janet, oh, Janet!

'... *may mean a new bridge – lower downstream – there is a place that would ease movement. I'll go into that.*'

Frank, Corn and West were absorbing Frannie's plans, nodding agreement from time to time. But Frannie was really speaking to Dar and Lew, they knew. Dar sat almost mesmerised by the stream of schemes – all obviously thought about over a long time, all good, sensible – all very much Frannie. It was breathtaking as the spate of ideas flowed so fast.

'... *need two new plunge dips, one on The Loop and the other on Venture. That can be done quite quickly once one starts. I'll move my cattle weighbridge, I think – over to The Loop – because we'll have the sale aminals over there...*'

Glory Halleluiah was looking at Libby, so settled now.

'Now. Dar – please will you think of this one? It's not my idea but came from George Geddes. Quite a few clients ask about the settlers and would love to see a settler farm and home. He wondered if, because he comes through The Loop quite often, he might bring clients to stay with you for a couple of nights? See the ranch, maybe do a bit of shooting if there's something you want rid of. Have a think. Bit more income – we could charge quite a lot. Libs would come over to deal with food. Think about it.'

Libby was sitting very quietly at Frannie's feet, saying nothing but glowing with warmth and happiness. All the time he was speaking he kept touching her, his hand never still yet his whole manner suggested total concentration on the recital of his plans.

'Of course it may not be practical but there's no other use for the land. If I can make a decent track then it would hold about a thousand sheep. Have to be Merinos. No-one's ever tried sheep here – worth a go?'

This was something that Corn and West had also considered but were constrained by too many leopards. Both were thinking the same – if Frannie was successful, they'd try it also. Get rid of the leopards and try sheep.

Glory Halleluiah wondered if Mumps had ever seen Frannie like this - assured, speaking well, ideas flowing. She thought it likely that Mumps, in her distorted mind, had only ever seen him as a disfigurement, never as a person. Yes, Frannie had been right to make a clean break with her, distasteful as the means had been.

Frannie bent to Libby who got up smiling. Lunch would appear soon. Frannie's plans were all out and the men were discussing some of the points. Dar wanted to say very little; this was Frannie's job now and he would back his son-in-law as much as he could but Lew said a few things as did the other men, all interested, all keen to see it happen. Frank had heard of a suitable lad to begin as an under-manager, Corn and West knew some of the sheep breeders in Kenya. There was a lot of discussion. Glory Halleluiah and Madge wandered over to the tents with Libby who showed them her new home with considerable pride. Two tents were facing each other with fly-sheets meeting. One end was their bedroom – there was only room for their big bed. The other end had dressing tables, wardrobes, shoe racks and other pieces; the fly-sheets made a passage between. The kitchen store and the linen store were admired. Guest tents were not yet up but would go over there. The shower and long drop were convenient to the main bedroom tent; staff tents were a slight distance away but not too far. With years of camping experience behind him Frannie had put everything on slightly raised ground. When it did rain in the Backlands it could produce a flood in an afternoon. Libby explained that they were going to store all the wedding presents and some furniture in The Gingerbread House until their own home was built. It was all practical yet homely.

After lunch everyone sat for a few lazy minutes and then left, Dar being the last to go. As he drove away he happened to glance in his driving mirror. There, clasped together in a deep embrace, were Frannie and Libby. He drove, almost choking with happiness. At last she was with the right man and the future of the ranches was assured.

CHAPTER 28

At the Government Hospital for Africans, on the same road as the Cottage Hospital but nearer town, Lew was sitting on one of the benches provided for all visitors along the front verandah of the hospital. It was a big hospital, serving a wide area and was made in the shape of two large courtyards with the operating theatre and other special rooms forming the central building; a cloistered monastery in design. The wards were round each side and the back; the front held offices, pharmacy, stores, staff rooms and other medical facilities. At the front there was a neat parking area and a flagpole. The D.C.'s office had a flagpole, as did the Police Station, but at those places the Union Jack was raised and lowered every day – with ceremony. For some reason the flagpole at the Hospital never had a flag. Lew was looking at it, wondering.

It was still early morning and Lew was in a state of bewilderment. He'd driven, as instructed, very, very carefully from the Backlands with Nzioka oddly stretched on a mattress in the back, moaning from time to time. To begin with he'd spoken, but then went ominously silent.

The doctor from the Cottage Hospital was there as well as the Government doctor; they helped each other over difficult cases. Early morning telephone calls had alerted the Government doctor that help may well be needed. Both men had come to the Land Rover and supervised moving Nzioka onto a trolley and took him into the hospital, leaving Lew bereft. All he could do was sit and wait. Two Africans, amazed at seeing a mzungu sitting waiting at their hospital, joined him on a neighbouring bench. Lew automatically greeted them in Swahili, but could cope with no more. The Africans didn't expect anything else.

Suddenly, blessedly, he thought, Janet arrived in her full uniform, bearing a flask and a packet.

'Lew!'

He couldn't answer but put his hand out and they held hands for a second.

'Drink this, Lew, tea with lots of sugar – and this is all I could find for food but please eat it, you'll feel better.'

He smiled his thanks. 'I'm O.K.,' he said.

She wanted to hug him, he felt that, and, swallowing, he managed, 'Thanks, Janet. I am O.K.'

'Yes. Look. I'll be back when I can, but there's a baby on the way and without Matron to-day I'm the only one with Maternity training so I'll have to be there. There's a hole in the hedge – short cut – it's only a minute away so I'll come. I must go now.' They held hands for a second and then she was gone.

Lew felt a lot better. What was it that women have? The power to comfort? The practicality? He needed the tea and the sandwiches; Janet understood that. Oh, Janet! How very typical that she'd stuck to essentials. Automatically he poured the drink and ate the food; Janet was right, he did feel better. The Africans beside him had moved away but others had come and he greeted them, too. They were extremely polite in the African way, greeted him but never asked his business.

With the mien of a queen the Government Hospital Matron came out. She was known as The Dragon because of her efficiency. Taking one look at Lew she said, 'Mr. Cooper? I'm glad you've got something to drink. I'll be back.'

She disappeared for about ten minutes, by which time he'd finished all that Janet had brought. He felt bad about not sharing it with the Africans around him, but they'd not expect it.

When The Dragon reappeared she asked him to come into the office.

'It's going to be a big operation – serious - and we're a bit short of blood....'

'Can I give?' he interrupted. She'd anticipated that and thought better not in his shocked state.

'Not yet but we do need help. Can you go to town and round up all the people you can to come and give blood? Send them here. Not the elderly or the very young – see what you can do. I'll set up a place for collecting blood. We need any at this stage (she was thinking of other operations due). The Africans have the same blood groups as us but in different proportions – so we need lots to get it right. Just send people, I'll be ready. The operation will start any minute; the doctors have done the preparation and Sister Stubbly has come to help.'

Sister Stubbly was Sexy Sarah from the Cottage Hospital; Lew realised how serious it must be if two extra medical people had come. Sexy Sarah had been theatre trained, he knew. Obviously the Cottage Hospital was not too full. A pity about the baby coming – he could have done with Janet by his side.

Lew said that he'd go at once and set off not too sure where to go first but then decided on the Club. He saw the elderly Secretary who was very solicitous and made a poster then and there to put at the entrance. It was too early for many people to be using the Club but the few who were there gathered round quickly to read the request for help. One man said he could go, he'd given blood before, knew the form.

From the Club Lew drove to the Kenya Farmers' Association main shop where he spoke to the manager, and from there to the K.F.A. stores – the maize store, other cereal store and the wool shed. Everyone was sympathetic and helpful. He then thought of the Police Station and the Veterinary Department. The latter was a bit out of town but he knew the men there and they were most helpful, two offering to go to the Hospital quickly. Back nearer town he visited the Kenya Co-operative Creamery depot where lorries were delivering milk in churns. The message left there, Lew drove into the centre of town and tried the main shops, almost all run by Asians. He went to the two large Grocery stores, then to the Chemist – Howse and McGeorge; there was a European manager there. He tried the bookshop and printer, the electrical shop, the three garages in town and the big Sikh workshop where agricultural machinery was repaired.

Running out of ideas he returned to the Hospital but behind him were many promises, both of help and that the news would be spread. In the hospital drive were eight vehicles and two more were arriving as he parked. Wonderful, he thought.

'Mr. Cooper – Lew. Can you help? When they've given blood they must have a little rest and drink a mug of tea – can you deal with that? There's the kettle, mugs, milk, sugar – make them have sugar even if they don't normally. I must get going. I'll be next door where we're taking the blood.'

Two at a time the volunteers were lying on beds attached to tubes that took the blood. No-one was saying much; those that talked did so in subdued tones. As they finished Lew made them sit and drink tea, which they found a bit sissy but agreed. They all had jobs to get on with, he knew. One strapping chap, a farmer from near Piet and Rena fainted. That shook Lew but not The Dragon. 'We'll prop him up. He'll be O.K. Let him come round – head on his knees, that's right. When he's better give him an extra rest.'

By the time eight men had given blood it became routine and Lew was able to thank them all. Then two ladies came in, which surprised Lew, but The Dragon accepted them without demur. Lew made more tea, persuaded people to rest, made them take sugar. The Dragon glanced at him. He was busy, that was good.

The Dragon said that they would need at least six pints but to get enough matching blood many more volunteers would be needed. Volunteers came. News had spread quickly around Chemchem that Frannie's special hunting companion, his tracker cum gun-bearer, the well-known Nzioka, needed blood.

'Are you O.K.?' a volunteer asked Lew.

'Thanks, yes, and thank you,' he managed to say.

The Dragon seemed to be doing a hundred jobs at once but the African nurses were helping. Unexpectedly Janet arrived in the room where Lew was holding sway. 'They'll give you lunch here. I've seen The Dragon. Did you give blood? Better not after all, perhaps. No baby yet – I'll be back.' She vanished but her presence, even for those few minutes helped Lew.

In the middle of the quiet procession of donors, now coming up to fourteen (more beds were being used to take the blood faster), a tray arrived for Lew. There was an enamel soup plate containing stew with a lump of posho; a spoon was provided. This was what the patients would eat. Lew was grateful and ate it quickly; welcome fare, if simple.

Fourteen stretched to eighteen and then Piet and Rena arrived with anxious faces.

'Oh, Lew – exactly a week! Tell.'

'Don't know much. Nzioka said a bit and then conked out. They got the lioness after a long wait. It was on the way back from the hide to the car. The buffalo came out of no-where. Dad said it must have been really old and stone deaf not to have heard the shot and get out of the way. Anyway – it was going for Nzioka – so Frannie had to act ...'

Piet patted Lew's shoulder and said, 'We'll both give blood – where? – oh, I see,' and they went.

As the number of blood donors slowly became fewer Lew was left with a far too vivid picture of the early morning. A runner came – no telephone until seven in the morning – and he woke Dar. They went as quickly as they could to the camp, having sent another runner to Frank and Madge, asking them to send messages to everyone else.

It was the camp's night guard who'd wondered why the Bwana and Nzioka had not returned. He woke the cook, who decided to wake Libby. She sent two men with torches; the bait was some way away but they could go straighter through the bush than a vehicle could on a track. When one man came back with news she sent a runner to Dar and messages spread rapidly.

By the time Dar and Lew arrived Nzioka was still conscious and they were able to put him on a camp bed to be carefully carried back to camp – all difficult and very slow in the dark. Frank arrived. Dar had gone a very odd colour and Frank made him go back and sit down in camp.

Libby had tears but was very much in control, giving orders. 'Please get a message to the District Hospital. Make tea – give it to Dar. Madge – please go to Mumps and stay with her.'

She seemed to have huge control somehow; seemed to be holding herself in – odd, Lew thought. It was all unreal, half dark and everyone behaving mechanically, but Libby being a Colossus amongst them.

Corn and West arrived, taking over the practicalities; they were shocked but capable. They dealt with things quietly and quickly, making Libby drink some tea. Libby asked Frank to take Dar home and be with him, leaving Corn and West to carry on. Eventually Glory Halleluiah arrived and Libby went straight to her.

At this point, as dawn was breaking, the group that had struggled to carry Nzioka through the bush came into camp. Corn and West immediately looked at him, got out tools, removed the back seat of Dar's Land Rover and laid Nzioka as flat as they could on a mattress in the back. Libby was still giving instructions, organising, being listened to, wiping tears but the centre and head of it all.

'Lew, go slowly, a telephone call should have reached the hospital by now – they'll be ready. And stay there until you know the result – good or bad – please. Don't come back before it's clear. You may have to stay all day but do it, please.'

There was blood all over the mattress; Lew wondered if Nzioka would survive the journey but he drove off slowly, not liking to leave Libby but Glory Halleluiah was by her side, Corn and West having gone back to the place where Nzioka had been found.

It was now full light and as Lew drove slowly out of Venture he passed Mario and Maria driving in. He called that he couldn't stop. Mario nodded and drove on.

Janet came back to the Government Hospital again.

'I should be off duty but the wretched baby still hasn't arrived. Have they got lots of blood? He'll need several pints. I'll come back as soon as I can.' And she was gone again.

But every little bit of Janet was a great support, Lew felt.

A few more blood donors appeared and Lew was kept busy again.

Another Sister arrived, taking over from the Matron; Lew carried on with the tea making. No-one talked much. No-one wanted to.

There was quite a stir with the African nurses, the orderlies and the patients, all of whom heard what was going on but Lew was ignorant of this. All those wazungu giving blood for an African! And he's not even a local man. He's an Mkamba from Machakos way – long way from here. But all those wazungu!

Again Janet appeared. 'At last the baby arrived – very quick at the end and I'm off duty. I'll go and see how things are.' She went into the inner part of the Hospital that Lew had not dared enter. He'd not asked for details, assuming that he'd be told in the end. To his surprise yet another couple of men came to offer blood. He helped the African nurse who was now dealing with collecting blood.

Janet reappeared. 'He's out of theatre. It's been bad, quite a few bones broken but less internal damage than they thought. Nzioka's in recovery now but this is often the difficult bit. Some Africans die of shock when they come round.'

Lew couldn't answer her; they sat together, just waiting; there was nothing more they could do.

After what seemed like a long time the Government doctor, a tall, wiry Scot, came to them.

'Mr. Cooper. Lew? He's conscious and I think if you could talk to him it might help. He called your name – or what we thought was your name – Bwana Fupi.' Janet accompanied Lew but stayed by the door so that Nzioka would not see her.

The doctor led Lew to Nzioka's bed where he was a mass of bandages with a tunnel over his lower body – or what Lew thought was a tunnel - and with tubes of liquid suspended above him, drips going into his body. But Nzioka seemed to be breathing all right. His eyes were closed.

'Nzioka!' The African's eyes opened slightly. Lew spoke in Swahili. 'Nzioka, it's me, Bwana Fupi.'

Nzioka managed to open his eyes a bit wider.

'You're going to be fine. The doctors are pleased. You'll be here for some time but they'll look after you very well. You've got some broken bones but they will mend – get better. You'll be hunting again quite soon. Just do what the doctors and nurses tell you. They are very good here. You'll be fine.'

Nzioka managed a croak.

'Bwana Chopi?'

'He's absolutely fine,' said Lew, who'd had time to think about this, 'Absolutely fine. Don't you worry about him.'

That seemed to please Nzioka who closed his eyes again.

'Nzioka, I'm going back to the ranch now. You'll be very well looked after here. You just sleep. I'll tell everyone that you are over the worst and that you'll be back to the ranch soon. Someone will come to see you to-morrow. Don't worry. Everything's fine.'

Lew left. Janet was waiting, 'Oh, Lew, that was good of you.'

'I'll have to go back now,' he told her.

'Yes, I know. Lew, you'll be all right. Really you will.' They held hands for a moment and then he leaned forward and gave her a quick kiss before getting into Dar's Land Rover. Someone had removed the mattress and washed out all the blood.

He drove slowly, too many thoughts crowding his mind. Libby! He'd never seen her as a strong person but this morning she had been amazing – in charge of everything – incredibly calm despite her tears. She was practical, dealing with things in turn, helping the staff who were thrown out of their normal behaviour. Women, he thought, how do they do it? They seem so emotional yet have this – iron, this – solidity, this – strength – and Lew ran out of words.

He stopped at the viewpoint. Below was the wonderful stretch of Venture, a lot of the river and part of The Loop. Beyond were the Littet Hills. It was a big country. Together, he guessed, the two ranches would make about a hundred and thirty thousand acres and carry at least twelve thousand head of cattle – or thereabouts – sometimes more. Down there were his friends, his life. Beyond the hills was the vast area where he and Frannie had hunted, marvellous country, wonderful, happy days.

Soon the light would fade. The sight below him was changing in a subtle way. Changing. Change.

Suddenly he couldn't think of the ranches any more; the morning's events flooded him. He dropped his head onto his arms over the steering wheel and wept, tears pouring out. Lew let it all go. Slowly it began to dry up and he used two handkerchiefs to help. He looked again at the land below.

Frannie was all right.

Lew knew what he had to do.

Putting his back straight, pushing his shoulders into position and grasping the steering wheel firmly, he drove on.

EPILOGUE

Glory Halleluiah was annoyed with herself. She was late spotting the advertisement in The Kenya Weekly News.

For sale. Chappell upright piano, tropicalised, good tone and condition. Stool and some music available if wanted. Family leaving Kenya. Tel: Rongai 6Y2

This was exactly the wedding present she wanted for Lew and Janet but when she phoned Rongai she discovered that the piano had already been sold. Strange, said the lady at Rongai, it's gone to your area; a gentleman called Mr. Twybitt came with a small lorry, and took it straight away, packed with mattresses.

Glory Halleluiah went to see Corn that evening.

'Oh, do try it. I've no idea if it's a good buy or a bad one but new ones from Nairobi cost a fortune.'

It was a very good purchase; despite the removal the piano was in almost perfect tune and had a clear, excellent tone; better, Glory Halleluiah thought, than her own Bluthner. She said that when Corn had moved it to what had been Mumps' house, ready for the couple when they came back from their wedding, she would call the Nairobi piano-tuner to put it right. He could tune hers as well. Oh dear, she thought, just what I would have liked to give them; never mind, the cheque can be bigger.

Mr. Evans had been unable to resist boasting about his future son-in-law's ability with a gun. Lions, buffaloes, elephants – leopards – he's shot them all. Habitues of the local pub had visions of some giant of a hunter with leopard skin around his hat, certainly a beard, maybe tattooed arms, weather-beaten, massive shouldered and probably rough, so when Lew arrived, small, quiet and mild mannered, there was some disappointment. This was quickly dissipated when, only three days after his arrival in Shropshire, Lew took part in a shoot, an invitation arranged by John Evans. It was November and the venue prided itself on producing very high pheasants. There was an expectation of about eighty birds with six guns; not a big day, but enough for everyone to have some fun. Lew was using Mr. Evans's shotgun that fitted him quite well. He missed the first bird, then got his eye in and never missed another. The guns either side of him stopped occasionally just to watch, giving Lew more scope. He had forty shots and got thirty-nine birds, leaving the keeper speechless. The other guns brought the total to eighty-two. Lew found sand-grouse shooting in Kenya more difficult than pheasants, however high. It was a good start to the three weeks before the wedding.

Lew and Janet, Dar, Frank, Madge and West flew to Britain together. Glory Halleluiah declined the invitation, feeling that she should help Libby, and Corn lost the toss over which brother was to go. Dar stayed with Hugh and Mary Constable, Edith's twin and her husband, only fifteen miles from the Evans' farm. Janet went to her parents; the others stayed at a small Guest House in the village (it was teetotal so the local pub did very well out of the Kenya visitors). Mario and Maria, very nicely, said that they couldn't accept the invitation but two of their remaining three 'boys' were to explore and enjoy London – have a holiday - before coming to Shropshire for the day, having flown ahead of everyone else.

The three weeks before the wedding were busy; it was necessary to hire morning suits (and grey toppers) for the men. West's breadth proved difficult, the final suit sat ill on him, he knew. The ladies had a flurry of shopping in Shrewsbury and the Evanses and Constables did a lot of entertaining. Dar was intrigued to find the John Evans' nine hundred acres was actually two farms combined and very well run indeed. Lew found it all very interesting on his first visit overseas but longed to get the wedding over and be with Janet.

When the actual day came the Kenya contingent looked quite imposing. Dar, Frank, Hugh Constable and Mario's sons were all tall men who looked very good in their morning suits, Marios's sons causing a stir amongst the girls at the wedding. Mary Constable and Madge were both handsome women; very well dressed.

West in his ill-fitting suit looked a bit like a heavy-weight boxer who had wandered into a Society wedding by mistake. He had to be Best Man, at Lew's request, and, standing by Lew in the Church he appeared more the great white hunter type that the locals expected, but he stood straight, played his part well and there was never a tease in sight. Janet's sister and brother-in-law played an unusual Oboe and Flute duet during the signing of the register, impressing the congregation. Everyone had to drive five miles to the only local hotel that could accommodate three hundred guests for a proper meal. Lew found it very formal but managed well, Janet being especially proud of his speech that they'd worked over together in Kenya.

The Kenya guests flew home soon after the wedding, leaving Lew and Janet to enjoy their honeymoon at a very quiet hotel deep in the middle of Wales where it rained almost every day. They hardly noticed.

The last baby Janet helped to deliver at the Cottage Hospital before she left was the healthy, perfect nine-pound son to Libby. The Doctor commented straight away, 'There's no question of that one's father!' and, even before Libby took the baby home, the nurses were calling him Frannie instead of Frank. Far too many well-wishers wanted to visit Libby and the baby at the Cottage Hospital and had to be stopped but they left a pile of gifts for Frannie's child.

It had been a fairly easy delivery. When she was given the baby Libby cried, then stopped, intent as she was on getting back to Venture Loop as soon as she could. With the overload of presents for the baby she left, saying to Janet, 'There's so much to be done at the ranches!' and she departed with her son to get on with the work.

Glossary

Askari	Solider, guard
Boma	Literally a rampart but meaning an enclosure
Bwana	Master, politely, Sir
Chaplain	Anglican clergyman serving the Settler community
Chopi	Lame
D.C.	District Commissioner
D.O.	District Officer
Dawa	Medicine
Dhobi	Laundry
Fupi	Short in stature
Jiko	Charcoal brazier
Kali	Fierce or sharp
Kikapu	Basket
Kikoi	Cloth commonly used by Europeans in Kenya as nightwear
Lekker	Good, true (Africaans)
Manyatte	Collection of mud plastered huts
Mbuni	Ostrich
Memsahib	Madam
Mungu	God
Mzungu	European white man, plural – wazungu

O.C.P.D.	Officer Commanding Police District
P.C.	Provincial Commissioner
Panga	Machete
Posho	Maize meal
Punda	Donkey
Punda Milia	Donkey with striper – zebra
Shamba	Garden or farm
Shuka	Cloth worn by Africans like a toga
Sufuria	Saucepan with no handles
Syce	Groom for horses
T.P.P	Temporary Permit to Posess (firearms)
Watu	People – African staff (in context)
Zoriba	Round thornbush blockade

Note: *Frannie's quotation is the second verse from the poem 'To a lady asking him how long her would love her by Sir George Etherege' (1635 – 1691).*